No Witness
But the Moon

Also by Suzanne Chazin

The Jimmy Vega Mystery Series

*Land of Careful Shadows**

*A Blossom of Bright Light**

The Fourth Angel

Flashover

Fireplay

*Available from Kensington Publishing Corp.

No Witness
But the Moon

SUZANNE
CHAZIN

KENSINGTON BOOKS
http://www.kensingtonbooks.com

KENSINGTON BOOKS are published by

Kensington Publishing Corp.
119 West 40th Street
New York, NY 10018

Library of Congress Card Catalogue Number: 2016947676

ISBN-13: 978-1-4967-0517-4
ISBN-10: 1-4967-0517-3
First Kensington Hardcover Edition: November 2016

eISBN-13: 978-1-4967-0518-1
eISBN-10: 1-4967-0518-1
Kensington Electronic Edition: November 2016

10 9 8 7 6 5 4 3 2 1

Printed in the United States of America

To Bill Hayes: you will always be family to me.

And that's why I have to go back
to so many places
there to find myself
and constantly examine myself
with no witness but the moon.

—Pablo Neruda

Chapter 1

He hoped this day would never come. He hoped he'd never have to cross the divide.

On one side were cops who never had to second-guess their instincts, never had to shield their consciences—that soft tissue of the soul—from the razor-sharp judgments of colleagues, friends, even strangers.

On the other were those who had to look in the mirror at three A.M. with a belly full of booze and a heart full of lead. The ones who had to whisper the worst question a cop can ask himself and then listen for that tumor of self-doubt in the echo: *Did I do the right thing?*

Jimmy Vega never wanted to be a cop in the first place. He wanted to be a musician. He wanted to move people with rhythm, not muscle. Then his girlfriend—later wife, later ex-wife—got pregnant. You could say he became a cop the same way he became a father: by backing into it and then trying his hardest to make it work out.

And it had. For eighteen years, it had.

Until tonight.

It was a Friday evening in early December, too early for real snow, even here some fifty miles north of New York City where the deer sometimes outnumber the people. There had been a dusting earlier today—the first of the season. Most of it had melted away but a sugary glaze still clung to the trees and stone walls, lending a festive atmosphere to the rolling hills and horse farms of Wickford, NY.

Vega, a detective assigned to the county police's homicide task force, had been in Wickford most of the day helping the local cops investigate a fatal robbery. The homeowner, a retired school principal, had suffered a heart attack during the break-in. Vega suspected the crime was part of a string of increasingly violent home invasions in the area. Four weeks earlier, just over the border in Connecticut, a rookie cop had been disarmed and pistol-whipped by four Hispanic men involved in a burglary there. Two weeks ago, a teenage babysitter in nearby Quaker Hills had been raped and savagely beaten by what appeared to be the same gang.

"Every day I'm getting a dozen suspicious vehicle calls," Mark Hammond, a Wickford detective, told Vega. "I swear, if we don't catch these mutts soon, we're gonna have some dead Wall Street CEO on our hands."

"Perish the thought," said Vega dryly.

Hammond made a face. Vega suspected the Wickford detective played golf with a few of them. He certainly dressed like he did.

At six P.M., Vega and Hammond had progressed as far as they could in the case. Vega was ready to call it quits for the evening. He phoned his girlfriend, Adele Figueroa, from the parking lot of the Wickford Police station, a brick and clapboard structure that looked like George Washington still slept inside. The entire village, with its cobblestoned sidewalks and whitewashed New England storefronts, could have sprung whole from a Currier and Ives lithograph. It was a cold clear night, the moon so bright it bleached the surrounding sky. A gust of wind bit right through Vega's dark blue insulated jacket. The air felt sharp enough to crack a tree branch. Tomorrow would have been his mother's sixty-fourth birthday. Vega had been trying to distract himself and not focus on it so much this year. It was supposed to get easier with time. That's what everyone told him.

"I just need to drop my car back at the station," Vega told Adele. "Then I'll be right over." He heard what he thought was a bark through the phone.

"*Nena?*" His term of endearment for her. *Babe* in Spanish. "Did I just hear a dog?"

"Don't ask." She blew her nose. "It's just for a little while."

"But you're allergic to dogs."

"Yeah, but Sophia isn't." Adele's daughter had been begging for a dog ever since Vega first met the girl eight months ago when he and Adele started dating. But even so, Adele's plate was full. Besides being the founder and executive director of La Casa, the largest immigrant outreach center in the county, Adele was on the board of the local food pantry and had also recently joined the advisory board of a Hispanic think tank in Washington, D.C. She barely had time to deal with the drama of being a divorced mother raising a nine-year-old, let alone take on a pet.

"One of my clients at La Casa had to move into a friend's apartment temporarily," Adele explained. "The landlord doesn't allow dogs. Sophia cried when she found out he might have to go to a shelter. It's just for a couple of weeks."

"Huh. Famous last words."

"I figure the walks will do me good. Lately my hourglass figure has too many hours and too little glass."

Vega laughed then wished he could take it back. He never understood why a woman with a Harvard law degree couldn't accord her body the same confidence she accorded her mind. "I think you look beautiful, *nena*. Even if you are picking up steaming piles of—"

"Mock me, *mi amado,* and I'll make you do it. See you in—what? An hour?"

"Sure thing." Vega hung up and drove his unmarked

Pontiac Grand Am out of the parking lot. He'd pulled the short straw getting this silver hunk of junk this morning. It had four wheels and working brakes but the interior lights worked only intermittently and the heater was lukewarm at best. He preferred the cars he used to get when he worked undercover in narcotics: Humvees and Land Rovers and Escalades. Drug dealers drove in style.

He kept his police radio on and listened for any reports of car emergencies or accidents in the area. Wickford was a lousy place to break down, especially in winter after dark. There were almost no streetlights and the estates were set so far back from the road, it would be difficult for anyone to summon help. Vega was anxious to be off duty. But even so, he'd never leave someone stranded if he had the power to help.

The radio was quiet so he took a shortcut he knew through the back roads of Wickford that would put him on the highway. He made a left then a right down several narrow, winding streets, some of them unpaved, all of them no wider than a cow path. He passed huge, dark velvet expanses of lawns slashed by moonlight and shadowed by hundred-year-old trees. A few miles to the west where Adele lived, Lake Holly's downtown blazed with delis, pizzerias, and row frames strung with Christmas lights and inflatable Santas on thumbprint lawns. But here, the darkness was broken only by the occasional high beams of a car.

A dispatcher's voice broke the silence. "Ten-thirty-two in Wickford. Report of shots fired."

Vega sat up straight. A ten-thirty-two was local police code for a home invasion. From the sound of it, an *armed* home invasion. Vega listened for the address.

"Private residence at Six Oak Hill. Homeowner reports push-in robbery and assault. One confirmed suspect though there may be others. Suspect is male. Hispanic. Medium build and complexion. Late forties or early fifties. Wearing a black puffy jacket, dark jeans, and a tan baseball cap. Suspect may be armed."

This is it. These are the guys we've been looking for. All of Vega's senses turned razor-sharp, as if he'd just gulped a double espresso. He'd stood next to the body of that retired school principal, dead of a heart attack these bastards caused. He'd seen pictures of that poor teenage girl in Quaker Hills, her flesh a map of swellings and bruises that only hinted at the even greater violation beneath. He'd heard the water-cooler rumors that that poor rookie in Connecticut was so traumatized after his encounter; he'd quit the force. If Vega could be the guy to stop it all, right now, that would be an absolute high—the kind of high every cop lives for.

He typed Six Oak Hill into his GPS. He was two streets away. He could be on the scene long before any of the Wickford patrols or an ambulance responded. He grabbed the speaker on his department radio.

"County twenty-nine," he said, identifying his unmarked vehicle to dispatchers. "I'm on Perkins Road in Wickford. I'll take this in. Alert local PD that a plainclothes Hispanic detective will be on scene in a silver Pontiac Grand Am." Vega didn't want to get shot by some townie cop who mistook him for the perp.

He turned off Perkins Road and raced over to Oak Hill—a steep ridge of newly constructed estates on four-acre expanses of lawn. Deep pockets of woods blocked the road from any of its neighbors and its high elevation kept the trees on adjoining roads from spoiling the view. There were only a few houses on the cul-de-sac. Six Oak Hill was a sprawling red-tile-roofed hacienda at the end of a long circular driveway. There were no vehicles parked on the street but that didn't mean one wasn't parked nearby. From what Vega had learned about the gang's operations, they sent a forward party of one or two guys. Only after they'd secured the property did they bring a getaway car.

He pulled the Grand Am to the curb and switched on his police grill lights. They bathed the perfectly trimmed boxwood hedge and pale stucco arches of the house in alternating flashes of red and blue. There was a fountain at the center of the driveway but it looked as if it had been turned off for the winter. The night air was still and silent save for the voice of a female dispatcher over his police radio giving the estimated time of arrival for backup. It would be at least four minutes.

Vega sprang from his car and began walking briskly down the driveway. He tensed as a door along the side of the house swung open. A short, Hispanic-looking man in a puffy black jacket and jeans stumbled onto the driveway. Floodlights bounced off the brim of his tan baseball cap. The man's right hand clutched his left shoulder as he tried to regain his footing. On his heels was a taller, movie-star-handsome man, also Hispanic-looking, waving a gun.

Vega pulled his Glock 19 service pistol from his holster and sprinted down the driveway.

"Police!" he shouted, pointing his weapon at the good-looking man. "Drop the gun! Hands up!"

The man immediately obeyed. "I'm Ricardo Luis," he called out in a Spanish accent. "Don't shoot! This is my home." His name sounded vaguely familiar but Vega was too pumped up to remember where he'd heard it.

The man in the baseball cap pitched forward and ran into the rear yard, still clutching his left shoulder. Then he disappeared.

"Stay where you are," Vega ordered Luis. "Keep your hands where I can see them. More police are coming." Vega scooped Luis's weapon off the driveway and tucked it into his waistband next to his handcuffs. Then he took off after the other figure in the baseball cap.

Bright floodlights blinded Vega as he plastered his body up against the side of the house and scanned the backyard for movement. Colored strands of Christmas lights flashed from a white columned pergola, illuminating a patio and pool covered over for the winter and a fenced tennis court to the far right. Nothing moved. Vega tried to catch his breath. He waited. And then he saw it—the shadow of a figure inching along the edge of the tennis courts. As soon as Vega took a step forward, the suspect broke from the bushes and began running straight for the woods in back.

"Police! Stop!" Vega shouted again. The man kept running. Even with a full moon out tonight, Vega knew the canopy of dense branches and pines would seal off the light. He had no idea how far the woods extended. In Wickford, it could easily go a half mile in any direction. Still, he couldn't hang back. He couldn't take the chance that once again, this gang would get away.

He ran to the pergola and took cover behind one of the columns. He felt like a pinball in an arcade game, zigzagging between bumpers, trying to stay out of the line of fire as he made his way across the lawn. His heart beat hard against his rib cage. Sweat poured down his body. The homeowner's gun was digging into the small of Vega's back. The cold had begun to numb his fingers around the handle of his gun. Vega wished he were back in uniform. At least he'd have a radio on his collar—not this bulky hand-held unit that only served to weigh him down. At least he'd be wearing his Kevlar vest. He still owned one but he hadn't expected to need it today.

Vega was at the edge of the woods now. He'd lost the suspect entirely. The darkness was like a wool blanket. Overhead, bright moonlight dusted the tops of the trees. But on the ground, there were only shapes and silhouettes. Thorny branches snagged Vega's pants and jacket. Logs and stumps half-hidden by leaves tripped up his feet. The cold made his nose run and his fingers tingle. He heard the whoosh of his own hard breathing in his ears. He couldn't turn on his flashlight. He had to mute the volume on his radio. Both would give away his location. So he was forced to stagger blindly across the uneven terrain, guided only by sound and shadow.

The land sloped steeply downward. Vega felt drawn by gravity and momentum. Ahead, he heard the snap of dry branches and the crunch of dead leaves. That made it easier to track the suspect's location but also for the suspect to track his. If there was a gang waiting to ambush Vega at the bottom of this hill, he was as good as dead.

Then Vega's right eye caught something in his peripheral vision. He swung his whole body in the direction of the movement and listened. He heard a crackle of dead branches. A scuff of pebbles. Vega's heart fisted up in his chest. He aimed his gun. The milliseconds felt like hours. Something darted out of the bushes. Something sleek and fast. Moonlight caught the white of its tail. A deer. It leapt over a log and scampered away. Was that all it was? Vega couldn't be sure. His own sandpaper breathing trumped every other sound.

And then—luck. Fifty feet farther down the hill, the suspect stumbled, his forward momentum carrying him right into a clearing that was lit up by a neighbor's floodlight. The man got to his feet, but before he could start running again, Vega caught up just short of the pool of light and took cover behind a tree.

"Police! Stop! Put your hands over your head!"

The suspect froze. He had his back to Vega but he was hunched over slightly, breathing hard, his jacket rising and falling with each intake of breath. Vega trained his gun on the man's torso and waited for him to straighten and put his hands in the air.

He didn't.

The suspect's left hand remained somewhere in front of him out of Vega's line of sight. His right one stayed planted on his left shoulder. *Was he shot? Reaching for a weapon?* From this angle, Vega couldn't be sure. In the time it would take to *be* sure, it could all be over. Several years ago while working undercover, Vega had witnessed one drug dealer shoot and kill another. One minute, they were standing around arguing the disputed weight of the merchandise. The next, one of the dealers was lying on the ground, bleeding out. It had happened that fast. Vega never saw it coming.

"Let me see your hands!" Vega shouted again.

No response. No compliance. *Was he stalling?* Vega scanned the woods. This was just how that rookie in Connecticut got disarmed. He thought he'd gotten the drop on one of the gang only to find himself surrounded by three more.

Vega switched to Spanish. *"Soy el policía! Déjeme ver sus manos!"* I'm the police! Let me see your hands!

Nothing.

"Are you deaf, *pendejo? Está usted sordo?"*

The man straightened but kept his back to Vega and his hands hidden. *"Hay una razón"*—the man choked out between gasps of air—*"por la que . . . hice esto."* There's a reason I did this.

So they were going to conduct this interchange in Spanish. Fine. At least now Vega knew. But why wasn't the suspect cooperating? What could he possibly hope to gain by refusing to obey a police officer with a gun pointed at him? "I don't care about your reason, *pendejo,"* Vega replied in Spanish. "Put your hands where I can see them."

"You are making a mistake," said the man in Spanish. *Was that a threat?* "Show me your hands! Now!"

Vega felt a burning in his gut—that fight or flight instinct that every officer has to conquer in order to survive. You can't back down when you're a cop. You can't negotiate a command or turn it into a request—or, God forbid, a plea. You're no good to anybody if you do. Not to other cops. Not to civilians. Not even to yourself. You have to own the situation or one way or another, it will own you.

"I'm not gonna tell you again," shouted Vega.

"But you don't understand. You can't do this—"

The man lifted his right hand off his left shoulder. Vega thought he was going to raise it in the air. Instead, he shoved it into the right front pocket of his jeans and spun around to face Vega.

One. Two. Two seconds. That's all the time a police officer has to make a decision.

One. Two. A lot can happen in two seconds.

An object can fall sixty-four feet.

A bullet can travel a mile.

And an indecisive cop can become a dead one.

Vega wasn't aware of squeezing the trigger. But he heard the shots. Like burst balloons.

Bam.

Bam.

Bam.

Bam.

The man crumpled to the ground. The confrontation was over.

The pain had just begun.

Chapter 2

Jimmy Vega's hands were shaking so much, it took him several tries before he could press the button on his radio.

"This is County twenty-nine," he said, trying to squeeze the breathlessness and panic from his voice. "I'm in the woods behind Oak Hill Road. Suspect on the ten-thirty-two is down on a four-four-four." Local code for an officer-involved-shooting.

It was like waking from a dream. Just fifty or sixty feet farther down the hill Vega could see the flashing lights of police cars bathing the woods in a strange, otherworldly glow. *Did they just show up? Or have they been there all along?* He'd been so focused on the suspect, he'd blotted out all other sensations.

Two uniformed patrol officers with heavy-duty flashlights began climbing cautiously toward him. Vega took a step forward into the pool of light. The suspect was lying on his back, not moving. From this angle on the hillside, all Vega could see were the soles of his sneakers and his tan baseball cap, now lying on the ground near him, soaked with blood. Vega wanted to rush over and begin CPR. That's what he was trained to do after a shooting. But he couldn't—not until these officers cleared him to move. He wasn't in uniform. For all the police knew, he was another perp. He dropped his gun to the ground, slowly removed his gold detective's shield from his belt, and cupped it in his left hand. Then he raised both hands in the air.

"Police officer! Don't shoot!" he shouted, waving his shield.

The two Wickford cops stepped into the floodlight. A man and a woman. The woman had a soft chin and frizzy bleached hair that reminded Vega of a dandelion. The man was shaped like a torpedo—with a shaved head beneath his cap and a wide torso made wider by his Kevlar vest. Both officers holstered their weapons as soon as they recognized him from the station house earlier. They were closer to the suspect than Vega was. Vega noticed the woman's mouth form a perfect O at the sight of the man. Torpedo raised an eyebrow and stepped back.

"No ambulance needed here, Detective. You got him good."

"Did you find anyone else?" asked Vega. He was still panting hard. His side had a stitch in it like he'd just run a marathon. "I think I heard someone else in the woods."

"There are police everywhere down there," said Torpedo. "If there's anyone else, we'll find them."

Vega retrieved his gun from the ground and ran over to the man he'd just shot. He was a homicide cop. He was used to pulling up on bloody, sometimes gory crime scenes. But he was unprepared for the damage he himself had inflicted. He'd aimed, as he'd been taught in his police training, for the center mass of the body—the torso. But as the man collapsed and fell backward, one of the bullets must have caught him in the chin and gone through his skull, cracking it open as easily as an egg. Blood and brain matter glistened, dark and gelatinous, across the fallen leaves. The suspect was unrecognizable from the neck up.

I've killed a man. Dear God, I fucking blew his head off! In Vega's eighteen years as a police officer, including five in undercover narcotics dealing with hardened gangbangers and felons, he'd never had to shoot anyone. He'd pointed his gun plenty of times and had guns pointed at him. He'd seen people killed. He'd wrestled suspects into handcuffs while they were trying to take a swing at him. But he'd never fired his weapon in the line of duty. The vast majority of police officers never do. You practice for it. Every couple of months you go out to the shooting range and train. But it's like a fire drill. You do it to stay sharp. You don't expect to ever really need it.

"Are you okay, Detective?" asked the woman cop with the dandelion hair.

"Yeah." Vega was shaking badly but he tried to cover it by pretending he was just cold. He began frantically walking the perimeter of the body. "Where's the gun? He had a gun."

Torpedo felt the dead man's jacket then stepped to the side and conferred with his partner.

"Anything?" Dandelion murmured. Torpedo shook his head. "He seems pretty sure he had one."

Vega paced impatiently. "No," he muttered to himself. "I just blow people's brains out for the fun of it." He hadn't even realized they'd heard him until he noticed the two officers looking his way. Both dropped their gazes and shined their flashlights on the ground to give them some extra wattage over and above the floodlights. They nudged the leaves with their boots. Nothing.

"He had one," Vega insisted. "I know he did!"

"We'll find it," Dandelion assured him.

More cops were heading up the hill now. Wickford's Detective Sergeant Mark Hammond was with them, carefully maneuvering his perfectly pressed khakis past the twigs and brambles that had snagged Vega's own pants.

Vega ignored them all. He crouched down next to the dead man. The suspect's bloody right hand was turned palm-side down. There was something underneath. It was too small to be a gun. *A knife, perhaps? A box cutter?* Vega knew he wasn't supposed to touch anything. But he had to know. He uncurled the fingers slightly. Staring up at him was a creased, blood-smeared photograph of two Hispanic men and a teenage boy.

There was nothing else in the dead man's hand.

Vega's stomach lurched. He felt light-headed and dizzy. He pushed himself unsteadily to his feet, ran over to the nearest tree, and vomited. He heaved again and again until there was nothing left inside of him. *The man I killed was involved in a home invasion robbery,* Vega reminded himself. *He ran after I identified myself as a police officer. He refused to surrender. He turned on me.*

He had no weapon.

That thought beat out every other in Vega's brain.

The other officers on the scene gave Vega space. No one said anything to him. They probably thought that's what he needed right now, and a part of him did. But another part of him would have given anything for someone to tell him he'd done the right thing. Instead, everyone went about their business like actors on a stage waiting for someone to feed them their lines. Nobody knew what to say. Two EMTs started up the hill but were quickly turned back. Vega watched their faces absorb the news in the ghoulish alternating flashes of red and blue light.

Hammond eventually walked over and patted Vega gently on the back.

"Come sit in my car, Jimmy. Okay? Maybe call your family? No sense you being out here."

Vega nodded, not trusting himself to speak as Hammond led him down the hill and into the front passenger seat of Hammond's unmarked Toyota.

"I thought for a moment you were gonna put me in back," said Vega.

It was meant to be a weak joke but Hammond's response gave Vega pause. "Take as long as you need to get your thoughts together, okay, Jimmy?" The detective's smile had too many teeth in it.

Hammond's unmarked Toyota smelled of peppermints and Lysol, but it calmed Vega down to be encased in this tomb away from the murmurs of other cops. He felt certain everyone was judging him. How could they not? He would.

Hammond got in the driver's side and radioed a request for the medical examiner and the county crime scene unit. The uniforms began cordoning off the area with yellow police tape. Vega felt like he was watching it all unfold underwater. Voices and sounds came at him disconnected from their sources. The dispatcher's voice over the radio provided a constant update of all the additional vehicles and agencies that were now being directed to this tiny lane in Wickford. All because of Vega. Because of what he'd done.

When Hammond left the car to go back up the hill, Vega took out his cell phone and dialed Adele. He could barely get the words out before he started to choke up.

"I just shot and killed a man."

"*What?* Oh my God! *Mi amado,* what happened? Are you okay?"

Vega's head was pounding. His eyes burned like someone had rubbed them with sand. He took a deep breath and heard it catch in his lungs. He hadn't felt the urge to cry this strongly since that day nearly two years ago when a Bronx detective called to tell him his mother had been found beaten to death in her apartment. At least then, no one would have blamed him if he'd broken down. The crime was brutal. It was still unsolved. But now? This was different. The police officers on the scene would take it as a sign of weakness. Worse, they'd take it as a sign of guilt.

Whatever you do, stay strong, he told himself. If he stopped believing that he'd had no choice about what he'd done, why would anyone else believe it either?

He tried to steady his voice and state the facts as dispassionately as possible. "Dispatch reported a home invasion and shots fired at a residence here in Wickford. I was nearby so I took in the call. The suspect refused to surrender and turned on me."

"Oh, Jimmy, how awful. Are you hurt?"

"No." He couldn't bring himself to tell her that the man he'd killed probably wasn't armed. He needed time to wrap his head around that one. He still didn't want to believe it was true.

A silence hung between them. It was just a moment's worth but Vega felt the sting. Was she judging him? Or was he judging himself so much that he read every hesitation as a criticism?

"It's going to be all right," she cooed softly. "Where are you? Peter was going to drop Sophia off after he took her to the movies." Peter was Adele's ex. "Maybe I can get her babysitter Marcela to come over."

"There's no point," said Vega. "They won't let you within a hundred feet of me."

"Have you given a statement yet? Spoken to counsel?" Adele had been a criminal defense attorney before she started La Casa. It was still in her blood.

"No." Vega squinted through the windshield. Already things were heating up. On the other side of the yellow crime-scene tape were civilian onlookers, news cameras, and more police cars. A lot more police cars. "It's going to be a long night," said Vega. "Can you call Joy and let her know?" Vega's eighteen-year-old daughter was a freshman at the local community college. She lived with Vega's ex-wife.

"Of course. I'll do that now." Adele hung on the line for a moment without speaking. "A delicate question," she said finally. "The uh—suspect. Was he white? Black?"

"Hispanic. He spoke to me in Spanish."

"Good."

"Why good?" asked Vega.

"Well, you're Puerto Rican," said Adele. "So you'll probably get a pass on the race issue."

Vega couldn't contain himself. "There is no race issue, Adele! I wasn't thinking about the color of his skin or the color of mine. My only thought was not getting shot!"

"Calm down, *mi amado*," she said softly. "I understand. I'm just trying to think ahead."

Ahead? Vega couldn't think through the next hour. "I don't need you to be my lawyer, *nena*. I'll have lawyers up the yin yang soon enough."

"Sorry." She exhaled. "You're right. I'll get in touch with Joy and check in with you later, okay? I love you."

"I love you, too." Vega hung up just as the driver's side door opened and Hammond slid in.

"Hey, Jimmy"—Hammond patted his shoulder and gave him a big, fake smile that was all pink gums and white teeth—"how you holding up?"

Vega wasn't interested in small talk. "Did you find a gun?"

"Not yet."

"A knife? Any sort of weapon?"

Hammond ran a finger along the pleats in his slacks without looking at Vega or answering his question—which was answer enough, Vega supposed.

"So that photograph?" asked Vega. "That was all that you found in his hands?"

"At the moment."

"How about accomplices?"

"The homeowner says he only saw one man."

"When I was in the woods, it felt like somebody else was there."

"My guys were at the bottom of the hill. Not sixty feet away. They didn't see anyone."

Vega winced. How could he not have seen them? "They were that close?"

Hammond nodded. "They had their lights and sirens on and everything."

"I guess I just—blocked it out or something."

Hammond put a hand on Vega's arm and squeezed it for

emphasis. "Don't talk, Jimmy—okay? You can only go through this story once. You go through it more than once and change something, some attorney's gonna eat you alive—or put me on a witness stand and eat us both alive."

Vega nodded. "Any indications that he was part of that gang?"

The temperature inside the car seemed to plummet twenty degrees. Vega could feel it instantly.

"Listen, Jim—I don't even know if I'm supposed to be saying this yet. But I just got a call from the chief of police? Over in Greenfield, Connecticut?"

Vega narrowed his gaze at Hammond. Cops aren't teenage girls. They don't frame statements as questions unless they'd rather not deliver the answers.

"Spit it out, Mark."

"The Greenfield PD just arrested the whole gang. Like maybe an hour ago. Four Hispanic men coming out of a big estate over there."

"The gang responsible for these home invasions? Are you sure?"

"One of the guy's prints matches a print we picked up on that robbery. The DNA on another matches semen from the rape in Quaker Hills. That Connecticut rookie they pistol-whipped positively ID'd two of them from mug shots. "

"So you're saying—"

"The man you killed probably wasn't connected to those other crimes."

Chapter 3

Vega had no idea how long he sat in Hammond's un-marked Toyota. Long enough, he supposed, for the county evidence techs to impound the two guns he was carrying (his and the homeowner's) as well as the ugly silver Pontiac Grand Am Vega had checked out of the station house lot that morning. They found four shell casings from Vega's Glock in the woods and one from the home-owner's Sig Sauer in the house.

Ricardo Luis. The homeowner's name came back to Vega while he sat slumped in the Toyota's front passenger seat. Vega figured out how he knew him, too.

Heat of my heart, beat of my heart . . . oh, oh, oh.

Vega couldn't remember the last two hours. He couldn't recall firing four—*four!*—bullets into an unarmed man. But he could sing the stupid chorus of that Latin pop star's wildly successful chart-topping song.

By the time Vega's friend, county detective Teddy Dolan, came to fetch him and drive him to their own police head-quarters, Vega felt wrung-out. Dolan was all forced good cheer, his voice casual and slightly country-sounding—the same voice Dolan used to talk down wife batterers and would-be bridge jumpers. Vega wondered if he fell into the latter category.

They weren't allowed to talk about the shooting so

Dolan tried to fill the space between them with distractions. He prattled on about last week's Giants game against Dallas, the upcoming division Christmas party, and how their boss, Captain Waring, was getting on everyone's case about detectives leaving litter in their cars. Vega couldn't even muster the energy for yesses and noes. There was only one thing that interested him.

"Who was he?" Vega asked softly.

Dolan bit the inside of his cheek and said nothing. He was a big, burly ex-Marine with a blond walrus mustache, a shaved head, and a Harley-Davidson tattoo on his right forearm. To look at the two of them, any civilian would think Dolan would be the one in this mess, not Vega. But Dolan was one of the most even-tempered cops Vega knew. Vega couldn't help but wonder whether the man he shot tonight would be alive right now if Dolan had been the officer he'd encountered instead of Vega.

"C'mon, Teddy," Vega pleaded. "In a few hours everyone's gonna know his name, and in a few days everyone's gonna know mine."

"It's not helpful to you right now."

"Let me decide what's helpful."

Vega already knew some things about the case from eavesdropping on conversations at the scene. He knew that the security footage from Luis's video cameras was useless because Luis had recently had his gutters cleaned and whoever cleaned them knocked all the cameras out of position. He knew that Luis had a bodyguard in Miami— his main residence—but not in Wickford where the Latin American community consisted of a thousand domestics and two transferred bank execs from Argentina. The police found no evidence of illegal drugs in the house or any other illicit activity. But they did find ten grand in small bills, which Luis claimed was cash he gave to his entourage in the form of tips and Christmas bonuses. No wonder he was a great robbery target.

"C'mon, man," Vega urged Dolan. "Cut me a break and give me what you got on the suspect. It's eating me alive."

Dolan cursed under his breath. "He had a social security card in his wallet under the name Antonio Fernandez," Dolan said finally. "He had a pristine-looking Atlanta, Georgia, public library card under the same name, too."

"You think the ID's real?"

"His wallet didn't contain a driver's license. My guess? The social security card is a forgery. He got the library card with it to establish another form of ID so he's probably here illegally. He broke into Ricardo Luis's house so I'm guessing he's probably got a criminal record. We won't know until we lift his prints and send them through the computer, however. That could take a few hours."

"Is that everything you found?"

Silence. Holiday lights on the passing houses flashed and faded in the glass. Vega had almost forgotten that Christmas was less than three weeks away. A few days ago, he and Dolan were bemoaning the glacial pace of promotions off the sergeant's list. Now they were on opposite sides of a divide that could never be breached. Vega wondered if he'd ever feel normal again.

"I didn't do anything wrong," Vega insisted.

"Nobody said you did."

"Then stop freezing me out of the loop here."

"Jimmy, you're not *in* the loop. You're sidelined. Nobody removes their own appendix, *comprende?*"

"I feel less like a patient at a hospital and more like the stiff at a funeral."

"There's not much to tell, okay? We found a paycheck in one of his jacket pockets. From Chez Martine."

"The French restaurant in Wickford?"

"Yeah, but it was made out to someone with an entirely different name at a Bronx address."

"You think he stole the paycheck?"

"That, or he was using multiple aliases from multiple states."

Vega nodded. They'd both experienced the frustration of arresting an undocumented suspect who used different parts of their name to confuse the police and make it harder to track identity or past arrests.

"Anything else to suggest a Bronx connection?"

"He had a New York City Metro card and ten Lotto tickets from a Bronx bodega in the same inside pocket as the pay stub. He had a small rosary with a crucifix in there, too."

"Great." Vega massaged his forehead. "So the suspect I shot just went from being a gangbanger who raped little girls to some religious busboy who just wanted to show me a picture of his family. Our department's storing the evidence, right?"

"Yeah. We're handling the homicide and Wickford's handling the robbery."

"So you can get access."

"And your point is?"

"I want to see the photo he had in his hands," said Vega. "I want to take a look at the contents of his pockets."

Dolan pulled a face. "No can do, Jimmy."

"A few quick shots on your iPhone. Come on, Teddy. What's the harm in texting them to me? I want to try to understand."

"You may *never* understand." Dolan shook his head. "In the Marines, we didn't spend a lot of time thinking about whether our enemies tucked their kids in at night. Nothing good can come of that. You've got to let it go."

"I will. I promise. Once I see that photo and the other stuff."

"Aw, for crying out loud—" Dolan went to rail at Vega but pulled back at the last moment. Vega read something awkward in his eyes. *Pity?* God, he hoped not. That was the last thing he wanted from anyone.

"I can't be your inside man, Jimmy. No promises. But let me see what I can do."

Captain Waring was expecting Vega and Dolan at the station house. Dolan ushered Vega through the back doors. Under the best of circumstances, their boss, Frank Waring, inspired a certain trepidation among the detectives in the homicide division. He wasn't a big man. He had the lean, angular look of a Depression-era dustbowl farmer and a voice that rarely rose above the decibel level of a librarian. But he was an ex-Navy SEAL and considered cops like Vega who hadn't served in the military inferior to those like Dolan who had. Vega and Waring's relationship had never been warm and fuzzy since Vega moved from narcotics to homicide two years ago. This latest incident wasn't likely to improve the situation.

"How are you holding up, Detective?" asked Waring. The captain's gray-blue eyes registered no genuine concern except perhaps for what this incident might do to his own career.

"Fine, sir," said Vega. You don't say "okay" to Captain Waring.

Waring turned to a uniformed sergeant named Lasky. "Sergeant? Please get the detective a glass of water." The water had nothing to do with any worry over whether Vega was properly hydrated. "Sergeant Lasky will take you down the hall for a urine sample."

"Yes, Captain."

Lasky, an old-timer nearing retirement, looked embarrassed by the request but Vega understood the procedure: everyone needed to be certain he wasn't under the influence of anything. Vega had nothing to hide. He wasn't even taking cold medicine. He sipped the water and then walked down the hall and whizzed in a cup while Lasky waited on the other side of the door. After that, the sergeant sat him in one of their interrogation rooms, a windowless space with a one-way mirror, a scuffed table, and a few folding chairs. That was it. No sound or light save the buzzing fluorescents overhead. Vega felt like a criminal—which he supposed he was in a way. He'd taken the life of an unarmed man. How much worse a crime can you commit?

"Can I get you anything, Vega? A sandwich? Some coffee?" asked Lasky.

Food was about as appealing right now as choking down carpet padding. Vega took the coffee but then watched it grow cold before his eyes. Several times cops mistakenly opened the door to the room, thinking it was available. As soon as they saw who was sitting there, they got wide-eyed and panicky, apologized profusely, and left. Everyone knew what had happened. They probably knew more than he did at the moment. When the door was open, Vega heard snatches of conversation.

". . . No weapon. Just some old photo . . ."

". . . This Latin pop star's house . . ."

". . . Three Hispanics in all of Wickford and they gotta rob and shoot each other . . ."

Vega had the attention span of a goldfish. He couldn't keep a thought in his head for more than two seconds. He typed stuff into his phone's search engine just to see what popped up. Already, the news had hit the Internet: *Police shoot and kill robbery suspect in Wickford . . . Robbery suspect breaks into Latin pop star's house.* Okay. Those were the facts. He could live with them. He typed in *Ricardo Luis* and came back with a dimple-faced Mexican man in his late thirties from the cover of his latest CD—the same man Vega had seen on that driveway in Wickford. Luis had recently published an autobiography too, called *Song of My Heart.* The cover showed Luis in a beefcake shot with his shirt undone to his navel.

There was a knock on the door.

"Yeah?"

A short, stout black woman with close-cropped white

hair entered the room. She wore big gold hoop earrings and round bright red glasses attached to a chain around her neck. Her feet were encased in orthopedic loafers and her navy blue pants suit and white shirt looked starchy enough to be a uniform. She closed the door behind her and stretched out a hand.

"Isadora Jenkins." She spoke with a throaty tremor. "I've been hired by your union to represent you in these proceedings."

She wasn't at all what Vega was expecting. He'd assumed his union would hire some jailhouse lawyer type with a paunch and a comb-over. Isadora Jenkins looked like a retired schoolteacher. A *long*-retired schoolteacher. All except for her choice in jewelry. On her bony hands, she sported several clunky costume-jewelry rings that seemed totally at odds with her drab attire. She looked like a Jehovah's Witness who'd gotten lost in a dollar store.

Vega rose from the table and shook her hand. "Pleased to meet you," he said woodenly.

"No, you're not. You're deep in the doo-doo, facing the worst day of your life and you're wondering what genius in your union decided to send somebody's grandma to represent you."

Vega bit back a smile. "I would never say that."

"Good. Then you've got enough brains not to say everything you're thinking. I like that in a cop." She grinned. "Hell, I like that in a man."

Jenkins plunked her briefcase on the table. It looked scuffed enough to suggest she'd had the same one since she graduated law school. Vega sat back down and waited for her to take a seat across from him. Instead, Jenkins folded her arms across her prow of a chest and began walking the room, staring at him from every angle. He flushed at the wattage of her scrutiny. He settled his eyes in his lap.

"Look at me, please."

"Huh?"

"I am walking around this room and keeping my eyes on you. Please do the same."

Vega forced himself to comply. He felt acutely uncomfortable. He began jiggling one of his legs nervously under the table. He started to sweat.

"I don't understand," he said after a minute.

"People are going to judge you from this moment forward. Like I am now. Keep looking at me. Don't back down."

Vega held her gaze and did as she requested.

"Good." She nodded, finally taking a seat. "You look away; people think you've got something to hide. You can feel sorrow. Sorrow is normal. No decent human being can be happy about what happened this evening. But if you act ashamed, then you're telling the world that you did something wrong—something that deserves punishment. You see what I'm driving at?"

"Yes, ma'am."

" 'Ma'am.' That's good." Jenkins nodded approvingly. "Lots of respect. Lots of deference. But no shame. You have to see yourself as you want a jury to see you."

"*A jury?*" Panic fluttered in Vega's chest. His stomach went into freefall. Jenkins dropped the possibility of Vega going before a jury like they were discussing whether or not it would rain tomorrow. "Am I going to go on *trial?*"

Jenkins shrugged. "Five years ago, I'd have said this could be cleared in-house. But police shootings are a political hot button these days. The moment the press hears the words *unarmed suspect* and that suspect is black or Hispanic, they're on it like vultures on carrion. I'm sure you know that. That's why we have to proceed as if anything could happen and be prepared for it."

Jenkins slid a business card across the table to Vega. Some law firm with many names, none of them hers. His union obviously didn't think him worthy of a partner.

"So," said Jenkins, "I've got two absolutes." She held up a hand with a large blue-green sparkly ring on it. Her veins stuck out like IV tubes and her joints looked like marbles. "My first rule is that you always tell me the complete, unvarnished truth. My second is that you never discuss the shooting with anyone. And by anyone I mean your significant other. Your family. Fellow cops. Your closest friends. You can't say *anything*. Nada. Zip. Not even to justify your actions or deny some false allegation. The last thing we need is for some attorney to bring your family and friends up on a witness stand. *You* don't want that. And *I* don't want that. Do I make myself clear?"

"Yes, ma'am." She had the hurricane force of Sister Margarita, the nun who ran Vega's old Bronx elementary school.

Jenkins pulled out a yellow pad and pen and set it down before her on the table. Vega took a deep breath and tried to gather his thoughts. His head was pounding. All evening, he'd been replaying the events on a continuous loop reel inside his brain. And now that he finally had someone to listen to him, he didn't know where to begin.

"You *do* know that you're legally allowed to ask for a delay in giving your statement if you feel you're under too much emotional distress—"

"No! I mean uh—no. I'm okay." That was all Vega needed: to cite "emotional distress." Captain Waring would have him stamped "unfit for duty" and laterally transferred out of homicide and over to the pistol licensing unit where he'd spend the rest of his career doing background checks on firearms permits. *No, thank you.* "I can give a statement."

"Good."

"You know that the suspect had a photograph in his hand, right?" Vega's voice sounded tight and weirdly out of tune, like guitar strings that had been pulled up to pitch too quickly.

"Yes. I'm aware of that," said Jenkins evenly.

"I don't know if he had any priors."

"Right now, I'm more interested in your actions, Detective. You are the sole living witness to what happened during the shooting."

"That's what everyone keeps telling me," said Vega. "But I feel like somebody else was in those woods."

"You were experiencing a common phenomenon that happens during a shooting," said Jenkins. "Tunnel vision. Your senses are so focused on the danger that they shut down or distort everything else."

Vega massaged his forehead. "I didn't see the cruisers at the bottom of the hill. Maybe if I had, I wouldn't have . . ." His voice dropped away. He couldn't bring himself to say the words *shot* or *killed*. It was too painful to contemplate what he'd done, let alone that it might have been averted had he paid more attention to his surroundings.

"So far, no officer has come forward to say he witnessed the shooting," said Jenkins. "Which is too bad, really. A fellow officer's testimony could have greatly bolstered the case that you were in fear for your life."

" '*Bolstered*'?" The word irked Vega. Did she think he had to invent excuses for what he'd done? "I don't need to *bolster* anything!"

"You have to understand," said Jenkins calmly. "Most civilians have no idea about the stresses and strains of being in law enforcement. They've never been in any sort of violent confrontation, let alone a shooting. They just see an armed and highly trained police officer against an unarmed civilian. We want to consider every possibility that would tip the scales in your favor. We don't have audio. We don't have video. A favorable eyewitness would have been a plus."

"I'll try to remember to send out invitations the next time dispatch tells me an armed suspect is on the loose."

Jenkins blinked at him behind the frames of her large red glasses. "Sarcasm is a bad tone to take here, Detective. And it's absolutely suicidal with a grand jury."

"Sorry."

Vega placed his sweaty palms on the table and tried to figure out where to begin. It was like swinging blindfolded at a piñata. There was something weighty and ponderous hovering just out of his reach, something he needed to split open. But his words kept glancing off the essence of his actions, never quite opening the core. He recalled the dense, claustrophobic darkness of the woods, the sudden brightness of that spotlight, those two seconds when the suspect dug his hand into his jeans and Vega's whole life flashed before him. He was blank on so much else.

He identified himself as a police officer—that much he was sure of. But he couldn't recall squeezing the trigger. He had no memory of firing off four shots. It had all seemed so clear in those moonlit woods, his actions so steeped in procedure, his choices so unavoidable. But now, under the bright damning fluorescents of this small interrogation room, he felt weak and ashamed of what he'd done. He wondered if Isadora Jenkins hated him yet. He certainly hated himself.

"Whenever I used to hear about cops shooting unarmed civilians, I always figured them for cowboys, you know?" said Vega. "Especially when the civilians were black or Hispanic. I figured probably the cops were profiling. Definitely they were undertrained and letting their emotions get in the way." Vega shook his head. "I never thought I'd end up right alongside them, being the kind of cop people hate—the kind of cop *I* hate. I don't want to end up on Ruben Tate-Rivera's Wall of Shame."

Jenkins nodded. Everyone knew about the former college professor who'd made a national reputation by spotlighting controversial police shootings, particularly of blacks and Hispanics. When he put a cop's photo on his Internet Wall of Shame, it was a virtual guarantee that that cop would go on trial, maybe even land in prison.

Jenkins rummaged through her briefcase and pulled out some unlined sheets of paper and a pencil. She pushed them across the table to Vega.

"Perhaps if you drew what happened?"

The paper helped. It took the onus off Vega's words and allowed him to concentrate on the three-dimensional rendering of events on the page. He spoke and drew and tried to give approximate distances. Jenkins asked questions.

She took notes. She helped him string together a coherent sequence of events. Gradually, Vega's stick-figure memories got a semblance of flesh and blood. But one thing kept bothering him.

"Do you know if the police found the suspect's car?" asked Vega.

"Car?"

"Wickford is very rural. Luis's house is in the middle of nowhere. It seems sort of strange that this guy just walked there. Plus, he must have planned to get away afterward."

"I don't believe the police found a car, but I'll check."

They went through Vega's actions until he felt comfortable explaining them. Then Jenkins excused herself to let Captain Lorenzo of internal affairs know that Vega was ready to make a statement to him and Captain Waring.

Vega had no illusions that Lorenzo and Waring were concerned about the dead man or even Vega, for that matter. All they were really worried about was negative publicity and lawsuits. Win or lose, a lawsuit would cost the county money. Which meant county officials would pass their displeasure on to the police brass who would in turn make Vega's life a living hell. Vega wondered why departments even bothered to give cops guns. They seemed to get you into far more trouble than they ever got you out of.

When Vega's session with Lorenzo and Waring was over, Sergeant Lasky came in with the paperwork that officially put Vega on paid administrative leave *until further notice* along with a referral to counseling. Vega didn't like the sound of either of those.

"How long before I can return to full duty?" The last thing Vega wanted right now was to have nothing to do but sit and brood.

"Typically, the administrative leave lasts for a week or two while your department and the district attorney's office sort through the evidence," said Jenkins. "After that, it's up to the department whether you go back to full duty or modified desk duty."

"In other words, punishment detail."

"That's an administrative matter, Vega. I have no control over that. The faster this is resolved in your favor, the better your chances of putting it behind you."

"Will my name be in the papers?"

"The department won't put it in any official releases for twenty-four hours. But it will be in the public record," Jenkins explained. "If the press wants to get ahold of it, they can. It just depends on how newsworthy they consider it to be." She thrust out a hand. "I'll be in touch if there are any developments."

They parted in the hallway. Vega began heading toward the back of the building to sneak out to his truck. Teddy Dolan caught up with him and began steering him to a conference room.

"I got you a personal escort."

"I don't need an escort."

"You'll want this one. Trust me." Dolan opened the door and there was Adele, sitting by herself at a long table. Her bob of silky black hair looked ruffled and static-charged from some hat she'd just removed. Her lipstick had long ago faded. Her mascara had gone soft like a water-color around her eyes. She was still the most beautiful thing Vega had ever seen.

"You came." His voice was hoarse and throaty. He tried hard to control the pitch.

Adele's full lips parted slightly. Her deep brown eyes searched his. She reached up a delicate hand and tucked a wad of hair behind one ear. It was such a simple gesture, one she did so often. But it brought an instant lump to Vega's throat. It made him want to bury himself in her arms and cry right there. But he knew he couldn't. And so he stood frozen in the doorway, afraid to touch her with his darkness, afraid to contaminate her world with the poison that was now his own.

"He needs to decompress," Dolan told Adele. "Take him out the back way." Then he flicked a gaze at Vega. "Take care, Jimmy. See you around, okay?"

The way Dolan said it made Vega wonder whether he ever would.

Vega hugged Adele as soon as Dolan left the room. He leaned over and whispered a husky thank-you into her hair. She smelled of vanilla and limes and something entirely her own. He wanted to take her to bed with him, huddle under the blankets, and never come out.

"My car's out back," she told him. "Leave your truck here tonight. You can fetch it in the morning. You're in no condition to drive home."

"But Sophia—" Vega knew Adele didn't like him sleeping over when Sophia was in the house.

"Peter agreed to keep her for the night."

"You didn't tell him, I hope."

"No."

Vega heard something sad and spent in her voice. And he understood what he hadn't wanted to before: he couldn't keep this a secret. Even if Peter didn't know tonight, he would know. *Everyone* would know before the week was over. Friends. Family. The cops in his band. His ex-wife's neighbors. Classmates Vega hadn't seen in twenty years. He was sticking his head in the sand if he thought he could keep this a secret.

They snuck out the back entrance. Everything felt shameful now. Vega laced his fingers into Adele's. He was hungry for her touch but it felt as tentative as her voice. When she smiled, there was something forced around the edges. He didn't press. They walked past Vega's Ford pickup, the black paint gelatinous under the cold wattage of floodlights. Adele's pale green Prius was in the visitor's parking lot, farther up the hill. She powered open the doors and Vega strapped himself into the front passenger's seat. The silence between them felt like a third person. Adele fumbled to undo the buttons on her coat. She had trouble steadying her hands. Vega gave her arm a gentle squeeze.

"It's okay, *nena*. It's going to be okay." He couldn't believe *he* was the one consoling *her*. But in an odd way, it made him feel better. By soothing her, he was soothing himself. It gave him an outlet for his pain.

They sat in the car for a moment, their breath clouding white. Adele didn't look at him. She stared out the windshield. "You didn't tell me he was unarmed."

Vega stiffened. He was going to tell her. Of course he was. But not like this. Not when everything was so fresh he could barely sort through it.

"Dispatch told me he was armed. I didn't know until—" He turned to her. "How did you find out?"

"I overheard some of the cops talking while I was waiting for you." Adele fiddled with a cross on a chain around her neck, sliding it back and forth. She seldom wore it. She was only nominally religious. "I drove over here picturing a gunfight. A struggle—"

"Would you rather I have been in intensive care?"

"Of course not!"

Vega picked at the skin around his cuticles until they bled. He didn't know what to say.

"People from La Casa are already calling me," Adele told him. "They're saying they heard that the police shot a Central American dishwasher in Wickford."

"You didn't tell them I'm involved, did you?"

"No. But it's bound to come out. I feel like I'm in the middle. My clients assume I know things I don't and I don't know things I do."

Silence.

"Jimmy, I need to know what's going on."

"There's nothing I can tell you. I'm not allowed to talk about the shooting. You know that."

"But you can tell me the man's name."

"I don't know it—not for certain, anyway. And even if I did, I couldn't give it to you until my department makes it public, and that won't be until after his next of kin are notified."

"Was he part of that gang? The one that raped that girl in Quaker Hills?"

"In all likelihood? No."

"He had a criminal record I assume."

"I have no idea." Did she think he ran background checks on suspects while he was racing to a crime in progress?

"Then how could you . . ." Her voice died away. They both knew what she was asking.

Vega ran a hand through his hair. It was sweat-dried and coated in grease. He needed a shower. "I know you want me to open up about everything right now. I want that, too. Believe me. Nothing would feel better than to unburden myself to you. But I have to do the right thing here. And the right thing is not to discuss the shooting. Not with you. Not with anybody. For your sake as well as mine."

"But people will assume that you did something wrong."

"I know."

"How am I supposed to defend what I don't know?"

"I'm not asking you to defend me, Adele. Just maybe not to—"

"Not to what?"

"Not to judge." Vega swallowed hard and kept his gaze on his hands. He was already failing Isadora Jenkins's shame rule. "People are going to say a lot of stuff about me in the coming weeks—bad stuff, in all likelihood."

"Why?"

"I'm a cop who shot an unarmed suspect. Turn on the nightly news and ask yourself who the media is going to believe."

Adele's cell phone dinged with a text message. She fished it out of her bag. "I just want to make sure it's not Sophia." She frowned as she read the text.

"Is Sophia okay?"

"The text isn't from Sophia. It's from Dave Lindsey." The chairman of the board of La Casa, Adele's Latino community center. "Dave says one of our clients heard from his cousin that the dishwasher who was shot worked at Chez Martine, that French restaurant in Wickford."

Vega looked out at the highway that ran alongside the building. Headlights flashed and faded like shooting stars across his field of vision.

"Jimmy? Is that true?"

He didn't answer. He felt like he'd flicked his finger at a domino this evening and the trail of tiles kept continuing to fall.

"Oh God, please say it's not true."

"Don't tell me you know this guy?"

"I've never met him before in my life," said Adele. "But if he's the dishwasher from Chez Martine, I know his daughter. She's Sophia's babysitter, Marcela."

Chapter 4

Marcela Salinez followed the sound of Spanish chatter and unfolding metal chairs. Her knees buzzed with the sweet reprieve of being able to sit for an hour. Today, she'd cleaned three large houses. Twelve bedrooms in all. Eleven bathrooms. A dozen mirrors. Walls and walls of glass. Then she rushed home, put a plate of tamales into the oven for her family, grabbed a quick shower, and headed out the door to La Casa, Lake Holly's Latino community center.

This was her Friday night routine. These women were the only people who understood her, truly understood her. Not her husband, Byron. Not even her other friends, the ones who could tuck their children into bed at night. For the hour Marcela was with these women each week, their children became more than just stilted voices over a long-distance phone line or grainy fishbowl images on an ancient computer screen. Here, in the safety of La Casa, they could laugh and cry as they shared stories of holidays and celebrations they would never know except through the time-lapse photos that papered their tiny apartments and au pair suites.

The women called themselves *Las Madres Perdidas*—The Lost Mothers.

Their children lived in locks of hair and lost baby teeth

that sat in boxes on the women's dressers, as if they could be mailed piecemeal over a border that would never let them reunite any other way.

This was the last time Marcela would ever attend one of their meetings.

She wasn't a lost mother anymore.

"Okay, everyone! Time to take a seat," said Rosa Ordoñez, the founder of the group, as she finished setting out cake and coffee beneath posters exhorting people in English and Spanish to *Dream Big!* and *Learn Something New Every Day!*

The women gathered in a semicircle in front of a dusty chalkboard and balanced cups of lukewarm coffee and store-bought cake on their knees. They chatted to one another about nanny and housekeeping jobs that never seemed to pay enough and rents that only went up. They compared currency exchange rates and the best places to wire money back home. Finally, the talk died down as Rosa took a seat.

"We have something to celebrate tonight," said Rosa. "As some of you already know, a 'special gift' has arrived." That was the euphemism they all used—*regalo especial.* They all knew what "special gift" meant. It was the only gift any of them wanted.

"Marcela," said Rosa. "Please share with everyone your good news."

Marcela took a sip of coffee and smiled shyly over the rim of her cup. She was thirty years old. There was a time not long ago when her dimpled smile and long dark eyelashes used to turn men's heads as they'd once turned Byron's. Fatigue had worn her down of late, made her eat more and sleep less. She compensated with home-color kits that turned her hair every shade of dark red and bright lipsticks that made her feel at least a little more attractive when she contemplated another day of scrubbing toilet bowls and ironing shirts.

She felt older than her thirty years even though she was

one of the younger women in the group. There were mothers in this room ten and fifteen years her senior, women who had left their countries when their children were babies and now worked to support two generations of offspring they could never see. Marcela wondered if her good fortune would only fill them with more sadness and frustration.

"My thirteen-year-old daughter, Yovanna, has arrived from Honduras," said Marcela softly.

A flurry of questions flew out of the women's mouths about the girl's journey.

How much did you pay?

How dangerous was the crossing?

How long did it take?

Did immigration stop her at the border?

Did she spend time in a detention center? "Ice boxes," the women called them. *Hieleras* in Spanish. The detention centers at the border were known for keeping detainees—even small children—in freezing cold quarters without blankets to punish them for crossing.

Outside this room, no one could speak of such things. Not to employers, some of whom didn't even know the women had children. Not to friends whose own children were here. Not even to the staff at La Casa. The staff knew that such things existed. But they could not partake—or even appear to partake—in anything illegal. This room on Friday evenings was the only place these women could share the photos and stories that kept them from being ghosts on the landscape of their children's lives.

Marcela tried to answer all their questions. The basic facts were easy enough to explain. The trip had cost ten thousand dollars—an unbelievable, princely sum. Even after years of saving, Marcela had had to borrow most of it from family. The journey had taken more than five weeks—a period in which Marcela could barely eat or sleep for fear of what would happen to her daughter. Would she be raped? Beaten?

Jailed at the border? Held for ransom with dozens of other desperate migrants in some brutal Texas safe house?

Yovanna hadn't been jailed at the border or held for ransom. Those two things Marcela knew. She'd prayed every day to Saint Toribio Romo, the patron saint of immigrants, for Yovanna's safe crossing. And her prayers had been answered. Sort of. No one had warned her about the nightmares. Or the anger. Or the fact that Yovanna would be so far behind in school that even in a special class for non-English speakers, she would be frustrated. No one had warned Marcela that she would leave behind a tenderhearted little girl and get back a sullen teenager who blamed her for everything. *I left for YOU,* Marcela kept shouting. But Yovanna only ever seemed to hear three of those four words: *I left YOU.*

"You are so lucky," said Guadalupe Carrillo wistfully, tucking her graying hair into a bun at the back of her head. Guadalupe was a live-in nanny who took care of three American children while her own three children grew up in Guatemala. Guadalupe had tried twice to get her oldest son here but he'd never made it farther than southern Mexico before getting caught and turned back. Since his last attempt, he'd suffered a broken jaw and the loss of his two front teeth after several gang members beat him up. He was only fifteen.

Ana, a Honduran who worked at a nail salon, couldn't hide her envy. Her nine-year-old son had lived apart from her practically his whole life. She narrowed her gaze at Marcela now.

"And how is your *husband* adjusting to having a stepdaughter live with him?"

Marcela played with her empty coffee cup. She had a sense that Ana knew even before she asked the question what the answer would be. It was the same for all of them who had new relationships here. But even so, she felt defensive. She chose her words carefully.

"He is—hopeful—that Yovanna will be a good big sister to our three-year-old son, Damon." Marcela tried not to think about Byron's real words to her when she told him Yovanna was coming: *We have a child already. Why must you bring your daughter here? Where will she sleep? How will you support her when we can barely support our son?*

Byron needed time, Marcela told herself. He was a good man. He was just very—practical. He carried his practicality with him everywhere, like the soles of his feet. They had a tiny three-room apartment. Marcela, Byron, and Damon already slept in the only bedroom. Yovanna was stuck with a borrowed cot in the living room. It was a cramped life.

My nineteen-year-old's in Honduras, too, he'd pointed out during that terrible argument. *You don't see me moving her in with us!* Marcela didn't remind Byron that his daughter was grown with a child of her own and a mother nearby. Nor did she point out that her sorrow was different from his. A mother's wholeness lives outside her body. It beats in the breast of another. How could he expect her to live the rest of her life with a divided heart? To inflict on Yovanna the same fate that had been inflicted on her as a child?

She had to go back to her early youth to recall a time when her heart hadn't felt divided. If she closed her eyes, she could still smell the perfume sweetness of ripe sapote fruit dangling from the tree in their dusty courtyard where her older brothers kicked around a bundle of wrapped tape and pretended it was a soccer ball. She could still feel the pearls of sweat on her father's neck as he hoisted her up on his shoulders to watch the priests in glittery robes carry a giant statue of Jesus through the narrow streets of San Pedro Sula. Later, in her teenage years, she could still see the boy with hooded eyes, big dreams, and fast hands who used to woo her in the back of a rickety delivery truck, despite her mother's warnings that neither the boy nor his dreams would stick around.

The women in this room understood. Here in this semi-circle of cold metal folding chairs, they were first and foremost mothers even if, in the rough economics of their world, loving their children meant leaving them.

The talk soon turned to the usual worries, the sense of impotence that distance and closed borders bring. Elena feared her daughters in El Salvador were being beaten by her in-laws. Elena called them all the time but the girls could never speak freely because the grandparents listened in on the phone. Ana's ex-husband had stolen their son from Ana's mother's house and dumped him at his own parents' farm where they worked him to death and refused to send him to school. Guadalupe's seven-year-old daughter was complaining of stomach pains regularly but Guadalupe's mother was too timid and old-fashioned to take the child to a hospital. So much was out of their control. They came here to earn money to provide a better life for their children. They lost their children in the process.

It was ten-thirty P.M. by the time Marcela returned to the old frame house where she and Byron rented their tiny apartment. She climbed the narrow wooden staircase. Behind the closed doors of the other five apartments, she heard game shows and soap operas blaring in Spanish from televisions. She heard salsa, rap, and cumbia rhythms from radios. Babies cried and adults raised their voices and lowered them again, aware that the thin walls were never constructed to shelter so many different families. The house was built up against the easement for the railroad tracks and every thirty minutes or so, Marcela heard the peal of the train whistle, followed by a push of air that rattled every window in the house. Pictures never stayed straight on walls and dishes left too close to the edges of tables often found their way onto the floor. She'd lived in this apartment for three years now. The rumble of the train had found its way into her dreams.

She heard raised voices behind her own front door as she unlocked it. Byron and Yovanna were in the living room, their angry faces lit only by the glow from the television that took up nearly the entire space along one wall.

"You're not my father!" Yovanna shouted before running into the bathroom and slamming the door. Byron paced the floor in front of the couch and ran a hand through his thinning black hair. "You think I wanted this? She goes or I do!"

In the doorway between the living room and bedroom, three-year-old Damon stood in his Thomas the Tank Engine pajamas, clutching his favorite stuffed dog and sobbing. Marcela walked over to her son and scooped him into her arms. He curled willingly to her body. She smelled the little-boy scent of baby powder and milky sweat at his neck. She held him close and shot her husband an angry look over the child's head.

"You woke him up! How could you?"

"*I* woke him up? *Me?* Your *daughter* did this," said Byron, gesturing to the locked bathroom door. "She's been nothing but trouble since she got here!"

Marcela swayed Damon gently back and forth, making shushing noises.

"Please, *mi vida,* she's been through a terrible journey. She won't even tell *me* what happened—"

"And that's *my* fault? *I* asked her to come? I work two jobs, Marcela. You work hard, too. We are exhausted. We barely get by raising Damon. How are we supposed to live like this?"

"Things will get better."

"How? How will they get better?"

Marcela had no answer. She was the mother of two children. They were like her right and left arms. Perhaps one was painful at the moment. Perhaps one didn't work the way she had hoped. But there was no question it was part of her body. She could not live without it. She opened her mouth to try to explain this to Byron. Her cell phone rang before she could get the words out. It was almost eleven P.M. Nobody she knew called her at this hour. She sat on the couch with Damon snuffling into her shoulder and fumbled with the phone buttons to answer.

"*Aló?*"

"Is this Marcela Salinez?"

The man on the other end was a native English speaker. Maybe the husband of one of her housekeeping clients. She rarely spoke to anyone but the women.

"Yes?"

"This is Detective Theodore Dolan with the county police. Are you home right now, ma'am? May I come by and speak to you?"

Marcela hesitated. "Why do you want to speak to me?"

"I think it would be best if we discussed this in person. Do I have your correct address?" The officer rattled it off. Marcela barely had the strength to confirm it.

"Thank you, ma'am. I will be there in ten minutes."

Marcela hung up, panicked and shaky at all the reasons a police officer might want to visit her house at this late hour on a Friday night.

Never in her wildest dreams could she have imagined the real one.

Chapter 5

Adele Figueroa was so preoccupied with the shooting this evening that she completely forgot about the dog in her kitchen until she heard the sound of nails tapping like uncooked rice on the linoleum floor. The brown-and-tan short-haired mutt jumped up to the gate Adele had temporarily installed between the kitchen and the rest of the house. He was a Golden Retriever/German Shepherd mix. People told her that such dogs were gentle like retrievers and smart like shepherds but apparently, this dog hadn't read the American Kennel Club manuals. He was dopey and skittish and an insomniac to boot. She was already regretting saying yes to keeping this monster, even for a couple of weeks.

"Hey there, buddy," Vega called out from the front foyer.

The dog's long, slender tail wagged hyperactively. His floppy upturned ears jiggled with excitement. His big pink tongue lolled out the side of his mouth, giving him a goofy expression. Adele felt a pepperiness at the back of her nasal passages. Time to pop another allergy tablet.

Vega threw his jacket on the coat rack by the front door. His eyes, so flat and hooded on the drive over, suddenly brightened. His whole body seemed to relax. They'd both been stiff and tentative around each other in the car. Every comment felt like a minefield.

"What's his name?" asked Vega.

"Diablo."

"*Devil?* He looks kind of sweet to me." Vega walked over to the gate and saw at once how Diablo had earned his name. "Uh-oh."

Adele came up behind him. "Oh my goodness. Bad dog! Bad, bad dog!"

The entire kitchen floor was littered with open cereal boxes, crushed chocolate-chip cookies, and chewed up bits of paper towel. To make matters worse, Diablo had peed over everything. The dog had no shame about what he'd done, either. He trotted about the chaos like an artist showing off his latest masterpiece.

"Huh. Well, I get the name at least," said Vega. "How about if I take Diablo for a walk and then come back and help you clean up?"

Adele sighed. "There's a leash by the back door. And a spare key as well if I'm in the shower."

Vega slipped his jacket back on and climbed over the gate, his boots pulverizing the mess even further. He fetched the leash and whistled for Diablo to follow. The dog bounded over, tongue panting, tail wagging furiously. He stood perfectly still while Vega fastened the leash to his collar. It had taken Adele ten minutes this morning to manage the same feat.

"Little piece of advice, pal," said Vega, scratching the dog behind the ears. "You want to stay in the señora's good graces, don't mess up like this again."

Vega looked over at Adele. She read the plea in those dark moody eyes. She wanted to reassure him that none of what had happened tonight made a difference to their relationship. But she knew him too well to lie. Instead, all she said was "I'll get my broom."

As soon as the back door slammed shut, Adele opened the kitchen gate and began sweeping the mess into several huge plastic trash bags. Cereal and mashed cookies crunched under her feet. Wet urine-scented bits of paper towel stuck to her broom. *Damn this dog! Damn the client who stuck him with me! And damn me most of all for my unforgiving little heart!*

Her insides felt like they were being torn in two directions at once. A part of her wanted more than anything to give Vega the comfort and reassurance he desperately needed. But the other part couldn't staunch the rage and grief over the fact that he'd shot an unarmed man. And not just any man: the father of a woman Adele knew and loved. A woman who had helped raise Sophia.

Marcela Salinez was more than her nine-year-old daughter's babysitter. She'd been with Adele through her early years as an insecure new mother. She'd lived through the fledgling years of La Casa when it was still struggling for a place in the community. She'd quietly endured the rockiest patches of Adele's former marriage. And Adele in turn had witnessed the blossoming of Marcela's life. Marcela met her husband, Byron, when he came over with a friend to paint Adele's garage. Adele was at their wedding. She was at the christening of their adorable little boy, Damon. And although Marcela no longer babysat full-time, she was still very much a fixture in Sophia's life. Now, with a single moment of callous indiscretion, Vega had destroyed everything. For Adele *and* Sophia, even if the child didn't know it yet. Adele couldn't imagine ever breaching this divide.

Worse still, Adele was now at the mercy of police protocol—and this angered her, too. As soon as Adele realized who the dead man might be, Vega called Detective Dolan from her car and gave him Marcela's cell phone number. Adele wanted to call Marcela herself but Dolan and Vega asked her not to. There was a procedure for such things. In police work, there was *always* a procedure. An officer—in this case, Dolan—had to deliver the news in person. Marcela had to be escorted to the medical examiner's office to make a positive identification. Adele was limited to offering up any information on other family members who might need to be contacted.

"I think he has a second wife and a couple of children in the Bronx," Adele told Dolan. She didn't have an address, phone number, or even the second wife's name—if she was indeed a wife at all. It was not uncommon for immigrant men to leave families back in their home countries and start new ones here. The years of separation and loneliness often became too much to maintain ties. Adele had no idea whether Marcela's father was such a man but given that Marcela spoke so rarely about him, it was a strong possibility.

Adele wrestled the garbage bags into the trash can out back. It felt good to put all her anger into something physical. *Who are you angry at?* she asked herself. *Jimmy? You knew he was a police officer when you started dating him. You knew this could happen.* Besides, as much as Adele loved Marcela, it certainly appeared that her father had committed a serious crime.

Yet no matter how hard Adele tried to accept that logic, she couldn't wrap her heart around the situation. If any other cop had been involved in the same scenario, as head of La Casa, Adele would be demanding a meeting with the county police to review the matter and putting pressure on the district attorney's office to convene a grand jury. Yet she couldn't do any of that here. In a few days—maybe less—everyone in the community would know that her lover was the cop who'd shot and killed an unarmed undocumented local dishwasher. Adele would look like a hypocrite if she sided with Vega. She'd look like a heartless careerist if she didn't. So she held her tongue—which was unfortunately attached to her heart—while they both stumbled about in their separate prisons of guilt and grief. His over what he'd done. Hers over what she could not do.

She ran a mop twice over the kitchen floor until she was sure she'd gotten rid of the smell. Vega and Diablo had been gone forty-five minutes. Adele decided to give him another fifteen before she called his cell. Maybe the walk was helping him clear his head.

She went upstairs to take a quick shower and slip into her nightgown. She drifted off to sleep briefly and then jumped up and blinked at the clock. Two A.M. Was Vega still out? The lights were off downstairs, all except for a dim glow coming from the kitchen. Adele grabbed her robe and padded softly down the stairs.

"Jimmy?"

"In the flesh," he answered hoarsely.

She found him seated on the step separating the mud-room from the kitchen. His blue button-down dress shirt was untucked from his pants and open to his white T-shirt beneath. His sleeves were rolled up. Diablo's head lay across his lap. There were three empty Corona bottles from her fridge by his side. He was staring at a picture on his cell phone screen, the faint light bleaching out the warm bronze of his face. He caught her looking at him and clicked off the photo. Even with only the fluorescent lamp above the stove for light, she could see that his eyes were red-rimmed and puffy.

"It's cold out there." He wiped a sleeve across his face. "The wind really gets to you."

Something heavy settled on her chest. The man she loved would rather pour out his anguish to a dog than to her. She knelt down beside him. The dog didn't stir.

"I must have dozed off," said Adele. "I didn't realize you were back."

"I didn't want to wake you." He ran his fingers along the black and white linoleum of the kitchen floor. "Sorry I got back so late. I'd have helped you clean up."

"It's okay. It didn't take that long. Come upstairs, *mi amado*. Take a nice hot shower and come to bed with me."

He shook his head. "I'm not going to be able to sleep.

And—uh—I don't know if I'm good for much else right now."

"We can just hold each other."

Silence. Vega stroked the dog.

Adele stared at the empty Corona bottles. "Drowning your sorrows isn't the way."

"I had three beers. Not a quart of vodka."

"Still, we need to find a better way through this." She touched his shoulder. "I know you say you can't talk about the shooting. But it's not like I would tell anyone."

"I can't, Adele. It's just wrong. For you. For me."

"Are you afraid that I might judge you?"

He tossed off a laugh. "You're already judging me. And don't tell me you aren't because I *know* you, *nena*. If we weren't sleeping together, you'd be calling for my blood right now and telling the DA that I had to have done *something* wrong or that man would still be alive."

"Well, maybe you're right. Maybe I would have. But I'm here, goddamnit. I didn't desert you. What more do you want me to say? That I'm okay with what happened? That my clients will be okay with it? I don't know that they will. You've put me in a bad place."

"I've put *you* in a bad place." Vega smiled sadly and got to his feet. Diablo danced nervously around his legs. "Maybe I should go."

He was like a man with a bad sunburn. The slightest chafe sent him into agony.

Adele blocked the doorway. "Please, *querido*. You don't have your truck. You've been drinking. The last thing you need right now is to be alone."

They stood staring at each other for a long, awkward moment. The dog gave a little bark of anticipation. Vega reached down and patted Diablo behind the ear. The dog leaned in closer. Vega could soothe that mutt in a way he couldn't soothe himself or Adele right now.

His cell phone rang in his pocket. He pulled it out and squinted at the number.

"Joy?" asked Adele.

"Nah. She called me earlier. When I was out with Diablo. It's Dolan. He's pulling an all-nighter, too."

For Teddy Dolan to be calling this late, Adele assumed it had to be bad news.

Vega turned his back to Adele and braced an arm against the doorframe that separated the kitchen from the mudroom. Adele couldn't make out the conversation except for his "Huhs" and "You sure?" and a scattering of curses in English and Spanish.

"Nah. You did the right thing calling. Thanks for texting over the pictures, too."

He hung up without turning to face Adele. He leaned his forehead on his arm and kept his eyes on the floor as he spoke. "Dolan got hold of Marcela. She ID'd the body. It's her father, Hector Ponce. She recognized the rosary in his coat pocket."

"Dear God. Poor Marcela."

Vega flinched. Adele could have slapped him and done less damage. She tried to recover. "Sorry. I'm just surprised Teddy would call so late just to tell you that."

"He didn't. He called to tell me that he ran a check on Marcela's father's fingerprints and nothing came back."

"No arrests? Not even a record of deportation proceedings?"

"No. I'm sure the press will be reporting this little tidbit as soon as it hits the wires so I thought you should know."

"Oh, *mi amado*." Adele hugged him from behind.

"Jesus," Vega said thickly. "Maybe I really did kill an innocent man."

"I'll try to do some damage control for you. I'll tell my clients and the community—"

"It's not going to matter what you tell them." Vega

turned to her. "This thing is already bigger than you and me. Dolan told me there's media interest from outside the area. You can't keep those dogs at bay for long. They've already found out about the photograph."

"Photograph? What photograph?"

Vega tapped his iPhone and pulled up the photograph Adele saw him looking at earlier. It was a picture taken before the digital age of three Hispanic males—two strapping men in their thirties and a teenage boy. Adele wondered if one of them was Marcela's father at a younger age. All three males were dressed in scruffy, loose-fitting jeans, baseball caps, and T-shirts. They were posed in front of a fruit stand with bananas hanging in bunches on a cord overhead. From the muddy road, broad leafy trees, and misty jungle mountains behind the stand, Adele guessed they were probably in Central America or southern Mexico. They stood next to each other, slightly stiff and self-conscious-looking but with the straight shoulders and shy smiles to suggest something hopeful about the occasion.

"Why is everyone so interested in the photograph?" she asked. It was evidence of some sort. From her defense attorney days, Adele recognized the long string of numbers—a case number—in the corner.

Vega didn't answer. He turned the screen away from her and went to scroll past the picture.

"Huh." He frowned.

"What?"

"Nothing. It's just—wait. No—" He wasn't looking at the photograph anymore. He was looking at a cell-phone shot of a pay stub with the same case number in the corner.

"Did that belong to Marcela's father?"

Vega ignored the question. He turned to where the light was better and enlarged a portion of the image on the screen.

"Holy—" He slumped against the doorway. "I don't believe it."

"I don't understand," said Adele.

"Look at the address on his pay stub."

Adele read it off. "Three fifty-four, One hundred and Seventy-Sixth Street in the Bronx. That was his home address I guess. So?"

"That was my mother's building."

Chapter 6

Vega crept out of Adele's bed on Saturday morning as the first light broke the sky. He slipped back into his clothes, which looked even worse in daylight. His blue button-down shirt was wrinkled and sour smelling. His dark khaki pants were snagged and muddy at the cuffs. He kept spare clothes in his pickup truck but it was still parked in the county police lot.

He hadn't slept at all. He felt like he had crystal meth running through his veins. A hot shower didn't help. He stayed under the blast an extralong time but his body still thrummed like a tuning fork. He kept whipsawing between two wildly different states of mind. In one, he was racked with guilt and shame at the thought that he'd killed Marcela's father, an unarmed man with no criminal record. In the other, he felt a burning frustration that a potential witness—or even, God forbid, his mother's murderer—had died by Vega's own hand before he could question him in her death.

Adele had insisted it was just a coincidence. "A lot of the restaurant help live in the Bronx. The rents are cheaper. You don't even know if your mother and Marcela's father lived in the building at the same time."

All true. And yet Vega couldn't make himself buy it. He

didn't believe in coincidences. He did believe in irony, however. There was a hell of a lot of irony to his having killed off his best lead.

He shoved his wallet, phone, Swiss army knife, and truck keys back into his pants pockets. That's when it hit him: he didn't have his truck. He'd have to fetch it from work. If he called a cab, Adele could sleep in this morning. He stepped softly into the upstairs hallway and turned on his iPhone. He'd walk Diablo before he left, but for the moment, he just wanted to concentrate on his own situation.

His screen lit up. There were over a hundred messages.

Not good. Not good at all.

The smart thing to do would be to dial a cab company and stay away from the Internet but Vega had a sense he needed to know what was going on. He opened a search engine and typed *Wickford, NY, shooting*. A Pandora's box of misery flashed across the screen.

Right away he knew he was in trouble. Although Vega's department hadn't formally released his name yet, the activist, Ruben Tate-Rivera, had somehow gotten hold of it. Worse, Tate had put Vega on his Wall of Shame, along with Vega's incredibly unflattering departmental photo. Vega had lifted his chin too high and blinked at the wrong time so he had a brutish look in the picture. His coloring was washed out too so he looked much whiter than he did in real life. Beneath the bad photo was his name: *James O. Vega*. The O was for "Orlando," his father—the only part of the man that stuck around. The middle initial gave Vega's name a Gaelic lilt. *Great. Just what I need. I'm now a brutish, white-looking Irish cop.* A perfect image for all his new Internet fans.

Vega scrolled through the copy on Tate's website. There was almost no mention of Ricardo Luis who'd mistakenly led dispatch to believe Marcela's father was armed in the first place. Instead, Tate told readers that the shooting happened in Wickford, NY, *one of the wealthiest towns in the United States.* It identified the dishwasher as Hector Mauricio Ponce-Fernandez (where the name "Antonio" or the Atlanta connection came from on his other ID was anyone's guess). It went on to describe Ponce as a *married father of two young boys with a steady work history and no criminal record.* Vega's stomach tightened to read about the boys, ages twelve and fourteen. Vega couldn't believe he'd robbed them of their dad.

But his guilt was quickly replaced by rage as he read on. Tate mentioned that Vega, a detective with eighteen years on the force, had shot Ponce four times and that *some of the shots had been delivered to the head, execution-style.*

Whoa. Hold on. Was Tate seriously suggesting to his almost one million website followers that Vega had executed the man? Here, Vega was forbidden to speak about the shooting, and this media gadfly who hadn't even been there was making unfounded accusations and turning him into a coast-to-coast whipping boy for all that was wrong with the police.

People were buying it, too. On Twitter, Vega's name suddenly popped up under hashtags like *#handsupdontshoot, #killercops, #immigrantlivesmatter,* and a hashtag created exclusively for him: *#shotforaphoto.* Under each was a torrent of hate mail:

I hope they lock up his sorry ass and throw away the key. . . .

Wait until he sees what happens to cops in prison. . . .

If I could do to him what he did to that dishwasher and get away with it, I would. . . .

He better never meet ME in a dark alley. . . .

He's gonna NEED a gun after this. . . .

Vega felt like he was going to explode from all the hurt and anger inside of him. He wanted so badly to punch something—anything—to get the rage out. But he didn't want to make any noise and wake Adele. She didn't deserve to be dragged through this. Their original plan had been to take Sophia to pick out a Christmas tree this morning at Our Lady of Sorrows Catholic Church in town. But Vega couldn't imagine doing anything so normal. Instead, he scribbled a quick note of explanation and left it by Adele's bedside. He hoped she'd understand. He didn't write what he was really thinking—what he didn't yet want to acknowledge. The kindest thing he could do right now was to leave and never come back. They'd been together only eight months. She didn't deserve to sacrifice a decade of hard work because of his two seconds of bad choices.

In the kitchen, Diablo greeted him warmly, jumping up for a scratch, dancing around the back door to go out. The cab could wait. Vega fetched the leash off a hook in the mudroom and attached it to Diablo's collar.

"Come on, pal. Let's take a walk."

It was a cold December morning. The air felt like peppermint in his lungs. Pale rays of sun lit up the hard frost on car windshields up and down Adele's street. Somewhere down the road, Vega heard an engine humming and the sharp sound of an ice scraper across glass.

Diablo was all good cheer as he trotted down the sidewalk, his tail and ears turned up on alert, sniffing every fire hydrant like he'd never before encountered such a thing of beauty. Vega had to fight with him a little to get him to heel but overall, the dog seemed comfortable with him. They soon developed a rhythm. While they walked, Vega pulled out his cell phone and checked his messages. They were multiplying like a virus. From friends. From fellow cops. Everyone wanted to talk to him about the one thing he couldn't talk about.

Vega was halfway to the next corner when Diablo began turning in circles behind a leafless sycamore and arching his back. Too late, Vega realized that he'd forgotten to bring a baggie to pick up after the dog. That was all he needed: to get Adele in trouble with her neighbors. He had to hope the dog would just be quick about it.

No such luck. Vega could hear the soft purr of a car engine slowly pulling alongside him as Diablo finished his business. Vega turned, ready to plead with some annoyed homeowner. He recognized the white Buick as soon as it pulled to the curb. The driver's door opened and a familiar figure hefted himself out from behind the wheel. A weak shaft of sunlight caught the top of the man's bald head as he frowned at Vega over the roof of his car. The man bent down and rummaged through a cellophane package for something. When he emerged again, he had a stick of red licorice in his gloved hand. He bit off a piece and chewed loudly.

"I'd ticket you, Vega. But I think you've got enough troubles already."

Diablo strained at his leash, jumping and whining until Lake Holly Detective Louis Greco walked around to the curb and gave the animal a scratch. "Is this a therapy dog?" Greco eyed the steaming pile of fresh doggie doo next to the tree. "Or are you just offering up a public statement on your current predicament?"

"So you've heard."

"The whole freakin' country's heard thanks to that mail-order professor with the Orville Redenbacher bowties. How he gets this shit so quickly, I'll never know. I got a friend on the Bronx detectives' squad who called me as soon as it went viral. Seems the perp you shot was from his neck of the woods." Greco shoved the rest of the licorice stick in his mouth. He rubbed two gloved hands the size of baseball mitts together. Everything about Greco was big. His wide, jowly face. His gut. His opinions. He delivered the last with gusto.

"I figured maybe Ruben Race-Hysteria would give you

a pass, you being Puerto Rican and all. But I guess being a cop trumps every other allegiance. That's probably the one thing that media whore and I can agree on."

"Glad to hear you two are in such cozy agreement," Vega said dryly. He wasn't in the mood to hear Greco's take on Ruben Tate-Rivera, the shooting, or the state of police work in the United States today. Besides, he already knew what they'd be. He and Greco had worked a few cases together over the past year and although Vega had initially been put off by the man's gruffness, he'd come to like and respect him. Even so, Louis Greco was a townie cop nearing retirement. His whole career had been spent in tiny Lake Holly handling small-time burglaries, car accidents, drug arrests, and domestic abuse complaints. The most deadly thing Louis Greco had probably ever done in his entire career was eat the two-week-old leftover potato salad at the back of the station house refrigerator.

Diablo tugged on his leash. "I've gotta get going," said Vega.

"I'm not out here looking for jaywalkers, you dope. I came to find you. Adele told me you and the dog had both taken off so I figured, follow the fire hydrants."

"I can't talk, Grec. Not to you. Not to anybody."

"I know that." Greco opened his front passenger door. "But Adele tells me your truck's in the county police lot and you need a ride to fetch it. Hop in. We'll drop the Poop King at her house and head over."

"That's not necessary."

"Consider me a taxi service."

"Look, I appreciate the offer," said Vega. "But I'd rather be on my own right now."

"Bad idea, buddy."

Couldn't this guy take a hint? "Listen, Grec," said Vega. "I know you mean well. But you've got no idea what I'm going through right now. And don't hand me that 'thin blue line' shit."

Greco was a head taller than Vega. He stared down at him. His eyes got dark and deadly serious. "You tried to drink yourself to sleep last night and it didn't work, did it? Next you'll start popping Ambiens like they're breath mints. They won't work either. That little film inside your head will just keep playing until making a cup of coffee feels like too much mental effort. You'll explode at every-thing and anything. Your relationships will fall apart. Friends will start to back off—or you'll back off, thinking everyone's better off without you. By the time they hand you back your service weapon, you'll start thinking that's just about the neatest and easiest solution. One bullet—no more pain."

Vega blinked at Greco. There was only one way he could know all that.

"How come you never—?"

"Like you said: How could anyone understand?" Greco rapped a knuckle against the open door. "Get in."

Greco kept the pearl-gray brushed velour interior of his Buick spotless. Vega was sure he had it detailed once a month. Which made Vega all the more embarrassed when Diablo licked the rear windows and muddied the seat with his paw prints.

"Sorry," said Vega after they dropped Diablo back at Adele's. "I owe you for a car cleaning."

"I'll put it on your tab."

Greco nosed the car along the highway, following the train tracks that zigzagged south through the county. They breezed past small, picturesque villages where nothing stood taller than the church steeples. All around them were bare gray trees and rolling hills dotted with deer and flocks of wild turkeys. The sun was trying to break through. The day looked far too promising for Vega's mood. His cell phone dinged. He took it out of his pocket and frowned as he scrolled through text messages and emails he had no in-tention of answering.

"Ah, social media," said Greco. "You can't take a leak these days without the whole world commenting on it. That was one thing, thank God, I never had to deal with."

"When did it happen?"

"Four years after I came on the job." Greco dug into his open bag of Twizzlers and pulled another out. He didn't offer Vega one. They both knew Vega would call it sugar-coated wire insulation and pretty soon Greco would be ribbing Vega about all the fried food Puerto Ricans eat and Vega would be countering that Italians couldn't eat anything not smothered in garlic, tomato sauce, and cheese. Working a case with a partner was a bit like being married. After a while you knew everything about the other person.

Or maybe you just thought you did.

"It was a domestic disturbance call," said Greco. "Sunday morning, February 27. That date will forever be etched into my brain. Me and my partner, Bryan Kelly—he's long retired now—we got dispatched to this nice, tidy little cape house over on Cliffdale Street. A seventeen-year-old girl had called nine-one-one to report that her twenty-year-old brother was holding a meat cleaver to their mother's throat." Greco shook his head. "For as long as I live, I will never forget that young man's face."

Greco went to take a bite of the licorice then changed his mind and stuffed it back into the bag. He'd lost his appetite. Vega could relate. He hadn't eaten more than a few bites since the shooting.

"Me and Kelly, we both tried to talk the kid into putting down the cleaver. Kelly—he's a veteran cop—he tries to distract the kid so I can get in a little closer and maybe disarm him. But the kid sees what we're about to do. He turns the blade from his mother and lunges at me. To this day, I keep wondering why I didn't just step back. Why did I shoot?"

"Because he could have killed you," said Vega.

"Yeah, well—you die a little anyway. I suspect you're already learning that by now. You're still in the denial stage, I imagine."

"The what?"

Greco pointed through the windshield to a red-tailed hawk hovering overhead. "Isn't that just the most beautiful creature? I swear I never get tired of watching hawks fly. All that beauty just so they can swoop down and kill something. Pierce it right through the heart. Oh yeah," Greco suddenly remembered. "The denial stage. You ever heard of the five stages of grief?"

"No."

"By the time you're finished with counseling you will." Greco ticked them off on his gloved fingers: "Denial, anger, bargaining, depression, and acceptance. Anyway, the first is denial."

"I'm not in denial, Dr. Freud," said Vega. "I know I killed a man."

"Yeah, but right now you're itching to prove to yourself and anyone who will listen that you did the right thing."

"I didn't have a choice."

"I know that, Vega. So does every cop out there. But you're looking for someone to *absolve* you. Like it never happened. That's what I mean by denial. You're not ready to accept that good intentions can still have bad consequences."

Vega found himself watching the hawk now. That magnificent wingspan, the way it just hovered above the earth on currents of air. Vega wished he could be above everything right now, just floating. "I never wanted to be this sort of cop."

"You think any police officer does?" asked Greco. "I've been doing this since you were having wet dreams, Vega. And sure, there are some cops who shouldn't be cops. They've got too much temper in them. They're too nervous under pressure. They see people as categories instead of individuals. But I've never yet met a cop who took this job because he wanted to kill people."

They were both silent after that. They'd worked two whole murder investigations together before this and they'd probably exchanged fewer words than they had this morning in Greco's Buick. Vega's cell phone dinged with more messages. More bad news. He was developing a Pavlovian response to his phone. Each ding made him queasy. He turned his face to the side window and tried to concentrate on the shafts of weak sunlight raking the bare trees. There was no yellow to the light this time of year. It was all gray and white, like the clouds that hovered so low they seemed like distant mountains.

"The man I shot?" said Vega. "Turns out he lived in the same building as my mother—the same building she was murdered in."

"Here we go again with the denial," said Greco.

"How is that denial?"

"You're hoping like hell you can fix your conscience by painting this guy as a murderer—your mother's murderer, no less. It ain't gonna happen, Vega. The NYPD's been all over your mother's case. If there were some connection, they'd have found it by now. All you're gonna do is alienate people."

"Like I'm not alienating them now, huh? You see the Internet this morning? I'm being compared to the Gestapo."

"It's going to get bad for a while, I'm afraid," said Greco. "That's where stage two—the anger—comes in. Everybody's Monday-morning quarterbacking you. Colleagues. Superiors. The media." He grinned. "Ruben Tweets-his-errors."

Vega allowed a smile.

"Meanwhile," said Greco, "your department's distancing itself from the whole mess. The victim's family is filing suit. It starts to feel like the entire world is running its mouth off while you're just standing there with your thumb up your ass, a bystander to your own life. The only people you'll have to take your anger and frustration out on are the people you love. But you do that"—Greco wagged a finger at him—"and it's over, my friend. You'll lose every significant connection in your life. Believe me, Joanna and I came close to divorcing during this period. It's going to be even harder for you and Adele. She'll be under pressure to distance herself from you."

Vega slumped in his seat. "She probably should. This will kill her career."

"Why you couldn't just date a nice nurse or school-teacher, I'll never know."

"I've got a thousand good reasons." Vega shrugged. "But if you were to reverse the question and ask how come she's with me? I can't think of one. And that was *before* this."

Greco tossed off a low-throttle laugh. It sounded like a furnace kicking in. "I can think of one."

"You can *always* think of one."

Greco pulled off the highway and turned into the county police parking lot. Several camera crews were already setting up near the front doors.

"I have a feeling those guys aren't there to film the latest budget talks," said Greco.

"My department's holding a press conference this morning to talk about the shooting," said Vega. "A bunch of brass who weren't there are gonna tell the world how I fucked up. And I can't even be there to defend myself."

"There should be a special circle of hell reserved just for the bureaucrats in our job," said Greco. "Which reminds me: Where does that Ricky Ricardo guy fit into all of this?"

"You mean Ricardo Luis?"

"Yeah. Whatever."

Leave it to Greco to turn every Latin singer into a knock-off from *I Love Lucy.* "He was a homeowner protecting his turf. His gun was legit. He called nine-one-one."

Greco frowned. "A Mexican entertainer? From Miami? And he doesn't have a bodyguard with him twenty-four-seven? You believe that and there's some swampland down in Florida I'd like to sell you."

"Nobody outside the Latin community knows who he is," said Vega. "And besides, he didn't kill Ponce—remember? I did."

Greco grunted as he pulled up to Vega's truck. Fortunately, from this vantage point, the building blocked them from the camera crews. Vega could make an exit without being spotted.

Greco put the Buick in park, pulled out a scrap of paper, and copied a phone number off his cell. Then he handed it to Vega.

"Who's this?"

"Dr. Ellen Cantor."

"A shrink?"

"She'll help you, Vega. She helped me. Call her."

"I don't know—"

"Your department's gonna make you do it. Why not get someone good?"

"I'd rather talk to you." Vega rolled his eyes. "Jesus—did I just say that? I must be in bad shape."

Greco grinned. "Nobody said you *can't* talk to me. Even in the middle of the night. I'll curse your unborn descendants. But I'll try to help you through this. That said however, I still think you should call her."

"I'll think about it." Vega tucked the slip of paper into his wallet. He put his hand on the door then hesitated. "Hey, Grec?"

"Yeah?"

Vega sat back in his seat. He didn't know how to formulate the question that was swimming around in his brain.

"You're still a cop," he said finally. "You're still married to Joanna." *Duh.*

"And you want to know how I got through it. You want a road map. Is that it?"

"Yeah."

Greco was silent for a long moment. Then he let out a long slow breath like the last vestiges of that terrible day had finally been expelled. "Make something good happen."

"Huh?"

"Something really bad happened here. You can't deny it. Can't run away from it. So? You gotta make something good come out of it."

"How?"

"In my case, I started reading up on how to handle mentally ill people. I pushed for department-wide training on how to de-escalate situations involving the mentally ill. A few years after the shooting, I talked a schizophrenic man out of taking his life and his girlfriend's life. If I'd quit the job, I'd never have done any of that. I found my good. And when I found it, it saved my life."

"What's my good?"

"I can't find it for you, buddy. You've got to find it for yourself."

"I don't even know where to look."

"You've got to start by realizing that you can't just go back to the person you used to be. That's where guys get in trouble. You either work on that or it works on you."

Greco frowned at the steering wheel. He seemed to want to say something and be afraid of saying it at the same time. "I heard the suspect was reaching for a photograph when you shot him."

"Yeah." It pained Vega more than anything to have to admit that. "I've got a copy of the picture on my cell. I keep looking at it even though I shouldn't. It just makes me feel worse."

Greco shifted in his seat so that the full force of his gaze was on Vega. He had dark, grandfatherly eyes. The kind of eyes that saw you for who you were but imagined in you something better.

"Think about it, Vega. You had a gun trained on this guy. And yet that photograph was so important, he gave his life to show it to you."

"I guess."

"You want to find your good? Figure out why that picture mattered."

Chapter 7

Marcela Salinez didn't sleep Friday night. There were calls to make. To her mother in Honduras. To Alma, the mother of her father's two young sons in the Bronx.

"The police will not get away with this!" sobbed Alma. "I will make them pay!" Alma had taken over her father's life when he came to the United States. Now it seemed she planned to take over his death as well.

"You must not listen to that woman. She talks crazy," said Byron early the next morning, as he got dressed for work. His "fish clothes," he called them. Jeans and T-shirts reserved exclusively for when he worked gutting and slicing fish at the smoked seafood plant in town. No matter how much Marcela washed those clothes, they always smelled faintly of fish, brine, and charcoal.

"Alma just became a widow," said Marcela. "And I lost my father. All because of a police officer's recklessness. We have a right to be upset."

"Of course you do," said Byron. "But not like this. Alma wants to tell the whole world that her sons' father was shot robbing a house. Is that a good thing for those boys? No! She can do what she wants. But you, Marcela? You must not talk to anyone about this."

"Not tell anyone my father just died?" Marcela put

down the spatula from frying his eggs. She was incredulous. She tried to keep her voice low. Yovanna and Damon were still asleep.

"Tell them he was sick."

"But it's all over the news."

"It's all over the news that the police shot and killed a Honduran dishwasher. No one has to know he was your father. You don't use his last name."

"You want me to deny my father?" Marcela couldn't hold back the catch in her voice.

Byron came up behind her and gave her a hug. Then he turned her around to face him. He was a broad-shouldered man with a nose like a block of granite and hair that had started to thin like beach grass across his scalp. She fell in love with him not so much for his looks but for his temperament. Unlike so many other Latin American men she'd known, he truly considered her his partner. They asked each other's advice on everything—which was probably part of the reason it pained him so much that she'd brought Yovanna here against his wishes.

"I would never ask you to deny your father," said Byron. "Only the circumstances of his death."

"You mean pretend I didn't see what the police did to him?"

Byron winced. He knew the enormity of what he was asking. "Tell as few people as possible then—and no *norteamericanos*, especially not your housecleaning and babysitting clients. If they hear that your father robbed a house and was shot by the police, they won't side with you. They'll side with the police. They'll figure, like father, like daughter."

"But they know I'm honest."

"It doesn't matter," said Byron. "They won't take that chance, especially with their children. They'll find a reason to let you go. They'll tell you it's for some other reason. But they'll still let you go."

He was right, Marcela realized. Something like this would

travel through the Lake Holly Moms Facebook page faster than a report of bed bugs or lice.

"We need the money," Byron pleaded with her. "You say you want this to work out with Yovanna? Then do as I ask. *Please*. Go to work today and don't tell anyone about what happened."

Marcela had just two houses to clean on Saturdays. The first was a couple whose son and daughter were in high school. They were all usually coming out of their own bathroom showers when she arrived, often draped in nothing but towels. Marcela was always amazed at how casual and informal *norteamericanos* were in her presence. The daughter and son usually had headphones on so they barely acknowledged her. Señora Garner was always friendly, if a bit frazzled, running around in her tennis whites with her cell phone at her ear. Señor Garner wandered in and out of the kitchen wearing a one-piece bright green spandex outfit, fluorescent orange sneakers, and a yellow bike helmet that jutted out like a wing in back. He looked like one of Damon's comic book figures. Marcela tried hard not to giggle. All the men she knew in town rode bikes to work— including her husband. They wouldn't be caught dead in a getup like that even if they could afford such a thing.

Señora Garner grabbed her tennis racket and car keys and motioned to Marcela that she'd left cash for her on the kitchen counter.

"Thank you, missus."

If the señora knew anything about the shooting, it wasn't apparent from the big smile on her face.

"We're all very excited," the señora told Marcela. "Jackson just got accepted to Brown."

"Congratulations, missus." Marcela knew from the tone of the señora's words that Brown must be something other than a color. But she had no idea if it was a team, a college, or a company. Not that she would ever ask. Being someone's housekeeper was both deeply intimate and oddly impersonal. She scrubbed the toilets and folded the underwear of people she rarely if ever saw. And yet she was privy to their deepest secrets. Husbands who slept apart from their wives. Closet drinkers who buried the evidence at the bottoms of their trash. The bulimic soccer moms who stashed huge bags of candy and bottles of laxatives in their closets. The teenagers who kept baggies of marijuana and packages of condoms under their beds.

And yet most of these families knew almost nothing about her—not how long she'd lived in the country or where she was originally from. Not her little boy's name or where her husband worked. Certainly not that she'd just smuggled her thirteen-year-old daughter here after ten years of them being apart. Most of her clients passed her with a smile and a wave as they headed out the door, their eyes on their watches and a cell phone at their ear. Byron had been right all along. The *norteamericanos* had no idea that Marcela was related to the man the police had just shot—if indeed they knew there'd been a shooting at all.

She wished she were cleaning for a family with lots of children today. She craved distraction. But the Garners all ran out the door early. Marcela was alone. She tried to lose herself in the rhythm of housework but she ended up crying openly as she scrubbed the Garners' marble bathroom tiles, her tears mixing with the vinegar cleaning solution (Señora Garner didn't allow bleach in the house).

Everything brought the horror of last night back: the chrome appliances in the Garners' kitchen. The rubber gloves by the sink. The smell of disinfectant. It still seemed unreal to Marcela to imagine her father lying on that shiny steel gurney in the medical examiner's office last night, his face so ravaged that the attendant left a sheet over it during most of the viewing. But worse than the carnage and the circuslike atmosphere was the aura of smugness and condescension in the police. As polite as that detective (*Dooley? Doyle?*) who spoke to her was, there was no mistaking that he believed her father was entirely at fault for what had happened to him.

Marcela took a quick break from cleaning and called to check on how Yovanna was faring babysitting Damon. Then she flicked on the Garners' kitchen television and caught the local Spanish-language news while she wiped down the countertops. She stared at yet another helicopter view of Ricardo Luis's Wickford estate with its swimming pool, tennis courts, and fountain. The footage was interspersed with headshots of police officers and reporters babbling on camera. There was a quick segment showing Alma, her tweezed eyebrows moving in angry animation across her puffy face as she held up one of those department-store portraits of her, her two boys, and Marcela's father. Next to her on camera was a black man with dark-framed glasses and a red bowtie. A lawyer perhaps. Marcela couldn't say. His Spanish carried an American accent. He seemed far more interested in criticizing the police than in getting restitution for her father's killing.

The news showed a small inset photograph of the police officer who had shot her father. In all the upset last night, Marcela had never asked his name. She'd assumed at first that he was this Dooley guy with his shaved head and blond mustache. Only later did she understand that it was someone else.

She stared at the inset shot and the name below it: *James O. Vega.* The newscaster said he was a county police detective.

James O. Vega. Detective James Vega.

Marcela stood frozen at the screen with a wet rag in her hand. This couldn't be the same man who drove her home several weeks ago when she babysat for Sophia. It was raining that night. He walked her to her door under his umbrella and waited until she'd made it safely inside. How could a man like that do something like this?

How could Señora Adele be involved with such a man?

Marcela's cell phone rang, interrupting her thoughts. She picked it up, expecting Yovanna with a question. Or Byron on one of his fifteen-minute factory breaks.

"Marcela?"

Marcela heard the sharp drawn-in breath, that familiar aggrieved tone that was always there, even before this happened. Of all her father's mysteries, none was more puzzling than why he'd chosen to settle down with Alma, a woman who defined her loyalties more by the people she held at bay than the ones she embraced. Loneliness and guilt can make you do strange things, Marcela supposed. She had only to look at her own life to realize that.

"Listen to me," said Alma breathlessly. "If you and your father made some kind of deal, that's *your* problem. Not mine! Don't drag me into this."

"What are you talking about?"

"You know what I'm talking about: your daughter!"

"Yovanna?" Marcela's heart hammered in her chest. "What about her?"

"Don't play dumb. I just got a call from the man you were dealing with. I gave him your cell phone number."

"What man, Alma? I don't know who you mean."

Alma's voice got soft and steely. "It's your fault this happened, you know. My Hector would never have gotten into this mess if not for your daughter."

"You're not making any sense."

"You think he broke into Ricardo Luis's house for no reason?"

"I don't know what to believe." Ever since Marcela had gotten that call from the detective last night, she'd tried to convince herself that the police were mistaken. Her father was no thief. But Alma's words gave her pause. She'd been apart from her father for too many years to say for sure that she really knew him. He'd lecture her on the importance of family and then go for weeks without calling. He'd complain that he couldn't afford new sneakers for

Aaron and Felix, his sons by Alma—and then for no reason at all mail Marcela fifty dollars. Sober, he blamed Marcela's mother—whom he'd never divorced—for his terrible, fateful journey to the United States. After a few beers, he always blamed himself.

"*Abuelita* hated him," said Yovanna last night after they got the news. Marcela's mother had been raising the girl and no doubt Yovanna had gotten an earful about her grandfather and how he'd abandoned the family. But Marcela had come to realize that her father's actions were more complicated than she'd believed as a child. She was a parent herself now. She'd seen how the border could slice families in two. No one ever came out of it the same.

The coyotes and moneylenders always told you it was easy. So easy. *Go to the United States! Make lots of money!* Everywhere in San Pedro Sula when Marcela was a girl, there were symbols of families with someone doing well in *El Norte*. New concrete homes with big American flags painted on their exteriors. Cell phones. Electronics. Stylish clothes with brand-name labels. She was ten when her father made his fateful journey. She didn't see him again for eighteen years. No one told any of them what the real cost would be. They were still paying it.

They would forever be paying it.

"This man who called you," Marcela said to Alma. "Did he give you his name? A phone number?"

Alma tossed off a bitter laugh. "Do you think this was one of your father's friends from the neighborhood? Someone he played dominoes with? Wake up, Marcela! This was not that sort of call. This man knew my address. He knew where Aaron and Felix go to school. We may live in New York. But even here, there are people who play by the same rules as the ones we left in Honduras. You don't say no to them."

"Did he say what he wants from me?"

Alma seemed to be weighing her words. "He called your

daughter—'collateral.' " Marcela heard the tightness in Alma's voice. As cool as the woman had always been toward Marcela, she was still a mother. She understood the gravity of what she was saying.

" 'Collateral'? Like for a loan?" asked Marcela. "But I didn't make any deal!"

"Then I guess you'd better make one now. If Yovanna's the collateral, I would hate to think what happens if you forfeit."

Chapter 8

Vega lived in a former summer cottage overlooking a wooded natural lake. When he bought his place after the divorce almost six years ago, friends told him he was crazy to bury himself in the middle of nowhere, a whole county north of where he worked. But there was one terrific thing about living in a summer lake community in December.

There was no chance of being followed by the media.

Vega's home address and phone number were unlisted. Even if someone tried to find him up here, it would be difficult. The mailboxes were at the entrance to the community. The streets were barely marked and his tiny cul-de-sac had only three houses.

Vega collected his mail at his mailbox—bills mostly. Then he drove his pickup truck along the main community road. He was still in the same clothes he'd worn since the shooting. He was dying to step out of them and into a hot shower as soon as possible. Through the trees to his left, he could see the lake, soft and milky like a pearl. It soothed him to see it. Nature always soothed him—which was funny in a way, when he considered that he lived his first eleven years of life in a Bronx tenement where the great outdoors consisted of a makeshift ball field in a garbage-strewn lot and a water view meant hanging out his mother's fire escape above an uncapped hydrant.

His mother. Today she would have been sixty-four. The shooting had nearly wiped her birthday from his thoughts. He owed it to her that he was living in a place like this at all. She was the courageous one, the one who left her home and her friends, first at seventeen to move from a mountain village in Puerto Rico to New York, and then again when Vega was eleven to move from the Bronx to Lake Holly. The second move was only a geographical distance of about fifty miles. But in many ways it was a bigger change. Lake Holly back then was a place where everyone spoke English with an American accent and parents traveled two by two. A Puerto Rican single mother was neither welcomed nor understood.

She didn't make the move for herself. She did it for him, because she believed he deserved a better life and a set of dreams that included college. He'd hated her for it at the time, hated sticking out like a Devil Dog in a sea of Twinkies. But it was because of her that he could effort-lessly swim and ice skate and ride a bicycle. It was because of her that he finished college. She moved back to the Bronx when Vega was grown. She missed her friends. Her world. But those years she sacrificed in between put Vega solidly in the middle class and gave him the skills to move comfortably between the Anglo and Latino worlds. He wouldn't have this life if she hadn't given up so much of hers.

He made two more turns and then headed onto his street. There was a white Volvo parked on his tiny gravel patch of driveway. Vega recognized the car. It had once be-longed to his ex, Wendy. Now it belonged to his daughter, Joy. Vega was touched that she'd driven all the way up here on a Saturday morning to see how he was doing. He was glad he'd given her her own key. He was also exhausted and needed a shower so he hoped her visit would be quick.

Vega pulled his truck to the side, so as not to block her car. As soon as he got out, he heard her music blasting inside—even through the closed windows. It was probably some female pop vocalist who was big on the college circuit right now. Joy had never had exactly rarefied taste in music.

He opened his front door. She hadn't locked it. She should have. He swallowed back his fatherly concern. He didn't want to greet her with a reprimand. He expected to see Joy right there in the open kitchen or adjoining living area. The house was only about a thousand square feet. The first floor was basically one big room with a fieldstone fireplace and a counter separating the kitchen from everything else. Upstairs were two tiny bedrooms and a bathroom under the eaves. It had the look and feel of a place owned by a man. Lots of electronics and dark wood. No curtains. Piles of bills and mail scattered across the kitchen counter. Nothing living, not even a plant. Vega turned off the music speakers. Joy had to be upstairs. He didn't want to scare her if she hadn't heard him come in.

"Joy?" Vega threw his keys and mail on the kitchen counter. His answering machine light was beeping. He didn't even want to think about how many messages he had. He was keeping his cell phone off for the same reason.

"Dad?" She peeked at him from the top of the stairs. Vega felt a catch in his throat when he saw those big dark eyes and long black lashes. He saw the woman and the child all at the same time. He remembered when she was all arms and legs and braces glinting from her teeth. He forgot for a moment that she was now eighteen.

She raced down the stairs and into his arms. She was a small girl with a ballerina's build, delicate as spun glass. Vega hugged her tight, thrilled and humbled that she hadn't stopped loving him even if right now, he felt supremely unlovable.

"It's going to be okay, *chispita.*" *Little Spark.* His Spanish nickname for her as a child, taken from a Mexican soap opera his mother used to enjoy. Even now, with too much eyeliner, long sparkly earrings, and jangly bangles, she was still his little girl.

"We'll get through this," he promised. She shivered beneath his touch. Even though the house was now insulated, it still tended to be cold in winter. Yet here she was, in nothing but a thin, long-sleeved shirt. She always tended to underdress. "Let me get you something warmer to put on." He broke away and noticed a suitcase and some boxes piled in a corner. "What's that stuff?"

"My things."

"Your *things?*"

"I'm moving in."

"What? Why?"

Her face dropped. "Don't you want me here?"

"Of course I do! You're always welcome. But—why now? This is so much farther from school and work than your mother's house."

"I don't want you to be alone."

Vega felt touched by her concern. But another deeper part of him cringed with embarrassment and shame. He didn't want to be the object of his daughter's pity. "I'm fine," he said stiffly. "I don't need anyone taking care of me—especially not my daughter."

"Don't get all defensive, Dad. It's not like I'm going to cook for you or anything."

"Thank God for that." The last time his vegan, gluten-free daughter cooked for him, she made a tofu lasagna that tasted like someone had mixed wallpaper paste and grass clippings.

"We can talk about this later if you want," said Joy. "After we get back from the Bronx."

"The *Bronx?*"

"Don't you remember, Dad? Today is Lita's birthday."

Lita—short for *Abuelita*—*Grandma* in Spanish. "You promised we'd go put flowers on her grave."

Vega collapsed on the lumpy corduroy couch in front of the stone fireplace and palmed his eyes. "I don't think I'm up to it, Joy. I need a shower and some rest."

"You could take a shower and nap and we could go later. I'll drive."

"In the Bronx? No way."

"You need to keep busy, Dad. Be around people. Talk things out."

"I can't talk about the shooting."

"You can talk about your feelings. You're going to make an appointment with a therapist, I hope."

Vega didn't respond. Joy's mother was a school psychologist. Therapy was Wendy's answer to everything—except ironically, their marriage. The phrase, "I'm pregnant with twins and you're not the father," kind of puts a dent in the notion of talking through your marital problems.

Vega noticed that the dining table across from the kitchen counter was covered in old photo albums, some of them open to yellowing snapshots of him as a child. He usually kept them in a trunk in the spare bedroom upstairs.

"Why are the albums out?"

"While I was waiting for you to come home, I thought it might be nice to look back through Lita's life," said Joy.

"Mmm." Vega never liked looking at old family albums. They just made him sad. Joy walked over to the refrigerator and opened the door. She was greeted by a can of coffee, a pint of milk, a six-pack of beer, and a bottle of hot sauce. She was probably just beginning to discover what living with her single father might be like.

"Are you hungry?" asked Vega.

"A little. I can go to the supermarket for you," she offered. "Stock up your refrigerator while you get some sleep."

"You don't know where the supermarket is."

"I don't need to," said Joy. "I have GPS."

Vega wondered if anyone under thirty could read a map anymore. He fished some bills out of his wallet and handed them to her. "I'm too tired to write up a grocery list."

"That's all right. I'll improvise."

"That's what I'm afraid of."

As soon as Joy left, Vega trudged up the stairs, showered, and fell into a deep sleep. In his dreams, he was running through a dark forest. But instead of chasing someone, he was being chased.

Someone is in the woods with me.

He stopped and slipped a hand into his back pocket, searching for the snapshot of Joy that he always kept in his wallet. It was gone. And then he heard it. The deep kettle-drum sound:

Bam.

Bam.

Bam.

Bam.

He woke up shivering and soaked in sweat. His head was pounding. His stomach was turning flips.

Someone was in the woods with me.

No matter how much Teddy Dolan and Mark Hammond insisted otherwise, Vega couldn't shake the feeling that there had been another person in the woods the night of the shooting. He threw back the covers and squinted at his watch on his bedside table. He felt like he'd been sleeping for days. He'd only been asleep for an hour. Joy wasn't even back from the grocery store yet.

He forced himself back into the shower and then toweled off and slipped into clean jeans, a T-shirt, and a button-down deep green Oxford. He was still shivering and achy. Deep regret felt like the mother of all flus. He checked his phone and saw that his lawyer, Isadora Jenkins, had texted him to see how he was doing. On the off chance that he was actually doing okay, she passed along a copy of Ricardo Luis's statement to the press calling Vega's "escalation" of the situation "regrettable." So much for civilian gratitude. He already hated that Mexican ham.

Everywhere Vega looked on the Internet, someone was selling him out. Ruben Tate-Rivera called him an "executioner" and compared today's police tactics to Nazi Germany. His own brass was quoted as vowing "a full investigation"—as if Vega had something to hide.

Hector Ponce, by contrast, was being readied for sainthood. Neighbors described him as "a devoted father and die-hard Yankees fan" who "held down two jobs."

Two?

The first one at Chez Martine Vega already knew about. The second stopped him cold:

Though Ponce worked nights as a dishwasher at an upscale French restaurant in Wickford, neighbors fondly remember him fixing leaky pipes and painting hallways in the Bronx building where he was both the super and a resident for the past eight years.

Vega felt an electric current zip through him. Ponce was the super in his mother's building? That meant he had a master key to every apartment. This guy had warning sirens going off all around him. He'd forced his way into Ricardo Luis's house. And now it turned out that not only had he lived in his mother's building at the time of her murder, he had access to her apartment as well. So how come Vega couldn't recall the Bronx detectives ever mentioning Ponce as a person of interest in her murder investigation?

You're looking to fix your conscience. Greco's words echoed in Vega's brain. So what if he was? He had the paperwork. He owed it to his mother to run down every lead.

Vega opened his bedroom closet and pulled down a brown cardboard box from the shelf. Inside were copies of nearly two years of NYPD paperwork concerning his mother's murder investigation. Witness statements. The autopsy report. Forensic analysis. The various detectives who'd worked the case had forwarded copies of their work to Vega piecemeal over the last two years as a professional courtesy. He'd read it all at one time or another. He'd made notes and charts and diagrams—all of it to no avail. Nothing had ever jumped out at him. *Nothing.*

Vega hefted the box down the stairs and onto the kitchen table. He pushed all of his mother's photo albums to one side to make room. Then he opened the box and began sorting through its contents. He'd never bothered to organize it before. Every time something new surfaced, Vega read it and placed it on top. As a result, the whole box was like an archaeological dig with information in layers going all the way back to the initial police report.

Vega separated out all the DD5s—the official form NYPD detectives use to follow up on a criminal investigation or complaint. Hector Ponce's name was not listed on any of them. There was however a mention of a Hector Fernandez who was listed as the building super. Vega checked the name of the interviewing detective: Mike Brennan. He was the first detective on the case and had since retired and moved to Florida. Vega was betting Brennan had made the classic Anglo mistake and assumed Hector Ponce-Fernandez's last name was Fernandez—his mother's maiden name—rather than Ponce. That's why the name never registered with Vega. But at least he'd been interviewed.

Vega began reading the DD5: *Fernandez states that on April 5th at 10:05 P.M. he went to fix a light in the third-floor hallway and noticed Lisa Rosario-Vega's front door partially open.*

Lisa. Vega gritted his teeth. His mother's name was "Luisa." He remembered how annoyed he'd been the first time he read the misspelling of her name. He couldn't ask

Brennan to redo the report because the guy was passing it on as a favor to begin with. But it made Vega wonder suddenly: if Brennan could be sloppy about Ponce's last name and his mother's first name, what else had he been sloppy about? He read on.

Fernandez states that he entered victim's apartment and found her beaten and unconscious near the front door. Dispatch indicates that Fernandez dialed 911 at 10:22 P.M.

Seventeen minutes? Ponce spent seventeen whole minutes inside his mother's apartment before dialing 911? Why hadn't this registered before? Had he been so annoyed with Brennan for getting his mother's name wrong that he'd completely overlooked the most important part of the report? Vega continued.

Fernandez states that he also used his cell phone to call the victim's priest, Father Francisco Delgado from St. Raymond's Catholic Church.

Vega knew Delgado. Everyone knew Delgado, even Adele. He was widely respected in the Latin American community.

First officers arrived at 10:26 P.M. and found Father Delgado in the apartment administering CPR to victim. Officers took over CPR while Delgado performed last rites. Fire Department EMS arrived at 10:27 and pronounced victim D.O.A.

Vega sat back in his chair and frowned. His mother lay beaten and unconscious in her apartment for almost twenty minutes after she was discovered and before any kind of help arrived. How had he missed this before?

He tried to remember that night but it was a blur. Sirens. Rubberneckers. Indifferent cops. People that he didn't even know rushing up to hug him. His mother's body bag being hefted from the apartment like an oversized piece of luggage. Some police officer on his cell phone arranging his girlfriend's birthday party. Father Delgado was there. He probably tried to talk to Vega but Vega was too distraught to remember the exchange. He hadn't even registered until now that the priest had performed CPR and tried to save his mother's life.

I killed Hector Ponce and Hector Ponce may have killed my mother. That was simplistic, he knew. But at the very least, Ponce's delay may have contributed to his mother's death. Was it incompetence? Or was there a much darker reason behind the man's actions? Vega noted that there was a security camera in the building's lobby that was wired into a digital video recorder. Brennan's notes indicated that the wire connecting the camera to the recorder had come loose and the DVD was blank. As the building super, it would have been easy for Ponce to yank that wire. Then again, as the super, he wouldn't have needed to. No one would have questioned his presence anywhere in the building—certainly not the lobby.

Vega thumbed through the painful forensic details of his mother's death again. She hadn't been raped, thank God. But aside from probably emptying a few bills from her wallet (she never carried much cash), she hadn't been robbed either. There was Chinese takeout food on the table (not something his mother normally ate), but the food could have been for one person or two—the number and placement of dishes didn't make that clear. There was no receipt from the purchase and no menu clipped to the bag, though there was a staple puncture from where a menu or receipt might have been.

A homicide detective named John Renfro who took the case over from Mike Brennan canvassed the area's takeout joints and their grainy video cameras but Vega's mother didn't appear on any of them, nor were they able to match up the very standard Chinese food items—dumplings, white rice, sweet-and-sour pork—to a specific customer. Renfro was only on the case a short time. He was promoted to a joint FBI task force on organized crime after that. Vega didn't even know where he worked in the city anymore.

Vega was desperate for new leads but he didn't see any. At the time, the police had theorized that his mother had opened her door expecting someone else and her assailant had pushed in and attacked her for her wallet. But the police were never able to come up with the person she might have been expecting. Her last call that evening, three hours earlier, had been to the apartment of her best friend, Martha Torres, who had recently been diagnosed with Alzheimer's. Unfortunately, when the police interviewed Martha after the murder, she couldn't remember his mother's call despite phone records that showed they spoke for at least twenty minutes.

Vega hadn't been a homicide detective back when his mother died. He still worked undercover in narcotics. Now however, with a few dozen homicide cases behind him and his mind less clouded by emotion, there were so many questions he wished he'd asked. Why the 911 time lag? How did the wire come loose from the building's security camera? Were there other videos from store security cameras in the neighborhood? From any of the Chinese takeout joints? In Vega's defense, he had to be diplomatic about backseat driving the NYPD. Everything they sent him was done as a courtesy; they could have rescinded it at any time. But still—he should have pushed harder.

Now he had to. He scrolled through his cell phone and was able to locate a phone number for Mike Brennan. He dialed. The phone number was no longer in service. The Bronx detectives division would have Mike Brennan's new number in Florida. They'd have John Renfro's too. But there was no way they'd give them to Vega. No cop was going to stick his neck out for Vega at the moment, especially a cop from another jurisdiction. Then again, maybe Vega didn't have to be the one who did the asking.

He dialed another number and got through on the third ring.

"If you're not about to jump off a building, can you at

least let me finish my lunch?" No doubt it was something smothered in tomato sauce, garlic, and cheese.

"Hey, Grec," said Vega. "You've got a friend in the Bronx detectives squad, right?"

Greco stopped chewing and swallowed. "Tony Carlucci," he said. "He lives in my neighborhood. Why?"

"I need him to get two phone numbers for me. One for a retired detective named Mike Brennan, and the other for a homicide detective who transferred to some FBI joint task force: John Renfro."

"And I ask again, why?"

Vega told Greco about Ponce being the super in his mother's building and what he'd found combing through the paperwork on her murder investigation. "These two detectives worked the case. I'm thinking maybe they can give me some background I'm missing. The cell I have for Brennan is no longer in service and I have no idea how to reach Renfro. Carlucci can probably get both numbers easily."

Silence. For a moment, Vega thought the call had been dropped. When Greco finally answered, his voice was barely above a whisper.

"Are you smoking that K2 shit or something? Have you been watching the news? Every immigrant group in the country wants to string you up by your cojones. They're building a shrine to Saint Hector the Light Fingered as we speak. And you want to start *investigating* him? You want me to ask Carlucci to put other cops on the spot? Do you have any idea how that's gonna look?"

"Nobody has to know," said Vega. "All I'm asking is for Carlucci to get the cell phone numbers of two colleagues. He doesn't have to say why. *I'll* make the calls. Brennan and Renfro don't want to talk to me? Fine. But what's the harm in my calling them?"

"No. I'll help you any other way, buddy. But I'm not feeding your paranoia."

"Ponce waited seventeen minutes before he dialed nine-one-one about my mother, Grec. Her priest arrived before the cops did."

"Yeah, so? Ponce was an illegal. You think he wants to call the cops and get questioned? He panicked and probably called the priest first and the priest told him to dial nine-one-one. If the guy was looking to hide his guilt, why call the cops at all? Why not just create a good alibi and let some neighbor find your mother and report it?"

Greco had a point. Vega walked over to the couch and sank down on one of the lumpy cushions. He felt drained. He couldn't think straight anymore.

"Where are you right now?" asked Greco.

"Home."

"Alone?"

"My daughter's staying with me. She went to get groceries."

"Good. When she gets back, go out someplace with her. Clear your head. Get some fresh air. Visit an old friend you've been meaning to see. You're driving yourself nuts. Remember what I said about doing something good?"

"I remember. I'll do something good."

He'd go with Joy to the Bronx. To visit his mother's grave. And while he was there, he'd take Greco's suggestion and visit an old friend—someone who was likely to know a lot more than any half-assed sloppy police report.

Father Delgado.

Chapter 9

Adele and Sophia bought a Christmas tree on Saturday morning at the stand next to Our Lady of Sorrows Catholic Church. It was a disaster. Someone watching them would have thought Adele was in the witness protection program the way she threw the hood of her jacket over her head and covered her eyes with the biggest, darkest pair of sunglasses she owned despite the fact that there was barely any sun. Get in. Get out. That was the plan. She grabbed the first tree she could find in her price range and stood it up for her daughter. A balsam. It smelled great even if it was shaped like an avocado.

"This looks good. Or this." Adele grabbed the one next to it that had a big bare spot in back. Burl Ives crooned "Holly Jolly Christmas" over the tinny speakers by the inflatable Santa Claus.

"But they're both so short!" complained Sophia.

"And fat, so there's plenty of space on them to decorate!" *Hmmm—new way to look at her own wardrobe.*

They bought the one that looked like an avocado. Sophia grumbled the whole way home.

"I thought Jimmy was going to help us," said the child. "Did you two have a fight?"

"No. We just have some things we—need to work out."

"That's what you said when you and Daddy separated."

Sophia was nine going on nineteen. Her sense of the world was growing almost as fast as her limbs. Adele tried to ignore it. That was her default mode for everything: the emails and texts pouring in, the phone calls from friends and colleagues, the grilling she got from her ex this morning. If Vega could shut down all questions, then so could she.

"We'll have fun decorating the tree together," said Adele. "We'll set it up in the living room and string it with popcorn. And maybe some cranberries."

"Diablo will eat the popcorn and cranberries," Sophia told her mother. She was probably right. This morning, Diablo had already turned one of Sophia's favorite sneakers into an open-toed sandal and eaten through the lining on her bike helmet. Diablo's owner had given Adele two toys for the dog to chew on. He hadn't touched either since he'd arrived.

"We'll just have to keep him away from the tree."

When they got back home, Adele fetched a stepladder from the garage and climbed up to untie the ropes that secured the tree to the car.

"It's so small," complained Sophia.

It looked like a bloody great monster to Adele, especially when she tried to tip it off the roof of the car. She ended up with a broken fingernail, a patch of sticky pinesap on her favorite suede jacket, and a head full of pine needles. She was shaking the mess off her shoulders and hair when she heard a familiar voice call to her from the sidewalk.

"Would you like a hand?"

Dave Lindsey stood at the foot of Adele's driveway with a backpack slung over one shoulder and his hands stuffed awkwardly in his jacket pockets. Though he lived in town and owned a real estate brokerage firm here, Adele couldn't remember the chairman of the board of La Casa ever stopping by her house before.

This wasn't a social visit.

Adele studied the tree at her feet. It was lying on its side like some hunter's slaughtered deer carcass. "Sure. Thanks."

Lindsey traveled the length of her driveway in three or four long strides. He had the slightly stooped shoulders and spider legs of a man who always got recruited for basketball as a kid whether he wanted to or not. He once confided in her that his shyness and size as a boy got him the nickname "Lurch," after the ghoulish fictional butler in *The Addams Family* television show. Adele wished he hadn't told her that. She could never see him now without thinking of the name.

Lindsey leaned over Adele's tree, poked a leather-gloved hand through the branches, and yanked the balsam into an upright position. The tip didn't even crest the underside of his chin.

"Is Santa growing his elves taller these days?" Adele quipped. "Or are you here to tell me I'm on the naughty list?" She wanted to keep the conversation light and playful. Sophia was still waiting impatiently on the front steps to get the tree into the house.

"We need to talk, Adele. And since you're not returning emails or phone messages—"

"I wasn't aware that my contract with La Casa required me to be on call twenty-four-seven."

"There's a fire blowing through this community. This is not the time to play hide-and-seek."

"Mom! I'm cold," said Sophia. "Can we take the tree in?"

Adele fished her keys out of her handbag and walked them over to the child. "Go inside. I'll be there in a minute, *lucero*." *Bright star*—her nickname for her daughter.

"But we were going to decorate the tree—"

"And we will!" She'd get this damn tree decorated today if it killed her.

Adele waited until the child had stomped off inside and she heard Diablo bark out a greeting. Then she turned back to Lindsey who was still holding the tree upright like some shield that could protect him from her wrath.

"Exactly *how* am I supposed to have this sort of conversation today? I have my daughter to take care of. She doesn't know about any of this. Nor do I want her to. Her former babysitter is the daughter of the man who was shot." Adele couldn't bring herself to say, "the man Detective Vega shot." She preferred to think of the shooting as some force of nature, spontaneous and ineluctable—not the willful actions of the man she loved.

Lindsey took a moment with Adele's revelation. "Have you spoken to her yet?"

"I haven't spoken to *anybody*. How can I? What would I say that wouldn't cause somebody in my life a lot of pain?"

"I understand your predicament, Adele. I do," said Lindsey softly. "But things are heating up. I'm not sure you realize just how much. Let me get your tree inside for you. Get Sophia settled in her bedroom or something for a little while. We need to talk."

If anybody else had shown up on Adele's front lawn this morning, she might have written it off as an overreaction. But Lindsey was no zealot. He'd started out a decade ago as a vocal opponent of an immigrant outreach center in Lake Holly, insisting at town meetings and demonstrations that such a place would encourage a greater influx of "lawbreakers" into the area, thereby weakening the economy, straining public services, and spurring white flight. He became a champion of La Casa when he discovered that the newcomers were hardworking people who kept downtown vacancy rates low and made it possible for small stores to flourish. He spoke softly, thought pragmatically, and shied away from political vitriol. If he was here this morning, it wasn't over some vague notions of injustice. It was because of something very, very real.

"Okay." Adele sighed. "Let's go inside."

Lindsey carried the tree into her living room and fitted it into the stand while Adele coaxed Sophia to play in her room and then went into the kitchen and put up some coffee. She hadn't realized she was holding her breath until she placed two mugs on the kitchen table and went to take a seat. She felt a stitch in her side.

"I'll be honest with you," said Lindsey, folding his long frame into a chair. His legs took up most of the floor space beneath. "When I first heard about this shooting, I didn't think it would end up quite so heated as this. But then word started coming in. First, that the suspect was unarmed. Then, that he had no criminal record. Then, that when his daughter went to ID his body at the morgue, he was unrecognizable from the neck up."

"That's not a rumor? He really was shot in the head?"

"Worse than the head. The chin. The bullet apparently caught him under the chin and obliterated his whole face."

"Dear God." Adele closed her eyes. There was only one way she could picture something like that happening.

She didn't want to think about it.

Lindsey gave Adele a puzzled look. "The police confirmed this at a press conference this morning. Haven't you spoken to Vega about this?"

"He can't talk about the shooting—not even to me."

"But you could call the DA's office," said Lindsey. "You have that contact there—what's her name?" For a businessman, Lindsey was terrible with names—especially Spanish ones.

"Myrna Acevedo." Adele had known her since law school. She and Myrna often traded things off the record. But this was different.

"Going to Myrna on this would feel like a betrayal," said Adele.

"If Vega's not talking—what choice do you have?"

"To wait for the results of the autopsy and police investigation before rushing to judgment."

Lindsey shook his head. "Normally, I'd leave a decision like that in your hands. But I think you're letting your personal feelings blindside you. This case is already garnering national attention. This morning, I spoke to both Ricardo Luis's publicist and Ruben Tate-Rivera."

"Ruben Tate-Rivera isn't even from this area! He's just looking for publicity."

"Well, he's going to get it. And you need to be ready." Lindsey leaned forward and held her gaze. "Vega joked about the shooting."

"What? That's nonsense! He would never joke about something like that."

Lindsey fished a piece of paper out of his backpack and handed it to Adele. "He did. Read the transcript. It's part of the interview the DA's investigator conducted with Wickford Police Officer Drew Franklin. Franklin and Alison Peters were the first two officers on the scene."

"How did you get this?" asked Adele. "Even *I* couldn't get this."

"Tate faxed it to me. He's got friends and media contacts everywhere."

Adele put on her glasses and read the highlighted portions.

DA: Did you see Detective Vega shoot the suspect?
Franklin: No, sir. But my partner and I heard the shots.
DA: How many shots?
Franklin: Four.
DA: How close were you to the shooting?
Franklin: About fifty feet downhill from the scene.
DA: Did you get a sense how close Detective Vega and the suspect were to each other when Detective Vega shot the suspect?

Franklin: They sounded close—maybe only a few feet apart. But I can't say for sure.

DA: How did Detective Vega behave after the shooting? Was he distraught? Nervous?

Franklin: Nervous. He kept insisting we find the gun.

DA: And what happened when you didn't?

Franklin: I commented to my partner that I wasn't sure the suspect had a gun and Detective Vega said, 'No, I just blow people's brains out for the fun of it.'

DA: He said this to you?

Franklin: I think he said this to himself but we both heard it.

DA: Do you think he was joking?

Franklin: Yes, I think he was trying to be funny.

Adele put the transcript down. "He was *trying to be funny?*"

"It was probably a nervous reaction," said Lindsey. "Nevertheless, Ruben somehow managed to get this interview. Which means it's going to become public if it hasn't already."

Adele knew from her days as a criminal defense attorney that people under pressure made spontaneous utterances all the time that bore no correlation to their real feelings. His "joke" was distressing. But something else in the interview was far more distressing. Officer Franklin said that Vega and Hector Ponce sounded like they were only a few feet apart. Vega never mentioned a scuffle. He had no defensive wounds. And yet Ponce was shot under the chin, which would be a difficult wound to inflict in a scuffle anyway.

If the officer's statement was correct that Vega was standing close to Ponce, then the only way Vega could have shot Ponce under the chin was if he'd aimed his gun up against the man's soft tissue and fired at point-blank range.

In other words, *executed him.*

Adele closed her eyes. She felt sick.

"This has to be wrong," she said in a shaky voice. "I could see Jimmy losing his temper and making those stupid comments. I could. But the way the shooting is described—I refuse to believe it."

"Adele—" Lindsey cupped his hands around his coffee mug. The mug disappeared between a wall of pale white fingers. "I'm not trying to hurt you or disparage the detective. But I wouldn't be doing you or La Casa any good if I didn't make you aware of all the evidence that's starting to come in."

"*All the evidence?*" Adele gave him a shocked expression. "There's more?"

"There may be. Ruben heard from his sources that there's a witness."

"A witness? Who?"

"The person hasn't come forward yet. Even Ruben doesn't know who he or she is. But the word is, this person is highly credible. And Adele—?" Lindsey hesitated. "This person saw Vega shoot Hector Ponce in the head at point-blank range. If that's the case, we're not talking about an accidental shooting anymore. We're talking murder."

"Oh God." Adele dropped her head into her hands. She felt like she was watching a car accident in slow motion. "What do I do?"

"Call for a grand jury investigation."

"You want me to ask the district attorney to put my— my—Detective Vega—on trial?" Adele felt embarrassed to use the word *lover,* and *boyfriend* felt so adolescent. It reduced her deep and satisfying affections for the man to something that could fit inside a Taylor Swift song.

"The evidence may exonerate him," said Lindsey.

"Or put him in prison!"

"That's not your call," said Lindsey. "That's the grand jury's. In the meantime, your friend Myrna in the DA's office may be able to give you a better picture of what's going on."

"The only thing that is going to give me a 'better picture,'" said Adele, "are the autopsy and forensic reports."

"The autopsy won't be ready for days," said Lindsey. "The forensics on the case could take weeks. Social media moves at the speed of light, Adele. You've got that symposium at Fordham University tomorrow. Gloria Mendez, the program coordinator, called me up this morning and asked if you could address the shooting in your keynote speech."

Adele gave Lindsey a panicked look. "You didn't tell her that Detective Vega and I are dating, did you?"

"Of course not," said Lindsey. "But that's just it. You're a leader in the immigrant community. You will be addressing the largest yearly gathering of immigrant leaders in the state. If you get on that stage at Fordham tomorrow and *don't* talk about the shooting and *don't* demand a grand jury investigation, people will start to wonder. Pretty soon everyone will be talking. You'll ruin your credibility. You'll ruin La Casa's credibility."

"I'm not getting up on that stage with a bunch of half-truths and innuendos."

"Then do your homework," said Lindsey. "Investigate the shooting. You're a leader. *Lead*. Which reminds me." Lindsey rummaged through his backpack and pulled out a book and CD. He slid them across the table to Adele. The book was Ricardo Luis's new memoir, *Song of My Heart*. The cover showed Luis in a black shirt unbuttoned to his navel. The CD was a headshot with a similar dimpled grin.

"Luis's publicist passed these on to you and all the board members this morning. Luis is hosting a small party in Lake Holly this evening before he returns to Miami on Monday. He asked us to attend as a gesture of forgiveness and solidarity."

"We're being used to scrub his image."

"Maybe so," said Lindsey. "But he wrote La Casa a check for five thousand dollars this morning and issued a public letter of apology for his role in the shooting. It serves no purpose to alienate him."

"I can't go," said Adele. "That would be a slap in the face to Jimmy."

Lindsey gave her a pained look. "This is your job. You can't just crawl under a rock when things get uncomfortable. The board doesn't want to have to exercise its power here. But I'm sure you realize we can if we have to."

Adele went very still. "Are you actually pulling rank on me, Dave?"

Although Adele was the founder of La Casa and ran its day-to-day operations, the budget, and ultimately the power to hire and fire, was controlled by Lindsey and the four other elected board members—all of them unpaid volunteers. For the board members, La Casa was a civic duty. For Adele, it was her livelihood.

"Think about what I'm saying, okay?" said Lindsey. "You've known this guy—what? Eight months? Be certain you understand what you're staking your career—your *reputation*—on before you go jumping off a cliff."

"And if I disagree with the board?"

Lindsey pushed back from the table and rose, a clear sign the meeting was over. "Then perhaps you really aren't in a position to do this job anymore, Adele. In that case, the board and I feel strongly that you should consider tendering your resignation, effective immediately."

Chapter 10

Jimmy Vega had forgotten how crowded the Bronx could be, especially on a Saturday before Christmas. Cars and delivery trucks jammed the intersections, sloshing through potholes and sending icy sprays of black water to the curbs. People crowded the crosswalks, maneuvering strollers, shopping carts, and children through the crush.

Joy wiped a sleeve of her skimpy black jacket across the passenger-side window of Vega's truck to clear the condensation. She balanced a grave wreath of pine boughs on her lap and frowned at the noise and confusion. They each saw this place so differently. Vega came back as a long-lost native, here to find the things he'd lost. Joy tagged along as a tourist, fascinated and bewildered by the grime and the chaos, her father's boyhood world as foreign to her as the Spanish he could roll off his tongue.

"Did you actually *like* growing up here?"

"At the time I did," said Vega. "I was angry when Lita told me we were moving all the way up to Lake Holly." He could still remember his first winter in the far northern suburbs. All that cold white land. All those cold white faces. "Of course if we'd stayed, I'd have probably never gone to college—or never finished, in any case." It was possible he never would have become a police officer either but he didn't want to dwell on those implications. "Your *abuelita's* decision to leave really opened up my life in ways I couldn't appreciate back then."

They turned a corner and Vega pointed to a storefront with a flashing red-and-yellow neon sign above a greasy plate-glass window. "See that place? Best little *cuchifritos* joint in the Bronx. Only place that could match your *abuelita*'s cooking. I'll take you there after we go to the cemetery."

"Daaad, do you really think I'm going to be able to eat anything in a place that specializes in deep-fried pork fritters?"

"Oh. Right." He slammed his brakes for a jaywalker and leaned on the horn. "In that case, you might have to survive on a glass of New York City tap water and a packet of hot sauce until we leave the Bronx."

Joy stuck her tongue out playfully at him. Vega smiled. Her presence distracted him from his pain as only a child's presence can. Vega lost himself in the moment. He delighted in pointing out the parochial school he used to attend, the one with wire mesh across the windows where all the nuns smelled like peppermint. He drove past Manny's Bodega where they still sold *El Diario* in the rack out front. He pointed out his old tenement building where he and Henry Lopez liked to hang out on the fire escape and throw water balloons at the girls jumping rope on the sidewalk below.

"How far away is Fordham?" asked Joy.

"The university?" Vega blew out a breath of air. "Geographically, it's just a little north of here. Emotionally, it's light-years away. Why?"

"Danielle's a freshman there."

"Who?"

"You know—my friend Danielle Camino? She's studying to be a teacher."

"Oh. You want to go see her today?"

"No. But sometime," said Joy. "I'd like to see the campus. Maybe apply there when I finish up at Valley Community."

"You want to go to school in the *Bronx?*" Vega pulled a face. "My mother killed herself to get me out of here—and her granddaughter wants to come *back?*"

"Not—here." Joy gestured to the gritty five-story brick buildings that rose like cell blocks on either side of the street. "The university."

"Have you checked out their premed program? You probably should before you start thinking in that direction."

Joy didn't answer. She hunkered down in her seat and played with the red velvet ribbon on the grave wreath in her lap. Every time Vega mentioned her old dream of going to medical school, she got quiet these days. He didn't understand it. Her grades were good, especially in math and science, so the problem wasn't academic. He wanted to talk to her about it but today wasn't the day. He could already feel himself deflating at the sight of the white marble cemetery arches. He could pretend Luisa Rosario-Vega was still alive when he wasn't here. He could not pretend in the presence of so many reminders that she was really, truly gone.

God, he missed his mother! Her backseat driving. The way she always fussed over him. In two languages. In public. She gave him so many things he needed before he ever knew he needed them: self-confidence. A genuine respect for women. The ability to dream. A love of nature. He'd never thanked her for any of it. Their time together was too short. It was like someone had ripped a book out of his hands a hundred pages before the ending. There was so much more he still wanted to know.

Vega nosed his pickup onto a path inside the cemetery and drove past the tight columns of headstones all lined up like Marine recruits. His mother's grave was tucked in a middle row. It was a smooth, thigh-high arch of gray granite with a cross etched into the center and a trail of ivy carved along one side.

"Oh look," said Joy. "Somebody remembered her birthday." There were flowers next to the gravestone already. A huge pink and white bouquet wrapped in cellophane.

Vega parked his truck on the side of the road. Joy smoothed the red velvet ribbon on the center of the grave wreath and handed it to him. A fierce wind stung their faces the moment they left the vehicle. A fire siren squealed somewhere in the distance over the steady whoosh of traffic on the Cross Bronx Expressway.

Joy slipped an arm through her father's and together they walked to the grave.

"Somebody left her lilies," said Joy. "How beautiful."

Vega couldn't tell one type of flower from another. All he knew was that they looked more inviting and cheerful than the grave wreath of pine boughs that he and Joy had bought up north.

"I wonder who they're from." Joy bent down and fished out a tiny note card tucked inside the cellophane. She frowned. "It's in Spanish." She handed it to her father.

Mi amada. Eres siempre mi ángel.

"It says, 'My beloved. You are always my angel,' " Vega translated.

"Wow," said Joy. "Sounds like a love note. Did Lita have a boyfriend?"

"She never mentioned one." Vega couldn't recall anyone coming up to him at the funeral.

"Maybe one of her friends would know."

"Martha Torres would have—before the Alzheimer's did her in. She was my mother's best friend. But I'm not even sure if she's alive anymore."

Vega began to tuck the note in a pocket of his jacket.

"Dad! What are you doing? That's not your note."

"What? You think Lita can read it? I don't know who wrote this, Joy. For all I know, it could be someone with information about my mother's murder. I'm not about to let it just rot at her grave." Vega handed Joy the wreath. She laid it on the grave.

"Want to say a few words?" she asked her father. "Maybe explain why you're stealing her love note?"

Vega shot Joy a dirty look. He was tired and spent. His daughter was shivering. "We're here. She's in our thoughts. That's what matters."

When they were back in the truck, Joy checked her watch and pretended not to.

"Got a date tonight?" asked Vega.

"I can cancel."

"You don't have to babysit me, you know."

"I want to spend the afternoon with you."

"In that case, can we make one stopover before we head back north?"

"You shouldn't eat all that fried food either."

"I'm not talking about the *cuchifritos* joint. I want to go to St. Raymond's and visit Father Delgado."

Joy looked surprised. "I thought you weren't religious."

"I'm not."

On the drive over to the church, Vega told Joy what he'd found earlier going through the paperwork on his mother's murder investigation.

"You're not seriously thinking the man you shot had something to do with Lita's death, are you?"

"It can't hurt to talk to Father Delgado about it."

"Look, Dad, I know you want to find some way to justify what you did—"

"I don't need to justify it. I didn't do anything wrong—"

"Honestly? You believe that?"

He didn't answer. The car was warming up. Joy shrugged off her jacket. It caught on the neckline of her ribbed sweater beneath, revealing for just a moment the bare bronzed skin of her left shoulder. Vega saw something he didn't expect to see when he glanced over. Something red. Bright red.

"What's that?"

Joy pulled the neckline up quickly. "What?"

"On your shoulder. I saw something."

"It's nothing."

Vega jerked the wheel toward the curb and double-parked alongside a row of cars. Drivers honked and gestured through their windows. Vega ignored them. He was a Bronx native. He was immune to expressions of frustration.

"Show me your shoulder."

"No, Dad. Leave me alone."

"I'm not moving until you show me your shoulder."

She pulled the neckline down and up quickly. "There. Satisfied?"

On her left shoulder was a red rose tattoo about the size of a shot glass rim, permanently etched into her flawless skin. The skin he used to bathe when she was a baby. The skin he rubbed sunscreen on when she was a little girl so that she wouldn't get cancer one day. And now she'd let some stranger stick a needle into it and inject permanent dye?

"You got a *tattoo*? When did you do that?"

"About a month ago."

"Does Mom know?"

"I didn't tell her until after I got it."

Vega hit the steering wheel and cursed back at the drivers who were honking and giving him the finger. He was probably the only male of his generation who was uninked and he intended to stay that way. All his musician friends had tattoos. A lot of cops did, too. Dolan had a great big Harley-Davidson eagle tattoo on his forearm.

Not Vega. He was squeamish about needles. He had a piercing in his left ear that he got back in his early twenties when he still thought he was going to make it as a guitarist. He'd nearly fainted from that. But even if he weren't squeamish, he didn't want his daughter marking up her body that way. A tattoo felt incompatible with her intellect and ambitions. How could anyone take her seriously as a doctor with that thing on her shoulder? Maybe it was simple prejudice on Vega's part. But he suspected a lot of other people felt the same way, if not about their own bodies, then certainly about their children's.

"How could you do that, *chispita?* Without asking either of us?"

"I'm eighteen. It's *my* body!"

"And you're *my* daughter!"

She turned to him. The light had left her eyes. "Yes, I'm your daughter," she said in a soft, steely voice. "The daughter you practically drove out of your house this morning. The daughter who's trying to take care of you when everyone else has turned away. I never judged you for shooting an unarmed man. And yet you judge me for getting a *tattoo?*"

"I'm just trying to make sure every door in life is open for you. Like Lita did for me."

"One little rose on my shoulder isn't going to close any doors," said Joy. "The problem isn't with the tattoo, Dad. It's with the way you see me." She took a deep breath. "I'm not sure I want to be a doctor anymore."

"Oh." Vega tried to mask his disappointment but it sat there between them like a deflated balloon. Joy had wanted to be a doctor since she was twelve years old. Her dream had become his. He didn't want to let it go.

"Can I ask what you *do* want to be?"

Joy rubbed a hand along the black fuzz of her jacket, stroking it like a kitten.

"I like working with young children a lot. Maybe a kindergarten teacher—"

"*What?* You want to waste your talents on—on—wiping snotty noses and teaching kids to crayon their ABCs?"

"Oh, that's rich." Joy rolled her eyes. "Coming from a man who shoots people for a living."

Vega turned away without saying anything. Then he shifted the truck into gear and nosed back into traffic.

"Sorry, Dad," she said after a minute. "I don't know why I said that."

"Forget about it."

"If you want to talk—"

"I'm okay."

Vega drove around St. Raymond's Church looking for parking. He couldn't find anything nearby so he parked about eight blocks away, around the corner from his mother's old building. They'd have to walk back to the church. Vega grabbed his aviator sunglasses and Yankees baseball cap from his glove compartment and slipped them on.

"It's not sunny out," said Joy.

"That's not why I'm wearing them," said Vega. "I don't want to chance getting recognized."

"Is that why you haven't shaved since you got home?"

Vega hadn't really thought about it. But yeah. Maybe. He wanted to hide from the world. A beard was one way to do it. If he stayed on administrative leave long enough, maybe he'd grow out his hair, too.

St. Raymond's was an imposing sandstone-colored church with filigreed stained-glass windows and twin spires that looked like cake decorations. The inside smelled of incense and lemon oil. There were no services going on so they were the only people in the nave with the exception of a janitor sweeping the pews, an older, heavyset Hispanic-looking man with a broad weathered face. Vega asked if Father Delgado was around.

"I'm not sure if he's in the rectory, señor. He was out making rounds at the hospital earlier. He will be here for Saturday evening Mass."

"Is there any way you could find out if he's in the rectory right now? It's important that I speak to him."

The janitor's dark, sad eyes settled on Vega's. He brushed a hand across his gray mustache. Vega sensed the man knew who he was. Was there no place any longer where his reputation didn't precede him?

"I will see if I can find him."

"Is there a bathroom around here?" asked Joy.

"I will show you, señorita."

Joy followed the janitor out of the nave and into a side hallway that presumably led to the rectory. Vega knelt at the edge of one of the pews and made the sign of the cross. Old habits died hard, he supposed. He slid himself onto the smooth wooden bench and folded his hands on the pew in front of him. Not in prayer. He'd been an altar boy long enough to know all the words. But they conjured no faith inside of him. He looked up to the ornate peaked rafters and stained-glass windows of saints and wished that all the glory and majesty of this place could quiet the hollow echo in his soul. He felt lost. So terribly, terribly lost.

I've killed a man. I've killed an unarmed man. For the first time, the full weight of those words fell upon him. He'd been looking for ways to relieve the burden. But Greco was right. If he ever wanted to make something good happen, he first had to come to grips with the unalterable nature of what he'd done.

"I was hoping you'd come."

The words startled Vega. He turned to see Father Delgado striding up the aisle toward him. For a man pushing seventy, he had a brisk way of moving. Vega could see why he was everybody's favorite priest. He had soft, deep-set eyes that never wandered when he was listening to you and a sort of Zen-like calmness that made you feel instantly like you were in safe hands. But he wasn't all prayer and mumbo jumbo, either. He was a die-hard Yankees fan, an excellent poker player, and a lover of all things spicy and fried. He was not above making priest jokes either—one of the reasons Vega supposed his mother loved him so much. They both shared an irreverent sense of humor.

Father Delgado bent down and crossed himself, then scooted into the pew next to Vega.

"I guess you've seen the news," said Vega. "I realize I'm not the most popular person to be seen talking to right now."

"Nonsense. Your mother would have been glad you reached out." Delgado pulled down the kneeling bench and clasped his hands in front of him. "Shall we pray together?"

"I'm not here for spiritual guidance, Father," Vega said sheepishly.

"Sometimes the thing we need most, we can't bring ourselves to look for."

"I can't lie about what I don't feel."

Delgado winked at him. "Politicians do it all the time."

Vega laughed. It was the first laugh he'd had since the shooting. The release felt good.

Joy walked back into the nave, said hello to Father Delgado, and then excused herself to return some texts near the doors.

"Shall we speak in my office?" Delgado asked Vega.

"Thank you. That would be great."

The church, with its heavy stone walls, wood rafters, and stained glass could have come straight out of the fifteenth century. Delgado's office however, was a pedestrian 1970s vintage with beige plaster walls decorated in equal parts crucifixes and Yankee memorabilia. Vega took a seat in a well-worn leather chair. Delgado took another chair across from him rather than choosing to sit behind his desk. Vega appreciated the priest's desire to make this visit as informal as possible.

"Father." Vega ran a hand through his black wavy hair.

He wasn't sure how to begin. "You knew my mother well. Did you also know the man who was—" *Own it, damn you.* "The man I killed? Hector Ponce?"

"Yes. I did."

"Was he a member of the church?"

"His family attends St. Raymond's. He was also friends with our church custodian. The man you just met."

That explained the probing look the janitor had given him. Delgado frowned and shifted in his seat. "Are you asking out of personal curiosity? I would assume, given the uh—situation—you aren't asking as a police officer."

"No, no," Vega assured him. "I have no police powers here. I'm asking because I read that Ponce was the super in my mother's apartment building."

"Yes. He was," said Delgado evenly.

"He was also the first person to come across my mother after she was beaten." Vega held the priest's gaze. "You were the second."

"Yes. Hector called me. I gave your mother last rites."

"You gave her CPR," said Vega. "And I never thanked you."

"I expect no thanks for being where God intended me to be."

"I wish God had put you there a little sooner."

Delgado took a deep breath. He looked genuinely pained. "I wish the same. Believe me."

"I went back through the time frame of the crime," said Vega. "It appears that Hector Ponce waited a full seventeen minutes before he dialed nine-one-one."

The priest put a hand on his knee and leaned forward. "Jimmy—may I call you that?"

"Sure."

"Your mother, God rest her soul, has been dead almost two years. Why are you revisiting this now? Do you honestly believe that Hector had something to do with your mother's death?"

"I don't know. But those seventeen minutes are giving me pause."

"I've known Hector many, many years—longer than I've known my church custodian even. He was a good man. A flawed man, perhaps. But a good man."

"What do you mean 'flawed'?"

Delgado shook his head. "I'm a priest, Jimmy. I will not speak against the dead. I can tell you this however: if he made any bad choices, they were done out of love and loyalty—never in hatred or anger."

"But—seventeen minutes," Vega repeated.

"Surely you must realize that given Hector's—immigration status—he was panicked about speaking to the police."

"And you think that's all it was?"

Delgado didn't answer. Vega tried a different tack.

"There's a picture the press has been circulating." Vega took out his cell phone and scrolled through it until he came to the photograph. "Ponce had this snapshot in his hand when he was—when I shot him," said Vega. "Have you seen it?"

"I'm trying to hold myself back from all the details of this case right now," said Delgado.

"I understand. But it would be helpful if you could tell me anything about the picture."

Delgado squinted at the screen. He pointed to the man standing on the right. "That's definitely Hector when he was younger. I know he had a younger brother and son who died a long time ago. That could be them." Delgado handed back the phone. "I'm guessing you aren't allowed to speak to the family."

"I'm not even allowed to do what I'm doing now," Vega confessed. "I'm just trying to see if there's a connection. You're telling me Ponce was a good man. Yet he broke into a celebrity's house and tried to rob him. And my mother was beaten to death and robbed in the same building where he was the super. What would you think if you were me?"

"I would ask the same questions," said Delgado. "But I'm afraid I don't have any answers. We're all capable of great deeds and terrible sins. Hector loved his two sons by Alma very much. And yet he abandoned his other children in Honduras. It went against everything he believed in. And yet he did it. Why? I don't know."

"If he could do that," said Vega, "maybe he did this, too." Vega rubbed his sweaty palms along his thighs. The adrenaline from last night had worn off but he still felt like a meth addict in withdrawal. He broke out in a sweat easily. He couldn't sit still for long. He got up and paced the room.

"It's tearing me up to think Ponce was right in my mother's building—all this time—and I never questioned him," said Vega. "I'm sorry to bring this to you but I've got nowhere else to go."

"You always have a place to go," said Delgado. He spread his palms and gazed up at the brown water stains on the acoustical tile ceiling. "God is listening, Jimmy. Make your peace with Him. Ask for His guidance and forgiveness." Delgado rose and made the sign of the cross.

"How can I just make my peace with God when I don't know who killed her?"

"The peace you need to make has nothing to do with your mother's life, Jimmy. It has to do with your own."

In the narthex, Vega found Joy texting. "Let's go home," he said to her. The Bronx felt too weighted with memory.

Joy glanced up from her cell phone. Her eyes traveled past her father to the front doors of the church. Her jaw muscles had a clenched look to them.

"Did you know that Ruben Tate-Rivera just finished holding a press conference at Lita's building? With Hector Ponce's widow?"

"No. I didn't."

"He wants the district attorney to put you on trial."

"He wants the DA to convene a grand jury, Joy. Not a trial. Not yet, anyway. Can we talk about this on the way home?" Vega zipped up his jacket. Joy stayed rooted in place.

"Dad? He's calling on his supporters to march in protest."

"Okay, so they're marching. That's their choice."

"The march just kicked off from Lita's building. That's right around the corner from where we parked."

Chapter 11

"Okay. Stay here. In the church. With Father Delgado," Vega told Joy. "You're safe in the church. I'll get my truck and come back for you—"

"But I want to come with you," said Joy. She sounded so young all of a sudden. All that charcoal eyeliner—even her rose tattoo—did nothing to hide the little girl she still was beneath.

"I'll be back in twenty minutes, *chispita*. Surely you can stay here by yourself for twenty minutes?"

"Why can't I come with you?"

"Because you can't!"

Vega hated the harsh tone he had to use with his daughter. But Joy had never seen how quickly a crowd could turn into a mob. She'd never witnessed the venom people could unleash when they knew they'd never be held accountable. He had. In uniform, he'd broken up brawls that started out directed at the brawlers and ended up directed at him. It was scary, all that anger. Like a wall of water coming at you. He didn't want to chance an encounter like that with his daughter by his side. He didn't want to alarm her, either.

"Look—" Vega put his hands on her shoulders. He spoke in a calm and measured voice. "Everything's going to be fine. It's just easier for me if you stay here and I come back for you."

"But you'll be okay? You'll keep your phone on?"

"Of course. I'll call you when I get to my truck."

He slipped back into his sunglasses and baseball cap. Disguise or no disguise, if anyone in that crowd had taken a good look at his personnel photo on TV or on any one of hundreds of Internet websites, he might as well be trailing a spotlight.

He left the church by a side exit. If he turned south and walked a couple of blocks before heading north, there'd be less of a chance he'd meet up with the protestors. He knew the neighborhood at least. He knew the pawnshops and check cashing joints with their brightly colored awnings and flashing neon signs in the windows. He knew the bodegas with their racks of cigarettes and forty-ounce malt liquors by the registers. He knew the narrow walk-ways along the sides of buildings that could sometimes take him from one street to another. If he could just avoid being recognized . . .

The cold helped. People didn't hang around in the cold. Vega turned left and then right. All the blocks in this area looked pretty much the same. Each side of the street was walled off by five- or six-story buildings the color of sand or mud with fire escapes zigzagging down their fronts like slashes of graffiti. In the windows, Vega could see air conditioning units and crosshatched metal gates, many strung with Christmas lights, some of them already aglow in the fading afternoon light. A few of the buildings had marble embellishments around their entrances attesting to a much grander past. But most looked liked their residents— sturdy and long-suffering. Along the curbs, dented sedans, some with faded and mismatched paint jobs, were parked nearly end-to-end. Fire hydrants, lampposts, and spindly trees sprouted from the pavements—all gunmetal gray this time of year.

His phone rang in his pocket. Adele's name was on the caller ID. He didn't want to pick up and let her know where he was. On the other hand, he didn't want her to worry if he didn't answer.

"Hey," he said breathlessly. "Can I call you back? I'm sort of busy right now."

"Whatever it is can wait."

Vega hoped the mob would be so accommodating. They were a block ahead of him, marching along the Grand Concourse. He saw raised fists and homemade signs. "Hands up! Don't shoot!" they chanted. It was a large group—much larger than a simple press conference would suggest. Vega wondered if they'd picked up supporters along the way.

"Look, Adele—"

She cut him off. "We have to talk. Not in an hour or two. Right now. Dave Lindsey came by to see me this morning. He wants me to use my keynote speech at Fordham tomorrow night to call for a grand jury investigation into the shooting."

Vega felt like he'd been kicked in the chest. "Sure. Why not?" he asked icily. "Why bother with all the niceties like due process, when it's so much more fun to string me up by my cojones right now."

"Jimmy, don't get defensive. I told him it was a bad idea."

"But you didn't refuse."

"I *will* refuse. But he's technically my boss. I have to have a reason."

"A *reason?* How about the fact that the ME hasn't conducted the autopsy yet? How about the fact that ballistics and forensics haven't weighed in? If I were one of your damned clients, would you and your zealot friends be calling for my head right now?"

Vega scanned the crowd one block over. He was close

enough to read the signs. I CAN'T BREATHE! NO MORE FER-GUSONS! IS MY SON NEXT? Worse than the words—at least for him—was the fact that his departmental photo was plastered on great big two-by-four signs. So if anybody had forgotten what he looked like, all they had to do was look up.

The crowd had grown, too. They were easily ten people across. And every one of them looked personally affronted, as if Vega were to blame for every slight in their lives. How come all these protesters only came out when they were angry with the police? Where were the marches against the gangs and drug dealers in the neighborhood? Against the proliferation of guns? Where was the political will to make the schools better? The projects safer? The parks cleaner for children?

"Do you think I want to be in this position?" asked Adele. "We're talking about the first step to possibly putting you on *trial*."

"I know what a grand jury is, Adele. You don't have to educate me." His nose was starting to run with the cold. He wiped it. He hoped he didn't sound like he was sniffling. "So . . . are you?"

"That's why I'm calling," said Adele. "I'm hoping you can give me the ammunition to dissuade Dave and the rest of the board."

"You know I can't talk about the shooting."

"Well, you damn well did last night!" she yelled. "I spoke to my friend, Myrna Acevedo, in the DA's office this morning. The Wickford cops are saying you joked about the shooting right after it happened."

"I *what?*" Vega ducked into a walkway on the side of a building. He didn't want to be having this conversation out in public.

"An officer by the name of Drew Franklin said that you stated in the presence of him and his partner that you blow people's brains out for the fun of it."

Vega's words came back to him now. Stupid, careless words. Muttered under his breath in a moment of panic and desperation. He couldn't even remember the two officers anymore, apart from the fact that one was a man shaped like a torpedo and the other was a woman with dandelion hair. He felt like some stray that had wandered into the middle of the Cross Bronx Expressway. He was about to be run over no matter which way he turned.

"Jimmy," said Adele. "Ruben Tate-Rivera has a copy of that interview. He's going to make it public if he hasn't already. If it's not true, you need to say something."

Vega kicked at some broken glass beneath his feet. The narrow passage smelled of rotting garbage. He closed his eyes. It *was* true. And either way, there was nothing he could say. He started walking again. He had to find a way past the gauntlet to his car. Maybe north? The mob on the boulevard just seemed to grow and grow.

"Where are you?" asked Adele.

"Running some errands," he lied.

"Look," she said. "Words are just words. I don't care what you said. I know you were under stress last night. I'm more concerned about this witness."

"*Witness?* What witness?"

"Hasn't your lawyer made you aware that a witness is about to come forward?"

Vega thought about the text he'd received an hour and a half ago from Isadora Jenkins, asking him to call her right away. He'd been at his mother's grave at the time. He'd thought it could wait.

"Jimmy—the DA is speaking to someone who claims to have seen you shoot Hector Ponce last night at point-blank range."

Vega's breath seized in his lungs. The sounds and smells of the Bronx pressed in on him. Diesel fumes. The squeal of brakes. Fast food wrappers. Babies crying from open windows. Car sirens. Police sirens. Or was that an ambulance? Vega used to be able to tell the difference when he was a boy. But he'd grown soft and out of touch with the sharp edges of city life.

"One of the bullets you shot apparently hit the underside of Ponce's chin," said Adele. "Your own department verified that. If what this witness is saying is true, the only way you could have made such a shot is if you—if you—"

"If I executed him," said Vega flatly, finishing her thought. Something burned in his nasal passages. The silence between them felt as deep and wide as the North Atlantic.

"It's not true, is it?" Adele's voice was almost a whisper.

Vega felt like he was being kneed in the gut with his hands tied behind his back. "Adele, please—"

"If you tell me it's not true, I'll back you all the way. No matter what. Even if it costs me my job. But you need to give me something."

"Anything I say could get you subpoenaed. You want that?"

"I want to be able to back you with a clear conscience."

"*Nena*, you *know* me."

"I used to."

Vega heard the brittle frozen edges of doubt creeping into her voice. He couldn't do or say anything to change that.

Silence. He waited. She waited.

"I gotta go, Adele." He hung up.

He shoved his phone in his back pocket, cursing himself for even answering it. He had enough to worry about right now. He turned the corner, hoping his luck might change.

It did. It got worse.

Chapter 12

O n the sidewalk, Vega found himself face-to-face with three young Latinos leaning in through the passenger-side window of a faded silver Nissan Sentra. The men were all wearing baggy jeans and hoodies. They straightened at the sight of Vega. Their hands shot out of their pockets. Their eyes tracked him while their heads pretended not to. Vega had been an undercover narc for five years. He knew instantly that he'd stumbled into a drug buy. He cursed under his breath and crossed to the other side of the street.

The biggest, heftiest of the three shoved something into the waistband of his jeans. He straightened and stepped back from the vehicle. Vega could tell just by the young man's stiff posture and the challenge in his eyes that the thing he'd just shoved into his waistband was a gun.

Vega was alone. He had no weapon. He had his badge, but showing it in a jurisdiction that wasn't his would only make things worse. He kept moving. He was no match for three armed gangbangers and God–knew–how–many–others inside the tinted-windowed sedan. The problem was, just as he could recognize a deal going down, they were equally good at knowing that aviator shades and a short, quasi-military haircut meant that he was a cop—unshaven or not. And not just any cop, but a cop who was trying to avoid them. That turned him from predator to prey in an instant.

The thug with the gun and one of the others crossed the street and began tailing him from a distance. The third guy broke away and headed up the opposite side. Some kid he'd never even seen before popped out of a doorway. Vega felt like he was being set up. Or maybe they were just playing mind games with him—scaring him off their block. He couldn't be sure. He kept walking. He heard one of the thugs behind him mutter, "Five-O." Yep, they'd made him. He decided not to engage. But then he felt their footsteps getting closer. The kid in the doorway began approaching from the other direction. Vega had to get control of the situation. If he didn't they might take it as a sign of weakness—which could turn out worse in the end.

Vega stopped in his tracks. He turned toward them and spread his arms in a way that was non-threatening but at the same time exuded the confidence of a man who had a gun and knew how to use it. It was posturing of course. But so much of police work was.

"Guess it's your lucky day, hombres," Vega said coolly. "I'm off-duty. Don't need the paperwork." He gave them a mock salute, turned, and kept walking, aware that their eyes were still on him. Sharks' eyes. His peripheral vision caught one of the shorter gangsters leaning into the window of the car, having a conversation with one of the occupants. The guy was pointing to the protest up ahead—to the giant poster some demonstrator was carrying with Vega's picture on it. Ricardo Luis had less face recognition to this crowd than Vega did.

"That's him," the gangster said to the faceless figure inside. "That's the cop they're marching about."

Vega kept walking. Up ahead he saw the protesters. Their chant had grown stronger and more heated. Somebody had even turned it into a catchy rhyme:

"Hands up! Don't shoot! Cops should never execute!"

Vega was trapped. There were no walkways to cut through. Nothing but solid fifty-foot canyons of brick and concrete on either side of him. There was a buzz of energy behind him now. A car door slammed—the Nissan's, he suspected. More feet on the pavement.

"Yo! Five-O! You the asswipe on those posters?"

Vega's heart pounded. A bitter, metallic taste settled at the back of his throat. If these gangbangers got ahold of him, they would beat him until he was as bloody as a side of beef and then finish him off with a bullet to the head—just like Hector Ponce. That's how they'd reason it, too. Retribution. Street justice.

Vega tried to calm his breathing and think. He had no weapon. He could fight as hard and dirty as any kid from the neighborhood. But he wasn't eighteen anymore nor was he particularly big or brawny. He saw only two choices: fight a fight he was bound to lose. Or run straight into the hands of the protesters streaming across the intersection who might very well do the same thing to him—albeit with more cell phone footage on YouTube.

He'd take his chances with the protesters. The ratio of college students-to-felons would be better. Not that that guaranteed anything. Vega had dealt with his share of drunken frat boys when he was in uniform. But at the very least, they'd be less bold about delivering a punch, more worried about losing teeth that their parents had spent thousands to straighten. He started running toward them.

"That's the cop! The one on the poster!" one of the gangbangers shouted to the demonstrators.

Most of the marchers were too busy chanting to notice what was going on. They probably thought it was a personal scuffle. That bought Vega time to weave his way into the center of the crowd. He took off his cap and sunglasses to make himself less recognizable to the gangsters. Unfortunately, that made him even more recognizable to the marchers. A big black man with a shaved head turned and frowned at Vega. He was holding up a sign that read JAIL KILLER COPS.

"Hey. Aren't you—?"

Vega didn't wait for more. He took off again. But it was too late. His presence rippled through the crowd. People began turning, pointing their cell phones at him. There was expectation in the air. Everybody was waiting for someone to throw the first punch.

It came from behind. A glancing shot just north of his kidneys. Vega felt the fire travel up his spine. If the punch had connected better, he'd be on the pavement now, and pissing blood in an hour. The punch was the invitation the rest of the crowd needed. Someone slapped his arm. Somebody else stomped on his foot. Another spit on his jacket. Vega shoved and kicked and tried to fight back but it was like being in the middle of a game of blind man's bluff. He never saw his opponents. He only felt them trying to push him to the ground. He had to stay standing. If he lost his footing, it would all be over. They'd kick him then. Break his nose, his jaw, his ribs. Give him a concussion. By the time the cops worked their way into the crowd and pulled them off, Vega would be unrecognizable, even to Joy.

A teenager stepped in front of Vega and tried to punch him in the face. Vega ducked and then swung to protect himself but he knew he couldn't keep this up. He was dizzy with panic, unsure which angle the next assault was going to come from. Suddenly a Latino man with a droopy black mustache and thinning hair stepped in front of Vega. He was dressed in sweatpants and a hooded sweatshirt. He wore a sweatband across his forehead and basketball sneakers on his feet like he'd just come from a game. He grabbed the teenager by the back of his sweatshirt and shoved the kid away from Vega.

"You're already on probation, Carlos!" he shouted in a mixture of Spanish-sounding consonants and Bronx vowels. "You want to add assault? I know your probation officer!"

Vega knew instantly that this was no stranger who'd saved him. This wasn't even the first time.

"Chill, hombres," Freddy Torres said to the crowd. "This guy you're messing with? He's old school. From the 'hood. Him and me go way back." He pushed Vega behind him and caught the eye of the gangsters who'd chased Vega into the march. "You got a beef?" Torres called out to them.

"No beef with you, Doc," said the one with the gun in his waistband. He held up his hands and backed off. Vega wondered if the gangbanger had long ago been a student at Torres's school, the Bronx Academy of Achievement. Even the protesters seemed chastened. Freddy Torres—*Dr. Fred Torres*—was respected in this neighborhood, even if the "Doc" was for his Ph.D.—not an M.D. They hesitated to cross some invisible line Torres had drawn around himself and Vega. Which gave Torres just enough time to grab Vega by the back of his jacket and yank him away.

"*Ay puñeta, carnal.*" Torres's smile parted the curtain of his mustache. "Why am I *always* saving your ass?"

Chapter 13

This was the third time in Vega's life that Freddy Torres had rescued him. The first, he couldn't recall. His mother used to tell the story. Torres was nine and Vega was seven. Their two-year age difference meant they traveled in different circles. Still, Torres knew Vega was a good ballplayer—one of the few things Vega was better at than Torres.

One day Torres let Vega join their street game. Somebody hit a high-pop foul and Vega dodged between two parked cars to run for it. He wanted to impress the older boys. But before he could make the catch, somebody grabbed his T-shirt from behind and pulled him to the ground. He hit the pavement hard, skinning an elbow. A second later, a car barreled past without even braking. Vega's mother swore that Freddy Torres had saved his life.

The second time was more humiliating. Vega was eleven. His grandmother had just died, his father had dropped out of his life entirely and his mother, a nurse, worked long hours at the hospital. Vega was feeling lost and adrift in a neighborhood teeming with gangs, drugs, and temptations.

A sometime friend had gotten hold of a couple of cans of black spray paint and suggested Vega join him and another boy to tag some buildings and earn points with the local gang leader. Vega took the can and followed the boys down the street—right past Freddy Torres who was thirteen at the time and babysitting his kid sister Donna, who had Down syndrome. Torres saw the can of paint sticking out of Vega's backpack, swiped it, and ordered Vega to quit hanging out with street toughs and go home. Vega, afraid to lose face, shoved Torres and demanded his paint back. Torres gave it to him, all right. He aimed the can and coated Vega's clothes with permanent black paint. They both ended up on the sidewalk in a hail of fists after that. But Torres at thirteen had the advantage of weight and size. Vega was quickly dispatched. The other boys jeered him and left.

Bruised, covered in paint, and burning with humiliation, Vega trudged home for the punishment he knew he was going to get, hatred for Freddy Torres in every pore. The following day he found out that the other two boys he'd been with had been arrested for vandalism. They were both so young; they probably got off with a warning. But still. Vega's mother was horrified. She moved them out of the Bronx soon after that. Years later Vega heard that one of those two boys went to prison for burglary and drug possession. The other died of an overdose. Vega often wondered if a can of black paint had spared him the same fate.

That, and Freddy Torres.

They crossed the street now, away from the mob.

"Listen, Freddy." Vega rubbed his sore back. He felt grimy and sweat-soaked. "I don't want to be the reason your school burns down or you get beat up."

Torres laughed. "I've survived a dozen mayors, urban renewal, and both the crack and the AIDs epidemics in this neighborhood. I think I can survive your little visit today."

Vega hadn't seen Torres since his mother's funeral nearly two years ago. His friend seemed to have grown old in the interim. His black hair had receded on the sides, leaving a little island of dark bird's nest fuzz in the middle of his head. His droopy black mustache did nothing to hide the sag of his chin. His shoulders sloped. He wasn't fat but beneath his hooded sweatshirt his belly had grown a little soft and pendulous. Vega had to remind himself that Torres had suffered even more losses than he had these past couple of years. His father died of cancer. Then his mother was diagnosed with early-onset Alzheimer's. Then his younger sister, Donna, the one with Down syndrome, slipped and fell to her death from the family's fifth-floor apartment window. Torres had an older sister, Jackie, but she lived out west somewhere, so Torres—never married and childless—had had to handle everything by himself. It couldn't have been easy. And now here was Vega, as usual, bringing more trouble.

"I hate to ask, but can I beg one more favor?" Vega told him about Joy, still waiting at St. Raymond's Church. "You wouldn't happen to have a car nearby, would you?"

"My SUV is behind the school. Happy to be your chauffeur."

"I owe you." An understatement.

Vega dialed Joy and told her he'd run into "an old friend" who was going to drive Vega to the church to pick her up. She chewed him out for taking so long to call but she bought the lie. That's all he was interested in.

"Good," said Torres. "Now let's get you cleaned up."

Torres's charter school, the Bronx Academy of Achievement was a block away. It was housed in a former tool-and-dye factory, four stories tall, with a fenced-in basketball court beside it. Everything about the building was square: square windows. Square flat roof. Square panes of glass in the front doors. What it lacked in architectural embellishments, however, it made up for in wow-factor. The entire stucco exterior was painted in tropical hues of lavender, orange, turquoise, and pink.

A knot of teenagers gathered by the chain-link fence of the basketball court next to the school, eyeing Vega and pretending not to at the same time. Reggaeton and rap music blared over a stereo speaker. Vega missed those sounds. In the suburbs, loud music was considered an assault, not an expression of joy.

Torres walked over to the fence and knuckle-rapped a few of the teenagers. "Game's over today, hombres." There was a collective groan. "Come back for the tournament tomorrow." Torres turned to Vega. "We're doing a basketball tournament in the indoor gym tomorrow at two. I'd invite you inside to wash up and take a tour of the school, but I've got painters redoing the stairwells at the moment and they don't even let *me* walk around." Torres nodded to the laundromat on the other side of the basketball court. "You can wash up at EZ Clean."

"They'll let me?"

"Carmela better." Torres smiled. "I own the place."

The Bronx had once been bargain-basement real estate. But no more. The guys who hung around and put a few dollars into the borough were reaping big profits now.

"So you're into real estate these days?" asked Vega.

"I own a couple of small businesses, that's all," said Torres. "Somebody's got to keep the neighborhood institutions going."

Carmela, the EZ Clean's manager, was an older Puerto Rican woman with a body like a water balloon and hair dyed the color of a new penny. She lifted her gaze from her magazine, greeted Torres as *"El doctor,"* and directed Vega to a bathroom at the back of the store. Silver Speed Queen washers and dryers rumbled along the floors and walls as Vega made his way down the aisles, dodging small children who were playing hide-and-seek and mothers chatting in Spanish on cell phones. The air was humid and detergent scented. The light had a truck-stop café brightness to it.

It had been decades since Vega had been inside a laundromat. He considered it one of the hallmarks of becoming middle class that he owned his own Sears washer and dryer and no longer had to waste time in a place like this. And yet being here filled him with such an unexpected sense of nostalgia. He could still see himself as that small boy enveloped in a warm, sweet-smelling cocoon of maternal embraces and children's chatter. If he closed his eyes, he could hear the chirp of the two parakeets that used to sit in a cage behind the front desk. He could still feel the static from the fresh-washed blankets as his mother removed them from the dryer.

Vega washed his hands and face in the bathroom and took a wet paper towel to the surface of his insulated jacket.

"Heads up," said Torres when Vega stepped out. Torres tossed a can of Coke from the vending machine in his direction. Vega caught it.

"Still got the old baseball reflexes, I see," said Torres. "I'd buy you a beer, but I figure you don't need to add a DUI to your troubles."

"You got that right. *Salud.*" Vega popped the tab and took a long pull. He wiped his mouth with the back of his hand.

"I never thanked you properly for today," said Vega.

"You don't have to thank me." Torres clinked his own soda can against Vega's. "Like I said out there, you're old school. There aren't too many of us dinosaurs left anymore."

Vega threw out half a dozen names of kids they both knew growing up. Two had gone into the army and left— the preferred exit route. Freddy's older sister, Jackie, had done the same herself. Two others had died—one in a shooting, the other from drugs. Another still lived in the neighborhood but was managing on disability after working construction and injuring his back. The last had moved to Atlantic City with a daughter to work in the casinos. There weren't a whole lot of escape routes.

"Hardest thing I have to do at my school," said Torres, "is convince my students there are worlds beyond this one."

"You did pretty well staying put," Vega noted. "Full scholarship to Columbia . . . a Ph.D . . . head of a prominent charter school. . . . My mom referred to you as *Doctor* Torres all the time. I'm not sure she ever figured out you weren't an M.D."

Torres laughed. "No wonder you were never all that jacked about coming back to the 'hood and seeing me."

Vega felt suddenly embarrassed. Did he sound envious? His mother never overtly compared him to Torres. Nevertheless, it was there. Torres got better grades than Vega. He attended an Ivy League school whereas Vega did four years at a commuter college. He was certainly a more involved son, taking care of both his mother and his sister after his father's death.

"I didn't mind," Vega lied. "Besides, it gave her a lot of joy. She'd watched you grow up. You were like a second son."

"And she was like a second mother. Hell knows, we needed second mothers. It's not like we had fathers to count on." Even though Torres's father was a presence in his children's lives (unlike Vega's father), he'd been a drunk and a brute. Torres and his sisters spent more time hiding from the man than bonding with him.

"Speaking of mothers," said Vega. "Is your mom—?" He didn't know how to ask. Fortunately Torres rescued him.

"She's over at Sunnycrest Manor."

"The nursing home on Webster Avenue?"

"Yeah. I couldn't keep her at home anymore. She went downhill fast after Donna died."

"Would she"—Vega hesitated—"know me?"

"She has good days and bad. But yeah, I think she would. You should go see her—when this blows over, I mean." Torres frowned at Vega. "Not to pry, Jimmy, but I'm kind of surprised that of all times to get nostalgic, you picked today."

"It's my mother's birthday."

"Ah. Hope you're not planning to go to her building. Hector Ponce was . . ." Torres's voice trailed off.

"My mother's building super, I know," said Vega. Clothes thumped in the dryers like a samba rhythm. Vega played with the tab on his soda can. "Did you know him at all?"

Torres shrugged. "After so many years here, I sort of know everybody."

"What was he like?"

"Like a lot of building supers. Sort of a *tigre*."

"You mean a hustler?" The Spanish word for *tiger* could be used as a compliment or an insult in the neighborhood, depending on context.

"You know the way it is down here. Things haven't changed. Everybody's got a hustle going on on the side. Especially the supers. Weed. Numbers. Women."

"So what was Ponce's?"

"I heard he liked to gamble."

"You don't mean Lotto tickets, I'm assuming." Vega recalled Dolan saying that they'd found expired Lotto tickets in Ponce's wallet.

"Everybody down here does that," said Torres. "That's financial planning in the 'hood. No. I mean like horses, numbers, sporting events."

"Do you know if he owed money?"

Torres stroked his mustache and smiled. "Everybody down here owes money, *carnal*."

"Yeah, but I'm talking big money. Enough to make him do something desperate like rob Ricardo Luis's house."

"Dunno." Torres gestured to Vega with his soda can. "You're the cop. Not me."

"Father Delgado made Ponce out to be this great guy. Very loyal and family-oriented."

"So's the mafia." Torres's phone rang in his pocket. He checked the caller ID. "Listen, Jimmy—I gotta take this call. But if there's something I can help you on with Ponce, just let me know. I'll drive you to the church as soon as I get off the phone."

Torres excused himself. Vega wandered up to the front of the laundromat in search of a garbage for his empty can.

"Here. I'll take that," said Carmela. Vega handed it to her. "The five cent deposits add up."

"Sure thing." Vega noticed that Carmela was reading a Spanish-language fan magazine with an inset picture of Ricardo Luis on the cover. Vega's stomach turned flips just seeing that Mexican heartthrob grinning back at him. He turned away from the counter and his eye caught a security camera pointed at the front door. It was a standard-issue, hardwired camera, not unlike the ones Vega saw in all the bodegas. Not unlike the one in his mother's building that hadn't been working on the night she was murdered.

"You ever get any problems with those cameras?" Vega asked Carmela.

She looked up from her magazine. "Problems?"

"Yeah, you know. Loose wires? The thing doesn't record? The DVD is just blank."

"No," she looked at him suspiciously.

"I'm not asking in order to rob the place. I'm thinking of purchasing one of those cameras for myself," he lied. "I've heard the wires can get loose."

"I don't know. It never happened to me. Besides, a loose wire just means the thing's not recording new stuff. It won't make the DVD blank. Whatever was last recorded on it will still be there."

"You're sure about that?"

"Yes. Of course. That's what happens when there's a power failure and I don't remember to change the battery backup."

"Huh." Vega thought back to Brennan's notes. He hadn't written that the security camera had failed to record the night's events. He'd written that the DVD was blank. There was nothing on it.

Someone had replaced the used DVD on the night of his mother's murder with a blank one. Someone with access to the security camera. Someone with an extra seventeen minutes of time before he dialed Father Delgado or 911.

Hector Ponce.

Chapter 14

The doorbell rang just as Adele was trying to zip up her blue silk dress, the one the saleswoman had referred to as "form-fitting." Adele wondered what form she was referring to. She was already late for Ricardo Luis's party. She didn't need any further complications. She tugged on the zipper, raced down the stairs, and shooed Diablo back from the door. The frame was warped. The door gave way all at once.

Adele's heart froze.

"Please excuse me, señora."

Marcela Salinez was standing on Adele's front porch in an oversized jacket with the hood bound so tight around her face that only her eyes and nose poked through.

"Marcela." It took all of Adele's energy just to say her name. Sweat gathered under the armpits of her shrink-wrapped dress. She blushed with a deep shame as if she had pulled the trigger last night. She opened the front door wider and hugged Marcela tightly. The coat was ice-cold to the touch and so soft; it felt like hugging snow. Marcela had obviously walked all the way from her house on the western edge of town.

"I am so sorry for your loss," Adele said in Spanish. Her words sounded weak and pathetic the moment they left her lips.

"Thank you," Marcela said woodenly. Adele beckoned her inside. She could feel Marcela's eyes taking in the shimmery festiveness of her dress. "You are going out." It sounded like an accusation.

"It's just a business function for La Casa."

"I really need to speak to you. Maybe just for a few minutes?"

"I'd love to, Marcela. Believe me, I would. But I can't talk about the—situation." Adele glanced up the stairs where Sophia was about to get into the shower. "She doesn't know," Adele whispered.

"I'm not here to talk about my father, señora."

Señora. Adele felt the full force of the word, the polite and stilted boundary it erected between them. Adele's own parents were undocumented immigrants from Ecuador. Adele did not see a divide between her and the people she worked with at La Casa. But they did. The honorific, which Adele had shrugged off as simple "good manners," now brought a dull ache of understanding to her heart. There was a chasm between her and Marcela that could never be breached, not even with the best of intentions.

Adele gave Marcela a pained look. "I grieve for you, Marcela. If there was something I could do right now, I would. But I'm already running late and I still have to take Sophia to her friend's house."

"It's about my daughter, señora. She's in danger."

"Yovanna?" Adele frowned. "But she's here now. She's safe." It was a miracle the child had made it at all. Adele heard so many terrible stories from clients. If a person was lucky enough to make it out of the cesspool of violence that was Central America these days, they faced rape, robberies, and beatings on the journey north through Mexico— assuming the Mexican authorities didn't deport them first. At the Texas border (that's where they almost always crossed), if they weren't detained by U.S. immigration, smugglers often packed them thirty to a room in safe houses and held them for ransom.

Every moment of the 2000-mile journey was frightening and perilous. But here? In suburban Lake Holly? This was where they could finally begin to decompress and deal with the longer-term problems of being undocumented, uneducated, and non-English speaking in a country that wanted to deport them. Stressful? Absolutely. But far less dire than what they'd already endured.

"By danger—do you mean from the immigration authorities?" asked Adele.

Marcela started to cry. In the nine years Adele had known her, she'd only see Marcela cry once: the day she got word that her brother Reimundo had been shot and killed in San Pedro Sula by a fourteen-year-old gang member on a bicycle. Adele put her arm around her.

"It's okay. Come. We can talk for a few minutes. At least until Sophia gets out of the shower."

In the kitchen, Adele got Marcela a box of tissues. She offered to make coffee but Marcela declined.

"I am fine. Thank you." Marcela perched herself on the corner of one of the kitchen chairs and blotted her tears. Adele took a seat across from her. There was a heaviness in Marcela that Adele had never seen before. Her shoulders looked weighted down. Her hair, dyed auburn for the fall, was growing out at the roots. She usually wore makeup, but not tonight. Her eyes carried an intensity that didn't need any embellishment.

"I need to borrow eight thousand dollars."

The words sprang from Marcela's lips so suddenly, Adele wasn't sure she'd heard correctly.

"*Eight thousand dollars?*" Adele repeated. "*Dios mío,* why?"

Marcela shook her head. "I can't say. Not to you. Not to anyone. But I promise you, I will pay you back. If it takes the rest of my life. If it takes the rest of my children's lives—"

"Does this have anything to do with why your father was at Ricardo Luis's house?"

"My father was not a thief!"

"I didn't say he was." Adele put a hand on her arm. "But you have to tell me what's going on. Is someone threatening you? Threatening Yovanna?"

It was a smuggler, Adele decided. It had to be. Yovanna had been in Lake Holly—what? A week? After probably a five- or six-week journey from Honduras. That sort of trip didn't come cheap. And now the smuggler was demanding repayment.

No. *That didn't make sense,* thought Adele. Smugglers always got paid up front. They disappeared as soon as a deal was completed—often before. This wasn't money to pay for the journey. It was money to pay someone *back* for the journey. That sort of borrowing only comes from two places: family and loan sharks. If Marcela was coming to her, then it wasn't to pay back family—unless family was the reason she was in this mess in the first place.

"Marcela, did your father borrow money from someone that he couldn't pay back?"

"Please, señora. There is nothing you can ask that will help me. It will only cause more trouble."

"Have you spoken to the police?"

"After what they just did to my father?"

Adele had a sudden panicked thought: was it possible that Marcela had no idea Vega was the man who shot her father? Adele didn't want to be the one to tell her. She didn't want to leave something like that unspoken, either.

"Marcela," she began slowly. "You do know—that is—the police officer who confronted your father—" Adele still had a hard time saying "shot" or "killed."

"I know about *el detective,* señora. I know what he did."

Marcela held Adele's gaze. Her eyes were hard. She had always been timid before this but anger had sharpened her resolve. "Now you understand how hard this is for me to come to you. But you are my only hope. I need to repay this money my father borrowed, or this man—he will kill my daughter."

"How did he contact you? By phone? The police can run a trace."

"They will never find him," said Marcela. "These sorts of people, they have a way . . ." Her voice died in her throat.

"Maybe in Honduras, that's true," said Adele. "But this man is probably here. In the United States. I'm sure the police—"

"Can do nothing!" Marcela shook her head. "It doesn't matter if he's in Honduras or Lake Holly or anywhere in between. If he loaned my father money, then he has the power to make my family pay. You cannot fight a man like that. You can only pay him or worse things will happen."

Adele got up from her chair and paced the kitchen floor. "Marcela—you're not seriously asking me to give you eight thousand dollars, are you? I don't have that sort of cash just lying around. I'm a single working mother."

"But you have important friends and donors. They do."

"Do you realize what you're asking? You're asking me to approach law-abiding citizens and prominent people in the community and ask them to contribute funds to pay off some gangster to aid in the smuggling of an undocumented—"

"But she's already here in Lake Holly. You aren't smuggling her anywhere."

"As far as the United States government is concerned, I'm engaged in facilitating the funding of an illegal enterprise involving the transport of an undocumented minor. That's a felony, Marcela. It doesn't matter whether I stick

her in my car and drive her over the border or pay off someone who already got her here."

"But you'd only be doing it to help me. Not for profit."

"Which means I'd get five years in prison, not ten.
That's the only difference."

"You could say you gave me money to go to school.
You had no idea what I was using it for."

"That would be a lie. Under oath, that would be per-
jury. I could be disbarred as a lawyer. I could go to jail and
lose custody of my own daughter. Not to mention the fact
that I'd be drummed out of La Casa and the entire immigrant services community for asking such a thing of others. There are people in this country who already believe
that the humanitarian work we do should be illegal. How
would it look if I do something that really is?"

"But I wouldn't tell anyone. Please, señora. She's my
daughter. And this man—he will kill her if he doesn't get
his money. He gave me a week. *A week!* I have no other
way to raise eight thousand dollars in a week."

"Does Byron know?"

"I haven't told him yet."

Adele stopped pacing and braced her hands on her
kitchen sink. She kept her back to Marcela and looked out
her kitchen window, past Sophia's pinch pots and clay tur-
tles that lined the sill. The refrigerator was covered in
Sophia's drawings of unicorns and rainbows. Adele couldn't
imagine a time when she wasn't a mother, when Sophia
wasn't the center of her universe. If she were in Marcela's
shoes, she would do whatever she had to to make sure her
daughter was safe. How could she ask Marcela to do less?

"Let me call Detective Vega—"

"No!"

"He did a terrible thing, Marcela. I understand that you
are furious with him. But he would try to help you now. I
know he would. He would put you in touch with the right
people at the very least."

Marcela leaned forward. Her eyes were dark and sober. "If you were me, after what happened, would you trust such a man with your daughter's life?"

I don't even know what happened, Adele wanted to say. That was the worst part. The not knowing. *No, scratch that.* The worst part was that Vega did know—and he wouldn't tell her. Was he holding back in some rigid adherence to duty? Or because he'd done something too terrible to admit, even to her?

He couldn't have.

He wouldn't have.

But we're all capable of the couldn'ts, Adele knew. They're often only a second of indiscretion away from our coulds.

The shower knobs squeaked off upstairs. The water stopped rushing through the pipes. "Mom!" Sophia called out.

"Be right there, Sophia!" Adele reached for Marcela's hand. "I understand your concerns—"

Marcela yanked her hand away. "No, you don't, señora. With all due respect, you cannot. Your daughter is safe upstairs. She hasn't spent the last ten years with a picture of you taped to her wall so she remembers what you look like. She didn't just survive a trip that no child should ever have to make only to die here because her family can't repay a loan. Do you know what she has endured already? She cries every night. I'm afraid to ask her about it. What can I say to make it better? All I can do is make her safe now. That's what I'm trying to do, señora: make her safe. If she was your daughter, wouldn't you do the same?"

"Yes, I would."

"Then you'll help me get the money?"

"Mom!" called Sophia again.

"Let me think about what to do."

Chapter 15

"So you're sure you'll be okay by yourself?" asked Joy as she finger-combed her long dark hair and checked her eyeliner in the reflection on the stove.

"I'm okay, *chispita*. Really. It's a Saturday night. You're a young girl. Go out with your friends. And then go back to your mother's place." Vega began hefting Joy's suitcase down the stairs before she could voice any protest.

"I can't believe you're throwing me out."

"I'm not throwing you out. I *love* when you visit. But it's not practical for you to be so far from school and friends." And not safe either, Vega decided. He'd been so consumed with grief last night and earlier today that he couldn't process his actions. But driving back from the Bronx this afternoon after his frightening encounter, he'd begun to take stock of his situation and the toll it could exact on the people he loved. Anyone associated with him was at risk—emotionally and, God forbid, physically.

"I'll make it up to you this summer," said Vega. "You can stay all summer if you want." He wondered if he were being overly optimistic to presume that by summer things would be better. He tried to imagine warmth and green but everything outside and inside of him felt cold and dead.

Joy hesitated by the front door. "So I spoke to Danielle today."

"Who?"

"Danielle Camino? My friend at Fordham? She said I could take the train down and visit the campus tomorrow."

Vega dropped her suitcase at his feet. "You want to go back to the Bronx? *Tomorrow?* Are you crazy?"

"I had fun today—"

"Look, Joy—"

"Dr. Torres said after I finished up at Fordham tomorrow, he'd give me a tour of his school and talk to me about what it takes to become a teacher—"

"No!"

"What do you mean, 'no'? Because you're still fixated on me becoming a doctor?"

"It's not that. It's just that—I don't like you wandering around the Bronx."

"I'll be fine. You worry too much."

He picked up her suitcase and carried it out to the trunk of her Volvo. She kissed him on the cheek. He wagged a finger at her.

"Keep a close eye on your surroundings. Don't travel alone. And whatever you do, don't tell *anyone* you're related to me."

"Roger that, Double-O-Seven," she teased.

"C'mon, Joy, I'm serious."

"Chill, Dad. I'll be careful—and in the meantime, you need to make an appointment to talk to a therapist."

"Mmm."

Joy frowned. "That sounds suspiciously like a 'no.'" Then she got into her car and Vega heard the pop and crunch of gravel beneath her tires as she backed out of his driveway. He watched her red taillights fade and then disappear.

He was alone. Already the sky had darkened, closing like a curtain around his house. He'd always liked his own company before this. But as soon as Joy left, Vega felt jumpy and restless. The normal sounds of the house—the creak of the floorboards, the hum of the refrigerator—all felt magnified and predatory tonight. He stared out the sliding glass doors onto his deck. The world was a solid sheet of black that reflected his face back at him. He looked older and gaunter. He still hadn't shaved. Could he really have aged in only twenty-four hours?

Food. He should eat. His stomach felt hollow but he had no appetite. He was afraid to get takeout right now. He was afraid some restaurant worker with a chip on his shoulder would recognize Vega and mess with his food. He searched the refrigerator for something that appealed to him but it was filled with Joy's gluten-free, vegan crap. Tofu. Organic beets. Soy burgers. Kale. In the freezer, he found a frozen Stouffer's Lasagna covered in ice crystals. He stuck it in the microwave then popped open a beer and drained it too quickly, feeling the slight buzz on an empty stomach.

Joy had left his mother's photo albums open on the dining table. Vega began to close them and return them to their carton. One day, he'd put all these prints onto discs. There had to be hundreds of shots here. Weddings and christenings in the Bronx and Puerto Rico. He had dozens of relatives but they lived mainly in pictures scattered all over his mother's apartment as a child, following Vega around like ghosts who didn't age or did so only in giant leaps between mailings. His mother and grandmother, *Abuelita* Dolores, always had one foot here and one foot back on the island. Their gossip was just as likely to do with a cousin's neighbor back in their mountain town of Barranquitas as it was one down the hall.

It wasn't any different on his father's side. Vega had three younger half sisters by his father, from two other women, all of them floating around somewhere in the New York area. His father was out there somewhere too, flawed and disappointing. That's why Vega couldn't look at family albums. They conjured up a longing for something he never knew he needed until those pictures reminded him that he did.

Vega closed one of the albums and began to heft it into the carton. An envelope tumbled out. Negatives, most likely. His mother loved to keep negatives so she could make copies of pictures for family back on the island. But it wasn't negatives. It was a letter, penned in Spanish on loose-leaf notebook paper. It took up about three quarters of the page. The script was beautiful—and not his mother's. It was addressed: *Mi amado.* My beloved. It was signed at the bottom: *Eres mi ángel.* You are my angel.

Mi amado. Eres mi ángel.

Vega smoothed the letter out on the dining table. Then he pulled his wallet out of the back pocket of his jeans, opened the billfold, and located the note card he and Joy had found inside the cellophane bouquet of flowers on his mother's grave earlier today. He laid the note card next to the letter.

The handwriting was identical.

An electric spark zipped through Vega. He picked up the letter and began to read it. He struggled a bit with the penmanship and syntax. Still, he could make out the gist of the words.

. . . *Oh, how I struggle with our being apart. I grieve that it cannot be otherwise.* Vega read the letter once, then twice. It was silly, frivolous stuff. It told him nothing about the letter writer or his mother. He searched the letter front and back for some sort of identification. He checked the envelope. He found nothing.

Who would write such a letter to his mother? Vega couldn't recall ever writing a letter like that. Not to Adele. Not even to Wendy. He was too much of a cop. He hated to commit anything to paper that might come back to haunt him. Or maybe he just wasn't romantic enough. Adele probably would agree.

Vega stared at the letter. So his mother had a secret

lover. Someone who was still alive and knew her birthday. Someone who never came forward to introduce himself at her funeral. Was he married to someone else?

Vega knew one person it wasn't: his father. Orlando Vega never wrote his mother so much as a child support check. He certainly never penned any love notes.

Then who?

The microwave dinged. Vega pulled out the soggy lasagna and slid the little container onto a plate. He grabbed a second beer and sat down at the table. He drained the beer but managed less than half the lasagna before throwing it in the trash. He couldn't find his once-robust appetite. Even the fried pork fritters that had looked so good in that *cuchifritos* joint earlier today couldn't tempt him now. He felt stripped of sensation, a vessel someone had forgotten to fill. A collection of liquor bottles sat in the far corner of the kitchen counter—bourbons and rums. He reached for one of the bourbons then put it back. It was too easy to go down that slippery slope.

What he needed was a distraction. He cleared the table, threw his plate and utensils in the dishwasher, and grabbed his guitar. His band had a club gig next week over in Broad Plains, but Vega couldn't work up the enthusiasm to practice.

Television. He flicked the remote. An HBO comedy. A Knicks game. An action thriller . . .

The news. *Coño!* He was being betrayed at every juncture. Ruben Tate-Rivera had leaked those stupid comments Vega had made at the shooting to the media. Someone in that demonstration today had posted YouTube footage of Vega trying to defend himself against that mob. The commissioner of the county police was looking grave and dismayed by all of it. Vega angrily shut off the TV. No matter what happened from this point forward, it would always be his fault. And why was that? He hadn't been drunk or angry or reckless when he shot Ponce. This wasn't personal. And okay, he'd made a judgment error. He'd had two freakin' seconds to react. *Two.* He'd like to see how well anyone in that mob would fare in the same situation. Or Ruben Tate-Rivera. Or his commissioner. They'd wet their pants.

If he could take it all back, he would. He just wished the world would let him say how *he* felt instead of making him out to be some sort of monster. Hell, when a doctor makes a mistake and the patient dies, his malpractice pays up and his life goes on as if nothing happened. No one even speaks about it in polite company. So how come Vega was facing the prospect of going before a grand jury and maybe even going to prison?

He wanted to crawl into bed and not wake up for six months. But he was too wired to sleep. What he needed was exercise and fresh air. He pulled on some sweatpants and track shoes and went outside. The air had a bite to it. He stretched and then started running, guided only by a sliver of moonlight through the trees. He saw one or two houses lit up in the distance but most of the places were dark and shuttered for the season. He turned down another community road and lost even those distant lights.

The first three miles felt good. He got his rhythm. His breathing turned hard and even, draining his thoughts. He was sore from the pummeling he took in the Bronx earlier. But even with all that, the endorphins were kicking in and making him feel better. He took bigger strides. He picked up the pace. He wanted to exhaust his body in the hopes that this would somehow exhaust his mind.

He went to leap over a tree limb that had fallen too close to the road in the last storm. But his back foot caught one of the branches. It held his body for the split second it took to lose his concentration and balance. His knee hit the pavement hard. He cursed. Nothing was broken at least. But his knee felt too bruised to run anymore. He would have to limp all the way back.

He began walking along the deserted road—a road he'd traveled a thousand times in all seasons. He could probably close his eyes and find his way home. And yet for some reason he couldn't fathom, his heart began to race. There were no streetlamps, only a dark wash of gauzy clouds that made the sky glow like a TV screen when the station has left the air. In the distance, he saw the blinking lights of an airplane. It was so high up that it trailed no sound.

He was exposed. Alone. Or maybe not alone—and that was worse.

Stop it, he told himself.

His body refused to listen. His heart beat so hard it felt like it would jump out of his chest. He broke out in a cold sweat. He couldn't catch his breath.

Just stop it.

He turned and turned again, his eyes checking and rechecking the woods for movement. Logic told him no one was here but he couldn't get his senses to agree. Every gust of wind through the trees, every crack of a branch or groan of a limb made him dizzy with panic. It sounded . . . It smelled . . . It felt like . . .

STOP IT!

It felt just like the woods last night.

He saw again that shadow of something to his right. He saw the slow, deliberate turn of Hector Ponce's body as he reached into the front pocket of his jeans. He heard those shots from his gun. In his head, they resonated like cannon fire.

Bam.

Bam.

Bam.

Bam.

"There is nothing out here!" Vega shouted.

The sound of his own voice surprised him. The hoarseness. The desperation. The trees closed in on him. A strong wind rustled the dead leaves. They sounded like fingernails tapping on a gravestone. He felt engulfed by a wave of nausea even though there was almost nothing in his stomach. What was wrong with him?

Goddamnit, what the hell was wrong with him?

And then he saw it—a faint glow of headlights on the next road. The vehicle was traveling at a slow creep. A homeowner? It didn't feel like it. It felt like the driver was looking for something. Or someone. Vega wiped the sleeve of his sweatshirt across his forehead and tried to catch his breath. Big white clouds of vapor formed in front of him, glowing like phosphorus in the moonlight. He watched the car turn onto his road and creep toward him, slowing as it approached.

He was unarmed. Trapped. His back ached. His knee hurt to run. He stumbled off the road and into the trees. He shivered as the sweat congealed on his skin. He'd become a feral shadow of his former self.

The car was a dark red SUV. Maybe a Honda. It stopped along the side of the road. Vega crouched behind some bushes. He couldn't see the figure that got out on the far side. The driver was alone. Could he outrun the person? Overpower them? Did they have a gun?

"Good Lord, Detective! Bad enough you don't return phone calls and I have to hunt you down in person. Don't make an old lady like me go running through the woods after you."

Isadora Jenkins. She pushed back the hood of her jacket. The moonlight caught her white hair. Vega parted the bushes and stumbled forward. He felt like an idiot. He was shaking all over.

Jenkins stepped around the car and frowned. "When did you last shave? You look like some mountain man who just wrestled a bear."

"I was running and I took a fall."

"You're running and falling, all right. And most of it ain't in your legs." She blew into her gloved hands and studied him a moment behind her big round glasses. "The first night after is the worst, you know. The adrenaline wears off and everything gets real scary real fast."

"I'm fine."

She tossed off a laugh. "And they say cops are good liars. What on God's green earth were you thinking going to the Bronx today and stepping into that protest?"

"I was trying to reach my truck," said Vega. "It's my mother's birthday and I wanted to visit her grave."

"Her grave is in the middle of the Grand Concourse?"

"I went to see a priest I know. Is that against department policy?"

"Unless he was giving communion on the center divide, I'd say so," said Jenkins. "Captain Waring wants to see you ASAP. So get cleaned up and, for God's sake, *shave*. You want people to treat you like a cop? Start looking like one."

Chapter 16

Vega shaved and showered faster than he'd ever thought possible. Then he got in his truck and followed Isadora Jenkins to the county police headquarters. It had been only twenty-four hours since he'd walked out of this building, but already it seemed like a lifetime ago.

He fantasized on the way down of unclipping his shield and throwing it across Captain Waring's desk when his boss started tearing into him. But whom was he kidding? Eighteen years in the county police meant no pension. Nada. Zip. What was he going to do at forty-two years of age? Stock shelves at Walmart? Resurrect his pathetic music career, or worse, his brief and extremely painful stint in insurance? He had mortgage and car payments. Joy was counting on him to help her with tuition. If his boss told Vega he had to file pistol permits for the rest of his career, then that's what he was going to do.

Vega daydreamed—not for the first time since the shooting—how much easier it would have been if he'd taken the bullet instead of Ponce. Live or die, at least he'd be a hero. Not this toxic embarrassment to everyone who'd ever cared about him.

Vega parked in police parking and walked over to the civilian area to meet up with Jenkins. She wagged a finger at him.

"What was my second rule after honesty, Detective?"

"Shut my big, fat mouth."

"Thank you. Now let's try to remember that."

They walked through the front doors and up to the desk sergeant who used to talk baseball with Vega. Now he just kept his head down and buzzed them in without a word. Doom and Gloom—a.k.a. Captains Waring and Lorenzo— were waiting for them in Captain Waring's office. Waring's office looked like a permanent Fourth of July celebration. There were stars and stripes and lots and lots of eagle depictions with tridents and guns—just in case you forgot Waring was a former Navy SEAL.

What was missing—what was always missing—was any mention of Frank Waring's other previous life as a professional Irish step-dancer. Vega had heard from some of the more senior guys in the division that Waring had been orphaned young and followed an aunt who'd raised him into the field. He was good—good enough to have had articles written about him. Yet Waring seemed even more embarrassed about his past than Vega was about the shooting. Maybe to a former Navy SEAL, high stepping across a stage in tight pants is worse than just about anything you could do with a gun.

Captain Waring was sitting behind his desk when Vega and Jenkins entered. It was impossible to tell from Waring's expression how much trouble you were in. Captain Lorenzo was no better. He was a gaunt, pasty-faced man who could make the words *You won the lottery* sound depressing. Lorenzo sat in the only comfortable visitor's chair in the room. Two conference room chairs had been pulled in for Vega and Jenkins. They were definitely not comfortable and weren't meant to be.

"Close the door," said Waring. His tone was soft. The softer it was, the more likely you were in trouble. Vega could feel his breath balling up in his chest.

"We haven't exactly been a good fit since you moved over to the homicide task force, Detective."

What was Vega supposed to say to that? Did he disagree and tell the captain he was wrong? Did he agree, which pretty much guaranteed his exit?

Vega said nothing. In the hallway he heard phones ringing and cops talking to each other in loud, carefree voices. Vega doubted he'd ever feel that way again.

"What you did today—publicly showing your face at that protest—was beyond stupid."

"But I didn't—"

"Captain," Jenkins interrupted. She shot Vega a sharp look. "Detective Vega is aware of his missteps and has already taken appropriate steps to get himself into counseling so this doesn't happen again."

Qué coño? Jenkins was telling his boss that he needed his head examined? Vega opened his mouth to contradict her. Jenkins glared at Vega, daring him. He shut it again.

Captain Lorenzo spoke. "How soon?"

Jenkins turned to Vega. She didn't ask. She ordered. "Tomorrow."

Tomorrow? Who was going to see him on a Sunday? That shrink Greco had given him? He had her name somewhere in his wallet. Maybe she'd do him a favor. Maybe they could meet for half an hour and he could check off a box and everybody would be happy.

"Yes," said Lorenzo. "I think that's a wise decision."

Waring already seemed bored with the topic. He didn't care if Vega got therapy or not. He folded his arms in front of him. "I need some straight answers on more pressing matters—starting with the Wickford patrol officer's testimony that got leaked to the media."

"Spontaneous utterances, Captain," said Jenkins. She and Vega had already been through the transcript before they arrived this evening. "Detective Vega was under stress—"

"I'm not talking about what he said," said Waring. "I'm

talking about where he was standing at the time of the shooting. Officer Franklin seems to believe Detective Vega was much closer to the suspect than fifteen feet when he shot him."

"Detective Vega and I have discussed the matter," said Jenkins. "He stands by his original statement."

Waring looked at Vega but directed his question to Jenkins. "Does the detective have any explanation he'd like to offer as to why one of the bullets entered beneath the suspect's chin?"

Vega fought the urge to defend himself. He silently counted to five and waited for Jenkins to answer.

"Detective Vega fired at the suspect's center mass, as per departmental training and policy," said Jenkins. "We believe the first three shots caused the suspect to collapse. The final bullet caught him under the chin as he was in the process of falling backward. My client is confident that ballistics will vindicate any suggestion that he aimed his weapon beneath the suspect's chin and fired at point-blank range."

"Confident, hmm," said Waring. He and Lorenzo traded quick glances. "The district attorney's office has uncovered a witness, Vega. Someone who swears they saw you shoot Ponce point-blank in the head."

"That's impossible!" Vega couldn't contain himself any longer. "I was never closer than fifteen feet from him!" He caught Jenkins scowling at him and sat on his hands— something he hadn't done since he was a kid in parochial school and Sister Margarita was trying to get him to sit still.

"Has the district attorney released the witness's name?" asked Jenkins.

"Yes," said Waring. "She lives on Perkins Road in Wickford. Her house is adjacent to the woods behind Ricardo Luis's estate. It was her spotlight that was shining into the woods where Ponce was shot."

Vega pictured a snoopy old dowager, wheelchair-bound,

skin like an oyster, half-addled with dementia, looking out her window and mistaking a deer for him. She was probably confused. Maybe a little lonely. Those big estates in Wickford had to get pretty lonely.

Jenkins must have been thinking the same thing because she asked Waring if he had a description of the witness.

"I have a few notes from the DA's office." Waring put on his glasses and read a printout before him. "The witness is a thirty-eight-year-old former bond trader for Goldman Sachs. She's now a stay-at-home mom with two boys, ages three and five. Her husband is a managing partner at Morgan Stanley." Waring put the sheet of paper down and stared at Vega. "And for the record? Her vision is twenty-twenty, courtesy of LASIK surgery she underwent about a month ago."

Vega felt the rope slowly tightening around his neck.

Jenkins, ever the good defense attorney, began exploring other angles. "So her mental and visual acuity are not in question, I take it. How about her politics? Would she have any reason to lie about what she saw?"

"She's on the board of a number of volunteer groups in Lake Holly," said Waring. "The hospital. The Junior League. A few other local charities. Her politics might be sympathetic toward immigrants. But her background seems pretty solid and community-oriented."

"In other words," said Jenkins, "her mere presence as a witness, coupled with all the media attention, is likely to force this shooting in the direction of a grand jury."

Waring and Lorenzo didn't answer. No answer was needed. They were all familiar with New York State law and protocol in police shootings. Most police shootings never went before a grand jury because the use of lethal force was considered legally justified. If the suspect brandished a weapon or was in the process of committing a violent crime. If there were witnesses who could verify that the officer reasonably feared for his life or the lives of others.

If there was video that backed up any of the same assertions. In these cases, the DA and the police wrote up their paperwork, cleared the shooting in-house and that was the end of it.

But if a shooting turned questionable or public reaction got heated, the DA might choose instead to convene a grand jury. It could take weeks for testimony to be presented. During all this time, Vega would be under a cloud of suspicion—so much so that even if a majority of the jurors eventually decided not to indict him, his credibility would be ruined. Every future arrest would be nitpicked by superiors. The slightest civilian complaint would earn him charges. Informants would mistrust him. Other cops would refuse to work with him for fear of becoming collateral damage. He might never be able to work a field assignment again. He might even be pressured to resign. Anywhere Vega went after this, his reputation would precede him. In the era of social media, he'd be an embarrassment to any law enforcement agency that considered hiring him.

And that wouldn't be the end of things, either. He could spend the next five years testifying. Even if the grand jury voted not to indict, the feds could decide Vega had violated the man's civil rights and convene their own grand jury to hear the case all over again. Or the governor could decide he didn't like the grand jury's decision and appoint a special prosecutor to restart the case from scratch. Not to mention the fact that Vega would be facing the same case in civil court when the family brought a lawsuit against him. Vega couldn't recall a police shooting in which a family *didn't* try to bring a case against the cop—even when the shooting was clearly justified.

But none of these scenarios even began to address the most terrifying one: Vega could get indicted. He could go on trial and be convicted. He could go to prison. Cops did these days. Not for twenty-five years, perhaps. But for three, four—even ten. All of it in protective custody since a cop in prison was a piñata in a room full of baseball bats. Everybody was just dying to take a swing.

Vega palmed his eyes. He was only just beginning to process what he was up against. "I did not execute Hector Ponce," he said slowly. "I swear. Won't the autopsy vindicate me?"

"It could," said Waring. "If there are no powder burns on that chin wound, that would argue against your having shot him at close range."

"Then again," said Lorenzo, "if you put the muzzle right up to Ponce's chin and shot, there wouldn't be any powder burns either. No opportunity for the powder to make contact with air."

Leave it to Lorenzo to kill even the suggestion of hope.

"Look," said Waring. His voice sounded a little kinder. He was a cop too, after all. "I believe the forensics will vindicate you if what you are saying is true. But the investigation could take weeks. Ponce was shot five times by two different guns—yours and Luis's. There is now disagreement on the range so every single investigator is going to want to double- and triple-check his findings."

"What do I do?"

"Stay out of the public eye," said Waring. "Don't eat in restaurants. Don't go to parties. Don't attend sporting events. Don't go to concerts. "

"But I'm a musician. I play in a band."

"Get someone else to fill in for you until this case cools down."

All Vega had was his music. That's how he lost himself. That was his therapy. And now he didn't even have that.

"I don't think the DA is going to make any decisions about whether or not to convene a grand jury until Monday at this point," said Waring. "In the meantime, the less you are out there, the better."

The meeting broke up and Vega walked his lawyer to her car. "Thanks for your help tonight," he told her.

Jenkins regarded him over the oversized rims of her big red glasses. "We're not through, you know."

"Pardon?"

"That wasn't just a line I said in there, Detective. You really do need to seek counseling."

"I will. When I have time."

"You have time now. That's about all that Waring has left you at this point. Do you have someone in mind or would you like me to set something up?"

"Aw, for cryin' out loud!" Vega raised his hands in frustration. "Look, I was married for thirteen years to a psychologist, okay? I've had my head examined more times than I care to count. And when all that was over, her lawyer examined my wallet."

"You're talking about your marriage, Detective. I'm talking about dealing with post-traumatic stress."

"Same thing, trust me. And for the record, I'm not suffering from post-traumatic stress."

"What do you call your behavior in the woods tonight when I came to see you? *Normal?*"

"I live out in the woods. It's normal to be concerned about intruders."

Jenkins shook her head. "This is not negotiable, Vega. You heard Captain Lorenzo. Either you get your butt into counseling or I'll do it for you. Which is it going to be?"

Vega ran a hand through his hair. He felt like an overripe piece of fruit some therapist was about to stick a knife into. No way would he slice up cleanly. If he opened up, it would be messy and sticky and God only knew what sort of rotten bits might be at his core. He was scared. Scared of what someone might find. Scared of what he might find most of all.

"What's it going to be, Vega?"

"This cop I know, he gave me a name of a shrink. I'll call her."

"Tomorrow." Jenkins shook her finger at him.

"Okay, okay. Tomorrow."

She got into her car. Vega watched her pull out of the parking lot. His cell phone rang as he walked back to his truck. It was Joy. Her voice sounded shaky.

"Dad? Can you come over to my campus?"

"Sure thing, *chispita*. What's wrong?"

"I'm here with campus security? I sorta don't want to alarm you. But somebody slashed all my tires in the parking lot and put a note on my windshield."

Vega tried to find his voice. His sense of command. It was fading fast. "A note? What did it say?"

" 'Killer cop's daughter.' "

Chapter 17

Adele smoothed the creases in her blue silk dress as she stepped out of her car. *This is just a business event like any other business event,* she told herself.

She wished she could make herself believe that.

Ricardo Luis had taken over the most expensive restaurant in Lake Holly for the evening, a new place called Harvest where a farm-to-table meal cost as much as six months' worth of groceries. It was housed in a graceful landmark Victorian that used to be a funeral parlor. Adele was pretty sure the celebrity chef who bought the place had no idea that when Dave Lindsey brokered the property as a "location to die for," he wasn't kidding.

Adele checked her coat at the entrance. Her blue silk cocktail dress was all wrong for the event. She saw that right away. She looked like she was the maid of honor at a wedding in 1953. Adele was used to attending events full of earnest academics, dowagers, and politicians where dressing in anything other than worsted wool made her look young and hip by comparison. But truly hip people, she now realized, didn't dress jazzy at all. There was an abundance of ripped jeans and linen jackets. The women wore clothing that was all about showing off skin, not covering it up.

Adele flattened herself against a pocket door and grabbed a glass of white wine off a passing tray. She searched the crowd for familiar faces. La Casa's board members were all here, including Dave Lindsey and his wife. They were clustered in a tight group at the edge of the event like kids at a first dance. Adele did not see Ricardo Luis, which disappointed her a little. She could dislike him for distancing himself from the shooting. But there was no denying the thrill of meeting a celebrity. Perhaps he was just going to put in a cameo appearance.

"Ah, we meet," said a booming voice over the chatter and music from a live salsa band in the next room. "And she's even prettier than I've heard."

Adele turned and took in the black-framed glasses and red bowtie. His trademark. Just in case you confused Ruben Tate-Rivera with some other black college professor-turned-activist. Or some other man who believed complimenting a woman on her looks still passed for high praise.

Adele forced a smile and extended a hand. She knew who Tate was. Everyone in the country knew who Tate was. Vega and other police officers hated him for his bombastic, antipolice rhetoric and penchant for publicity. They accused him of distorting facts to suit his preconceived notions of the world. But Adele had always argued that a free society needed a single-minded person like Ruben Tate-Rivera who embraced the claims of the poor and disenfranchised simply because they were poor and disenfranchised. She didn't like his style. She didn't think everything he said was true. But he forced the police and the media to take note of things they might otherwise brush under the table.

She wondered if she'd feel the same way now that someone she cared about was caught in his crosshairs.

"So nice to meet you, Professor," said Adele. She'd heard he liked to be referred to as "Professor." He was surrounded by a gaggle of young, fresh-faced assistants who no doubt called him that.

"I'm looking forward to hearing you speak at Fordham University tomorrow," he said.

"You're coming to the symposium?"

"Absolutely."

The symposium was the largest annual gathering of immigrant coalitions in New York State. Strictly speaking, Ruben Tate-Rivera's constituency wasn't immigrants. It was activists concerned about police abuse of power. The two areas overlapped of course. But Adele liked to think that her clients were far more concerned with fair wages and a pathway to legal residency than they were their day-to-day relations with the police.

"I spoke to Gloria Mendez, the event coordinator, this morning," said Tate. "She's most anxious to hear your comments on yesterday's shooting. I understand a lot of media will be there, too. This is an excellent opportunity to pressure the district attorney to convene a grand jury—maybe even get the governor to appoint a special prosecutor for the task."

Adele froze. "I never said I was going to do any of that."

Tate narrowed his gaze. "It would be—unfortunate—if you turned timid, Adele. The media is expecting a forceful response."

"Why? Because you told them that's what I was going to say? Who gave you the right to hijack my speech?"

"Would you prefer I tell them the *real* reason for your trepidation?" Tate's eyes bored into hers behind those heavy black-framed glasses. He knew. Adele suspected the source of the leak. She searched out Dave Lindsey's face just beyond Tate's entourage. Lindsey tried to duck into the crowd but since he was a head taller than everyone, he was easy to spot.

"My private life is no one's business," said Adele. "Least of all yours, *Professor.*"

"Oh, come now," said Tate. "I hope you aren't seriously going to try to make excuses for this cop. His actions are indefensible. His comments since the shooting have been callous and outrageous."

"How can you say that?" asked Adele. "How can anyone who wasn't there speak about what happened?"

A small smile curled the edges of Tate's lips. "But someone was, Adele. A witness. My sources tell me she saw Vega shoot Ponce point-blank in the head."

"I've heard that. And I don't believe it."

"Why? Because the detective *told* you it didn't happen?"

Adele seethed. She hated Tate for his arrogance and condescension. But she hated Vega too for putting her in this position. Here she was defending a man who wasn't even willing to defend himself.

"Who is the witness?" asked Adele.

"I'm awaiting official release of her name," said Tate. "She's a neighbor, I think. When I find out, I'll let you know. And then I suggest you rethink your position. You go on that stage tomorrow and don't demand a grand jury investigation, you can kiss off a career in this field, Adele. Not a single person or group in that audience will be with you."

"I will."

The voice came out of nowhere, floating above the music and chatter and movement of waiters. It was a melodic voice with a strong Spanish accent. It carried a hint of the breathy vibrato he was known for. Adele had hoped she'd get to meet Ricardo Luis this evening. She hadn't planned on doing it this way.

Everyone turned in Luis's direction. For a celebrity, he seemed rather shy up close.

"I'm not saying I can defend what this police officer

did," Luis said hesitantly to Tate and the crowd. "But I did not sense any anger or hatred in him. Maybe he did what this witness is saying. Maybe he didn't. But perhaps it is best to let the courts handle it from here, yes?"

His words took the heat right out of the conversation. Adele could have kissed him, she felt so grateful. Tate nodded curtly to Adele and eased away, surrounded as always by his assistants. Even Dave Lindsey backed off. Adele assumed Luis would too, but he stood there, holding out another glass of white wine to her. Adele couldn't deny a little skip in her breathing. She'd never been this close to a celebrity before—and a good-looking one at that.

"Thank you," she said shyly. "For the wine and for . . . um, coming to my rescue."

"Politics bore me," said Luis. "I'd much rather talk music and food. Life is too short for so much anger, yes?"

He was charming. She expected him to be charming in a crowd. But not like this. Not up close. He was shorter than he appeared onstage. Probably all of five-seven. He was probably pushing forty though he had none of the crow's feet or random strands of gray that Adele had begun to notice when *she* looked in the mirror. He was dressed in a fitted black shirt that managed to look stylish and indifferent to fashion at the same time. He was attractive of course. But even beyond the dimpled smile and perfectly sculpted body, there was something magnetic about him. He radiated star power. Was that always there? Or just a result of his fame?

Stop it. You sound like a groupie.

"I don't normally make a scene like that," said Adele. "I must apologize, Mr. Luis—"

"Ric. Call me Ric. Everyone does." He had a killer smile: lots of white teeth that shone almost as brightly as his liquid brown eyes.

"Adele." She pressed a palm to the chest of her dress.

Her sweaty fingers stuck to the shiny silk for a brief moment, which made her feel even more embarrassed at her choice of attire this evening.

"You don't have to apologize, Adele," said Luis. "I think it's very—how do you say . . . open-minded?—to be head of an immigrant organization and still be able to defend a police officer."

Adele laughed. "I'm not as open-minded as you think," she said. "You see, the police officer who shot Mr. Ponce is my, my—I'm dating him."

"*Ay caray!*" Luis smacked his forehead. He had a performer's sense of gesture. Every emotion had an accompanying physical tic. "I had no idea."

"Then you're the only one Ruben Tate-Rivera *hasn't* blabbed to. That's why he was going at it so hard with me. He knows I'm not open-minded. Just torn."

A stocky Latino in a black beret put a hand on Luis's shoulder and whispered in his ear. Luis's face slackened and then regained its trademark smile. He obviously could pull it out on command, like a pair of sunglasses. Adele assumed he would glad-hand her like a politician and slip away but he waved the man in the beret off and turned back to her.

"We are similar, you and me? You and I?" said Luis. "Forgive me. I learned my English the way most immigrants do. While working my butt off."

"Your English is fine," said Adele. "It's you and I. But we can switch to Spanish if you'd prefer."

"No. I need the practice. Thank you."

A waiter walked over with a platter of colorful finger foods that took longer to explain than to eat. Adele would have been fine with pigs in a blanket.

"What I'm trying to say is that I'm also torn," said Luis. "I'm very grateful to the police officer for coming to help me so quickly. But I'm sad that a man died as a result."

"I wish you could say that publicly," said Adele.

"I have," said Luis. "I issued a statement through my publicist. And I gave a donation to your organization."

"No. I mean what you're saying about Detective Vega."

"Ah."

Another person came up to Luis, a black woman with platinum-blond hair whom Adele vaguely recalled seeing on the cover of some fashion magazine.

"Adele." Luis touched her arm. "I would like to talk more to you about this officer and his situation. Can you give me—maybe forty-five minutes to greet everyone? Then can you meet me by the back doors of the kitchen? I'll need a cigarette by then."

"You smoke? But your voice?"

Luis winked at her. "Don't tell my agent, okay? He thinks I've quit."

Dave Lindsey caught up to Adele when Luis slipped away.

"That didn't go too well with Tate back there."

"It might have." Adele held his gaze. "If my chairman of the board didn't see fit to broadcast my private life to the public."

"People *know*, Adele. Whether I tell them or not. Some already knew and now they all do. Besides, how else could anyone explain your behavior? You spoke to the DA's office. You confirmed all the incriminating facts. And yet you're still refusing to call for a grand jury investigation."

"I'm not refusing. I'm weighing it."

"What's to weigh?"

Adele blinked at him.

"Okay. I get it," said Lindsey. "If you stand up on that stage tomorrow and call for a grand jury investigation, your life with this man is over. But let me ask you this: if you found out he executed an unarmed man at point-blank range, would you really *want* a life with him after that? You've spent ten grueling years building La Casa. You've spent what?—a few months?—dating this guy. Are you really willing to stake your whole career—La Casa's credibility—on what he did in those woods?"

One of the board members pulled Lindsey aside to ask him a question. Adele used the excuse to disappear into the crowd. She felt lost and was reeling. She wished she knew what to believe. She wished Vega would tell her. Why couldn't he just tell her?

After forty-five minutes, Adele grabbed her coat and found her way out through the kitchen. Minutes ticked by. Luis wasn't there. She turned to go back inside.

"Finally. My nicotine fix." And there he was, dimpled grin on command, smiling at her as he stuck a cigarette between his lips and lit it. "You smoke?" He held the pack out to her.

"No. Thanks." She shook her head. His presence one-on-one turned her shy.

Luis regarded the glowing embers of his cigarette. "I keep trying to quit but I've been smoking since I was thirteen."

"That young?"

Luis shrugged. "I was a street kid in Nogales, Mexico. You grow up fast."

"Did you always sing?"

"Sang. Danced. You name it, I did it."

"I guess people noticed your talent."

Luis laughed. He could act, too. He was acting like he cared what Adele had to say. "Nobody notices anything when your belly's empty. Believe me, I spent years dressing up in ridiculous costumes and doing stupid gong show routines on *Sábado Gigante*. One wrong move and I could end up back there." Adele knew the Spanish-language variety show. She used to watch it as a child. "Despite what everyone sees, I was not an overnight success."

"So how did you get your big break?"

He shrugged. "You make the right connections and then

just do whatever you need to keep them. You got my book, right?"

"Um, yes. Thank you." She hadn't cracked the spine.

"See, that's where I am right now. I just wrapped up my first American movie. It's coming out in July and my agent and a whole bunch of people in Hollywood think this is the career move that's going to break me out of the Latin market and into mainstream audiences. This shooting—it could ruin everything."

"I'm sure you've got an army of publicists handling that," said Adele.

"Yes. I do," said Luis. "But when you told me just now about your connection to the police officer"—he sighed— "I feel bad. I never wanted things to go like this. I know the detective was just trying to do his job."

"It would be great if you could say that publicly."

"I wish I could, Adele. But the media, the fans—they could turn against me in an instant. It's bad enough that I shot this man. All the anti-gun people now hate me. Never mind the fact that every celebrity in Hollywood who is anti-gun walks around with an armed bodyguard. The double standard is ridiculous."

"You don't have a bodyguard?"

"I do in Miami. I have to. Here for the most part, I can escape from all of that."

"Sounds like you don't like fame all that much."

"It's got its upside, sure." He held his cigarette between his thumb and forefinger and took a long pull. Up close like this, without a camera or spotlights, Adele could see the scrawny Mexican street kid he'd once been.

"The problem is, everyone wants something from you," said Luis as he exhaled a long blast of smoke. "Even when you give, it's never enough. They always want more. When I made that nine-one-one call, I just wanted it to be over."

"It? You mean the robbery?"

Luis leaned against the building's shingles and looked past Adele to the parking lot. "If there was a way I could make things better without destroying my career, I would. I didn't grow up like this." He gestured to the Mercedes, BMWs, and Escalades that lined the lot, their chrome and paint sparkling like they'd just come out of the showroom.

The man in the black beret whom Adele had seen earlier hung out the kitchen door. "Ric. You're needed inside."

Luis stamped out his cigarette. "See what I mean?"

"It's a shame," said Adele. "Under different circumstances, Jimmy would have been thrilled to meet you. He's a musician, too."

"The detective? What does he play?"

"Guitar. In a club band. They call themselves 'Armado.' "

"Hah." Luis laughed. "Sorry. It's just—*Armed*—that doesn't sound like the best band name for a man who just uh, did what he did."

"I know. All the band members are in law enforcement. That's where the name came from."

"Hold on a moment, please." Luis went into the kitchen and emerged a few minutes later with a scrap of paper. "This is my private cell phone number. Please tell the detective that if he would ever like a tour of my home recording studio or guitar collection in Wickford, I would be happy to give him one."

"Thank you," said Adele. "That's very kind of you. But I doubt his department would let him."

"I understand. I'm just trying to offer a—*cómo se dice?*—a peace offering?"

Adele tucked the scrap of paper into her purse. "I'll let him know." She ducked back through the kitchen and found Dave Lindsey.

"I've got to go." Adele didn't want to pick Sophia up too late from her friend's house. The girl's family was doing her a favor as it was.

Lindsey leaned in close to speak over the music. "Margaret Behring," he shouted.

"What?"

"Do you know a Margaret Behring?"

"I'm on the board of the Lake Holly Food Pantry," said Adele. "Of course I know Margaret. She coordinates all the volunteers who help stock the shelves." Many of the pantry's needy clients were also clients of La Casa.

"Margaret lives in Wickford. On Perkins Road. Right behind Luis."

Adele stepped back as the realization of what Dave Lindsey was saying sank in.

"You don't mean. She's not—"

"Tate just told me. She's the one who witnessed the shooting."

Chapter 18

Rage coursed through Vega's veins. The sort of rage he'd never known his entire life, not even when Wendy told him she was pregnant with another man's twins. It bypassed all logic and reason. It clawed at his core, snarling and feral, ready to leap out at the son of a bitch who'd threatened his daughter.

I will kill the hijo de puta who slashed my little girl's tires. I will bash his brains in. I don't care if they send me to jail. I'm going anyway.

How was it possible that he'd killed a man last night and felt only guilt and regret? And now, not twenty-four hours later, he felt only desire to do the same thing?

You want a killer cop? Bicho es! I'll give you a killer cop!

He could barely keep his mind on the road as he drove to the community college campus. He tailgated in the left lane, driving too fast, taking the turns too quickly, whipping in and out of traffic like he had some sort of death wish for himself and anyone who came into contact with him. *I'm toxic. Stay away from me, cabrones. The world hates me and I hate the world!* If he could find a bumper sticker to proclaim it, he would.

Up until this moment in his life, he'd always tried to find the essential goodness in people. And sure, with some, you had to paw through a pile of manure to uncover it.

But he never quit looking. He wanted to help people. He wanted to keep them safe. He wanted to guide them through their time of crisis to that moment when things would get better. He believed that even when they lied to him or cursed at him or took a swing at him that it was only the uniform or his position of authority that they were angry at. They were acting out of impulse. It wasn't personal. When everyone calmed down, they would see that. Things would improve.

He wasn't sure he could believe that anymore. Never had humanity looked darker or more threatening to him than in these last twenty-four hours. Never had he felt so vulnerable and alone.

Do whatever you want to me! he felt like screaming. *But spare the people I love!* He was a man with a bull's-eye on his back. Everyone he cared about was likely to become collateral damage.

Valley Community College was county police jurisdiction. *His* jurisdiction—if he weren't on administrative leave. He managed to keep himself together long enough to ask his department to send over two officers to file a formal report. He didn't want this swept under the rug by campus security.

He tried to force himself to calm down enough so that he didn't look like a raging lunatic when he pulled up to the campus security building. It was a portable trailer that looked like a giant Twinkie with a handicap accessible ramp in front and two flowerpots that seemed to be used mostly for cigarette butts. There was a small parking lot facing the building with one campus patrol car in a marked spot and an aging Nissan sedan across from it. Joy's car wasn't here. It was probably in the student lot. Just as well, thought Vega. He wasn't ready to face the casual viciousness of the crime yet. He parked his truck next to the Nissan and walked inside.

The trailer was one long overheated room. It smelled of

burnt coffee and damp wood. Joy was sitting on a plastic chair between two girlfriends who were hovering protectively around her. All three of them looked like variations on the same theme, with their skintight, ripped jeans, ponytails, and childish accessories. The girl on Joy's right was black with Rudolph-the-Red-Nosed Reindeer mittens on her hands. The one on her left was blond with freckled skin and a wool hat adorned with pom-poms pulled low across her forehead. Vega wished he knew their names, wished he paid more attention to such things.

Everybody stared at Vega when he entered. Besides the girls, there were three officers in the room. There was the campus security officer, a black guy with the ramrod posture of a retired soldier. There were also two uniformed officers Vega recognized from his own department—Wilson, a white guy with soft eyes whose father used to work with Greco in the Lake Holly PD, and Duran, a fellow Puerto Rican who was short-listed to make detective soon. At this rate, maybe he'd take Vega's job.

All conversation stopped when Vega entered. The only sound was the squawk of the department radios. Vega nodded to the three officers. There was no point in introducing himself to the campus security guy. Anybody who hadn't been under a rock the past twenty-four hours knew who he was.

"So what do you have so far? Any witnesses? Any video footage?"

"No witnesses," said Duran. He had a weight lifter's physique—all shoulders and biceps and pecs—probably a compensation for his relatively short stature. He lifted his gaze to meet Vega's but his eyes seemed to be focusing on a spot just past Vega's earlobe. "We've pulled the video. One suspect. A white male, maybe five-nine, a hundred and fifty pounds wearing a dark hoodie."

"That's like a third of the student body."

"The video's very grainy," said the campus officer. His

nameplate read STEVENS. "The county hasn't appropriated any funds to update our security equipment in a long time so we've got no clear facial shots. We do know that he got into a dark-colored jeeplike vehicle with someone else behind the wheel. Though again, we've got no idea who that person is."

"Model? Color? License plate?" asked Vega.

"Can't tell from the video," said Stevens. "It looks like a Jeep. Maybe a Renegade. Black or dark blue or maybe even dark green."

"You can't cross-check the Jeep with student-registered vehicles?"

"We did. But right now, we have no proof it was a student. The campus has no perimeter security so in theory, anyone could have driven in."

Vega turned to Joy. "Can you narrow the field of suspects, perhaps? Any boy you rejected? Or who thinks you rejected him?"

"That's sexist, Dad."

"How is that sexist?"

"To assume that I'm somehow to blame for this."

"I'm not blaming you. I'm just wondering if maybe you sent out the wrong signals to someone."

"That's not blame? Look at the note, Dad! It's about *you*, not me."

There was an uncomfortable silence in the room. Now Vega was not only a killer cop, he was a chauvinist as well. He tried to run with his mistake.

"Okay. So this is about me." He turned to Stevens. "Has someone on campus been active in antipolice protests?"

"We have several student organizations that would fit that bill," said Stevens.

"The whole campus knows!" said Joy. "You'd be hard-pressed to find anyone who hasn't seen something about it." Vega could have been on death row and been more popular, apparently. He turned back to the cops.

"Are you interviewing students?"

"Duran and I are on that now," said Wilson. "Kids often brag about this sort of vandalism."

"It's more than vandalism," said Vega. "This *student*—and I use the term loosely—made terroristic threats against my daughter."

"Actually, right now, the charge *would* be vandalism," Duran interrupted. "Criminal mischief, to be more precise. There is no threat, implied or otherwise."

"This *cabrón* wrote 'killer cop's daughter.' That's not threatening?"

"I'm afraid we get a lot of this type of vandalism," said Stevens. "Some are fraternity pranks. Others are students who are angry at their professors or looking to get revenge against an ex-boyfriend or ex-girlfriend—"

"What Stevens is saying," Duran interrupted, "is that we can't justify a bigger charge in this case without explaining why all those other cases fall under the heading of 'criminal mischief.' "

"So that's it? You just file the report and let these *pendejos* skate?"

"Nobody's letting anyone *skate*." Vega could tell Duran was getting frustrated with him. Vega was frustrated, too. He'd never been on this side of the divide, standing before cops, feeling helpless and victimized.

"Stevens is going to keep an eye out for your daughter," said Duran. "We'll run checks on the student-registered vehicles. We'll ask at the fraternities. It could take a month or two. But we'll catch these guys, I'm sure."

"And they're gonna be real scared when you charge them with criminal mischief and all they pay is a freakin' fine."

"Dad!" cried Joy, tugging at his sleeve. "Let's go home."

"I don't make the laws, Jimmy," said Duran. "And neither do you. My suggestion in the meantime? Buy your daughter some pepper spray. A lot of the girls on campus carry it."

"Pepper spray? That's your answer?"

"Quit it, Dad! You're embarrassing me." Joy ushered her father out of the trailer and into the parking lot.

"Pepper spray?" Vega asked again as their feet hit the asphalt. "You're attacked and all these guys can do is suggest I buy you some *pepper spray?*"

"I wasn't attacked. Just my car. Dad, please! Can we concentrate right now on getting the car home?"

Joy had already called a tow truck to meet them in the student parking lot. They just had to wait for it to show up. Vanessa, the black girl with Rudolph mittens, hugged Joy and got into her car next to Vega's truck. Vega thanked her for being there for his daughter.

The other girl, the freckled blonde, just stood there fiddling with the pom-poms on her knit hat.

"You need a ride?" asked Vega as he beeped open his truck doors.

Freckles didn't move.

"Tell my dad what you just told me," said Joy.

"But it'll get my boyfriend in trouble!"

"If you don't tell, I will," said Joy.

"Tell me what?" asked Vega. "Does she know the guys who did this?"

"No," said Joy. "Tell him, Katie."

Vega found himself suddenly scrutinizing this Katie more closely. She wore a suede jacket and supple high leather boots that were fashionable rather than warm. Even her slouchy cherry-red messenger bag looked like something his ex-wife would buy on her second husband's hugely inflated Wall Street salary. While a lot of kids at Valley Community were struggling financially, Katie didn't appear to be one of them.

"Where's your car?" Vega asked the girl.

"In the same lot as Joy's."

"Hop in. I'll drive you over and we can talk."

The girl squeezed into the back seat of Vega's truck and removed her pom-pom hat. A crackle of static filled the air.

"Katie's from Wickford," said Joy.

"Mmm." Vega had no idea if this was small talk or significant. With teenage girls, you never could tell.

"Her folks live on Rose Lane. Off Perkins Road."

"Huh." That was right around the corner from Ricardo Luis. Vega's palms began to sweat just thinking about those dark woods. That full moon. He willed himself to listen and not float off into his own loop of fears.

"Dad? If Katie tells you something, does it have to get reported to the police?"

"Depends." Vega caught Katie's eye in the rearview mirror. He needed to engage her directly. "I'll do my best to shield you from any embarrassment. But I have to work within the law."

"I'm like, more worried about my parents than the law," said the girl. She pulled a brush and compact mirror out of her messenger bag and began combing her long blond hair, no doubt getting it all over Vega's back seat. He often wondered why women considered it perfectly reasonable to fix themselves up in public. What would they say if he brought out his shaving kit right now?

Vega pulled into the student parking lot. On the far end sat a tow truck with flashing lights. A man who looked like Santa Claus in coveralls was securing Joy's Volvo in preparation for the tow.

"Hold your thought," said Vega. He kept his pickup running and the heater on for the girls as he hopped out. He didn't want this guy taking Joy's Volvo anywhere until he was sure what it would cost. Wendy had been helping Joy with the cost of maintenance and repairs but Vega suspected she'd argue that Vega was the cause of this situation and therefore he should pay. It was in his best interests to negotiate the price at the outset.

The price, it turned out, was non-negotiable. Santa Claus simply showed Vega his rates. Ninety-five dollars for a hookup and $5 per mile to Wendy's mechanic in Lake Holly ten miles away. Vega figured he was going to pay now or pay later, so he put the $145 on his credit card and walked back to his own truck to warm up.

"Thanks, Dad," said Joy.

"No problem." His social life was going to consist of Chinese takeout by himself in front of the TV for a long time to come so he probably wouldn't feel the pinch too badly anyway. Then again, he hadn't factored in the cost of four new tires yet.

He turned to meet Katie's eyes in back. "So you live with your parents in Wickford?"

The girl nodded. Vega was right about her family having bread.

"What did you want to tell me?"

"Last night?" said Katie. "I was with my boyfriend?"

Vega suppressed the urge to roll his eyes. She had that annoying habit of turning statements into questions. "Go on."

"He, um . . . We like to um . . . He has a friend we scored some weed from."

Vega shot a sharp glance at Joy. *This* girl was her friend? First the tattoo and all that talk about not wanting to become a doctor anymore? And now potheads for friends?

Joy flared her nostrils at him. For the moment anyway, Vega had to keep his feelings in check.

"My boyfriend's friend met us near the woods on Stillman Lane," Katie continued. "That's like, right around the corner from Perkins Road? He delivers pizza."

Talk about leveraging your business interests.

"So he like, dropped some stash off on his way to a delivery. Me and my boyfriend—we were just about ready to turn back to my house—when we saw this Hispanic-looking dude run out of the woods. Like somebody was chasing him."

"Was this before or after the gunshots?"

"We didn't hear any shots," said Katie. "The car windows were closed and we had our music turned up."

"Do you remember what time you saw this man?"

"Around six-thirty?"

Vega frowned. "Are you sure about that?" He couldn't believe he was asking a stoner if she was sure about anything. But he needed to pin her down since the shooting occurred right around six-thirty.

"Pretty sure," said Katie. "We were watching the clock on account of, my boyfriend had to get me back home and pick up his mom from her personal trainer at seven. Her Mercedes was in the shop. She'd have grounded him if he were late."

Vega wondered if *Mom* knew that while she was flexing her abs her son was smoking blunts. And then driving afterward.

"This man," asked Vega. "Where did he go after he ran out of the woods?"

"He ran a little on Stillman Lane."

"Toward Perkins Road? Away from it?"

"Away. He cut through one of the lawns and just sort of disappeared."

"Did you see him get into a vehicle?"

"Nu-uh. Maybe it was parked somewhere else, but I didn't see one. Then like, right after that, we drove off and saw all these flashing lights over on Perkins Road. My boyfriend thought the cops were coming for him." Katie looked at Vega with pleading blue eyes. "I'm not going to get anyone in trouble, am I?"

"We'll work that out later," said Vega. "Right now, I need you to remember everything you can."

"I don't remember anything else."

"What was the man wearing?"

"Dark jeans, sneakers, and a dark jacket, sort of like the one you're wearing now."

"And you say you have no idea whether you saw him before or after shots were fired."

"It had to be before."

"Why do you say that?"

"'Cause in the newspaper? I saw a picture of the man who got shot?" said Katie. "And see, the thing is? He looked exactly like the man I saw running out of the woods."

Chapter 19

"Please tell me you're not smoking dope," said Vega. "Nobody calls it 'dope' anymore, Dad. And no. I don't use drugs. Or smoke cigarettes. I don't even drink and pass out like every other college freshman I know."

"You got a tattoo."

"And you killed someone—and then joked about it. I saw the tweets about what you said right after the shooting."

"I did not joke!"

"Well, that's what it sounded like! Somebody told me there's footage of you on YouTube as well." So far, Vega had managed to keep that mob incident in the Bronx today away from her. He didn't want her seeing that. It would frighten her too much.

The tow truck was heading up to Lake Holly Motors to drop off Joy's Volvo. There was no way Vega was going to be able to get new tires on that thing until Monday. They both needed to decompress.

"How about we go somewhere and get a bite to eat?" Joy suggested.

Vega hesitated.

"C'mon, Dad. The Star Diner's right off campus. A lot of cops go there—not just college students. The food's good. And it's cheap."

"I guess that'll be okay."

The diner was hopping on a Saturday night. The red Naugahyde booths were full. Even the stools at the counter had clusters of young people and cops by the register grabbing coffee on their breaks. Waves of laughter and chatter rippled through the space, ebbing and flowing like voices on a beach.

Vega and Joy waited for an empty booth. The waitress presented them with menus long enough to be chapter books. The bright lights and noise comforted Vega. Being here with Joy took away some of the anger he'd felt earlier. He could almost feel his appetite coming back. Joy ordered a salad. Vega ordered a burger. The waitress brought tea for Joy and coffee for Vega. The coffee was hot and strong. His hands felt good wrapped around the mug.

"So, this Katie girl," asked Vega. "Is she reliable?"

"Yeah, I guess. We're partners in chemistry class."

"I'll bet Katie knows a *lot* about chemistry."

"Dad! You are such a hypocrite. When you were my age, you formed that band, Straight Money. You told me yourself that they were all stoners."

"But I wasn't!"

"Well, neither am I!"

The waitress brought their meals. Joy dug in. Vega surprised himself with how hungry he was. The hamburger tasted good. Greasy and salty. Since the shooting, Vega had felt robbed of the pleasure of everyday sensations. The sun on his face. The sweet reprieve of dreamless sleep. The tingle in his body when he thought of Adele. Even food had lost its allure. But this burger—it made him feel like maybe he could get those sensations back. Maybe they weren't lost forever.

He asked Joy about her classes and listened but he found his mind drifting back to Katie's eyewitness account. No way could she have seen Hector Ponce running out of those woods at six-thirty, the time of the shooting. It had to be before. But then why would he be running *out* of the woods?

"...So I talked to my advisor about switching majors..."

Vega nodded at Joy. But his eyes were drawn to three hulking young men who were passing by their booth. College students, he was sure of it. The first was a big white kid wearing a rust-colored knit hat with a ridiculous fringe of wool like a Mohawk. The second was black. He was wearing a Giants football jersey that was supposed to hang loose but revealed a soft, bread-dough body beneath. The third, another white kid and the shortest of the three, had on a Valley Community hooded sweatshirt with the hood pulled up and his pants hanging loose and low, the crotch halfway to his knees like some toddler with a soggy diaper. Vega saw Mohawk glance at him and elbow Giants jersey. Giants jersey gave Mohawk a puzzled look. Then Mohawk extended his index finger and curled the others to form the shape of a gun. He pointed it at Giants jersey's head and puckered his lips.

"Pow," he said. Diaper boy laughed.

Vega put down his burger and rose.

"Dad?" asked Joy. "What's wrong?"

Vega didn't answer. He turned to Mohawk. "You think you're funny?"

"What?" asked Mohawk.

Vega stepped out of the booth. "What kind of car do you drive?"

Diaper boy and Giants jersey backed up. Mohawk frowned. "What's it to you?"

"I asked you a question."

Joy rose now, too. "Dad! What are you doing?"

Vega pointed a finger at Mohawk's face. "Answer the goddamned question."

"Go to hell, man. I don't have to say anything to you." Mohawk turned his back on Vega. "Asshole," he said to his friends. They laughed. Vega felt a heat rise inside of him. These had to be the bastards who'd threatened his daughter. No way was he about to let them get away with it. He grabbed Mohawk by the back of his hooded jacket.

"Dad! Stop it!"

Everything happened fast after that. Mohawk turned and punched Vega in the shoulder. Vega punched back. Giants jersey joined in, landing a hard right to Vega's cheek. A dish and glass fell to the floor and shattered. People in adjoining booths and nearby tables stepped back. Joy began crying. Two uniformed officers jumped into the fray. Vega recognized Wilson throwing his body between Mohawk and Vega while Duran grabbed Vega's shoulders from behind. Vega hadn't even seen them come into the diner.

"He put his hands on me!" shouted Mohawk. "I didn't do anything. That cop is fucking nuts!"

Vega, his cheek already beginning to swell, tried to lunge at Mohawk again. Duran tightened his grip.

"*Qué coño,* Jimmy! We come in on our coffee break to this?"

Vega felt only rage until he looked at his daughter's face. She turned away. A great wave of shame welled up inside of him. Whatever good will she still had toward him after the shooting had just dissipated in a stupid fight in plain view of dozens of witnesses and two members from his own department.

"These are the guys who slashed Joy's tires," said Vega. He didn't even sound convincing to himself.

"Where's your car?" Wilson asked Mohawk.

"My car's been at the mechanic's since Friday with a busted tailpipe," said Mohawk. "Matt doesn't have a car. Andre drove." He nodded to Giants jersey.

"Where's your vehicle?" Wilson asked Andre.

"Right there," Andre said, pointing out the window to a silver Toyota sedan gleaming under the floodlights of the diner parking lot. It wasn't a Jeep. It wasn't even dark-colored.

Duran and Wilson exchanged looks. They didn't need to say a word. It was too late for words anyway. Vega's fists had done enough talking already.

Chapter 20

Officer Duran forced Vega to sit in the booth with some ice on his swollen cheek and not engage anyone. The three young men went outside with Wilson. Joy, meanwhile, took herself off to a stool at the counter and never once looked in Vega's direction. A boy and two girls she seemed to know from the college came over to console her.

"You gonna arrest me?" Vega asked Duran.

"Right now, we're trying to save your ass," said Duran. "Wilson's convincing those punks that if he locks *you* up for assault, he's gotta lock them up too and let a judge figure out who started it."

"They're gonna say I put my hands on him first."

Duran shrugged. "In the heat of a fight, who's to say?" They held each other's gaze across the table. The diner was back to its normal hustle and bustle—all except for Vega in the far corner booth with a plastic bag of ice wrapped in a towel from the kitchen staff. His left cheek was swollen. His left eye felt like it was starting to bruise. Some of the diner patrons craned their necks to see what the commotion was about. Vega felt embarrassed. He held the towel over much of his face and stared down at the chipped Formica table.

"They didn't slash Joy's tires, I take it?" said Vega.

"It was a big leap on your part to ever think they did. I told you, Jimmy, we'll take care of the campus situation. But it's gonna take time. And it'll take even more if you keep going Rambo on us."

Vega studied his hands. His knuckles were swollen. His fingers hurt to move. He hadn't broken any of them, but he felt like he'd sprained every one. "So if Wilson gets them to take a hike, am I free to leave?"

"I can't do that."

"But you just said—?"

"I said, we're trying hard not to arrest you. But that doesn't mean I'm just letting you walk out of here. Not the way you're behaving. You're emotionally unstable. No better than any EDP we get called out for. Your daughter doesn't even want to be around you right now. We're taking her home."

Vega swallowed hard. He saw Joy shoot a sideways glance in his direction and quickly look away.

Wilson walked through the diner doors and gave Duran a thumbs-up. Duran nodded. "Okay. We're doing well here. The students left without pressing charges. Your daughter's going home with us. Your ride is on its way."

"My *ride?*"

"Wilson says you're friends with this Lake Holly detective his dad knows. He's on duty. He'll be your driver. You're staying in Lake Holly tonight."

"*What?* Where?" *Not with Joy, that was for sure.* No way would Vega stay at his ex's house. He'd rather sleep in a motel than lower his pride and go there.

"Your daughter called your girlfriend for you. You're staying with her tonight until you cool down."

"Oh no. No! I want to talk to Joy. I want to go home."

"She doesn't want to talk to you, man."

"Neither does my girlfriend."

"Look, Jimmy, your daughter called her and she okayed

it. Either you cooperate with us and do things the way I'm telling you, or we haul you down to county psych for twenty-four hours' observation. What's it going to be?"

"So can I drive there at least?"

"Your truck stays here for the night. I told you, you're getting a ride. Detective Greco should be here any minute."

"Do they have a word in Spanish for 'world-class jerk?'" Greco asked Vega on the fifteen-minute drive back north to Lake Holly. "You're just lucky it was Wilson and Duran who came into that diner tonight or you'd be spending this lovely December evening in the county lockup kissing your career good-bye."

Greco fished a Twizzler out of a cellophane bag on the console next to him. He'd signed out an unmarked dark blue Ford Focus for the drive so he could keep in radio contact. The car smelled faintly of cigarettes the officers weren't supposed to smoke but did so anyway. It was better than the pieces of junk Vega's department usually stuck him with. Vega reclined his seat slightly so he wouldn't chance being seen by anyone who might know him. He knew he looked a mess. His left cheek felt like tenderized meat. He was too old for fistfights. With age was supposed to come wisdom. But with him, all that seemed to come were stiff joints and slower reflexes.

"I don't want to go to Adele's," he said.

"And I don't want to take you, so we're even. I don't even return your phone calls. They give me too much agita. Not to mention watching that footage of you and your fan club on YouTube."

"You saw that, huh?"

"Last time I looked, it had ten thousand hits."

Vega waited a respectable five seconds before asking a question he knew would send Greco's blood pressure through the roof.

"Did you ever get ahold of any contact numbers for those NYPD detectives, Brennan and Renfro, from your friend Carlucci?"

"Jesus, Vega!" Greco hit the steering wheel. "Your problems are multiplying faster than freshmen at a keg fest. And you're still on about Ponce and your mother?"

"There was a security camera in my mother's building. Brennan wrote in his notes that the camera wasn't working because of a loose wire."

Greco shrugged. "It happens."

"Yeah, but the DVD was blank. I spoke to a storeowner who has a similar camera and she said a loose wire wouldn't result in a blank DVD. A loose wire would only affect the current recording—not whatever was on it before."

"So?"

"The only way that DVD could have been blank was if somebody switched it with the one that was in there before. The only person with that sort of access would have been Ponce."

"So Ponce switched DVDs—*maybe*. It's also possible he never hooked up the camera," said Greco. "Or he accidentally erased all the images. There's no way to know."

"It sounds to me like he was covering for something. Or someone."

"Or he was incompetent. Either way, he's dead," said Greco. "Whatever he did or didn't do, it's over, man. You've got to let it go."

"In other words, you never asked Carlucci for Brennan or Renfro's contact numbers."

"I did. Brennan retired to Florida. He doesn't have the paperwork and says he barely remembers the case. You're not going to get anything there. As for Renfro? He's on a joint task force out of Brooklyn now. Carlucci said there's nothing he's likely to be able to tell you anyway. He didn't work your mother's case except for a few odds and ends. He knew her as a complainant, not the deceased."

"What do you mean, 'a complainant?'"

"Apparently, your mother made an appointment to speak with Renfro before she died. She never told him what it was about so if it was related to her death, the evidence died with her."

"My mother made an appointment to speak to a *homicide detective?* As in, she suspected someone of murder? Were you planning on sharing this with me at some point? Or were you just going to slip it into my Christmas stocking?"

"There's nothing to share, Vega. Renfro doesn't know any more than I'm telling you right now."

They were in Lake Holly now. Greco made several turns and headed up Pine. Adele's street.

"Duran and Wilson aren't going to know if you just circle the block and drop me somewhere," said Vega. "I can take a cab back to my truck."

"No can do. That wasn't the deal."

"Screw the deal! Look, Grec—Adele doesn't deserve this. The farther I am from her, the better."

"You really think you can go this alone?"

"At least until this thing is over."

"This *thing,* as you call it, will never be over, Vega. *Ever.* The paperwork and procedures will end. The whispers and rumors will die down. But taking a man's life? That's always going to be a part of who you are from this moment forward. You think it's not a part of me? It's been two decades and it's *still* a part of me. Every single day. That's why I gave you that therapist's name. Don't you get it? You're different now. You're going to have to find a way to live with that. And if you think you can do it alone, then God help you, buddy."

Greco's words pierced something inside of Vega. He'd been holding himself together until now, trying to sooth himself with the notion that if he could just hang on, this nightmare would have a back end to it. And now suddenly, here was Greco telling him that there was no back end—not now. Not ever. He could never wash the stain from his skin. It *was* his skin now. And he'd wear it until the day he died.

Vega felt tears gather in his eyes, the salt stinging his swollen flesh. His nasal passages loosened. His lungs shuddered of their own accord. He turned to the passenger side window and wiped the sleeve of his jacket across his eyes. *Coño!* Of all the people to break down in front of, it had to be Louis Greco.

Greco kept his eyes on the windshield and his hands on the wheel. His voice spilled out of the darkness, deep and gruff but strangely soothing. "It's gonna be different, Vega. But that doesn't mean it's not gonna be okay. Call Dr. Cantor, will ya? I swear, she won't be as bad as you think."

They were both silent after that. Greco pulled into Adele's driveway. Her porch lights were on. The colored lights on her Christmas tree glowed softly through the sheer curtains in her front window. She and Sophia had managed to buy a tree, lug it home, and put it up. Without him. Life went on.

Vega stared at his swollen knuckles. Every part of him felt broken. "What if—what if we can't make things right between us?"

"Then shouldn't you find that out?"

Adele opened the front door and stood in the doorway, her hand on Diablo's collar, the two of them backlit by a soft honeyed light. Vega saw the shimmery blue dress he'd always loved on her. She'd been out tonight. Without him. He sank down in his seat, afraid to move, afraid that every single thing he did and said to her from this moment forward would be their last.

Greco waved a hand like he was brushing crumbs off the seat.

"Go."

Chapter 21

Even under the sodium haze of streetlight, Adele could see that Vega had gotten the worst of the fight. His left cheek and eye were swollen and bruised. He was holding his right hand at a funny angle. She was so shocked by his appearance that she accidentally let go of Diablo's collar. The dog bounded down the porch steps and jumped up on him, trying to lick his face.

"Down, Diablo!" shouted Adele.

Vega gave Diablo a scratch behind his ears. "Well, I've got one fan at least." He tried to smile. It looked like it hurt.

She opened the door wider and stood shivering in her stocking feet. She hadn't even removed her blue dress from this evening. Her heart felt like it was doing a rumba in her chest.

Vega planted a work boot on the bottom porch step and stood there with his hands in the pockets of his jacket. There was a tear in the sleeve and the gray lining poked through like a wound in need of stitches.

"Are you going to come in?" she asked. "Or are we going to stand here freezing like this all night?"

Vega trudged up her front porch steps and into the foyer. Diablo raced ahead like he owned the place, which

Adele supposed he sort of did given how his hair covered every surface in the house.

Adele closed the front door behind Vega. A chill lingered in the air. He did not unzip his jacket.

"Let me get you an ice pack for your face and some aspirin and—"

"Stop." Vega put his hands firmly on her shoulders and turned her to look at him. "The kindest thing you could do for both of us right now is to call me a cab so I can get back to my truck."

"The police said you needed to be here tonight."

"I don't care what they said. I don't want to put this on you. Last night I couldn't think straight. Tonight I can."

"This?" She gestured to his ripped jacket and swollen face. "This is thinking straight? Getting into fistfights? Pushing everyone who loves you away? You're behaving like an idiot."

"I'm trying to spare you."

"You're trying to self-destruct. That's what you're trying to do," said Adele. "You want to get yourself good and hurt on the outside to match the hurt within. Make yourself so unlovable that everyone who cares about you just tosses up their hands and walks away."

"You want to psychoanalyze me? Go ahead. Everyone else does!" Diablo ran out of the front foyer and up the stairs. Vega was too caught up in the argument to notice. "As far as Ruben Tate-Rivera and all your freakin' rights groups friends are concerned, I'm an executioner!"

"You're not helping matters when you refuse to defend your actions."

"*Ay, puñeta,* here it comes!" Vega threw up his hands. "You will *never* forgive me for what happened. *Ever.* It doesn't matter what I say."

"But you don't. What do you expect me to think?"

"I did my job!"

"If you believe that, then we definitely don't belong together!"

There. She'd said it. In anger, yes. But there was some truth to her words. Witness or no witness, Adele wasn't sure she could ever reconcile the man she loved with the man who took an innocent life.

Sophia appeared at the top of the stairs in a T-shirt and fuzzy pajama bottoms with brightly colored cupcakes emblazoned on the fabric. Her long dark brown hair was tangled. She rubbed her eyes. Diablo panted and danced by her side.

"Mommy? You and Jimmy are yelling. I can't sleep."

Vega shrank into the darkened archway of the dining room. He didn't want to frighten the child with his battered face. "I'm sorry," he whispered to Adele. "I didn't mean for things to—I'll leave."

"No." She put out a hand to stay him. "Not like this." She turned to Sophia on the stairs. "Go back to sleep, *lucero*. We're just having a discussion. It's okay. We'll be quieter, I promise."

Sophia looked down at Diablo. "I want a glass of milk and I think Diablo needs to pee."

"I'll take him out," Vega offered.

"No. Stay there, out of the way." Adele turned to Sophia. "Come down and get your milk, *lucero*. I'll take the dog out."

Sophia was in a half sleep so she glided right through the foyer without even lifting her head in Vega's direction. Adele guided her around through the living room to the kitchen so that she wouldn't see Vega. The dog followed dutifully behind. Adele got the child a glass of milk and secured Diablo's leash to go outside.

"I want to take Diablo outside," Sophia insisted.

"It's late. You should go back to sleep."

"You never let me take him out. I'll watch him. I promise."

"Okay. Just in the back yard."

The child grabbed her purple coat, snow boots, and mittens and went out through the back door. In her wake, there was nothing but cold air and silence. Adele walked back into the foyer where Vega was standing in the shadows. His skin was a tapestry of bruises.

"I should go," he said. "I'm like a wrecking ball right now."

"No, please. We both need to cool down. And besides, I need your advice on something. Something police-related. But if I tell you, I need your assurance that it will stay between us."

"Adele, I can't know that until you tell me what it is."

She closed her eyes, caught between keeping a confidence and maybe saving a life. "It has to do with—a child."

"Sophia?"

"No. Come into the kitchen. I'll make some coffee."

The bright lights in the kitchen felt like an assault. Vega blinked and rubbed his red-rimmed eyes. He eased himself into a chair while Adele scooped coffee into the coffeemaker. He studied her shimmery blue silk dress from behind, the way it pulled tight across her backside. Where had she gone in his favorite dress? Without him? He wiped a swollen hand across his chapped lips. He wanted her. God, he wanted her.

"So you went out tonight?" He asked the question as casually as he could.

"A business function." After a few beats she added, "A party. Given by Ricardo Luis."

"Huh." He felt like someone had stuffed an old sock into his chest where his heart used to be.

"Jimmy, it wasn't my choice. Dave Lindsey ordered me to go. What could I do? The man gave La Casa a donation after the shooting."

"How nice for him. He gets applauded and I get lynched.

Maybe I should start unbuttoning my shirts down to my navel and sing forgettable songs."

"He offered for you to go see his guitar collection sometime."

"I'm sure Captain Waring would be thrilled for me to have a heart-to-heart with someone who might very well testify against me."

"It was still a nice gesture. He gave me his cell number if you ever change your mind."

"He gave you his *cell number?*" Vega noticed Ricardo Luis's autobiography lying on the kitchen table. "And you're reading his book, too?"

"He gave autographed copies of his book and CD to all the board members. You don't have to get jealous."

"I'm not jealous." Vega began thumbing through the well of photographs. The more current shots were full of color and life—even the candid ones of Luis roughhousing with his three children by an enormous pool next to a whitewashed mansion surrounded by palm trees. The old photos were much grittier and darker. His dimpled smile was absent. His closed lips were a slash devoid of emotion. There was only a gritty, hard-muscled look to his body and a dull, hungry cast to his eyes. Even his facial proportions were different. His nose was broader. His cheekbones were less defined. His eyelids had more droop. This wasn't genetics. This was plastic surgery. No doubt every tooth in his head had been straightened or replaced as well.

"I started reading the book a little this evening," said Adele. "He wrote a lot about his childhood in Nogales, Mexico. It was pretty rough."

"He didn't *write* anything, Adele. It's fluff—probably made-up fluff—written by some ghostwriter. I'll bet Ricardo Luis isn't even his real name."

"Well, it's *part* of his real name. His full name is Jesús Ricardo Luis Alvarez-Da Silva."

"Man, you really *do* have a crush on him!"

"I do not!" Her eyes told otherwise.

Vega slammed the book shut and tossed it on the table. "It doesn't matter." It felt better to tell himself that. "You said there was a child you wanted to talk to me about."

"Yes." She hesitated. "A thirteen-year-old girl. She just came over from Honduras."

"You mean she was smuggled over," said Vega. "Nobody just 'comes.'"

Adele poured water in the coffeemaker without answering.

Vega sighed. "Not a pretty choice—deciding whether your kid's safer in the hands of a bunch of sleazy coyotes or walking the gang-infested streets of Honduras. But if she's here now, what's the problem? She's got a court date with immigration or something?" They both knew that even if the child had been caught at the border and ordered to plead her case with immigration, court cases could drag on for years so she was in no immediate danger of being sent back.

"I wish it were that simple," said Adele. "To pay for her passage, her family took out a loan and now some gangster is trying to collect on it. The girl is the collateral."

"If the family gives me a cell phone contact for this loan shark," said Vega, "I can get one of my guys to run a trace and maybe set up a sting. If it crosses state lines, I might even be able to pull the FBI into this. Who's the family?"

Adele hesitated. "Is it risky? To the girl or her family?"

"It was risky the moment they decided to smuggle her over here," said Vega. "It was risky the moment they started working with gangsters. So yeah, of course it's risky. The police don't make guarantees, Adele. Give me the family's number. I'll contact them."

"The mother's afraid to work with the police."

"If she wants help, she's going to have to trust somebody."

"She trusts me."

"Then the question is, do *you* trust me? Or is that the deal breaker these days?"

Her silence told him everything he feared.

She turned away and looked out her kitchen window at the blackness of her backyard. Something shifted in her face. Her eyes narrowed and took on a singular focus. All the color seemed to drain from her skin. A small gasp escaped from her lips.

Vega came up behind her and stared out at the yard, trying to understand what had spooked her. For a moment, all he noted was the reflection of their faces in the glass. It took him another second or two to comprehend what Adele had seen—or rather, what she hadn't.

"Where's Sophia?"

Chapter 22

Adele turned to Vega. "I don't see Sophia outside."
Vega raced to the back door and opened it. "Sophia?"
he called out across the yard.

Silence. No little girl laugh. No jingle of dog tags. Vega
ran into the backyard and called her name again. Adele
grabbed her coat and shoes and Vega's jacket from the
coat rack in the foyer and went out the front door. Maybe
Sophia and Diablo were in the driveway.

"Sophia!"

Nothing. Vega ran around front to find her. He held up
his hands. "She's not in the backyard either."

"She wouldn't just leave like this."

Vega stuck his thumb and middle finger in his mouth
and made a loud, long whistle. They both listened but all
that greeted them was the hum of a car on an adjoining
street and the disembodied voice from a television when a
neighbor opened a door.

Adele tried to calm the panicky flutter in her chest. *How
far could they have gone?* It was a safe neighborhood.
Well-lit. Plenty of people on the block knew Adele and
Sophia.

But it was winter. And dark. People were inside. Who
would notice a stranger? An unfamiliar car? A moment of
youthful indiscretion?

"Where could she be?" Adele could feel the cinch in her vocal cords, the tight knot of worry that had traveled from her throat to her chest. What kind of mother was she to get so carried away arguing with her boyfriend that she hadn't noticed her child running off into the night?

"She took Diablo on the leash, didn't she?" asked Vega.

"Sure. But she wouldn't just wander off with him."

"Maybe she lost control and chased him." Vega grabbed his jacket from Adele. "Stay here. I'll find her."

"I'm coming with you."

"No," said Vega. "Better we split up. You go left and I'll go right and if we spot them, we can check in by cell, okay?"

"Okay." She walked quickly down the sidewalk calling out her daughter's name. She'd walked this short distance thousands of times in her life—when Sophia was a baby in her stroller and later when the child was learning to ride her bike. She'd walked it to cool off after fights with Peter. Or just to get fresh air on a nice spring day. But the terror in her step now obliterated every past journey. It was as if she were walking the block for the very first time. Every buckle in the sidewalk, every shadow of a tree or lip of a driveway felt foreign to her. The sharp bite of air felt serrated in her lungs. She was breathing too hard. Or maybe the problem was, she wasn't breathing at all.

She felt as if she were watching herself from a great distance. She was in a movie playing Adele looking for her daughter. This couldn't really be happening. She tried to push the darker thoughts from her head. Vega was clearly a target right now. Someone had just slashed Joy's tires because of what he'd done. But surely no one would hurt a child.

Surely.

She was a block from her house when her cell phone rang. Relief flooded her body when she heard Vega's voice. "You've got them?"

"I've got Diablo. He's by himself."

"Oh no!"

"His leash is still attached. He seems to want me to follow him. I'm on the corner of Pine and Sequoia heading toward Spring. Can you catch up to us?"

"I'm on my way."

It felt like an eternity before she caught up with them. Spring Street was a road full of capes and ranches on quarter-acre plots of hyperpruned bushes, swing sets, and stubby fruit trees. It dead-ended beside a deep thicket of woods and streams. Adele never let Sophia play near the area. In summer, teenagers and homeless people congregated in those woods. The police made regular sweeps to clear out the vagrants and trash left behind. But this time of year, the woods were dark and silent, the bare limbs like iron bars to a prison that no one was meant to enter or leave.

Vega was breathing hard, keeping a tight grip on Diablo's leash. Adele noticed the leash was muddy and wet. Where had he been?

"Damn this dog!" said Adele.

"Don't damn him yet," cautioned Vega. "He may be the only one who can lead us to Sophia."

Diablo strained at the leash. His floppy triangle ears were on alert. His tail was curled like a giant question mark. His nose glistened in the moonlight. His whole body seemed poised and ready for action. But what sort of action?

They left the pavement and stepped onto the gravel at the end of the cul-de-sac. Diablo jumped over a fallen tree limb. His leash snagged on a branch and Vega undid it. Adele wondered if the dog would just run off but he waited while Vega tucked the leash in his pocket and pulled out a small flashlight.

"Stay here. I'll find her." Vega began scrabbling over the limb.

"I'm coming, too."

"Adele—"

"She's my daughter!"

He held out his hand and helped her over the limb.

"Sophia!" she called out. Her voice felt tight and raw. No answer. A montage of frightening possibilities flashed through her head. Sophia had been abducted. She'd fallen and hit her head. She'd been struck by a car crossing the street. She was lying in a ditch bleeding. Her baby. Her life. There was nothing she wouldn't do to save her.

Nothing.

Diablo continued to push on. There were no real trails back here. Just uprooted trees, skeletal bushes, and thickets of dead limbs that tore at their clothes. Vega could barely keep up with the dog. Adele could barely keep up with Vega.

"Sophia!" Vega called out. His voice was deeper and stronger. It seemed to rattle the darkness. There was a note of desperation in him, too. She could hear it.

And then she heard something else. A child's soft whimper.

"Sophia!" cried Adele. "Where are you, *lucero?*"

Vega waved the flashlight in an arc before him. Thorny bushes and dead limbs absorbed the yellow haze. Beneath an overgrowth of dormant vines was an overturned metal shopping cart. A wheel stuck up out of the dirt, rusty and bent. Sophia was here somewhere. Why wasn't she walking toward them?

The dog raced down an embankment and then backtracked to Vega. Adele followed them both until she could make out the silvery thread of a stream. It had the viscous glow of liquid mercury under the haze of moonlight. And then she saw it. On the other side of the stream. A purple coat and a pair of mud-streaked fuzzy pajama bottoms.

"There!" she said.

Sophia was curled into a ball, rocking back and forth, rubbing the ankle of her muddy snow boot.

"Mommy!" At the sight of her mother, Sophia burst into tears. "I dropped Diablo's leash! He ran when I tried to pick it back up. So I chased him. I'm so sorry!"

"It's okay, *lucero*. We're coming!"

"My ankle hurts."

"Call nine-one-one," said Vega. "Ask them for an ambulance and fire truck response. Tell them to meet you at the entrance to the woods on Spring Street." He handed her his flashlight.

"Don't you need the flashlight?"

"I'm not sure I can carry Sophia back up this muddy incline."

"What are you going to do?"

"If I can't move her? Stay with her. What else?"

Diablo panted beside Vega. He turned and rubbed a knuckle against the dog's head. "Good dog."

"*Good dog?* Are you kidding?" asked Adele.

"He found Sophia."

"He's the reason she's in this mess in the first place!"

Vega frowned. Even in the pale glow of moonlight, his dark eyes registered the truth: *We're the reason she's in this mess. Not the dog.*

Adele watched Vega's shadow fade into the blur of darkness, the dog at his side. The embankment was steep. Even in heavy-soled boots, it would be hard for anyone to negotiate at night. Adele took out her cell and dialed 911 and gave them the information Vega had instructed. On the other side of the embankment, she heard loose stones scatter like rice down the rocky, crusted hillside. Branches cracked and snapped in the darkness. There was a quick, deft splash of water—likely Diablo—followed by a heavier sloshing sound that was likely Vega. She heard her daughter's soft, panicked cry and Vega's soothing voice.

"It's okay, *mija*. I'll wrap you in my jacket. Put your arms around my neck and I'll see if I can get you out of here."

Adele pointed the flashlight down at her feet and maneuvered through the broken branches and tree limbs until she found her way onto the street. The pale yellow wash of street light felt glaring after the darkness of the woods. The trip into the woods had seemed so long. The trip out, so short. What felt interminable now was the wait. She bobbed up and down on the curb to stay warm, her breath clouding up before her, and waited for the sound of the sirens.

Sophia would be all right. Adele knew that. Despite the adrenaline coursing through her veins, the nervous pins and needles draining the feeling from her limbs, her logical mind knew that Sophia was not in mortal danger. Even if the child's ankle was broken, she was with Vega. They would get her to the hospital. Sophia would be fine again in a few days or so with a great story to tell her friends. This wasn't anything like what Marcela's daughter, Yovanna, probably just experienced on her 2000-mile trek from Honduras to here. This wasn't anything like the terror that Marcela and her family were experiencing now.

And yet in those moments before Adele and Vega found Sophia, Adele's pain had been as acute as any of the women in *Las Madres Perdidas*. Her heart blew up in her chest until it felt like it was going to explode in desperation. She couldn't breathe. She couldn't feel cold or dampness or hunger. At that moment, she would have struck any bargain, risked any punishment, and paid any price to assure her daughter's safety.

Just like Marcela.

She heard the sirens before she saw the red flashing lights. The police arrived first. Two young officers whom she knew by face, though not by name. She could barely form the words but they knew what to do. The ambulance came next. Then a fire truck. The firefighters helped Vega and Sophia up the embankment. Sophia was lost in the folds of

Vega's jacket. She wasn't crying anymore. She was holding tight to Vega's neck while Diablo danced around his feet.

Vega was shivering. His shirt was muddy. His boots and pants were soaked to the shins.

"She's gonna be fine," Vega told Adele. He gave her a wink. "She's brave like her mother."

The EMTs loaded Sophia into the back of the ambulance. One of them handed Vega back his jacket. He slipped into it gratefully.

"Thank you," Adele said to him. Those words didn't begin to cover her gratitude.

"You ride over to the hospital with Sophia," said Vega. "I'll take Diablo back to your house, grab your car, and meet you there."

The EMTs were closing the doors of the ambulance. Adele needed to hop inside.

"Jimmy—" There was so much she wanted to say and no time to say it.

"I'll be over as soon as I can."

Chapter 23

Marcela pulled her hood tightly around her face and slipped into her father's building. Darkness fell early this time of year. In the Bronx, the concrete canyons ate up the natural light, replacing it with the glare of streetlights and hallway CFL bulbs that offered neither warmth nor clarity.

Marcela desperately needed both at the moment. Alma wasn't expecting her. Alma would not be happy to see her.

For ten years, Marcela had lived about fifty miles north of her father and his second family. But it was only two years ago that she and her father were finally able to come to a truce. His priest had brokered it. Father Delgado. He was one of the few people her father had ever told about his trip across the border.

"I know you're angry that your father abandoned you," the old priest had told her. "But your father wants your forgiveness." By then Marcela was well versed in what the border does to parents and children. She was a parent, too. So she swallowed the anger and tried to turn her thoughts to their early years together in San Pedro Sula. The corn-husk doll her father once made for her. The time he bought her a bag of cotton candy at a street fair—a memory so strong that even now, the smell of that sugary confection brought back that day, the sun on her shoulders, her hands and face covered in sticky sweetness that melted into every pore of her being until even her toes curled with delight.

They did not talk about that last morning together in Honduras—the one when she said good-bye to her father and sixteen-year-old brother under the broad canopy of a huanacaxtle tree. Marcela could still see Miguel waving good-bye from the back of that truck overloaded with people and backpacks. He would always be that gangly young prince who hefted her over deep puddles in the streets after it rained and spoke with hope in his chest of what he would do in *El Norte*. He seemed so old when she was ten. He seemed so young now. Three years, it was supposed to be. Only three years before they would all be together again.

Of all the lies people tell you about journeying to *El Norte*, this was the biggest lie of all.

"I want to make it different for you and Yovanna," Marcela's father told her one day a few months ago. All of a sudden. With no pretext. That was Hector Ponce. Marcela could never read his mind. She didn't question why or how. She didn't want to know the details then.

She knew too many now.

Marcela stepped inside a black-and-white-tiled hallway that smelled of roach defogger, chili powder, and cooking oil. She walked down a flight of stairs to her father's basement apartment. Her father's sons, twelve-year-old Aaron and fourteen-year-old Felix, were standing outside the front doorway, huddled against a wall with friends, trying hard to look defiant and tough, though Marcela could see the freefall in their eyes. She could feel their loss like a magnet, drawing her in. She wanted to comfort them. She knew that was impossible—even dangerous at the moment.

"Marcela," Felix called softly. He was a stocky teenager with his mother's square chin. He had a tendency to stutter when he got excited. "I can't believe this is h-h-hap-pening."

Marcela gave the boy a hug. She wanted to feel her father's blood coursing through his veins but all she could feel was Alma. These boys, they were not like Miguel with his cougar grace or Reimundo with his dark liquid eyes. She could never look at either of them without thinking of what Miguel and Reimundo might have done with their lives had they been born here instead of Honduras. At the very least, they would be alive.

The front door of the apartment was open and packed with Alma's relatives and men in suits. *Lawyers.* Here it was, twenty-four hours after the shooting and Alma was still surrounded by people while Marcela had to pretend like nothing had happened.

She was getting very good at pretending.

Alma was propped in a chair, surrounded by people hovering protectively over her and holding her hand. She was a short, stocky woman who favored bright red lipsticks and tweezed her eyebrows until they were just slash marks across her brow, which gave her a harsh look. She came here from Honduras when she was sixteen and had had the good fortune of squeezing in under the amnesty so she was legal, unlike Marcela and her father. She worked at a bakery off the Grand Concourse. Between Marcela's father's job as a dishwasher and building handyman and her job in the bakery, they squeaked by. Without Marcela's father's wages, it would be a struggle—which was why Alma had wasted no time in securing an attorney and filing a lawsuit.

Alma sat up straight when she saw Marcela. Her eyes narrowed suspiciously.

"Marcela. You came." Nothing in that greeting sounded like a welcome. Marcela noticed others eyeing her so she bent down awkwardly and hugged Alma. Then she leaned into her ear.

"I need to talk to you," she whispered in Spanish. "Privately."

Alma pressed her red lips together and dabbed her eyes. She rose unsteadily. One of her friends patted her hand. "I'm okay," Alma assured the woman. Then she turned to Marcela. "In the bedroom, yes?"

Marcela followed Alma down a short, overheated hallway with framed photographs of Aaron and Felix on the walls. There were no photos of Marcela, her two dead brothers or her sister who now lived with her husband and children in Costa Rica. It was as if none of them had ever existed.

The basement apartment had two bedrooms at the end of the hall. Felix and Aaron's bunk beds were in a room on the right. On the left was a bedroom that looked out on a concrete retaining wall. The only light came from the harsh ceiling fixture overhead. The room had barely enough space for a queen-sized bed and a chest of drawers. Alma closed the door and sat on the bed. She began speaking as soon as she sat down.

"Why are you here? The wake and funeral, I understand. But that has not been arranged yet."

"My father told me a while back that he left an envelope for me in his bedroom. With some old family pictures and mementos inside. He wanted me to have them if something happened to him."

"Mementos? What kind of mementos?"

Marcela gathered her words carefully. "I really don't know. I'm just wondering if you've seen the envelope?"

Alma narrowed her gaze. "Did that man call you today? The one who was asking for money?"

"No," Marcela lied. Besides, it wasn't money he wanted anymore. He had his eye on something more valuable—at least to him.

Alma frowned. "He seemed pretty insistent about getting his money."

"Maybe he changed his mind." *Or circumstances changed it for him.* Marcela tried to keep her voice as even as possible. "Perhaps my father tucked this envelope in a drawer?"

"Everything in this apartment belongs to me!" Alma said sharply. "There is nothing here that concerns you."

Marcela leaned against the dresser drawers. There was barely any floor space left in the bedroom. She nodded to the hallway. "Those lawyers out there? What would they say if I told them you aren't Hector Ponce's legal wife?"

"I am the mother of his two sons!"

"Yes. That's true. But you aren't my father's legal wife. I'm his blood relative. Maybe you aren't entitled to any money at all." Marcela didn't know if that was true, but she knew it would scare Alma—scare her enough to make her think twice about chasing Marcela out of the apartment when it would be easy enough to hand her a bunch of old pictures and mementos that Alma would just throw out anyway.

Alma reached into the cleavage of her blouse and pulled out a hanky. It was hot in the bedroom, the old steam radiators hissing and clanking. Slowly she got up from the bed and opened one of the chest drawers. She poked around underneath some of her father's clothes. They smelled of his spicy aftershave. She pulled out a book. It was Ricardo Luis's recently published memoir: *La Canción de Mi Corazón. Song of My Heart,* the Spanish-language edition. On the cover was a picture of the sexy Mexican pop star in a black unbuttoned shirt.

Marcela frowned at the book. "What was my father doing with Luis's autobiography?"

"I don't know," said Alma. "But whatever it was, he was up to no good. Your father had no interest in Luis's music."

"He wasn't stealing."

"Well, he was doing something illegal. That ID he was

carrying in his wallet when he was shot? I've never seen it before. Your father's middle name is Mauricio. Why would he have fake ID in the name of Antonio—ID from Georgia, a state he's never even been to—unless he was doing something illegal?"

"Have you shown the book to anyone?"

"Of course not," said Alma. "The police came this morning asking for his comb and toothbrush and a few other things. I gave them what they asked for but I'm not giving them an excuse to wash the blood off their hands. Maybe your father did some things he shouldn't have. Maybe he borrowed money from someone he shouldn't have. But he didn't deserve to die."

Alma opened the book now. Inside was a manila envelope addressed to Marcela. It had been torn open. Alma handed it to her.

"You—opened this?"

"I didn't know what was inside."

You wanted to make sure there was no money, thought Marcela. But it served no purpose to say what each of them knew. Marcela reached into the envelope and examined the contents. She saw a jumble of grainy and yellowed photos of her and her sister hugging, of Miguel posing with Reimundo by a corrugated fence, Reimundo smiling through two lost baby teeth. She pulled out the photo she'd seen on the news of her father, his brother Edgar, and Miguel posing by a fruit stand as they began their journey north.

So there were two copies of that photo the police confiscated. Of course. It made sense.

And then she saw it. A thick religious tract about Jesus in Spanish. It was inside a clear plastic envelope. It looked like some free piece of literature one of the religious societies might give away. She could feel the hard press of something tucked inside the tract. Something round and flat. The size of a saucer. A disc. Yes. This was what she was looking for. This was where her father had stashed it. Marcela nearly wept with relief to think she'd found it.

She carefully folded up the envelope and tucked it into her bag. "Thank you," she said to Alma. She meant it for once. Without knowing it, Alma had just turned over the one thing that would wipe out her father's $8,000 debt.

And more importantly, it would spare her daughter's life.

Chapter 24

"Her name is Yovanna," said Adele as she handed Vega a cup of coffee from the emergency room vending machine. Vega took the cup gratefully just to feel the warmth in his hands. His pants and boots had mostly dried but he'd been so cold out there in the woods with Sophia that he couldn't shake the chill.

"You mean the Honduran girl you were telling me about earlier?"

Adele nodded. Her gaze shifted to the emergency room doors. It would be a while before Sophia's ankle got X-rayed. Adele's ex was in with the child now. Vega got the impression Peter blamed Adele for what had happened tonight.

"Would you like me to speak to him?" asked Vega, nodding to the doors. "This whole situation is really my fault."

"He'll blame me no matter what you do," said Adele. "And let's face it, I blame myself." She stared down at her blue silk dress. Splotches of mud covered the front. Her makeup had gone blurry around the eyes. Vega squeezed her hand. He didn't know what else to do. He'd started out the evening determined to keep his distance from both Joy and Adele, to spare them the pain of his association. Yet somehow he'd loused things up anyway. But even so, for a moment tonight, when Sophia was wrapped in his jacket and they were making their way up that muddy embankment, he'd felt a great sense of purpose. He saw himself as the man he used to be—the man he wanted to be again. He just didn't know how anymore. So he sipped his coffee, which tasted like sweetened water, and tried to hang on to the notion that he could still do good in the world even if he'd done something bad.

They settled into an area far from the television and vending machines. "So tell me about this girl," said Vega.

"Her mother and stepfather live here in Lake Holly." Adele played with the chain around her neck, sliding the cross back and forth. She was still wearing that thing. Vega wondered who she thought she was praying for. If it was Vega, God had a wicked sense of humor. She cleared her throat. "The girl's mother is Marcela."

"*Huh?* I thought Marcela had a little boy."

"She does. Yovanna was living with Marcela's mother in Honduras. She just arrived about a week and a half ago."

Vega felt the knowledge roll like a bead of dew across the surface of his brain for a moment before slowly sinking in. "Wait, do you mean to tell me that you spoke to Marcela *today?* You didn't talk about *me,* did you?"

"I wouldn't do that. And besides, what *could* I talk about? You don't tell me anything."

He let the dig pass. "Did she tell you about why her father went to Ricardo Luis's house?"

"She insists he's not a thief. But I also gathered from the conversation that Hector borrowed money to pay for Yovanna's passage and he hadn't paid it back."

"So you knew her daughter was coming?"

"I knew she'd arrived," said Adele. "I can't ask more than that. It would be—inappropriate—given my position."

"Not to mention that what she did is illegal."

"A child belongs with her mother, Jimmy. Look what

we just went through with Sophia and tell me you don't believe that."

"In my heart? Of course I believe it. In my head? I don't have an answer." Vega shot a glance at the doors beyond the brightly lit waiting area. A television screen glowed across the faces of anxious people waiting their turn to be admitted. His mind was racing. He wasn't really thinking of Marcela and her daughter. He was thinking about Hector Ponce.

"So Ponce borrowed money to smuggle his granddaughter from Honduras," said Vega. "Presumably from someone with far less friendly repayment terms than Hudson United—and no free pens. How much did he owe?"

"Eight thousand dollars."

Vega let out a long whistle. "Not bond-trader big. But certainly a huge chunk of change for working people, never mind immigrants." Vega was already building a case in his head. Vega's friend, Freddy Torres, had said that Ponce was a gambler. Maybe Ponce was counting on a big score and when it fell through, he got desperate. Ricardo Luis dined regularly at Chez Martine where Ponce worked. The Wickford police had already established that. It would have been a simple matter for Ponce to lift Luis's address from credit card receipts and make the hit.

Except Ponce didn't have a car or a means to get away.

"Jimmy? Are you listening to me?" Adele sounded frustrated. "This isn't about Marcela's father. It's about Yovanna. Marcela told me this gangster gave her a week—*one week*—to come up with eight thousand dollars or he'd kill her daughter."

The cop in Vega could see it coming a mile off.

"Let me guess." He crumpled up his coffee cup and aimed for the wastebasket. It flew in cleanly. "Marcela wants you to give her the money."

"Not give. Lend. Or find a way to raise it."

Vega grabbed her hand. "Come."

"Where?"

"Tell the front desk to call you on your phone if they need you."

"But why?"

"Because I'm not having this conversation in a public waiting area," said Vega. "That's why."

He walked Adele to her car in the hospital parking lot. Neither of them spoke. Adele got in the driver's seat and slammed the door.

"What?" she asked him.

"You're getting snowed, *nena*. And you don't even see it."

"Snowed?" He could sense her tensing. She saw everybody as a broad, open surface of good intentions. He was a cop. He saw the sharp edges and angles.

"Marcela wants a payoff. Guilt money."

"*What?*"

"Isn't it convenient that she should approach you, knowing you're the girlfriend of the cop who just killed her father?" asked Vega. "And isn't it convenient that you're so wracked with guilt right now that she could ask for just about anything and you'd give it?"

"What do you take me for? An idiot?"

"No. Never an idiot," Vega said softly. "Just a very trusting person."

"Who can't tell the difference between a con and a sincere request."

"You're upset right now. You're not thinking clearly."

"And you are?" She threw up her hands. She had a point there. "You don't know Marcela like I do. She's not that sort of person."

"She's the daughter of a thief. You think blackmail's beyond her?"

"She came to me because she was scared."

"But not scared enough to contact the police. In fact, she doesn't even *want* you contacting the police."

"Oh, and contacting the police is really going to accomplish a lot." Adele gave him a sour look. "I'm sure Detective Greco is going to fall all over himself to help the daughter of the man you just shot protect the child she just smuggled!"

Vega slouched in his seat. He felt impotent as a cop, impotent as a man. He couldn't do anything right these days. "Look, I'm not saying Ponce wasn't in hock to someone. It makes sense. And maybe this thug did contact Marcela and threaten her. But true or not, you can't give her money. You'd be aiding and abetting—"

"A felony. I know, Jimmy. You don't have to educate me on the law."

He touched her knee. He felt her whole body relax beneath his touch. He still had that effect on her. That was something at least.

For a moment, he felt the old energy, the spark of desire to undress her right here, right now. But something strangled it as quickly as it came. All emotion and sensation had gone dead inside of him since the shooting. Hunger. Lust. Deep, dreamless sleep. Light, playful laughter. He caught glimmers of those things but they were like trains speeding through a station. He couldn't latch on no matter how hard he tried. Would anything ever come back? Would he spend the rest of his life at the bottom of this cold, dark well? He couldn't tell anybody how scared he was. Not even, sadly, Adele.

"What do you want me to do?" he asked her softly now. "Tell me and I'll do it."

Adele sighed. "If I had anyone else I could go to, I would. I know you've got enough on your plate. But this is a desperate situation. Is there some way you could make a few inquiries without letting Marcela know I told you?"

"My department impounded the cell phone that was on Ponce when he died," said Vega. "I'm sure Teddy Dolan got a warrant for a record of all his calls. Not that it's necessarily come through yet, but if Ponce knew this loan shark personally, there might be a traceable number on there. You borrow a big sum like that; I suspect it's not a faceless transaction. I can run it by him at least."

Adele huddled deeper into her coat. "Marcela asked me not to go to the police. I feel like I'm betraying a confidence."

"You can't just sit on your hands. What if her daughter really is in danger?"

"You won't take it beyond an informal discussion with Dolan?"

"Let me see what he comes up with—okay?"

Adele locked up her car and they walked back into the building. They'd just sat down when Sophia's doctor opened the doors of the emergency triage area and beckoned Adele to follow. She rose. "I've got to go. Will you—?"

"I'll be waiting here when you come out."

Adele disappeared through the doors. Vega pulled out his cell phone and texted Dolan to see if he'd gone through Ponce's phone records yet. Vega didn't say why he needed to know. He thought it would be better to discuss the situation in person. Not that Dolan was answering his texts anyway, it seemed. He checked his messages. There was one from Isadora Jenkins:

Name of therapist? Date and time of appointment? Answer NOW.

Coño! She wasn't going to leave him alone about this. He was fine. When he was helping Sophia in the woods this evening, he felt strong and in control.

But would I have been if I'd been alone? he wondered. *If I wasn't focused on helping someone else?*

He pulled out his wallet and rifled through the billfold until he found that scrap of paper Greco had given him with Ellen Cantor's name and phone number. He left a message on her answering machine with his name, number, and a request for an appointment. At least it would get his lawyer off his back.

He walled himself off from the noise and commotion of the emergency room waiting area. All around him he heard babies crying and children whining for candy. Across from him he noted several glassy-eyed teenagers who'd clearly gotten into daddy's booze and were now regretting it. He hoped they didn't decide to get sick right now. His clothes had been through enough these past twenty-four hours.

An ambulance barreled up to the sliding glass doors of the emergency entrance. Vega lifted his head to see two EMTs hustling a bloody man on a stretcher through the doors and into the back. The man's face was covered with an oxygen mask. A saline drip hung from a bag. On a Saturday night, he could be anything from a motorist in a car wreck to a drunk after a fistfight. Still, he looked to be in bad shape. He'd take precedence over all the sprains and broken bones in the waiting area. Adele might be awhile.

A Lake Holly uniformed patrol officer walked over to the admitting desk and began giving the nurse some basic check-in information. Vega went back to scrolling through his messages. He looked up just in time to see a familiar face hustling through the doors with a red licorice stick in his mouth. He took the licorice out of his mouth and began talking in low murmurs to the uniformed officer.

This was no car wreck. Detective Greco wouldn't be wasting his Saturday night in the emergency room for that.

Vega got up from the couch and sidled up to Greco while he was speaking to the nurse. Greco turned, a sour look on his face.

"What are you doing here, Vega? You're supposed to be under the equivalent of house arrest and you end up in the emergency room? I don't even want to *know* what you two were up to."

"Adele's daughter sprained her ankle. I'm just waiting for them now." Vega nodded his head toward the emergency room doors. "So is that the victim? Or a suspect you leaned on too hard?"

Vega expected Greco to toss off some snide comment and tell Vega to beat it. It wasn't any of Vega's business who the man was or what the Lake Holly PD wanted with him. Instead, the big man's jaw set to one side and he studied Vega.

"Come. We need to talk." Greco showed his badge at the security desk and ushered Vega into a waiting area by an operating room. He jerked a thumb at the doors.

"Call came in right after I dropped you off," said Greco. "Couple of teenagers found him on the banks of the Brighton Aqueduct right near the pedestrian bridge."

"A jumper?"

"That's what I thought. Until I checked his wallet."

"He was robbed?"

"Maybe. I don't know. But that wasn't the most interesting thing about him. It was the picture I found inside his wallet that got me. One of those department store Christmas photos. Of a man, a woman, and their two boys."

"It's gonna be a tough Christmas for them," said Vega.

A door to the operating room opened and a doctor in scrubs emerged. These guys all used to look so ancient and biblical when Vega was a kid. Now they all looked like pro golfers in shower caps. The doctor pulled down his face mask and fixed his gaze on Greco. His eyes looked grim. "Are you the detective who brought him in?"

Greco nodded. "He didn't make it?"

"Afraid not."

"All right. Thanks." The doctor went back into the operating room to clean up. Greco kicked the chair. Vega had never seen him so visibly distressed over a victim before.

"You probably couldn't have saved him," said Vega. "I guess you're going to have to break it to his family that he's dead."

"That's the problem," said Greco. "They already think he is. The photograph I found in this guy's wallet? It's a picture of Hector Ponce with his family."

Chapter 25

Vega paced the waiting area, barely able to breathe. He heard the rattle of metal trays, surgical instruments, and gurney wheels on the other side of the operating room door. The dead man was being spirited away down to the hospital morgue.

Doctors always get to bury their failures. Cops usually have to live with theirs.

Vega wanted to feel some measure of peace from the news. If what Greco said was true, Vega hadn't killed Hector Ponce. Then again, Ponce was dead either way and Vega had still killed *someone*. Some other unarmed, Hispanic man. Some other human being with a family who was about to get the devastating news that a loved one was gone. The stain on Vega was no less great just because the name had changed.

The human being in him grieved. The cop in him wanted answers.

"Are you sure that was Hector Ponce in the operating room?" he asked Greco.

"No. But I just tagged the evidence in his wallet," said Greco. "That family photo is *identical* to the one Alma Ponce released to the media. Do *you* keep pictures of other people's families in your wallet?"

Vega leaned back against the wall of the operating room

waiting area with its soothing watercolors of sunsets and flowers. He wondered if Adele was looking for him. He wondered how he'd explain where he was. He couldn't tell her about any of this. Not until the police made it public— and they weren't about to do that until they knew a whole lot more.

"I don't understand it," said Vega. "Marcela ID'd the other man as her father."

"Marcela ID'd a man whose face you shot off."

Vega flinched. Greco's words were true but they still pained him greatly.

"Most likely," Greco continued, "what Marcela Salinez ID'd was her father's coat and the pay stub in the pocket. As I understand from Mark Hammond over in Wickford, the ID in the man's wallet listed an entirely different name."

"Antonio Fernandez," Vega remembered. "Still, it seems to me, a man is more likely to part with a family photo than he is his paycheck."

"Unless Ponce lent this Fernandez guy his coat and was planning to take it back after the robbery." Greco tossed off a laugh. It sounded like someone sawing wood.

"What's so funny?"

"I'm picturing the look on Ruben Tate-Rivera's face when he realizes that he's built an entire media scandal around you shooting a guy only to have him show up dead twenty-four hours later."

"I killed *somebody*, Grec."

"Yeah, you did. But that's too complicated for Tate and the media to handle. They like things they can fit into a hundred and forty-character tweet. No one can even say for sure which one of these two bodies is Ponce's until Dr. Gupta compares the DNA, and those results won't come back until tomorrow at the earliest. And that's the *least* of my problems."

Vega nodded. They both knew that the Lake Holly PD would have to treat this as a homicide investigation for the time being. Most likely, Vega's department would be involved too, given the serious nature of the crime and its connection to the Wickford shooting. "You think he jumped? Or was pushed?"

"We're looking at video in the area, trying to figure out how he got there."

"Any video from the bridge?"

Greco shook his head. "The town board was talking about installing security cameras at both entrances awhile back. But the price tag made them decide to just not install any nighttime lighting on the walkway instead."

Vega raised an eyebrow. "Those cameras will look cheap next to the lawsuit the town could be facing."

"Yep." Greco agreed. "Ponce's family may get richer claiming he couldn't see and took a fall than they ever would've with you shooting him."

"That is, *if* he fell."

"Ah, the million-dollar question," said Greco.

"More like eight thousand."

"Huh?"

Vega closed his eyes. There was no way around this. Adele had told him that Ponce was in hock for $8,000 to some gangster who'd threatened Yovanna's life. She'd handed Vega the motive for Ponce's robbery. And now Ponce was dead under suspicious circumstances, so that motive was more crucial than ever to the case. As an officer of the law, he couldn't hold back evidence of this magnitude.

"Hector Ponce owed eight thousand dollars to a loan shark at the time of his death."

"*What?*" asked Greco. "Where did you hear this?"

"Marcela told Adele," said Vega. "In *confidence.*"

"Ain't no such thing in a police investigation and you know it," said Greco.

Vega gave Greco a dirty look. Yes, he knew it. But he also knew that Adele would feel betrayed. She'd wonder how Vega could refuse to confirm or deny a single shred of information on the shooting to her, and yet so freely divulge *her* confidences to another police officer. It would sever Adele's relationship with Marcela. It would break trust between her and the immigrant community. Worst of all, it would break *them*.

Vega's defense—his only defense—was that he was doing what he was supposed to do as a police officer. Then again, he thought he was doing the same thing Friday night, and look where that got him.

Vega slumped against the wall and woodenly offered the facts as he knew them. He told Greco about Yovanna, the loan, and the threatening calls to Marcela for repayment. Greco listened, his face contorted in stomach distress or concentration, Vega couldn't say which.

"So Ponce owed some thug eight thousand dollars," said Greco, trying to recap the basics. "Presumably borrowed to finance Yovanna's little excursion to the U.S. When the thug heard Ponce was dead, he leaned on Marcela for repayment."

"In a nutshell," said Vega.

"But this opens more questions than it answers," said Greco. "Where was Ponce Friday night?"

"In the woods at Luis's house, I think," said Vega.

"Where's the proof?"

Vega told Greco about Joy's friend Katie who saw a man who looked like Ponce running out of the woods. "She never heard the shots so she couldn't say if she saw him before or after. But now I'm wondering if it was after."

"I don't know, Vega. A pothead scoring weed is not my idea of a good witness. And don't forget, a neighbor gave the DA a statement that she saw you shoot Ponce point-blank. She didn't see anyone else. For that matter, neither did Luis."

Luis. Vega straightened. "Luis said he shot Ponce."

"So?" asked Greco. "Luis wouldn't know who he shot until the police told him the guy's name."

"Yeah, but unlike me, Luis *saw* the face of the man he shot. In good light. At close range. Ponce's picture was all over the news. If the man Luis shot wasn't Ponce, why didn't he say anything?"

"Luis probably never gave the guy more than a passing thought except as to how it might affect his career."

Greco's phone dinged with a text. "My guys just brought Marcela in." Greco sighed. "I hate telling people their loved ones are dead. And I *really* hate delivering that news twice."

Vega left Greco and returned to the emergency room waiting area. It felt like hours had passed but it had only been twenty-five minutes. Adele still hadn't come out. Vega was glad. He couldn't tell her any of what he'd just found out.

He pulled out his phone and played a game to distract himself. He never felt normal hunger anymore, only sudden waves of intense desire for sugar or caffeine. He walked back to the vending machine, bought a Snickers bar, and another weak cup of coffee, and sat at a small table in the snack area trying to eat slowly and feel the food travel from his mouth to his stomach. The sweetness soothed him. He brought the cup to his lips—and froze.

Two uniformed police officers walked by. Between them stood Marcela and her husband, Byron, both of them looking grim-faced and cowed in the presence of so much authority. Vega ducked his head. He felt the cup shaking in his hands. It was only a few weeks ago that he'd driven Marcela home in the rain. He remembered walking her to her door, both of them huddled under his umbrella. How could he have guessed their lives would become entwined under such horrible circumstances?

Marcela didn't see Vega, thankfully. She was too focused on her little boy, who looked like he'd just awoken from a deep sleep. The child was still wearing his pajamas and clutching a stuffed dog. Marcela handed him off to a young teenage girl accompanying the family. *Yovanna?* The teenager took the sleepy child in her arms and started heading for the vending machines.

Vega felt trapped, as if he'd been caught spying or shoplifting. He shoved the rest of the candy bar in his mouth and threw the wrapper in the garbage. He picked up the coffee to leave when the teenager walked into the small snack room with the little boy in her arms. The child was fully awake now. He'd spotted the candy in the machines.

"*Quiero caramelos!*" the boy whined. He wanted candy. The teenager shushed him. "I have no money," she told him in Spanish.

Vega fished some change from his pockets and held it out to the girl.

"Here," he said in Spanish. "For you and the little boy." Vega couldn't remember the child's name. But he wouldn't have used it anyway. It would have frightened the two children to think this stranger knew who they were.

The girl shook her head no and kept her eyes on the floor. Adele had said she was thirteen but she looked much younger than that. She had her mother's dark skin, wide face, and Asian-looking eyes. Her clothes looked too small on her and more suited to spring than winter. She wore only a light pink windbreaker. Vega wondered if this was all Marcela had had on hand for her when she arrived.

"Candy! Candy! Candy!" the boy cried again in Spanish.

The teenager bounced the boy on her hip. "We'll get candy later maybe," she offered. But the boy kept up his chant.

Vega took the money he'd offered her and fed it into the vending machine. "Please," he said to her. "Have what you want."

The girl regarded Vega from the corner of her eye. She lifted a skinny little hand to the machine but it just hung there. Vega realized she had no idea how the machine worked.

"Would you like this?" He pointed to a Snickers bar. "It has peanuts and chocolate. Or maybe this?" He pointed to a Mounds bar. "It has coconut. Or maybe this?" He pointed to a Milky Way.

She pointed to the Mounds bar. Vega pushed the buttons and the bar spiraled forward and down into the delivery tray. The girl just stood there. Vega reached into the tray, pulled out the candy bar, and held it out to her.

"Here. Enjoy."

"Thank you," she said in a voice so tiny, it was as if she hadn't spoken at all. Not once did her eyes leave her feet. Vega tried to think back to what Joy had been like at thirteen. She giggled. She gossiped with her friends. She spent hours playing with her hair in mirrors. She was afraid of spiders, sure. And scary movies. But she walked through the world like she owned it. This girl looked so frightened and diminished by comparison. She seemed both younger and older than Joy had at the same age. Vega thought about the terrible stories he'd heard of undocumented minors traveling through Central America and Mexico. The life-and-death rides atop freight trains. The brutal desert treks where death by thirst or snakebite were common. The shifty-eyed coyotes who routinely beat or raped their charges. No wonder she looked so cowed. Vega felt the same way right now. Traumatized. Angry. In despair. He wished he could give her Dr. Cantor's phone number. She'd probably make better use of a therapist than he would.

"Jimmy?"

Vega turned at the sound of Adele's voice. He drained the last of his coffee and switched to English.

"How's—?"

"It's just a sprain. She'll need a boot brace for a week or so and then she'll be fine. Peter wants to drive Sophia home." Adele frowned at the children sitting at a table by the vending machines. The girl was carefully parceling out the candy bar for the boy and herself. "Damon?" Adele called to the little boy.

He smiled at Adele. The girl's body language grew suspicious and defensive. She hunched closer to the boy. Vega realized that the teenager hadn't yet met Adele.

"Damon?" asked Adele. "Is that your sister?"

"Yovanna, yes," said the boy.

Adele turned to Vega. "These are Marcela's children," she said in English. She sounded alarmed. "What are they doing here?"

Vega swallowed hard. "I don't know," he lied. He couldn't say anything that would jeopardize an ongoing investigation.

Adele addressed the girl in Spanish. "Yovanna? I'm a friend of your mother's. Is she okay?"

"Yes." The girl kept her eyes on the table.

"She's not hurt?"

"No."

"Byron? Is Byron hurt?"

"No."

Adele turned back to Vega. "What's going on?" Vega beckoned her out of the room.

"Marcela and Byron aren't hurt or in trouble. I can't tell you anything more than that."

"But you know what's going on?"

"Some of it. Look, Adele—" He took her hand. Her fingers had gone clammy and cold. "This whole case is changing right now. You have to trust me."

"What about Marcela's situation?" Adele must have read it in Vega's eyes. She pushed his hand away. "You didn't *tell* anyone what I told you, did you?"

"*Nena,* I had to let the police know that someone threatened the family."

"You *told?* After I asked you not to?"

"I had to. It's going to go to Dolan and my department anyway."

"But not like this! Not for the police to use any way they want! What's going on?"

"I can't say. Not yet."

"Oh, *you* can't say. Goody for *you*. You can't talk about the shooting. You can't tell me why Marcela's children are here. You betray my confidence and won't tell me why—"

"C'mon, *Nena*. Don't be like this. Things are happening. I have a duty—"

"Don't tell me about your *duty*. Your *duty* got Marcela's father killed!"

Vega stood there, feeling everything, saying nothing.

"Just—" Adele held up her hands and backed away from him. "I think you were right, Jimmy. I think it's best we took a break from each other. You'd better call a cab. I don't think I can handle having you around right now."

Chapter 26

Vega's cell phone rang by his bedside on Sunday morning. He rolled over to grab it and felt the ice-pick sharpness of strained muscles and bruised skin. Every inch of his body ached, right down to the shafts of his hair. Even the sunlight peeking through the cheap room-darkening shades felt like an assault.

He squinted at the name that came up on the screen. He was hoping it was Adele. Or Joy. Or even Teddy Dolan or Louis Greco with an update. The name on the phone read: *Ellen Cantor.*

Greco's shrink. No way did he want to talk to her. No way did he want to call her back, either.

"Yeah?" He hoped his hoarse clipped voice would indicate his displeasure at being called so early.

"Is this Jim Vega?"

If she'd listened to his voice mail properly, she'd have realized that he identified himself as "Jimmy." How could she help him if she couldn't even get his name right?

"This is Jimmy Vega."

"This is Ellen Cantor. You called me yesterday?"

"Yeah." Vega searched for his manners. Why was he being so hostile?

He knew why. One word: *Wendy.* His ex-wife. He could never look at any kind of counselor and not think of her.

The therapy queen. The woman who believed talking things out could solve all your problems—and then promptly cheated on him and left with nary a session of marital counseling. They'd been divorced almost six years now. She was long remarried. Joy was grown. Those twin rug rats that Alan had impregnated her with while she and Vega were still together were in kindergarten now. It was time to stop hating her for how she'd hurt him. But for some reason, the wound never closed. His psyche felt like a minefield that poor Ellen Cantor was glibly planning a picnic on.

"Thanks for calling me back," said Vega finally. "I, uh—don't know if you know who I am."

"You're the police officer who was involved in that shooting incident."

Involved-in-that-shooting-incident. That was kind. Better than he'd have said.

"I've been—sort of—*ordered*—by my job to get some counseling before I return to work and uh, a friend gave me your name."

"When would you like to meet?"

"I don't know," said Vega. *How about never? Is never good for you?* "Next week? The week after?"

"I've been following the news. I think we should meet sooner than next week. Are you free today?"

"*Today?* On a Sunday?"

"Unless your religion precludes it."

Does football count?

"I'm pretty booked all week otherwise," said Cantor. "I don't normally do appointments on a Sunday. But I'm happy to put the time aside for a patient who really needs it."

Coño! She thought he was a head case. He hesitated.

"Let me guess," said Cantor. "You would rather have a colonoscopy than visit a psychiatrist."

Vega laughed. "Yeah. I guess I would. Okay. How about ten A.M.?

"That would be fine." She gave him an address in Wickford. He was hoping not to have to go back to Wickford so soon.

"Is that an office?"

"My house. I have a private office entrance. Sort of like some dentists."

"I'd rather have root canal."

Vega hadn't been back to Wickford since the shooting. He told himself it was just a place. No big deal. He texted his lawyer and Joy to let both of them know he was seeing a shrink like they'd wanted. He hoped this might make up for his behavior with Joy last night. He didn't hear back.

Wickford was almost an hour south of his house. He managed the first part of the drive just fine. He felt calm and reasonably collected on the highway. The sky was a hard shell of blue and pierced with a bright morning sun that promised to fade quickly under December's heavy baggage of night. Vega kept his mind blank by alternating his music CDs with sports talk on the radio.

But as soon as he made the turnoff to Wickford, everything changed. A headache throbbed at the back of his head. His neck felt like someone had tried to dislocate it from his shoulders. His fingers developed pins and needles. He flexed and unflexed his hands at the steering wheel as he navigated the winding roads and backcountry horse farms. He relied on his GPS to get him to Ellen Cantor's place and damned if it didn't take him in practically the same direction as Ricardo Luis's house.

You're behaving like an idiot, he told himself. *You're acting like some traumatized kid—like Marcela's daughter at the hospital last night.* That poor girl had had no hand in the cards she'd been dealt. But Vega? His misery was of his own making.

Calm down. Control your breathing. He was sweating profusely. The trees, the stone walls, the white clapboard houses—all of it filled him with dread. He rolled down his windows and gulped in air that had the same bite of wood smoke mixed with decaying leaves that he'd smelled Friday night.

The scent took him back, hard and fast. His mouth went dry. His stomach tightened. He tried to think about anything except how much he wanted to puke up the bagel he'd grabbed on his way out. He drove past the road where all the cop cars had been parked on the night of the shooting. Just seeing the bent signpost where yellow crime scene tape still fluttered made his whole body shake.

Bicho es! He was going to be sick. Vega pulled his truck to the side of the road and vomited in the leaves by the woods. Thank God this wasn't Adele's neighborhood where every inch of grass was mowed and trimmed. Thank God this wasn't Luis's driveway. At least here, maybe the rain would wash it away.

He grabbed some water from his truck and tried to wash out his mouth. He popped breath mints and left his door open to cool himself down while he tried to gather his composure. His striped Oxford shirt felt clammy and sweaty. He'd nicked his chin shaving this morning. *I can't even be trusted with a razor anymore. How can I ever be trusted again with a gun?*

By the time he showed up at Ellen Cantor's office door on the side of her sprawling white colonial, he looked every bit the mess he felt. He begged his stomach to obey him as he rang her doorbell. Whatever else he felt about visiting a psychiatrist, he did not want to upchuck on her doorstep.

Ellen Cantor looked nothing like Wendy, and for that, he was grateful. She was short and stocky with curly silver hair and thick eyebrows that overshadowed all her subtler features—her swanlike neck, her high cheekbones, her small, dainty mouth. She had beautiful hands with long, expressive fingers. Piano fingers. He wondered if she played.

She flicked her eyes down him as she extended a hand. Her touch was warm and firm.

"Detective Vega? Are you all right?"

He'd forgotten how beat-up he looked from the fight last night. Plus, he was pale and shaky from the sudden bout of vomiting earlier. He wasn't about to tell her that, however.

"I think I'm coming down with a virus."

She didn't buy it. He didn't care. She opened the door wider and beckoned him in. She had a small, cheerful waiting area with yellow checked gingham furniture and flouncy curtains on the windows. Martha Stewart on steroids. Fortunately, her office was a little more sedate. Deep rust-colored couches and chairs. Some leather and dark wood. It was hard enough talking to a psychiatrist he'd never met before. It would be harder still in a room that looked like a sorority den.

He took a seat on a plush leather sofa. He didn't know where to begin. Was he allowed to talk about *everything?*

"This is confidential, right?" he grunted.

"I am bound by HIPAA laws, Detective. I can't reveal anything about our sessions without your written consent, not even to a court of law."

"Okay." He didn't know if he should tell her that he might have killed a different man. Did it matter for therapy purposes? Dead was dead, wasn't it?

She got him a glass of water. He sipped it and tried to recount all the salient details he could think of about the shooting. Time. Date. Place. Number of shots. Wounds to the victim. Whatever he'd told Isadora Jenkins would probably work for Ellen Cantor. He left out last night's fistfight and his lovely little vomiting session this morning. Then he sat back, looked at his watch, and pretended not to at the same time. Forty minutes to go and he'd be finished.

Cantor had a yellow legal pad in front of her but she

didn't write down a single word he'd said. Not one. *Jesus.* He interviewed people all the time and he wrote down *everything.*

Vega shifted his weight on the leather couch. He jangled his keys and change in his pocket. He felt like a kid in the principal's office. *Thirty-seven minutes to go.*

"I'd like you to call me 'Ellen.' May I call you 'Jimmy'?"

Vega shrugged. "Sure. Whatever."

Cantor leaned forward. "You don't want to be here, do you?"

"No offense, ma'am—Ellen. But my ex is a psychologist and I never saw any of this stuff working for her or me or anyone else."

"By 'stuff,' what do you mean?"

"You know—" He stretched to avoid her gaze. "Having people sit around navel-gazing and talking about the time they didn't get what they wanted for their birthday when they were ten."

"I agree."

"You do?" *Good.* This would be faster than he thought.

"Which is why I would never put you through that. Tell me, how are you eating?"

"How am I *eating?*" The question surprised him. "Okay, I guess."

"Did you have breakfast this morning?"

"A bagel. But uh"—he jiggled his legs—"I kinda threw it up on the way over."

"Is that happening a lot?"

"No. But—I'm not really hungry most of the time."

"How about concentration?"

"I don't know . . . I'm sort of like a goldfish right now. I can't think about anything for more than two seconds."

"So you feel restless and antsy a lot?"

"Yeah—like I've got about ten cups of coffee in me."

"How about sleep?"

"What's that?" He threw out the comment lightly but

one of the things he was hoping Cantor would give him today was Ambien. He really, really needed a good night's sleep, and if he had to induce it chemically—well then, so be it. "I can't sleep for more than maybe an hour and a half at a stretch. Maybe you can like, give me a prescription?"

"Pills are a short-term solution at best," said Cantor. "I'm not a big believer in them."

"Oh." *So much for pills.*

"Are you talking to friends?"

Vega tossed off a laugh. "More like avoiding them."

"Why is that?"

"I'm not allowed to talk about the shooting. And all their shit—*stuff*, sorry—it sort of gets under my skin. I've been yelling at my teenage daughter a lot and she doesn't deserve it. Everything sets me off."

"Do you have a girlfriend?"

"I did. We're sort of on the outs at the moment. She runs an immigrant center—"

"Oh my."

"Yeah, 'oh my' is right," said Vega. "This whole situation has hurt her professionally. She's hearing stuff that makes me sound like a mafia hit man."

"Such as?"

"There's this witness. A neighbor who claims I executed the suspect—shot him at point-blank range. My girlfriend wants me to tell her it's not true. But I can't."

"*Is* it true?"

"Of course not!" His vehemence seemed to startle Cantor. Vega realized belatedly that the woman wouldn't know what was true and what wasn't.

"You can't tell your girlfriend what you just told me?" asked Cantor.

"It's not that simple," Vega explained. "If I tell her what's *not* true, then, in effect, I'm also telling her what *is*. My lawyer ordered me not to say anything. I'm already in trouble for some stupid comments I made at the scene. I can't risk another mistake."

"Have you told her that?"

"It wouldn't make any difference."

"Why is that?"

"Because she's gotta deliver this keynote address to a bunch of immigrant groups this evening at Fordham University. She's supposed to go up on stage and call for the district attorney to convene a grand jury against me."

"And how do you feel about that?"

"How do you think I feel? Like she's knifing me in the back." Vega heard the anger in his voice and shook his head. "She's got the clout to make it happen, too."

"You must feel deeply betrayed."

Vega sighed. "I do, of course. But in another way, I sort of get it. If you asked me to protect someone who did something very wrong, no matter how much I loved them, I couldn't go against my conscience. That's sort of what I'm asking of her."

"And when you tell her that, what does she say?"

"I can't tell her," said Vega. "I can't talk about any of this stuff without exploding."

"And you're exploding a lot, I gather."

"Kind of." He crossed and uncrossed his legs.

"Hmmm," said Cantor. Vega didn't like the sound of that. "Tell me," she said. "Are you having a lot of dreams?"

Vega closed his eyes. He saw the woods. Shadows moving in the darkness. A noise like cannon fire. Four shots. Four punctuation marks that signaled the end of life as he knew it. His stomach roiled. Sweat gathered at the back of his neck. His mouth tasted like old pennies.

"I guess—I'm sort of getting these uh—physical reactions."

"Post-traumatic stress."

Vega made a face. "That's for soldiers and rape victims and people who've survived atrocities. I'm a cop. Cops carry guns. Guns kill people. If I can't handle the basics of my job, what kind of cop am I? Hell, what kind of *man* am I?"

"Is that what you're worried about? That if you admit you're having a hard time processing this, you're less of a man?"

"Look"—Vega ran a hand through his hair—"I know I made a mistake. I know that. But Jesus—I should be doing better than I'm doing."

"So that image of a police officer you had as a little boy—you're afraid you're not living up to the dream?"

"It was never my dream," said Vega. "Maybe that's the problem. Being a police officer was not a lifelong ambition for me. I wanted to be a guitarist in a rock band."

"What happened?"

Vega shrugged. "Life got in the way I suppose. I had college loans to pay off. My girlfriend got pregnant. I became a cop for all the wrong reasons." Vega ticked them off on his fingers now. "Security. A pension. Health insurance—"

"Oh come now, Jimmy." Cantor regarded him over the tops of her glasses. "You've been a police officer for eighteen years. I very much doubt medical benefits kept you on the job."

"No. I like the work," he admitted. "I like making people feel safe and protected. I like the adrenaline rush of a good collar." He closed his eyes and tried to put something into words he never had before. "I feel like—what I do matters. And when I'm doing it, *I* matter."

"Then those are good reasons for why you stayed."

"So how come I look in the mirror and feel like a fraud? All these other guys I work with—they wouldn't be falling apart the way I am. What the hell is wrong with me?"

Cantor laced her long piano fingers in front of her and smiled reassuringly. After all the terrible stuff he'd just told her, she still seemed to think he was worth saving.

"Nothing is wrong with you. You're experiencing a very normal human reaction. You took a life. It's not something you intended to do and you're coming to grips with the weight of that. Because you did it as a police officer, you're having to come to grips with it in a very public and humiliating way."

"The media's making me out to be some kind of monster. I can't defend myself against the lies. I can't even say I'm sorry for the stuff that's true. Not that anyone would forgive me anyway."

"Do *you* forgive you?"

"I don't know." Vega tossed up his hands. He didn't have an answer. "I just want to stop feeling scared all the time."

"That's something we can work on." Ellen Cantor winked at him beneath her mop of silver hair. "No navel gazing necessary."

Vega had no memory of what they talked about after that. The time flew. He discussed things he never expected to: his former marriage. His relationship with Joy and Adele. The shooting, of course. But also his mother. He hadn't realized how intensely her murder had affected him, especially since the killer had never been caught. It was like a giant open sore that never seemed to heal.

"I feel like I let her down," said Vega. "She's been dead almost two years and here I am, a homicide detective, and I still have no idea who killed her. If that's not bad enough, now I find out that she had a lover all these years she never told me about."

"You said your mother's best friend is still alive," said Cantor. "Perhaps you can talk to her."

"Martha has Alzheimer's. She couldn't remember talking to my mother on the phone three hours before she died. How is she going to be able to tell me anything?"

"Jimmy—" Cantor lifted her glasses to the top of her head. Her eyes were softer and warmer without them. "Sometimes it's not about what people tell us. It's about what being with them helps us tell ourselves. You're hurting so badly right now over your mother. Maybe just being around her best friend could be of comfort to you."

"Perhaps."

Cantor turned to her computer and pulled up a file on the screen. "In the meantime, we'll work on your PTSD in a completely scientific way." She printed out some sheets with eye and breathing exercises designed to control his flashbacks and calm him. Vega looked at the pages and frowned.

"You don't want to do it?" asked Cantor.

"No. I'll give it a try," said Vega. "I was just thinking about this teenage girl I met last night at Lake Holly Hospital. She just arrived here from Honduras. Her mother's undocumented and the girl . . . Let's just say it probably wasn't the easiest of journeys."

"That's a brutal trip, especially for a child on her own."

Vega nodded. "She seemed so . . . I don't know—"

"Traumatized?"

"Yeah." His heart ached for her. The shooting had rubbed all his nerve endings raw. He felt everything acutely now—even other people's pain.

"I keep thinking that that girl needs therapy even more than I do," said Vega. "She's thirteen years old and in a strange country. She doesn't speak the language. She hasn't seen her mom in ten years. And God only knows what her journey across Central America and Mexico was like."

"I've worked with some of those children," said Cantor. "And you're right. Many of them are suffering from PTSD. They've endured terrible traumas. It's no wonder they have nightmares and can't concentrate."

"What's the prognosis for a girl like that?" asked Vega.

"I haven't met her so it's difficult to say," said Cantor. "But I'm guessing she's having adjustment issues being away from her mother for so long. If there's a new husband and children, that can add further burdens. There are the language barriers and the fact that she's likely behind in school. Then of course there's the fact that she's undocumented so her future here is uncertain at best. It's easy for a child like that to feel overwhelmed and fall into depression and self-destructive behavior."

"And if she got the services she needed?"

"The prognosis would be much better, certainly. She can't focus in school until she feels safe and she can't feel safe until her PTSD is addressed." Cantor studied him. "Jimmy, I'd love to say I could help every child. But without some framework in place, one or two therapy sessions would do nothing for a child like that."

"I understand," said Vega. "I'm just—"

"Trying to help." She smiled. "Because that's why you do what you do. So we're going to concentrate on getting you well again. And then you can use that energy to help others."

Chapter 27

"Mom! Hurry up! I'm going to miss Hayley's birthday party!" Sophia cried. Fortunately, Sophia's friend's ninth birthday was a movie-and-pizza affair, not an ice-skating or rock-climbing event. Adele had already had enough guilt from her ex-husband, Peter, last night about Sophia's sprained ankle. She didn't need her daughter adding more.

"Are you sure you're up to it?" asked Adele, glancing down at the soft cast on her daughter's foot.

"I'm fine."

The party was being held at a small movie theater in downtown Wickford in a beautiful old landmark building that had yet to succumb to the megaplex syndrome of all the other movie houses in the area. It had the look and feel of an old concert hall of the 1800s, with large white columns in front and a chandelier in the lobby. Hayley's parents had taken over the theater for the latest Disney release and the pizza party afterward. Adele didn't even want to guess what such a party had cost the family or what they would do for an encore when Hayley got into the double digits.

Adele dropped Sophia off at the party. Then she sat in her car and tried to quiet her nerves for what she was about to do. She picked up her cell phone and dialed. A woman's voice—breathy and confident—answered on the second ring. It turned brittle as soon as Adele said her name.

"Unless this has to do with food pantry business, my attorney says I can't talk."

"I understand your situation, Margaret," Adele replied. "And I'm not asking you to alter any statement you've made to the police. I'm just asking if—given our previous relationship—you might at least walk me through what you saw Friday night."

Adele had known Margaret Behring about five years—ever since Margaret and her husband moved north from Manhattan. She'd been a bond trader at Goldman Sachs before she had her two children, and she brought her brains and organizational skills to the food pantry and a host of other charities in the area. Adele respected her. That was one of the reasons this was so difficult.

"You're not a disinterested party, Adele."

"I know I'm not. But I'm about to walk on a stage this evening and set the tone for how every major immigrant group in this state regards this shooting. Detective Vega won't say a word to me. If you won't talk to me, what do I have to go on?"

"You're not going to like anything I have to say."

"I'm prepared."

Silence. Adele's car was cold and yet she felt sweat gathering on her skin.

"There's a shipment of canned corn and carrots coming into the pantry around four this afternoon," said Margaret. "No one else is going to be there to receive it but me."

"So if I show up, you'll talk to me?"

"We never had this conversation. Is that understood?" Margaret hung up.

Adele had a long list of errands to run while Sophia was at the party. Her younger sister Grace's birthday was coming up. There was a drugstore next to the French restaurant, Chez Martine, that sold birthday cards. Adele began walking over. She heard someone call out her name. She turned to see a teenager in restaurant whites sweeping the sidewalk.

"Omar!" Adele couldn't remember his last name. He was a Guatemalan, about seventeen, short in stature with a round, impish face. She hugged him. "I didn't know you worked at Chez Martine."

"I got the job maybe two months ago, señora."

Adele culled her memory for what she could remember about him. His mother used to attend that Friday night support group at La Casa, *Las Madres Perdidas*. She worked for years as a live-in maid in Wickford. Omar had come over recently. There were probably other siblings still left in Guatemala. Adele didn't think he attended school. Most likely, he hadn't been to school in years—which made it next to impossible for him to go back. Besides, the trip over had probably burdened him and his family with enormous debt. He needed to earn money to pay it back. He probably didn't even have time to take English classes.

"Are you happy here at Chez Martine? Are they treating you well?"

"Yes, thank you. I just got a promotion to a better shift." His face turned solemn. "Only I am sad because of the reason. It's because our head dishwasher, Hector, died. Did you know?"

"Yes. I heard. I'm sorry." Omar was so young and so new to this country that he probably had no idea how Adele was connected to the shooting. "Did you know him well?" she asked.

"Oh yes. He was a very good man. I don't care what the police say." Omar waved his hands in front of Adele. They were encased in heavy padded black gloves. "These? Hector gave them to me. I didn't have a pair. I didn't know how cold it gets here. He gave me a wool hat, too."

None of this sounded to Adele like a man who would rob a house.

"Omar, did the police talk to you about Hector at all?"

"They talked to all of us after the shooting, yes. They searched his locker."

"Did they find anything unusual?"

"I don't think so. They didn't even find his extra jacket in there. Hector always kept one in his locker in case the weather changed. He didn't like the cold. Maybe he gave it to his friend."

"A friend at work?"

"No." The teenager looked over his shoulder and kept sweeping.

"Omar, is there something you didn't tell the police?"

"I don't want to get in trouble."

"This isn't Guatemala. The police won't do anything bad to you."

Omar kept his eyes on his broom. "I have to go peel carrots."

Adele squinted inside the mullioned windows. Chez Martine wasn't open for lunch on Sundays. The staff would just be cleaning the place out and preparing for Sunday dinner. "Do you have a break when I can talk to you?"

"Maybe you can come around back? I will speak to my boss."

Omar's boss, a hefty Colombian who seemed to tower over his largely Central American staff, growled at Omar in Spanish that he had "five minutes" to speak to Adele. Then he handed Omar a giant bucket of carrots. "Peel while you talk." He had a commanding presence. Adele felt as if she were being ordered to don an apron and do the same.

"I don't want to get fired," said Omar. He worked fast as he spoke. Adele watched the carrots flying through his fingers, the knobby orange peels gliding across his sun baked hands. His fingernails were chipped and uneven. They looked like they belonged to a hand much older than seventeen years. There were fresh pink scars across the knuckles. She wondered what sort of journey he'd endured to make it to see his mother here in Wickford. She wondered how they were faring as a family now.

"Nobody is going to fire you for telling the truth," Adele promised him.

"Even when the truth is against an important person?"

"What important person?"

Omar wiped his hands on his white apron. He licked his chapped lips. He seemed to be weighing some secret he was deciding whether he could trust her with. Adele sat very still.

"My mother," he said finally. "She still lives at her employer's house. Here in Wickford."

"She's still a live-in? I thought after you arrived . . ." Adele's voice trailed off. She saw at once what the boy was telling her. His mother's living accommodations weren't sufficient to take him in.

"Omar," she asked softly, "where are you living?"

Omar kept his eyes on the carrot peeler. "I have a cousin. He lets me sleep on his couch sometimes. My mother does my laundry when she can at her employer's. But some nights, my cousin has no room. So I—" Omar nodded back at the restaurant. The lovely cobblestoned restaurant with the glass mullioned windows. It was a great place to dine. It was no place for a seventeen-year-old boy to live.

"Does your employer—?"

"Jorgé knows. He sounds mean but he has a good heart. He is only the kitchen manager, however. The chefs don't know. And the owner definitely doesn't know."

"Do you stay over at the restaurant often?"

"Not so much—until the weather got cold."

Adele knew what the boy was saying: *When it was warmer, I sometimes slept outside.*

Omar kept his gaze on his work. Adele could only imagine the stress he was under. He had no place to live. He didn't speak the language. He'd endured a traumatic journey. After so many years apart from his mother, he probably didn't even really know her anymore. Nor could she take care of him. If it hadn't been for the fact that Adele was asking about Hector, no one except his boss, Jorgé, would even know the teenager's situation.

The boy must have sensed something in Adele's gaze because his shoulders straightened. "I'm seventeen. A man. I can take care of myself," he said. In his world, seventeen *was* a man. Adele decided to let his problems go at the moment and concentrate on his account.

"So—when you were staying at the restaurant, did you see something?"

He glanced up at her and then quickly looked away.

"Omar, please. If this has something to do with the shooting, I need to know. Hector's *family* needs to know."

"I want to help," said Omar. "But I have family, too. I need this job. I have loans to repay. If I don't pay, there is a man in my town back in Guatemala—he will take it out on my older sister!"

"I promise you," said Adele. "I will not tell anyone where I got the information." After Vega's breach of confidence, she would never divulge anything ever again.

Omar took a deep breath. "Hector was one of the last people to leave the restaurant every night. Usually, Jorgé drove him and a bunch of the staff to the train station in Lake Holly. But one time, maybe three weeks ago, Hector told Jorgé he didn't need a ride. Someone was picking him up. I didn't want Hector to know I was sleeping here. I didn't want to get Jorgé in trouble. So I pretended to leave and then came back and let myself in with the key Jorgé gave me."

"This friend of Hector's? Was he the one who picked him up?"

"No. His friend came by taxi to the parking lot. I saw them from the office window upstairs. That's the room I sleep in because it faces the back so nobody can tell when a light is on. His friend didn't have a warm jacket. Just a sweatshirt. I saw Hector give the man his spare jacket from his locker. Hector seemed concerned about him. Like they were good friends."

"What did this man look like?"

"I think he might have been Central American, too. He was about the same height and build as Hector. I thought maybe they had some sort of night job together. I just watched because I have nothing to do at night when I stay here. It gets sort of—lonely."

Adele felt something thud in her heart. She knew half a dozen La Casa volunteers who would gladly take this boy in. She just hadn't known about his plight. How many other children, she wondered, were wandering around Lake Holly and Wickford and all these other little upscale villages in the same distressed state as Omar? Some, she knew about. The vast majority, she didn't. Probably because—even if she did—there was little she could do for them. She barely had the funds to provide basic services to adult clients and their American-born offspring. She had nothing left for these lost children who were pouring in.

"So who picked them up? Another taxi?" Adele asked the boy.

"No. After about ten minutes, a black Mercedes pulled into the parking lot. Hector and his friend got in back. The driver powered down his window and threw out a cigarette he was smoking. That's when I saw him."

Adele noticed Omar's voice had turned to barely a whisper. His hands had grown shaky and he was having more trouble peeling the carrots.

"This driver—is he the important person you were talking about?"

Omar nodded. "Hector and his friend were probably hired to help at a party."

"A party?" Adele frowned. "But this is after Chez Martine closed for the night. You serve until ten P.M. So this had to be after midnight, yes?"

Omar shrugged. "Maybe they stayed at the man's house and worked the next morning."

"That's possible," Adele agreed. "But why wouldn't you mention this to the police?"

"Because everyone keeps saying that Hector went to his house to rob him. How can I say that I saw him pick up Hector and his friend in the restaurant parking lot maybe three weeks earlier? Nobody would believe me."

Adele felt something seize up inside of her. "Omar—are you saying that the driver who picked up Hector and the other man was Ricardo Luis?"

"I must be wrong. If Hector worked for him before, how come nobody has mentioned it?"

Yes. How come?

"Thank you for sharing this with me," said Adele. She fished a card out of her wallet and handed it to the boy. "This has my cell number on it. You find yourself without a place to stay some night, you call me. There are people at La Casa—board members and others—who will make sure you have a real home to stay in."

"I'm okay," he said. "I can take care of myself."

"Please, Omar. I know you're strong. But I'm a mother. I don't want to see you worrying about this in January and February."

"Okay. Thank you." He tucked her card in his shirt pocket. "I will think about it."

Outside Chez Martine, Adele checked her watch. She had a little over two hours before she had to pick up Sophia. Her sister Grace's birthday card would have to wait. She fished that scrap of paper out of her wallet with Ricardo Luis's cell phone scribbled across it.

It wasn't guitars she wanted to see anymore. It was him.

* * *

There were only five houses at the top of Oak Hill Road. Four of them were clapboard-and-cobblestone colonials set back from the road with wide front porches and gabled roofs. In the middle was a fifth house, a Spanish hacienda the color of a sun-bleached lawn flamingo. It had a red clay tile roof, stucco arches and enormous windows with black wrought-iron grilles. Adele wondered what the old-money CEOs thought of this second coming of the Alamo among their stately gray-and-white New England charmers.

Adele parked her Prius by the curb and walked down the driveway, past several sedans and SUVs. It looked like Luis had other guests this morning. A housekeeper answered the door and Adele gave her name. She'd called before she drove over. She'd have never had the nerve to show up otherwise.

The housekeeper told Adele to wait in the marble entrance hall by a sweeping staircase. Children's laughter floated up from somewhere inside the house. Luis's family must have flown in last night or this morning to be with him. Adele wondered if she'd get a glimpse of his fashion model wife, Victoria. From the pictures in Luis's book, Victoria was an elegant Panamanian, slightly taller than her husband with blond-streaked hair and high cheekbones.

Oh God, she was becoming such a groupie.

The housekeeper reappeared. "The señor will see you now."

Adele followed her through a hallway with a vaulted ceiling and dark polished wood floors. Their footsteps echoed. They turned and turned again until they were in a hallway lined with framed gold records and photographs of Luis holding up Grammy awards on the covers of various Latin magazines. The woman entered a small paneled room and gestured for Adele to have a seat. It felt like a doctor's waiting area. Then a door opened. Adele recognized the stocky Hispanic man in the black beret from last night at Harvest. He nodded to her but didn't give his name. Adele already knew it from speed-reading through most of Luis's memoir last night when she couldn't sleep. This was his producer, Oscar Cifuentes.

"Ric's in the studio."

"I interrupted a recording session? Oh my."

"Nah. We're just fooling around. If he were really doing a recording session, you couldn't be anywhere near the place. But he's just hamming it up for a magazine photo shoot. Come," said Cifuentes. "I'll show you."

Cifuentes led Adele into a recording booth. A console that looked something like an air traffic controller's workstation stared back at her. On the other side of the sound-proof glass was Luis. He was dressed in a bright blue T-shirt with a swordfish on the front and a chambray work shirt over it. A set of headphones straddled his tousled black hair. His feet were bare, his khakis, unpressed. On one side of him was a guitarist, a black man with a shaved head. On the other was a Hispanic drummer with a skinny pony-tail that looked like some pelted animal had died and ossi-fied on his back.

Vega would have been in seventh heaven to be in a recording studio like this with musicians of the caliber of the men with Ricardo Luis. Adele felt guilty she was here without him. Then she remembered last night at the hospi-tal—the way he'd so cavalierly betrayed her. The way he'd refused to tell her anything about why Marcela and Byron were even there.

There was a photographer in the recording studio along with Luis and the two musicians—a young Asian woman with a long braid of silky black hair. Luis mugged for the camera, offering up his trademark dimpled grin, pretend-ing his drummer's ponytail was a microphone. He was a natural comedic actor who could make his features bigger and bolder on command.

"He's just having fun in there," said Cifuentes. "Do you sing? Play? You're welcome to join him."

Adele thought about Vega's frozen smile when she tried to sing and shook her head.

"I'm afraid growing up I showed more skill at torturing notes than carrying them," said Adele. "So they stuck a sword in my hand instead."

"A sword?" asked Cifuentes.

"I fenced as a teenager."

"Yeah? Me, too."

"Really?" Adele seldom met anyone who fenced.

"Sure." Cifuentes winked at her. "You wanted a new set of hubcaps or a stereo, I was your man. That was fencing in *my* neighborhood."

Mine, too, Adele wanted to say. But it was too exhausting to explain that she was a scholarship kid in a YMCA program who happened to show some talent. Poverty was always exhausting—first, when you're in it and later, when you try to explain how you outran it. So she changed the topic.

"Do you think I could borrow Mr. Luis for a second? I have a couple of questions I want to ask him."

Cifuentes pushed a button on an intercom. "Hey, Ric. The lady from La Casa's here. Can you take five?"

Luis took off his headphones and stepped into the booth.

"Hey, where's the detective?" He probably thought that's why Adele was here. She didn't make it clear over the phone.

"It's just me, I'm afraid."

" 'Just you' is good, too." He touched her arm. "What can I do for a pretty lady?"

She blushed. "Is there someplace private we can talk for a few minutes?"

"My office is good." Luis told Cifuentes he would be back in ten. Adele sensed he said it as much for her as for his producer. Ten minutes was all she'd get with him. She had to make it good.

Luis's office was just down the hall from his home recording studio. The furniture was a glossy dark teak with maroon leather chairs. The bookcases were crammed with awards and photos of the singer next to presidents, recording stars, and athletes—even the Pope. There were photos of his model-wife and three beautiful children as well. But what drew Adele's eye most was a grainy shot of a very young-looking Luis in a striped T-shirt and jeans that were too short for him. He was clasping a microphone and singing on a stage with a backdrop of corrugated tin.

"My first performance in Nogales, Mexico, when I was fourteen," said Luis. "It was at a talent show. They called me *tobillos*." He laughed. "I think you can see why. That's all anyone remembered about that performance: my ankles."

"I'm three-quarters the way through your autobiography," said Adele.

"You are a fast reader."

"It's captivating. So you were nineteen when you came to the United States?"

"*Came*." Luis smiled. "I like that. It sounds very— *friendly*. It wasn't. I hopped the border, as they say. Walked through the desert. Dodged immigration every step of the way." He shook his head. "That's why I give La Casa money now. I understand these people. I *am* these people. God just happened to bless me with a voice, that's all. And now I'm an American citizen." Luis spread his palms as if he were about to belt out a song. Even up close, there was a certain larger-than-life quality about him. Adele wondered if he'd always had it or if he'd honed it over two decades of climbing the showbiz ladder playing two-bit dives and dressing up in ridiculous costumes on *Sábado Gigante*.

Luis gestured for Adele to have a seat. He rummaged

through his drawers and pulled out a pack of cigarettes. "Do you mind?"

Adele shook her head no. She hated cigarettes but hey, it *was* his house.

He lit one and took a drag. Then he propped himself on the edge of his desk. "You came to ask me something, yes? My lawyer called me this morning and said the police wanted to arrange another meeting before I head back to Miami tomorrow. Maybe you know what it's about?"

"I don't, unfortunately."

"Your boyfriend didn't tell you?"

"No." She swallowed back a mixture of anger and embarrassment at having to admit that.

"Maybe we will both know more after your speech this evening."

"You're coming?" asked Adele. "I thought that was— you know—?"

"A Mexican 'yes'?"

Adele laughed.

"It's true," said Luis. "We Mexicans have a very hard time saying no. But in this case, I really am planning to come. My publicist thought it would be a good idea. So did Ruben Tate-Rivera."

"Oh." Adele felt sick to her stomach every time she thought about getting on that stage. "Mr. Luis—"

"Ric," he offered.

"Ric," said Adele. "I don't know how to ask this. But did you ever meet Hector Ponce before Friday night? Maybe you hired him for a private event or something?"

Luis stiffened. "I already spoke to the police about everything, Adele. I don't think this is a conversation that either of us should be having."

"I know. You're right. It's just that—someone I met claims they saw Hector get into a black Mercedes you were driving."

"*What?* When?"

"A few weeks ago."

"Where?"

"Here in Wickford. I can't be more specific than that. This person isn't comfortable coming forward."

"And yet you are comfortable making an accusation."

"It's not an accusation," Adele assured him. "I'm only asking because I'm desperate to understand what happened in those woods with Detective Vega. If I go on stage tonight and call for a grand jury to review the shooting, I've ruined his career. If I don't, I may very well ruin mine. I'm searching for any morsel of information that could help make my decision."

Luis leaned against the edge of his desk. He took a deep inhale of his cigarette and studied her for a long moment. He smiled but there was something forced around the edges. His easy warmth was gone, replaced now by stilted politeness.

"I wish I could help you, Adele. I do. But I have nothing to offer."

"So it's not true? You never gave Hector Ponce a ride?"

"I will say again: I have already made my statement to the police." Luis stubbed out his cigarette. He walked over to his office door and opened it, a clear invitation for Adele to leave. "I wish you good luck tonight, Adele. I hope you find the answers you are looking for. I hope that Ruben is wrong about what's going to happen."

Her insides turned to jelly. "What did he say?"

"It was a compliment in a way, I guess. He said you were a good lawyer once and maybe you should go back to being one."

Chapter 28

Vega called Joy from Dr. Cantor's driveway.

"I did it," he said. "I saw the shrink."

A heavy silence hung on the line. "And that's supposed to make everything okay?"

"No." He felt small and powerless. He wanted so much to earn back his daughter's respect. He had no idea how.

"About last night—" he began. "I was only trying to protect you—"

"Dad, when are you going to learn to quit rationalizing things and start owning up to them?"

Vega closed his eyes. He wanted to do better. Joy deserved better.

"I know I suck at apologizing." It took all his willpower to admit that. "It probably cost me my marriage to your mother. Or helped, in any case." He took a deep breath. "But for what it's worth, I'm really, truly sorry for what I did. All of it. The shooting. My behavior on campus. And especially that fistfight last night at the diner. I embarrassed you. I embarrassed myself. I can't bring back a man's life. But I can try to make things right between us. I want to do that, *chispita*. If you'll let me."

Silence. Vega felt a sudden panic that he'd said the wrong thing. Everything that came out of his mouth toward his daughter—about her tattoo, her career choices, her friends—was wrong. He wondered if it was already too late to earn back her trust.

"Do you know," she said finally, "that's the first time I've ever heard you really apologize?"

"I guess it was overdue."

"By about a decade." And just like that, a light switch flipped back on. Her whole manner toward him changed. Was that how it worked? Vega wondered. Could genuine remorse, honestly expressed, really be that cathartic between people? He felt embarrassed that it had taken him all these years to figure that out. Then again, you could say sorry for a fistfight and maybe put the pieces back together. No amount of sorrys brought back a life. Maybe that's what Greco meant about being forever changed.

"You aren't anywhere near Lake Holly, I suppose?" asked Joy.

"I'm in Dr. Cantor's driveway in Wickford. Why?"

"Mom and Alan and the boys had to go to an event at the synagogue" said Joy. "Can you give me a ride to the train station?"

"You're still going to see your friend today?"

"At Fordham. Yes."

Fordham. Just the word made Vega's stomach ricochet like he was on some carnival ride.

"Dr. Torres is also going to give me a tour of his school after the basketball tournament is over this afternoon."

"Look, Joy, maybe you want to hold off. People hear you're my daughter and—"

"I'm not walking around with a banner over my head, Dad. I'll be fine. See you in ten."

Vega drove to Lake Holly taking the same local roads he'd driven on the way over. He was testing himself. Testing his nerve.

I can handle this.

He went back to the signpost with the crime scene tape. He tried to breathe and found that he could. *Good.* He swilled some water in his mouth and made the turn onto Oak Hill. He'd do one drive around the cul-de-sac and then head back down. *So far, so good.* He wasn't shaking. He was breathing steadily. His stomach was a little off. But okay, that was to be expected.

That was before he saw Adele's pale green Prius parked by the curb.

He knew it was Adele's. She had a Lake Holly Elementary School bumper magnet on the hatch and a little soccer ball with the Ecuadorian flag dangling from her rearview mirror. What was she doing here? Vega's insides felt like they'd been folded, creased, and sent through the shredder.

He quickly reversed his car and sped down the hill. He turned on the radio to distract himself. "Heat of my Heart" blasted out of the speakers. *Goddamn this guy!* Vega angrily punched the radio button off. All his misery these last forty-eight hours began and ended with Ricardo Luis. There was so much Vega wanted to ask him and couldn't. Why was he alone in that house Friday night? How come he answered the door? Did he ever see a second assailant?

What was he doing with Adele?

Vega tried to push the last question out of his head and concentrate on Friday night. He wished he knew what Luis was thinking when he dialed 911. But the police would have that audiotape under lock and key at county dispatch now, given that it was part of an ongoing investigation. Vega would need a case number to access it. And nobody on the investigation was about to give him that—especially not after the way he'd been behaving.

Then again, maybe he didn't need to ask. In Joy's driveway, Vega pulled out his phone and scrolled through his photos until he came to the evidence pictures Dolan had sent him Friday night. There it was, on the upper right hand corner. His way in.

"So what are you planning to do today, Dad?" Joy asked him on the drive to the train station.

"Oh, this and that."

Joy raised an eyebrow. "I don't like the sound of that."

"I won't get into any fistfights, I promise."

She kissed him on the cheek as she left the truck. "Stay out of trouble."

"Always." He could hope.

The county's emergency dispatch headquarters was located in a shoebox of a building on the state medical college campus, a sprawling patchwork of parking lots that cobbled together the most unlikely collection of services. Besides the county hospital, there was the county jail, rimmed in double razor wire so no one mistook it for the equally unattractive hospital. There was also the medical examiner's office, a shelter for battered women, and the county's emergency dispatch service. Each division had its own unattractive beige cement building complete with a parking lot, a couple of ugly rotting picnic benches, and itty bitty signage so that if you didn't know where you were going, you probably shouldn't be there.

Dispatch was conveniently located right across from the medical examiner's office. Just to make doubly sure no one knew what he was doing, Vega parked in the ME's lot and crossed over to dispatch.

The vestibule door was alarmed, but he showed his ID to the video camera and immediately got buzzed through. The front reception area had all the warmth of a post office. The ceiling was acoustical tile, the floor was linoleum. There was a collection of flags—American, New York State, and county. At the front desk was a young white guy, not long out of college. He had close-cropped hair and wore a dark blue dispatcher's knit polo shirt that looked as if it had been pressed, certainly not by him. Vega suspected he still lived at home with his parents.

Vega showed his badge and added a little push to his voice, hoping his rank and seniority might keep the kid from asking too many questions.

"I need to pull the tapes on the Benito Diaz shooting." Diaz—a.k.a. Lil—was a teenager who had been gunned down in a lover's triangle back in September. Vega was the lead investigator on the case so nobody was likely to question his motives.

The dispatcher buzzed Vega through the doors. Vega followed the hallway to a room with cubicles, computer monitors, and headsets. It reminded him of language lab when he was a kid. He expected to be listening to someone discuss their vacation in French. For all Vega's fluency in Spanish, he couldn't order off a menu in French.

The screen required him to type in his badge number and the number of the case he was looking to access. It meant there would be a record linking him to audio he wasn't authorized to listen to. But who would bother to look?

Vega pulled out his phone and copied the case number from the evidence pictures Dolan had sent to him. Then he put on the headsets and hit *play*. A flat, emotionless female dispatcher's voice came on the line:

"*County dispatch 911, what is your emergency?*"

A male voice answered in a heavy Spanish accent.

"*Ah, I was home? By myself? And this man? He, ah—he broke into my house.*"

Vega frowned. It took Luis three full sentences to get around to stating his emergency. In Vega's experience, people got to the point pretty quickly: *I've been shot! My baby's not breathing! My house is on fire!* And okay, Luis wasn't a native speaker. He was likely scared and under pressure. But why was every statement framed as a question? The only people Vega knew who framed statements as questions were teenage girls and lying suspects. And Ricardo Luis was not a teenage girl.

"*Where is your house, sir?*"

"*Six Oak Hill Road. In Wickford.*"

"*Is the suspect there now?*"

"*Ah, I'm not sure. I think they—he ran away? After I shot him.*"

They? Did Luis confuse singular and plural? Or did he know there were two men? If so, then why lie to the police?

Unless he didn't want the police to go looking for a witness.

"*You shot him? Where did you shoot him?*"

"*In the hallway.*"

"*No. I mean where on his body?*"

"*I don't know. He wouldn't listen. I told him to get out. It's his fault he got shot.*"

The more Vega listened, the more the 911 recording filled him with unease. When Vega was in uniform, he regularly responded to 911 calls. The contents—relayed by dispatchers—were nearly always some variation of *Get over here now. Help. Save me. Hurry.* The callers couldn't care less what happened to the people who were hurting them. They never thought to justify their actions. The one time Vega remembered listening to a 911 transmission like this was on one of his first serious child abuse cases. A man called 911 to report that his girlfriend's toddler had "fallen" down the stairs while he was caring for the boy. Vega arrived to find a man more interested in explaining how "naughty" the child was and how he was always "tripping" rather than in whether Vega and the EMTs could save him. They did save the boy, thankfully. But the man eventually confessed to beating the toddler when he wouldn't stop crying.

So what was going on here? The dispatcher's voice came on again.

"Okay, sir. Stay on the line with me. Police will be responding shortly."

"Chingada madre! He's still in the house."

Okay. Here, Luis sounded genuinely upset. He cursed. He gave factual information. Vega believed that whatever was going on, Luis definitely was afraid to have this guy still in his house.

"Can you get someplace safe in the house until police arrive?"

Luis took the phone away from his mouth and shouted in Spanish to someone in the room. The words were garbled. They sounded like . . . but no. That didn't make sense.

Or did it?

"Sir? Sir? Are you still on the line? Police are on the scene."

The dispatcher lost contact with Luis after that. The rest of the radio communication had to do with Vega and the Wickford Police. Vega went back to the beginning and played the tape again. He heard those garbled words more clearly this time:

"Largo de aquí, joto!" *Beat it, faggot!*

Was Luis calling the intruder a homosexual? And if so, did that have something to do with why the man was there in the first place? Was that what Luis was hiding?

Vega left the building, still trying to make sense of this development, when a man stepped out of the front doors of the medical examiner's office and began walking toward the only other car in the lot. He had a shaved head, broad shoulders, a blond walrus mustache, and the distinctive chest-forward walk of an ex-high school linebacker who still played in weekend leagues, albeit with increasing sprains and pulled ligaments. *Dolan.*

Vega stopped in his tracks. "Thanks for returning all my calls, Teddy."

"I've been a little busy trying to save your ass." He took in Vega's bruised face and frowned. "What the hell happened to you?"

"Duran and Wilson didn't tell you?"

"No."

"Huh." Vega figured the two officers would have blabbed to everybody in his department by now. He'd behaved like a bastard to them last night and they'd still covered for him. He owed them big time. "I tripped."

"On what?"

"My good intentions."

"The worst kind." Dolan swept a gaze behind him to the video cameras mounted on the side of the building. "For a former undercover narc, you sure pick lousy meeting spots. The brass sees me here with you, we'll both be stamping pistol permits."

"You're breaking my heart."

"Get in my car at least, will ya?" said Dolan. "If I'm going to talk to you, it's not gonna be out in the open like this."

Vega hopped into the passenger seat of Dolan's un-marked—a late-model gray Toyota Camry. Dolan always managed to draw the better vehicles. Vega started talking as soon as Dolan slid behind the wheel.

"Have you listened to the nine-one-one tape of the shooting?"

Dolan shook his head. "Not yet. The robbery's Wickford's jurisdiction."

"Wickford is Boy Scouts with guns. Listen to it when you get a chance."

Dolan gave Vega a sour look. "I gather you already have."

"That would be against department policy."

"Yes, it would." Dolan played along. "So assuming a *friend* heard it, why is it worth listening to?"

"Because my *friend* thought it didn't sound like Luis was getting robbed. It sounded more like he was having a homosexual encounter that went wrong. And by the way, Luis may have known there were two guys on his property."

"We checked the gay angle," said Dolan. "It didn't pan out—least as far as Luis is concerned."

"Wait." Vega frowned. "Why would you check that angle if you haven't yet heard the nine-one-one tape?"

Dolan fixed his gaze at the windshield and delivered his best hundred-yard stare. "Turns out the phone in our possession didn't belong to Hector Ponce. It belonged to the other man—the one you shot. And a lot of the contacts on it are gay men. But Luis's closest associates assure us he's not gay or bi. We have no evidence to the contrary."

"Hold on a moment, back up," said Vega. "Are you confirming that the man I killed wasn't Hector Ponce?"

"The DNA from Ponce's toothbrush and hairbrush match the body from the Brighton Aqueduct. Dr. Gupta verified the results this morning."

"So who's this other guy? A gay friend of Ponce's? Someone entirely unrelated?"

"Neither," said Dolan. "When Gupta originally ran the DNA from Ponce's hairbrush and toothbrush against the man you shot, some of it was a match."

"What do you mean, 'some of it'?"

"Gupta originally thought the samples had been corrupted," said Dolan. "So she ran the test again. The second batch indicated that the man you shot had the same mitochondrial DNA as the mitochondrial DNA on the hairbrush."

"That's the DNA a person gets from their mother, right?" asked Vega.

"Affirmative."

"So you're saying the man I shot was Hector Ponce's *brother?*" Vega blinked as it sank in. "How come nobody in the Ponce family told the police this?"

"Because they thought he was dead," said Dolan. "Hector Ponce only had one brother, Edgar. He was supposed to have died in the desert twenty years ago."

Chapter 29

Vega pulled out his phone and scrolled to the picture Dolan had texted to him Friday night—the one Edgar Ponce held in his hand when Vega shot him. Vega pointed to the man standing next to Hector Ponce by the fruit stand, the one with the slightly narrower face and soft smile. "This is Edgar? The brother who was supposed to have died in the desert?"

"That's him," said Dolan. "Edgar *Antonio* Ponce-Fernandez. That's where the ID with the name 'Antonio Fernandez' came from, as well as the Atlanta, Georgia, connection. We're just piecing all of this together now. We haven't even notified next of kin yet so you can't talk about this."

"I understand." Vega closed his eyes and tried to wrap his mind around this new development. He hadn't killed Marcela's father. He'd killed her uncle. There were people who loved and cared about him somewhere—in Georgia perhaps. They would never see him again. Changing the name didn't change anything.

"So the family didn't know he was alive?" asked Vega. "I'm assuming Hector knew."

"That's what I'm gathering so far," said Dolan. "It seems the brothers crossed the border together twenty years ago, got separated, and each thought the other was dead. I think in Fernandez's case, he saw no future as a gay man back in Honduras so he decided to stay dead to his family."

"Okay," said Vega slowly. "I get why he might want to disappear if his family was very traditional. But—why resurface now?"

"That's the part we don't know yet," said Dolan. "Fernandez has an ex-partner in Atlanta who told us that he left for New York about three weeks ago to reunite with his brother. But his ex didn't know any more than that."

"So who was Fernandez staying with in New York? Not Hector and his family, I'm assuming. A gay lover? It seems like *somebody* in the Bronx would know."

Dolan's cell phone dinged with a new text. "Stay out of this, Jimmy. You're sounding a bit too interested for my taste."

Dolan checked his text and began tapping out a reply. Vega's mind drifted. *Twenty years. The brothers had been apart for twenty years.* So what sparked their reunion? Some criminal enterprise? Vega the cop suspected as much. But Vega the man wondered if the motive could be something much simpler. Whatever else family was, it was shared recollection.

Vega could understand the hunger for such a thing. He'd felt it himself since his mother's death. He had no brothers or sisters to soften the pain of her passing with stories of their life together, no presence of a father to color in the faint outlines of early childhood. All the rituals of his youth were sealed away inside of him. He was a soda can with a broken pop top. Even Martha, his mother's best friend, couldn't reminisce with him now. Vega wondered if maybe that's why Fernandez and Ponce reconnected. There was too much shared memory not to.

"I've gotta go, Jimmy." Dolan leaned across the empty seat as Vega stepped out of the car. "Hey, when this thing's behind us, come over and have a couple of beers at my house, okay?" He wasn't looking for a response. He was looking for an escape. "In the meantime, try to stay at least twenty feet back from every one of your good intentions."

Vega watched Dolan drive away. He had the day to himself—and he didn't have a clue what to do with it. He couldn't handle being with friends. He wasn't allowed to attend anything public. Adele wasn't speaking to him— and in all likelihood, in a few hours she was going to be speaking *about* him.

Vega felt a queasy sensation in the pit of his stomach that he could only describe as homesickness. He wanted to sit at his mother's kitchen table while she fussed over him, piling too much fried food on his plate, straightening his shoulders, mussing his hair, and complaining that it needed a cut. He wanted to talk in shorthand about people and experiences long in the past. He wanted comfort without expectation and chatter that required no rejoinders.

In short, he wanted to feel like a child again.

He thought about what Ellen Cantor had said about visiting Martha Torres. She was not his mother. She was not even really Martha anymore. But she was the one person who had known him almost as well as his mother. If Vega wanted to start healing himself, he had to go back to a place before the pain began.

He was long overdue.

Chapter 30

The lobby of Sunnycrest Manor had the look and feel of a preschool. There were snowmen cutouts on the windows and glittery handmade stars on the tile walls. The staff wore overly bright smiles and big name tags. But as soon as Vega left the lobby, there was no mistaking it was a nursing home. In the hallways and dayrooms, old people sat about in wheelchairs—some aware of their surroundings and some not. The air was overheated and smelled of canned soup, overcooked vegetables, and the faint but unmistakable odor of urine.

Vega asked at the front desk and again at the nurse's station until he found his way to a double room on the top floor with Martha Torres's name on the door. He hadn't seen Martha since his mother's funeral almost two years ago. She seemed shell-shocked and barely coherent even back then. In the four years before Vega's mother's murder, she'd lost her husband, been diagnosed with early-onset Alzheimer's, and buried her youngest child, Donna. Vega's mother's death must have seemed like the last blow.

He had no idea what he'd find on his visit today.

Martha was sitting alone in a wheelchair by the window. She was wearing baggy bright pink sweatpants and a matching hooded jacket. She'd never been a big woman, but the disease seemed to have compacted her even further.

She inhabited her clothes the way a turtle might a shell—sinking deep into the folds and crevices. Vega inched into the room.

"Doña Martha?" He used the respectful greeting, then added, "It's me, Jimmy. Luisa's son?" He wanted to bend down and kiss her but he didn't know if she'd recognize him anymore and he didn't want to frighten her.

The blue skies of the morning had given way to clouds and a gray light washed across her face. Vega had expected to see fear or confusion but there was a blank sweetness to her features. No raisin ridges on her forehead. No commas by her lips, and only the softest crosshatch of crow's feet by her eyes. It was as if the struggles of the world had slid from her shoulders and left her with only a vague but simple gratitude for the moment. Like Donna. That's how Vega would always remember Freddy's disabled sister.

Martha slowly turned her face from the window. She smiled broadly and spread her arms like a child awaiting a hug. "You came. I knew you would come."

Vega hesitated. He had no idea he'd made such an impression on her all these years or that she'd been anticipating this visit. His mother and Martha were very close, of course. Even after Vega left the neighborhood, he was often dragged back for visits. But still, it surprised him that a woman who couldn't recall what she'd done yesterday could reach across the chasm of years and remember him so fondly.

He bent down and gave her a hug, afraid that he might crush her, but her grip was still surprisingly strong. She wrapped him tightly in her embrace. He caught a whiff of cologne—something vaguely musky that had gone out of fashion the same year men in the neighborhood stopped wearing qiana shirts. He felt a catch in his lungs. He knew that scent. Not from Martha. From his mother.

His mother used to say that she and Martha met over a bag of dropped onions. That was the short version. The long one was more painful. Vega's mother was barely seventeen when she left her tiny mountain village in Puerto Rico to come to New York. She didn't speak a word of English. She was boarding with a stern aunt she barely knew. It was February. She didn't have a good winter coat, boots, or any money to speak of. And nobody in New York had patience for some backwoods *jíbaro*.

One day her aunt sent her to the local bodega to fetch a quart of milk, some onions, and a bag of rice. The milk carton was defective and started to leak. On the way home, the paper bag split. Milk, rice, and onions tumbled onto the slushy pavement. Vega's mother started to cry, certain that her aunt would yell at her (and beat her, Vega suspected though his mother never liked to talk against the family). People passed by without giving Luisa Rosario a second glance. Only Martha stopped. She was twenty-four then—seven years his mother's senior—and fluent in English, having lived in New York since she was thirteen. She not only helped Luisa salvage what she could, she marched her back to the store and harangued the owner into letting his mother have a new bag of rice and quart of milk (though Luisa always suspected Martha had ended up paying for it.) The two became fast friends after that. Their friendship never wavered for almost forty-five years.

"Come. Sit down." Martha patted the bed next to her. She grasped Vega's hand in her own. Her palms were as soft as a baby's skin. Her bob of steel wool hair had been pinned back from her face. "We must talk. We *need* to talk."

Her urgency surprised Vega. He took a seat on the bed. The room was hot. He stripped off his jacket and placed it beside him.

"What would you like to talk about?"

"We need Donna here first," she said. "Is Donna in the kitchen?"

Vega started to panic. He'd never been good with peo-

ple who suffered from cognitive issues. Even as a cop. He
wanted to do the right thing but he was never sure what
that was. Did he play along? Did he tell Martha the truth
that her daughter had died in a fall from their apartment
window more than two years ago? He had no idea what
the playbook for this sort of thing was. Clearly, some part
of Martha's brain still believed Donna was alive. Vega didn't
want to be the one to break it to her all over again.

"We can talk without Donna," Vega offered. Martha
nodded, appeased for the moment. He felt relieved.

She leaned forward as if someone might overhear them.
"I know Donna can be difficult." Martha patted Vega's
knee. "But you must not be angry with her. She doesn't
understand."

"I always liked Donna," Vega insisted. "I used to give
her candy when we were kids, remember?"

"You and Jackie always used to steal it from her."

Vega stared at Martha, stunned. It wasn't true! Bad
enough that he had to deal with some witness telling the
world that he'd shot an unarmed suspect point-blank. But
now, his mother's oldest friend was accusing him of stealing candy from a little girl with Down syndrome?

Vega went to defend himself. Martha shook a finger at
him. "You know what you did, yes? So does Luisa. That's
why she wants to talk to you."

Martha had told his mother this? Vega was dumb-
founded.

"I don't know what you're remembering. But I swear, I
always tried to be nice to Donna."

Martha's voice quaked. She was growing more agitated.
"You need to say you're sorry. You need to get your head
right with God."

Ay, caray! This was not going well. Martha couldn't
know about the shooting. And yet she was talking like she
did. "Okay. I'm sorry," said Vega. He was sorry for so many
things, he couldn't even choose between them anymore.

"Where is your sister? Where is she?"

"My *sister?* Donna's not—" And then it hit him. Martha was confusing Vega with Freddy. She had no idea who he was.

He grasped what was happening, but it saddened him all the same. He wanted so much for Martha to remember him—or at least, to remember his mother. He noticed a photo album on a shelf above the television. He walked over and pointed to it.

"May I look through this album?"

Martha's face had gone blank again. She smiled at Vega as if he'd just walked into the room for the first time, like there was a reset button in her head and it had just gone back to "start."

Vega pulled out the album and sat down next to Martha. He slowly turned the pages. The laminated inserts crackled like a cheap shower curtain. Inside were the usual yellowed assortment of communion shots, weddings, christenings, and holiday celebrations, the gray concrete symmetry of the Bronx contrasting sharply with the verdant chaotic hillsides of Puerto Rico. Some of the people in the pictures Vega recognized. Some, he didn't. He picked out Martha as a young schoolteacher. He saw her brutish husband grimacing for the camera. Other pictures showed sweet Donna who never seemed to age, Freddy with his sober, serious expression, and Jackie who, even then, looked like she wanted to be somewhere else.

Vega turned a page and ran his hand over a picture of his mother, looking firm-faced and impossibly young in a bright red dress. She was posed in front of a Christmas tree with a trim, good-looking, dark-skinned man. Vega's father, Orlando. Vega was a toddler, flopped on his father's shoulders, looking sleepy-eyed like he couldn't wait to be poured into bed. Vega went to turn the page. Martha grabbed his hand to stop him. Something flashed across her face.

"I remember the onions," she whispered. "I remember. She cried when she dropped them in the snow."

Vega straightened. He stared at Martha. Her face, so blank a minute ago, flooded with light, like a piece of stained glass lit from behind. She knew who Vega was. She knew who his mother was. He swallowed back the dizzying sensation. The scent of her musk cologne. The picture of his mother in that red dress. The memory of those dropped onions. For one tiny moment, everything in the world was right again. His mother was here. With them. In this room. *Alive.*

"That's how you and Luisa met," Vega said softly. He squeezed her hand. "You remember, Doña Martha. You remember."

Martha's soft cheeks suddenly grew taut. Her mouth pressed in. "Luisa is dead." Her eyes registered the moment like it had just happened.

Vega nodded. "Yes. But she is still alive in us."

Martha dropped Vega's hand. She looked suddenly distressed. "It was terrible. So terrible. She cared about him. How could he do that?"

"Doña Martha, do you know who killed my mother?"

"She trusted him. We all trusted him!"

Vega thought about that love note he'd found in Spanish at his mother's grave. *My beloved. You are always my angel.* Martha would have known who her mother's lover was. They were too close not to have shared that. Could this be the man who killed her?

The room felt hot and close. In the hallway, two orderlies rolled a heavy cart across the linoleum floor and discussed the Jets' loss against the Dolphins. Vega felt like he was walking on a carpet of spun glass. Her memory was so fragile. The slightest misstep could fracture it.

"Doña Martha, if you know who killed Luisa, please tell me," said Vega. "She called you three hours before she died. Please try to remember. Anything at all. I beg you."

Martha drew back from him. She looked frightened by his intensity. He'd come on too strong. He tried to scale it back.

"It's okay," Vega murmured. "Take your time. We can work through this slowly." But already he felt something slipping from his grasp. The fade on a movie screen. Some synapse deep inside her brain had snapped again. On the other side of those neurons were forty-five years of memories with his mother that Vega wanted to connect to—none more desperately than those very last ones before she died. But they were already floating out to sea, a blurry point on the horizon.

A nurse's aide appeared in the doorway, a young black woman with a chirpy Caribbean accent. "Mrs. Torres?" she said brightly. "It's time for your shower."

Vega turned his back on the aide and tried to get Martha's attention. Her gaze had shifted to the window.

"It's like that sometimes, I'm afraid," said the nurse's aide. "They're so alert one minute and the next, it just vanishes."

"Will it come back?"

"Possibly. But when and where, no one knows."

"Is she lucid like that a lot?"

"She doesn't get many visitors so it's hard to say. Her priest comes to visit regularly."

"Father Delgado?"

"That's him. He sees a lot of the old people here."

Vega rose from the edge of Martha's bed. He kissed her on top of her head. She didn't respond.

"See you soon, Doña Martha." She didn't look like she'd even heard. The lines had smoothed out on her face. She was at peace again.

Even if he wasn't.

Chapter 31

Marcela felt shaky and queasy as she moved away from the warmth of Byron's body and sat up on the edge of their bed. Damon was asleep on a cot in the corner, his little arms wrapped around his stuffed dog. A Metro North train rattled past, shaking the window frames. Damon barely stirred. His mouth was open, his eyelids fluttering from a dream. A good dream? Or a bad one? She hoped he was too young to process the last two days. She hoped by the time he was old enough to understand, the heartache and fear would be behind him—behind them all.

I lost you and found you and then lost you again, Papi.... Marcela grieved this second death almost worse than the first. It had felt like a miracle to hear her father's voice on the other end of her cell phone yesterday afternoon and to know he was alive. True, he was on the run and in a lot of trouble. But he'd devised a plan to get them out of this $8,000 debt, a plan that wouldn't require any money at all. It gave Marcela hope. And then within hours, he was gone—truly gone—and she had no idea if it had to do with the money he'd borrowed, the DVD he'd asked her to retrieve from his apartment, or the worries he harbored in those final dark hours of his life.

Marcela broke down and told Byron everything last

night. About the borrowed money, about the phone calls and threats if they didn't pay it back. She even showed him the DVD her father was convinced they could trade in place of the $8,000 for Yovanna's life. She and Byron played the DVD on the old laptop computer Señora Adele had passed along to Marcela after Damon was born. They fast-forwarded through several hours of time-stamped security footage of people coming and going from her father's apartment building. Men. Women. Teenagers. Old people. Some were carrying shopping bags and knapsacks. Some carried nothing at all. Since the camera was positioned high above the front doorway, most of what Marcela and Byron saw were hair and hats—all of it through a fish-eye lens. All of the people looked so ordinary; Marcela had no idea why this video would be worth so much to anyone.

Her father's desperation told her otherwise. "When you get it, call me right away," he'd told her yesterday. But when she called, his phone went to voice mail. She was now left wondering if this little silver disc could have saved him or whether the knowledge of it spelled his undoing.

Byron was furious that Marcela had held so much back from him.

"All of this misery happened because you brought your daughter here!" he shouted. "If she had stayed in Honduras, our family would be safe now! Your father would still be alive!"

Marcela started to cry. "If I could take it back, I would!" How could she say such a thing? With Yovanna in the next room? Maybe Damon was asleep, but Yovanna most certainly was not.

"If the gangster your father borrowed money from wants this video," said Byron, "it's because it shows a crime. If your father knew about it, then he was a witness. Maybe that's why he's dead. Just having this DVD in our apartment is dangerous. I don't want it here!"

"But nothing happens on the camera," Marcela argued. "People are just walking in and out of the building."

"Then it wouldn't be worth eight thousand dollars—maybe even your father's life. But it is, Marcela. We should destroy it or we will be next."

"And if we destroy it, what do we have to repay the loan?"

"Maybe we should take the video to the police," he suggested.

"The police don't care about us," said Marcela. "If we show them this video, they'll just take it and tell us to lock our doors. They'll only show up after somebody is hurt or dead to fill out the paperwork."

Around and around they went until they were both so spent, Marcela coaxed her half-asleep daughter onto her living room cot and they all went to bed.

Now, in the dim morning light behind the lank, drawn curtains, Marcela threw back the covers on her side of the bed. It was stifling in the small room. The old radiators always sent out too much steam in winter. Still, she felt a sudden chill. She grabbed her robe and shifted her weight to get out of bed. The movement of her body made Byron stir. He rubbed his eyes and sat up. They stared at each other a moment, hesitant to speak in case they woke up Damon sleeping in the corner or Yovanna in the living room.

"Let me start breakfast," said Marcela. "After church, we'll figure out what to do."

In the living room, a slash of light angled its way through a broken slat in the blinds, illuminating the silver garland on the artificial tree in the corner. It shimmered with false promise. Their first Christmas together as a family. How long Marcela had dreamed of this! How hard it had turned out to be.

Marcela's eyes moved from the draped garland on the

tree to the cot wedged up against it. Yovanna's cot. The sheet and blanket were pulled back. The pillow was plumped.

There was no Yovanna.

Marcela stepped closer. The clear plastic two-drawer bin where Yovanna kept her clothes was empty. She opened the drawers even though she could see that there was nothing inside. She walked over to the front door. Her daughter's blue backpack was missing from its hook along with Yovanna's pink windbreaker. Her sneakers were absent from the mat.

Marcela wandered the room as if Yovanna were simply hiding in plain sight. Maybe she'd gone out for something. Maybe she'd left a note. Marcela rounded the counter into the kitchen. The only sounds were the tap-tap-tap from the leaky faucet and the soft hum of the refrigerator. On the kitchen table, the manila envelope Marcela had taken from her father's apartment lay open, a jumble of her childhood snapshots on top.

The DVD was missing.

Marcela walked back into the living room and opened the laptop. She pushed the eject button on the DVD slot. It was empty. She began opening drawers and cabinets. She felt under the couch cushions and beneath her daughter's cot. She searched the shelf above the television. The DVD wasn't in the apartment.

Yovanna was gone, along with the one thing that could save them all. Or kill them all.

Marcela wasn't sure which.

Chapter 32

Adele could hear the thump of rap and salsa beneath her feet as she walked the corridor of the Methodist church. The church's basement housed a teen center that appeared to be in full swing on a Sunday evening. But here, along the classroom corridor, all was quiet save for the sound of a cardboard carton sliding along a tile floor and the scrape of canned goods being loaded onto shelves.

Adele peeked her head into the classroom that now served as the Lake Holly Food Pantry. Margaret Behring was standing in the middle of the room, clipboard in hand, surrounded by three-foot-high piles of mostly empty cardboard cartons. She was dressed in jeans and a sweatshirt, but there was something different about her. Maybe it was the loose gathering of her honey blond hair. Or the fact that she wasn't wearing any makeup or jewelry. She looked younger somehow. Perhaps she'd just had a round of Botox. Half the women in Wickford had their dermatologists on their speed dials.

Adele rapped a knuckle on the doorframe so as not to startle her.

"Margaret?"

Margaret put down her clipboard and turned to the doorway. Her blue eyes looked flat and slightly wary. Adele noted again that there was something different about her.

Behind her was a table full of canned corn and carrots. She was checking expiration dates before she loaded them onto the pantry shelves. She flicked her eyes at the flash of red dress beneath Adele's black wool coat.

"Going out I see."

"Out would be good," said Adele. "This is more like presiding over a funeral." Adele threw her black leather clutch on a table next to the canned carrots. "I have to deliver a speech tonight to a coalition of immigrant groups. And when it's over, somebody's career is going to be over, too. Either mine or Detective Vega's."

"I see." Margaret grabbed a can of corn and studied an ink stamp on the top. She held it out to Adele. "Do you see an expiration date on this? The stamp doesn't seem to correspond to anything."

Adele fished a pair of glasses out of her clutch to check the tiny print. "That's not a sell-by date," said Adele. "I think it's safe to give to clients." She handed the corn back to Margaret. That's when it hit her.

"You're not wearing glasses." Adele had never seen Margaret without her wire-framed glasses. "Did you just get contacts?"

"I was never any good with contacts," said Margaret. "I had LASIK surgery about a month ago. For the first time since first grade, I don't have to have a piece of glass between me and the world."

"So you didn't need glasses on Friday night, I take it?"

"I can see perfectly without them now."

Great, thought Adele. Vega not only shot and killed a man in front of a witness, he picked one with twenty-twenty vision.

Margaret turned her back to Adele and began stacking the cans on a shelf. There was an uncomfortable silence between them, punctuated by the bass thump of music and teenagers' voices below. Adele got the sense Margaret had offered up this meeting and then instantly regretted it.

"I spoke to my attorney again, Adele. I don't see how anything I say to you is going to be helpful to either of us."

"We won't know if you don't tell me." Adele grabbed a can of carrots off a shelf and studied the label. Some off-brand with a wholesome picture on the front that bore no resemblance to the mushy contents inside. "I lived off this stuff when I was a kid. To this day, I can't eat anything canned."

Margaret stopped stacking and turned to her. "Your family shopped—*here?*"

"There was a place in Port Carroll where I grew up," said Adele. "Not this nice. Or maybe it was just the times. I remember it stank of cheddar cheese."

"I'm sorry."

"Don't be," said Adele. "I don't mention it for the most part. It's not something I like to dwell on." Even now, some thirty years later, Adele could still see the pain in her mother's face when she had to line up in front of that warehouse by the library for stale bread, hunks of cheese gone hard and white around the edges, and nearly expired cans of vegetables.

"Your parents lost their jobs?"

"My parents worked every day of their lives," said Adele. "They were teachers in Ecuador. Here, they cleaned office buildings. But they dreamed of something better. So they started a business. Sort of like a FedEx store for immigrants. Wire transfers. Courier services. Phone lines in the era before cell phones. That sort of thing."

"And it failed?"

"No. It was a huge success. So much so that their neighbor stole it from them."

"You're kidding," said Margaret. "Couldn't they file a police report or something?"

"The neighbor was the business owner on paper. On account of the fact that she was here legally and my parents weren't. End of story as far as the police were concerned."

Adele still burned with the memory of her father trying to file a theft report—and the police laughing at him.

"There was nothing my parents could do," she explained. "When you don't have papers, you don't count and neither does anything you try to accomplish. My parents lost all their savings. After that, we had to make choices. If my sister or I got sick, a doctor's visit meant my father couldn't afford bus fare for the week and had to walk three miles to work. A school trip to the museum meant a week of no lunches for my mother. People used to heckle us when we visited the pantry. They'd shout 'Learn English' or 'Get a job.' My parents did everything they could to build a better life for our family. And in one fell swoop, it was gone."

Margaret leaned against the table and studied Adele for a moment. "Is that going to happen tonight?" she asked softly.

Adele felt embarrassed. She didn't want this woman's pity. "I'm not my parents," she said stiffly. "And Detective Vega's a big boy, too. We'll survive. I'd just prefer to know the truth, that's all."

Margaret exhaled. She seemed too spent to argue anymore. She grabbed one of the empty cardboard cartons and began ripping it apart and flattening it for recycling as she talked.

"I was getting my three-year-old out of the bath around six-thirty," Margaret began. "My son's bathroom window overlooks our side yard. I looked out and saw two men standing on the edge of a pool of floodlight in the woods adjoining our yard. They were standing right next to each other."

"Can you describe them?"

"One was wearing a dark puffy coat and the other was wearing a smooth nylon one that was also dark in color. They both appeared to be Hispanic, at least from my vantage point. I dried off Tyler, picked up the phone, and dialed nine-one-one. The dispatcher told me the police were already on the scene. Right after that I heard gunshots and looked out the window. The man in the puffy jacket was lying on the ground and the other man was backing away."

"Wait," said Adele. "So you didn't actually *see* Detective Vega shoot Hector Ponce?"

"Adele—I saw them standing very close together and thirty seconds later, I heard gunshots and saw one man down and the other backing away. What does that sound like to you?"

Adele paced the scuffed beige floor. She stared at the colorful posters on the walls showing kids scarfing down fruits and vegetables she had to bribe Sophia to eat.

"I don't understand," asked Adele. "Why was there even a floodlight in the woods?"

"The floodlight is ours," said Margaret. "Last weekend, some professional installers put up Christmas lights on our house and garage. In the process, they knocked a lot of our floodlights out of alignment. One of them accidentally got aimed into the woods."

"So you looked out. You saw two men standing together. How do you know one of them was Detective Vega?"

"I don't," said Margaret. "But there were no other people in the woods. So what I saw corresponds to your detective friend and that Chez Martine dishwasher."

Adele bristled that Margaret had chosen to refer to Vega and Ponce by their jobs, not their names. They weren't people to Margaret. They were occupations.

"The dispatcher told you the police had arrived," Adele noted. "But you didn't see flashing lights?"

"Not from my vantage point. I suppose they were there," said Margaret. "They may have been closer to the bottom of the hill. The trees are very thick, even this time of year."

Margaret stacked the flattened cartons up against the wall. She was finished for the evening. She looked anxious to leave. "Look, Adele, I'd love to tell you something that would make you feel better. But I can't lie about what I saw."

"I know that. I'm not asking you to."

They shut off the lights. Margaret locked the pantry doors. Evening had fallen by the time they returned to the parking lot. Margaret cupped a hand over her eyes.

"Ever since I had the LASIK surgery, everything is so much brighter at night! It's quite amazing."

"Mmm." Adele couldn't care less about the wonders of LASIK surgery. She was more concerned about the weather. The sky had a thick wash of clouds across it. Snow was in the forecast. She hoped it would just be a few flurries. She didn't want to have to deal with a winter storm tonight on top of everything else.

Adele walked Margaret over to her Land Rover. A car sat idling in front of her own Prius. Its headlights were on and rap music thumped from inside the closed windows. *Teenagers.*

"I'm sorry to keep coming back to this," said Adele. "But you didn't actually *see* Detective Vega shoot Hector Ponce, did you?"

"Look, Adele—even if I were standing right next to them, I'm pretty sure I wouldn't *see* the bullet."

"No," Adele agreed. "But there's a difference between seeing something and *assuming* you saw it."

"If you saw two men standing next to each other and seconds later, one was lying on the ground and the other was backing away, what would *you* assume?"

"I guess you're right," said Adele. Margaret beeped her electronic key and unlocked her door. Adele thanked her for her time and walked back toward her Prius. She knocked on the window of the Hyundai sedan idling right in front of it. A young man powered it down.

"Can you move forward?" asked Adele. "You're blocking my car."

"Sorry. No problem."

Adele straightened and went to back away from the young man's vehicle. Out of the corner of her eye, she caught a set of chest-high headlights barreling toward her. *Right* toward her.

"Stop!" Adele waved her arms frantically.

The headlights grew larger. A strangled cry squeezed out of her throat. Or was that coming from the teenagers inside the car? She couldn't tell. Her limbs turned to Jell-O. Her heart stuttered like a windup toy. A cold wave of sweat flooded every pore in her body.

Brakes screeched. Tires squealed. The Land Rover jolted to a stop just inches from Adele's body, close enough that she could smell the faint burn of rubber and hear loose bags slamming against one another in the trunk of the vehicle. Had the snow already started—had there been even the faintest coating of sleet on the pavement—Adele would no longer be standing.

The door of the Land Rover flung open. Margaret Behring raced over to Adele. Even under the hazy lights of the parking lot, Adele could see that the woman's face had drained of color. There was a glaze of sweat on her upper lip.

"Oh my God! Are you okay?"

"Mmm." Adele had forgotten how to speak. She was just relearning how to breathe.

"I'm so sorry!" she kept repeating. Her voice sounded choked, as if she were about to cry. "The lights—they're so bright. I didn't see you. I just didn't see!"

The two women stared at each other, their short panicked breaths clouding the night air. Adele held Margaret's gaze. When she answered, her voice was calm and steely, and strangely self-assured.

"I know."

Chapter 33

Vega hustled up the brick steps and through the heavy wooden doors of St. Raymond's Catholic Church. Incense and lemon oil wafted over him. He hadn't planned on being back here so soon. But he couldn't leave the Bronx without trying to make sense of his visit with Martha Torres today.

A late-day Spanish Mass was just ending and parishioners were streaming out of the church. Father Delgado had a long line of people waiting to speak to him after the service. Vega sat in a rear pew and watched them, wishing he could feel what they felt in this place, wishing it could give him the solace it seemed to give them. He took out his cell phone and scrolled to that picture of the two brothers and Ponce's son at that fruit stand. He touched a finger to the soft, shy face of the man once known as Edgar and now, as Antonio. He'd looked at this picture so often, he felt like he knew them all.

"Perhaps if you offer a prayer," said a voice behind him in Spanish. "A prayer always helps."

Vega lifted his gaze. Standing over him was the grizzled, leathery face of the old janitor he'd seen sweeping the pews here the other day. The man was dressed in a white shirt and dark slacks today. His gray hair was freshly washed and still sported wet grooves from where a comb had raked through it.

"Father Delgado told me you were Hector's friend," Vega said to the old man in Spanish.

"Yes."

Vega slipped his phone into his pocket. "I'm sorry for your loss."

"Thank you." The man nodded to the pew. "May I?"

"Of course." Vega scooted over.

The man bent with effort and crossed himself. He sat next to Vega and pulled down the kneeling bench. "Are you a Catholic?" he asked.

"A long time ago," Vega admitted.

"But you know the prayers, yes?"

"I know the usual stuff: Ave Marias, the Lord's Prayer."

"I think an Ave Maria would be nice." The man knelt on the bench. His shiny black patent leather shoes squeaked. Vega sensed he wore them rarely and had never broken them in. Vega felt awkward following the old janitor's lead and just as awkward not to. So he lowered himself beside the man, clasped his hands together, and followed along in whispered prayer the Spanish words he'd known so well as a child. His voice caught on the familiar line: *Ruega por nosotros pecadores—Pray for us sinners.* He needed those prayers himself now.

Vega and the janitor sat on the bench after that in a moment of silent communion. All around them people poured out of the church. A few old ladies in black stayed up front, mumbling prayers to their rosary beads, their silhouettes framed by the light of rows of flickering candles beneath jewel-colored glass.

"I don't even know your name," Vega apologized.

"Humberto Oliva," said the man. He extended a large hand. Vega shook it. His palms felt like old burlap but his grip was firm. "I know yours, of course."

They sat in silence while parishioners drifted past. Vega

kept his eyes on Father Delgado up front. He was anxious to talk to him. "Does the Father have any Masses after this?"

"No. Usually after this he makes the rounds of some of the faithful who cannot get to church."

"If you'll please excuse me then, I need to ask him something." Vega started to rise.

"About Hector's brother, yes?"

Vega sank back down onto the hard wooden bench. "So you know?"

"That he is dead? Yes. I spoke to Alma this morning."

"Did Hector ever mention him to you?"

"He didn't know Edgar had survived until about a month ago. That's when he told me. We were both so happy."

"Why both of you?"

Oliva stared at his squeaky shoes. "That picture. On your phone? It's the one I saw on the news, yes?"

Vega pulled his phone out of his pocket again and brought up the picture of the two brothers and Hector's son on the screen. "This one, you mean?"

"It was taken in Guatemala," said Oliva. "Near the border to Honduras. In a place called El Floridio."

"Hector told you that?"

"No." Oliva pointed a thick stubby finger to his white shirt. "*I* took that picture. I was with them on that journey. That is how I know Edgar."

Vega felt as if someone had wrung all the air out of him. "You crossed the desert with them?"

Oliva's dark eyes held Vega's. "Yes." Then he faced forward and laced his thick-knuckled hands on the pew in front of him. His voice took on a soft trancelike quality. The noise and people in the cavernous interior fell away and Vega found himself transfixed by the man's words.

"I met the two brothers and Hector's son on the journey from Honduras. By the time we reached northern Mexico, some of the Hondurans in our group had gotten sick or hurt or caught by the Mexican police and deported back. There were only twelve of us left," Oliva said slowly. "Nine men. Three teenage boys. Near the border, we were handed off to a coyote who was supposed to guide us across the desert and into the United States. He was no older than the boys."

Oliva's voice was measured and even, almost devoid of emotion. He barely moved when he spoke, except to lick his chapped lips. "We each carried three plastic gallon jugs of water and some tins of sardines. The water was heavy and hard to carry but it was enough to last us for three days." Oliva held up three cracked and callused fingers. "That's what we were told the journey from Mexico to Arizona would take." He said the last words like a small child who still believed that saying something would make it true.

Oliva stared straight ahead. His voice turned husky and barely rose above a whisper. "On the second day, we ran out of food. On the third day, we ran out of water. On the fourth, we drank our own urine. We were lost. The coyote told us to give him all our money so he could buy water and get help. We never saw him again."

"He abandoned you?" asked Vega.

"Yes. After that, some became too weak to travel. The group began to split up. Hector's son, Miguel, got bitten by a scorpion. Hector had to walk much slower for the boy's sake. I was by myself. I had to keep going. My family in Honduras was depending on me."

"How did you know where you were going?"

Oliva pointed to the vaulted ceiling of the church where a fresco of saints acted out their own life-and-death dramas. "I followed the North Star at night. That was all I could do. My nose bled. My tongue swelled. My skin felt like it was on fire. On the fourth day, I spoke to the mountains." He closed his eyes. "On the fifth, they answered back."

Vega felt stung by the enormity of such suffering—the sheer loneliness of it. To die in the desert is to die twice. Once in the body. Once in the soul.

"The doctors told me that when two good Samaritans found me by an Arizona roadside, I had only hours to live," said Oliva. "At the time, I believed I was the only one of the twelve to survive."

"You didn't know that Hector and Antonio—um, Edgar—had survived?"

Oliva shook his head. "How could I know? We did not travel under our real names. We could not draw attention to ourselves or our situation once we were here. I didn't even know the name of the coyote who abandoned us. We called him *"Chacho"* because he had this little bit of facial hair beneath his chin. He was so young, I think that's all he could grow, even after we were out there several days."

"How did you find out Hector was alive?"

"Years later, when I lived in Queens, I met Father Delgado and told him my story. That's when he introduced me to Hector. I moved up to the Bronx and began to work at the church. Neither of us knew that Edgar had survived. Not until Edgar contacted Hector through a cousin's Facebook page."

Oliva brushed a hand along the beveled edge of the pew in front of him. "You need to understand," he said slowly. "Edgar wasn't trying to be hurtful when he disappeared from his family. He was just living a very different life than they would have been comfortable with."

Vega nodded. "They wouldn't have accepted his homosexuality?"

"Probably not," said Oliva. "At least not then. This was twenty years ago."

"So what made him come forward now?"

"Edgar saw the book."

"The book?"

Oliva rose. "Come. I will show you."

Oliva ushered Vega out of the nave and into the hallway that connected the church to the rectory. They walked past Delgado's office until Oliva came to a small janitor's closet full of mops and brooms and cleaning supplies. Oliva felt around on a shelf for something.

"This is why Edgar contacted Hector."

Oliva pulled a book from the shelf and handed it to Vega.

"*Song of My Heart?* A celebrity memoir? Why would Edgar care?"

Oliva took the book from Vega's hands and thumbed through the well of pictures. "Look."

Oliva pointed to a faded photograph of a young Luis in a hoodie and loose jeans. He was standing next to a graffiti-covered wall and talking to several Latino men, some of them old enough to be his father. Luis's nose was broader than it was now. His cheekbones were less defined. Even his body was different back then. He had a teenager's narrow and undefined torso. He was ropy from lack of food, not physical conditioning. His squint however, carried the same dazzling self-assurance he could still summon on a dime.

But it wasn't Luis's appearance that caused Vega to rear back. It was the man in the center of the group that Luis was talking to. A man with a soft chin and shy smile.

Vega lifted his gaze from the picture and stared at Oliva. He felt his lips forming around a question too terrible to contemplate. But he already knew the answer. There was only one way that Jesús Ricardo Luis Alvarez-Da Silva, a Mexican from the northern state of Sonora, could have ended up in the same photograph with Edgar Antonio Ponce-Fernandez, a Honduran trying to cross the border. Luis was "Chacho," the teenage coyote who had gotten those men lost in the desert and then abandoned them twenty years ago. Luis was responsible for the deaths of six men and three teenage boys, including Hector's sixteen-year-old son, Miguel.

"So that's why Edgar and Hector went to Luis's house. They *knew*."

Oliva nodded. "Once Edgar saw the book, he was consumed with revenge. He wanted to find a way to get even with Luis. It was different for Hector. For him, it was all about Miguel. He never forgave himself for what had happened to his son. He thought the only way to find peace would be if he could make things up to his daughter, maybe by bringing his granddaughter here. So Hector and Edgar asked Luis for money. A few weeks ago. And he paid. But then . . ." Oliva's voice trailed off. He looked suddenly embarrassed.

"But what?"

"I think maybe they got greedy. Maybe Hector gambled the first money. I don't know. He changed after that. They both did. The money seemed to make things worse. It was like, no amount of money could ever be enough. They went back a second time. That's when all the bad stuff happened."

"And you? You went with them?"

"No." Oliva waved his hands in front of him. "I told them that what they were doing would not bring them peace. Only God can do that. They wouldn't listen. That journey—it took so much from me. My health. My dignity." He took a deep breath. "And now, my friend and his brother."

"Huh." Vega stared at the book. "Why didn't you come forward after the shooting?"

"I didn't want to get my friends in trouble. I am talking to you now because now they are both dead. Nothing can hurt them anymore."

"You'll still need to make a formal statement to police."

"No." Oliva shook his head. "I told you what I know. I

gave you Edgar's book. I will not speak publicly against Luis."

"But why?" Vega frowned. "Luis murdered all those people. He nearly killed you. Doesn't it bother you that he's beloved by the world and yet he did this terrible thing?"

"God will judge him. I will not," said Oliva. "I gave my life over to God in that desert. You do what you need to do, Detective. But I am an old man. I have no stomach to fight anymore."

"We will need to speak more about this."

Oliva seesawed his head. "Father Delgado will leave if you don't hurry."

Vega could see that he wasn't going to get any more from the old janitor today. He tucked the book under his arm and headed back into the nave.

"You should light a candle for your mother while you are here," Oliva called after him. "It was her birthday yesterday, no?"

Vega stopped in his tracks and turned to Oliva. "How would *you* know it was her birthday yesterday? Do you memorize the birthdays of all the parishioners at St. Raymond's?"

"No. I remembered because I saw the flowers Father Delgado bought for her grave."

Chapter 34

Father Delgado had already left the church. Vega spotted the priest half a block ahead on the sidewalk. He could be headed in any direction. To a parishioner's apartment. To the hospital. To a nursing home. Vega had to sprint before he lost him completely. He shoved Luis's book inside his jacket. It was a softcover, thankfully. But it was still awkward to carry while running.

"Father Delgado!" Vega called out breathlessly.

The priest turned, his bushy silver eyebrows raised in surprise. He waited for Vega to catch up to him. "You came to Mass?"

"I came to see you. Vega huffed. "I'd be lying if I said I came for the Mass." His eyes settled on Delgado's for an extra beat. "I visited Martha Torres this morning. At Sunnycrest."

"I'm glad to hear that. Your mother would have been pleased."

"I think so, too. But not for the same reasons." Vega caught his breath. The cold air felt like crushed glass in his lungs. He spoke the Spanish words before he could attach to them their full meaning:

"Eres siempre mi ángel."

Vega noticed a twitch in the folds beneath Delgado's right eye. Vega waited.

Silence. Delgado stood very still. The gentle smile was gone.

"Do you recognize those words?" asked Vega.

Delgado met his gaze. The priest's deep-set eyes looked more sunken than thoughtful. He'd always looked much younger than his nearly seventy years. Suddenly, with his white hair and shapeless black coat, he seemed thin and frail and not long for this world.

"Jimmy." He exhaled the word. "Why are you asking me this?"

"I think you know." Vega's voice felt as frozen as the tips of his ears. "Tell me, are those the words of a priest to one of his parishioners?"

Delgado put a hand on Vega's arm. "Maybe we should discuss this back in my office."

Vega shook his arm away. "No! I want to know now! Were you in love with my mother? Did you kill her?"

"*Dios mío*, Jimmy! I would never hurt your mother! Never!"

"Martha Torres was lucid enough this afternoon to make me believe the person who killed my mother was someone she and my mother trusted," said Vega. "*You* were at the apartment when the police arrived. *You* were covered in my mother's blood. Ponce was covering up for somebody. That, I'm sure of. And that somebody was *you*."

They were near the entrance to the D-line subway. Delgado gestured to the stairs. "Please, Jimmy. If you won't come back to the church, then let's at least not have this conversation on the street."

Vega reluctantly followed Delgado down the steps into the subway tunnel. Stale, humid air rose to greet them, along with the vague scent of urine and fast food. On a Sunday afternoon, it was empty save for a homeless man in a shabby coat curled up sleeping beneath an advertisement for mattresses. Vega's and Delgado's steps echoed on the concrete. Delgado's thick white hair looked as washed-out as a blank sheet of paper. His eyes had lost their sparkle.

"I did not kill your mother, Jimmy. I tried to save her life. I gave her CPR."

Vega looked at him sharply. "You gave her more than that."

"Yes." Delgado exhaled. "I did." He leaned against the grimy white tile wall of the station. He looked almost too feeble to stand. "I should have come forward a long time ago. I know that. I was weak and in my weakness, I caused a greater sin." The old priest's eyes turned watery when he met Vega's. "She was the love of my life. But as God is my witness, I never once hurt her."

"How long was this relationship between the two of you going on?"

"A long time." Delgado closed his eyes. "I wanted to leave the priesthood over it at one point but she urged me to return to my vows. She believed this was what God had called me to do. She said if I left, I would always feel diminished in some way and she didn't want that. So we kept our relationship platonic after that. But I never stopped loving her on an emotional level. Or spending time with her." Delgado held Vega's gaze. "Including on the day she died."

"So how am I supposed to believe you didn't kill her?"

"I was at a benefit dinner at the Holy Name Society when she died, Jimmy. A dozen priests saw me there. The police checked it out."

Vega paced the grimy concrete. He wanted to haul off and hit the old priest for holding back all these years and maybe costing him a lead in her murder. "Ponce waited seventeen minutes before dialing nine-one-one," said Vega. "Plus, he called you first. Why?"

"I really don't know," said Delgado. "I still think he panicked. But maybe it also had to do with the Chinese food."

"The takeout food? That the police found on her dining table?"

"I bought it for your mother. She loved spareribs. Since I had a dinner engagement, I couldn't stay."

"So the missing receipt? The menu—?"

"Would have traced back to me."

"That's why you got rid of them."

"No." Delgado shook his head. "I would never do that. But maybe Hector did. He was not blind to what was going on between your mother and me. He saw me in the building all the time. I think he was trying to save me the embarrassment of the situation—save your mother as well. She wouldn't have wanted it to come out, either."

"He did more than destroy a receipt and menu for you," said Vega.

"What do you mean?"

"He used those seventeen minutes before you arrived to disconnect the security camera in the front lobby and swap the recorded DVD for a blank one."

"I didn't ask him to do that! I never asked for any of this!"

"But you didn't come forward, either," Vega noted.

Delgado was silent.

"The DVD would have had footage of you entering the lobby with Chinese food," said Vega. "The police would have been able to put you in my mother's apartment—"

"And shown me *leaving* before her murder as well."

"Well, there was somebody on that DVD who *wasn't* innocent. And now we'll never know who."

They were both silent for a moment. Vega collapsed against the wall beside Delgado. He felt drained. A train rumbled into the station. There was a push of warm, fetid air, then a strong vibration and then a screech of brakes like two cats in a standoff. It felt like the perfect soundtrack to his derailed life.

"So that's it?" Vega asked as the train left the station.

He pushed himself off the wall and faced the old priest. "This murderer walks because of a DVD Ponce probably destroyed almost two years ago? Because you couldn't man up about what you'd done? At least I'm facing *my* mistakes."

"You're right, Jimmy." Delgado patted his shoulder. "I've confessed and repented my actions many times. And I'd gladly come forward now. But without this DVD you think existed—I don't think anyone would be very interested in what I had to say."

"When did you leave her that night?"

"At around six. I brought the food but she wasn't hungry then. She said she'd have it later."

"Was she expecting anyone?"

"No. She had no plans, as I recall."

"Did she mention that she was going to call Martha Torres?"

"No. But they spoke often. It wasn't unusual. Especially after Donna died."

"Did Martha know about you and my mother?"

"Could she have guessed? I'm sure. Would your mother have told? No. She was a very private person. Even I didn't know everything that was going on in her life."

Vega stepped back, disgusted with Delgado, disgusted with himself. "Well, you should've known, Father. We both should've." He threw up his hands and hustled up the subway stairs. The last pale gasp of daylight had slipped from the horizon. The sky was dark and glazed with thick clouds. It was snowing lightly now. Big fat flakes fell like ash, gray and gritty, melting quickly on the pavements. Night descended early this time of year. The store windows were cataract-clouded with steam or shuttered completely beneath roll-down metal security gates. Vega zipped up his jacket. He felt the cold in his bones. He still had Ricardo Luis's book underneath his jacket. He felt unclean even carrying it.

He kept his baseball cap on as he trudged back to his truck. The snow made people bundle up and forget about anything but getting home. He wanted to do the same. He wondered if Joy had left the Bronx yet. When he got to his truck, he shrugged out of his jacket, threw Luis's book on the seat, and dialed her cell. A part of him knew he should stay away from her right now. But another part of him craved the warmth and reassurance of her presence.

"Hey, *chispita*. I'm in the Bronx. Want a ride home?"

"What are you doing? Tailing me?"

"Nah. Visiting Freddy's mom at the nursing home. I'm not far from the Bronx Academy. How about I swing by and pick you up?"

"Can you come in like, an hour?"

An hour? He didn't want to hang around the Bronx for another hour. Then again, he didn't want his daughter wandering around by herself down here in the dark and snow, either.

"Yeah. Okay. Sure."

Vega hung up and studied the frosting of white across his windshield. It was too cold to stay in his truck. He could trudge around trying to find a place to get coffee, but the Bronx didn't have a Starbucks on every corner. He could drive somewhere but he didn't want to lose his parking spot and have to find another. If he showed up early to Freddy's school, Joy might accuse him of spying on her. Vega needed someplace near the school that would be open on a late Sunday afternoon. Someplace warm and dry where he could hang out as long as he liked without being hassled.

And then it came to him. The place that had always made him happy as a child. The only thing missing was the two parakeets.

Chapter 35

EZ Clean was packed on a Sunday night. Little children scampered up and down the aisles, playing hide-and-seek while their mothers chattered in Spanish on their cell phones. Groups of young men talked sports while they shoved what looked like every item they owned into dryers. People were at the candy machine and the soda machine. The air was warm and humid—more like July than December.

Carmela wasn't working this evening. There was another older woman at the front desk, her hair dyed so black that the gray roots looked like snow in her parting. She gave Vega a passing glance because he had no laundry in his hands. Not that that mattered in this neighborhood. People in the Bronx always treated the laundromat as a social club so it was conceivable he was just stopping in to visit a girlfriend. A patron called out to Snow Lady that he was having trouble working the card machine so Vega was able to breeze past without comment.

He used the bathroom at the rear of the building and bought himself a soda at one of the vending machines. Then he unzipped his jacket and settled into a molded plastic chair along a wall where he checked his cell phone to the conga rhythm of wet clothes thumping away in the dryers.

He was hoping for a message from Adele. There wasn't one. He took that as a bad sign. Should he send her one? *No.* That looked too pathetic, too much like he was begging for mercy. His pride wouldn't allow it. He thought about calling Dolan and telling him about Humberto Oliva and Luis. But that sort of conversation was best handled in a more private space than a laundromat. He'd call Dolan about it first thing tomorrow. As for what Father Delgado had told him? Vega had no idea how to handle that. His mother's murder was under NYPD jurisdiction and nothing Delgado had told him altered the case very much at this point. Vega wondered if he'd do more harm than good if he exposed the old priest's confession to any sort of public scrutiny.

Vega played a football fantasy game on his phone to distract himself. He stretched out his legs, careful not to trip anyone walking by. At home, he might have lost himself in the game. But not here. His eyes flicked up at regular intervals, scanning the rows for trouble—seen and unseen. It was the cop in him. He could never be totally oblivious to his surroundings. But even so, he still might have overlooked the dark-skinned Hispanic girl with the Asian eyes walking down the center aisle of the laundromat.

If not for her light pink windbreaker.

What was she doing here? Was she running away? He couldn't think of any other reason why a thirteen-year-old Lake Holly girl, fresh from Honduras, would be wandering around a Bronx laundromat on a Sunday night.

Vega watched her walk into the bathroom with a blue backpack slung over one shoulder. He put away his phone and rose from his chair. He didn't want to be obvious about following her so he bought a Snickers bar at the candy machine and pretended he'd just seen her for the first time as she stepped out of the bathroom.

"*Mija.*" *My daughter*—a gentle endearment. "What are you doing here?" he asked in Spanish. "Do you remember me? I bought you and your brother candy last night at the hospital."

Yovanna's eyes flared in surprise for a brief moment, then she looked down at her feet. Vega noticed that her purple canvas sneakers were soaked from traipsing through the snow. She had no hat or gloves. What parent would send a child out in spring clothes on a night like this?

Marcela hadn't. This was the teenager's own doing. That much was becoming crystal clear.

Vega crouched down next to the vending machine and held the Snickers bar out to her. He wanted to meet her downcast eyes and make himself as small and unthreatening as possible. "I bought the wrong item. Would you like it?"

Yovanna looked torn. If she was running away, she was probably hungry. On the other hand, she clearly didn't want to engage him.

"It's okay," Vega said softly. "I won't hurt you, *mija*." He didn't tell her he was a cop. That wouldn't soothe a Honduran teenager who'd just seen what passed for justice on both sides of the border. So he concentrated on associations. "I know your mother, Marcela. She used to babysit for my girlfriend's daughter. My name is Jimmy, by the way."

Vega waited for her to tell him her name. She didn't. Instead, she took the candy bar from his outstretched hand and settled into one of the chairs along the wall. She sat the backpack in her lap while she unwrapped the bar. She bit off a huge chunk and chewed noisily. She was hungry. Vega sat down in the chair next to her and kept his gaze straight ahead so she would feel less threatened.

"Does your mother know you're here?" he asked softly.

The girl didn't answer. Vega had to let Marcela know her daughter was safe but he didn't have her number. He decided to bluff.

"Okay, *Yovanna*." He used her name now to let her know he meant business. "I'm going to have to call your mother. I can't let you just wander around New York City without your mother knowing where you are."

"No!" That woke her out of her stupor. She looked at him now. "Please. I have to do this."

"Do what? Run away?"

"I have to meet a man."

Vega felt sick. No man who wanted to meet a thirteen-year-old girl was up to anything good. Vega pumped her for information. "So this man—he's supposed to meet you here?"

"No. In front of a dollar store a few blocks from here. He's picking me up in an hour. But it's cold and I needed someplace warm to stay until then."

"Do you know his name?"

"No. I just have a phone number for him." *Probably a burner,* thought Vega. These sorts of low-lifes have dozens of disposables they use once and throw away.

"Do you know what he looks like?"

"No. But he said he will know me."

"Yovanna, getting mixed up with some *rastrero* who will abuse you is not the way."

Yovanna frowned. "But I'm not. I'm just giving him something. Something that will fix all of my family's problems."

"You are thirteen years old, *mija.* If your family is having problems, it's not because of you."

"But it is! If I weren't here, my grandfather would still be alive. My mother said so. I heard her!"

"*Ay.*" Vega dropped his head in his hands. He felt terrible that this poor girl had to carry this burden at such a tender age.

"My mother said she wished he'd stop calling and the situation would go away," said Yovanna. "So I got his phone number off her cell. I can handle this myself."

"And what exactly are you supposed to give this man that is going to fix all of your family's problems?"

"Just this." Yovanna unzipped her backpack and pulled out a shiny silver disc—a CD or DVD—wrapped in a single sheet of newspaper. The grooves caught the overhead lights and sparkled. Yovanna flipped the disc over to the cover side. Someone had scribbled numbers across it in black magic marker. A date.

Vega's heart froze.

He was never good at remembering birthdays. He and Wendy once had a terrible fight because he forgot their anniversary. He had to write down every date on his calendar for the littlest thing or it slipped his mind. But he knew that date: it was branded onto his heart.

That was the date his mother was murdered.

This was the missing DVD. And on it, most likely, was video security footage of his mother's murderer. Vega snatched the DVD out of Yovanna's hands.

"Hey! That's mine!"

Vega got to his feet and held it out of her grasp. "Where did you get this?" he demanded. He forgot for a moment that he was talking to a frightened thirteen-year-old child.

"Give it back! If I don't hand it over, he'll hurt my family!"

"And if you do, he'll kill you. The man you're meeting with is a murderer, Yovanna."

"Give it back!" She started to cry. Loudly. Loud enough that even over the rumble of washers and dryers, people heard her. Three young Hispanic men in the adjoining aisle walked over, forming a wall between Vega and the front door.

"Are you messing with this girl?" the stockiest one demanded. He had a snake tattoo running down the side of his neck. His buddies were behind him. Vega could feel the machismo radiating off their bodies. They were already priming themselves to throw a punch in defense of her honor. *Coño!* He'd had enough fistfights in the last twenty-four hours to last him a lifetime.

Vega slipped the DVD into the pocket of his jacket and flashed his badge. "I'm a police officer and this girl and her belongings are part of a criminal investigation."

Snake tattoo thrust out his chin at Vega's badge. "What the hell is that? That ain't NYPD. You some kind of mall cop or something? That don't count for shit here, man."

Snake tattoo's words emboldened the dozen or so people beginning to gather around Vega and Yovanna. "Give her back her stuff!" yelled an obese young woman in a Mickey Mouse sweatshirt. She flung a wet towel at Vega. He ducked.

Yovanna clawed at Vega's pocket for the DVD. He grabbed her by her arms and began maneuvering her out of the store. "Help me!" she cried to the onlookers in Spanish. "This police officer shot and killed my grandfather. And now he wants to hurt me, too!"

The crowd pressed in as Vega half dragged, half carried Yovanna and her backpack out the door. "Let her go!" they began chanting. Vega knew he had to act fast before they cut off his exits.

"You are coming with me," he told Yovanna in Spanish. "You are thirteen years old, your family has no idea where you are, and whether you believe me or not, your life is in danger if you turn over that DVD."

He thought the people inside EZ Clean would give up once he hit the street. He thought the cold and snow would be enough to keep the two dozen or so patrons inside. But they were worked up now. And the crowd was getting bigger. The commotion had attracted the attention of two guys drinking outside a bodega on the opposite corner. Soon several more people from the bodega joined in. Word had started to spread that Vega wasn't just *any* cop. He was the cop who'd shot a dishwasher from the neighborhood. "Let-her-go!" was soon replaced by the chant, "Kill-er-cop!"

Things were escalating—and fast.

Vega backed up toward the school. Torres owned the laundromat. People around here respected him. Surely he could calm them down. But would he even know what was happening right now? God forbid Joy should walk out into this.

"I'm trying to save your life," Vega hissed at Yovanna. *Crash.* Somebody tried to throw a beer bottle at his head and missed. People had their fists raised in the air. Their mouths were hard and angry. Vega wasn't sure he could hold the crowd off much longer. He tried to speak but his voice was drowned out by the chanting.

"Let me go!" Yovanna shouted. "This has nothing to do with you!"

"That DVD has evidence of a murderer on it. My *mother's* murderer!" Vega shouted.

"You're lying," she insisted.

"I'm not." Vega tried to maneuver her up the steps of the school. He heard the click of a push bar behind him. A door opened.

"Everyone! Please! Stay cool. We can work this out."

Vega had never been so happy in all his life to hear Freddy Torres's voice.

Chapter 36

The gathering was supposed to kick off with cocktails at five, followed by Adele's keynote speech at five-thirty followed by dinner at six. It was an awkward arrangement, sandwiching Adele between the buzz of booze and the rumble of empty stomachs. Normally these events were a clubby affair, more akin to a college reunion than a political caucus

But not this year.

Adele saw the news vans as she nosed her Prius off the main tree-lined roadway of Fordham University and into the parking lot of Keating Hall, a fortresslike building with turrets befitting a medieval castle. At first Adele thought the media presence had to do with the fact that Ricardo Luis had planned to attend. But Luis wouldn't be a household name to the mostly white student body.

Adele got out of her car, already cursing her little open-toed red sandals, which scooped up the falling snow with every step. The sky was skillet black but the building's security lights were bright enough for Adele to pick out a small gathering of what looked like students on the front steps. It had to be students. They were all carrying backpacks and wearing ridiculous wool hats with pom-poms and fringe. At least they were dressed for the weather, unlike Adele. Ruben Tate-Rivera was at the center. Not only was he hijacking the event, he was bringing his own media entourage to make sure he got top billing.

Adele bundled her coat around her and ducked past the crowd. She wasn't about to give Tate the satisfaction of being pulled into his interview.

The lobby of Keating Hall had marble floors and a high, arched ceiling with dark beams cutting across it. It did not hold heat well. Adele was freezing. She had chosen to wear a sleeveless cinched-waist chiffon in a dazzling shade of ruby red. The choice had been deliberate—to show the audience she wasn't hiding and didn't intend to. But at the last minute, she'd grabbed a red-and-tan silk scarf to mute the effect.

Already, she was chickening out.

She'd scrapped her speech on the way over. She had no idea what she was going to replace it with. The symposium's theme this year was "Healing a Divided Nation." How could she talk about healing a divided nation when she couldn't even come to terms with her divided self? She didn't believe that Vega had executed Hector Ponce—not after getting a near-fatal firsthand glimpse of Margaret Behring's night vision. But that didn't mean she thought Vega was innocent, either. He was still a police officer who'd shot and killed an unarmed man. She couldn't go against her conscience and sweep that under the rug. In time she'd come to hate herself—and hate him, too—for such a decision.

So where did that leave her? She had no idea.

She followed the crowd down a long marble corridor. She felt relieved when she couldn't place any of their faces. The annual event drew immigrant advocacy groups from all across the state. Adele was hopeful that the shooting wasn't as big a news item in Buffalo or Schenectady.

At the door to the reception room, a pretty young Latina was checking in guests.

"Can I have your name?" the young woman asked Adele, checking her roster.

"Adele Figueroa." It came out as a near whisper.

"I'm sorry. I didn't hear you."

"Adele Figueroa."

The chatter around her stopped instantly. People eyed her and pretended not to at the same time. *They know my connection to the shooting.* She suspected she knew why: *Ruben Tate-Rivera.*

"Ah, Adele. The lady of the hour."

And there he was, in his trademark red bowtie, giving her a smile that was halfway between a smirk and a leer. He was surrounded, as always, by a gaggle of young, good-looking female assistants.

He sidled up to her. "Ricardo Luis isn't coming."

"He's not?" She couldn't deny a little dip of disappointment.

"His handlers have decided that he needs to keep a low profile from here on out. His publicist called me earlier and said he's making no further public appearances or statements related to the shooting."

"What changed his mind?" But even as Adele asked this, she knew. Her questions had made him uncomfortable today. Why, she couldn't say. Still, none of this explained the media's extreme eagerness to cover what amounted to a collegial gathering of activists.

"I saw you talking to reporters on the front steps," said Adele. "There were more cameras out there than I've seen in all my years at one of these events."

"The media goes where there's a story."

"And what story is that? Nothing I say—or you say—tonight is going to change the immigration debate in this country one iota."

Tate frowned. "You really don't know, do you?"

"What?"

Tate took her arm. "Come." He turned to his assistants and told them he would catch up with them later.

"Where are we going?" He never traveled anywhere without an entourage.

"Someplace quiet."

Farther down the hallway was an alcove with windows that overlooked a broad expanse of lawn and several gothic fieldstone buildings that made Adele forget she was in the Bronx. It was snowing harder now. Tiny flakes imprinted on the lead glass and then melted. The drive home was going to be hell.

"He didn't call you?" asked Tate.

"Who?"

"The cop. Vega."

"What are you talking about?"

"There's an impromptu demonstration going on right now outside a charter school off the Grand Concourse. Know what they're shouting? 'Jail killer cops.' "

"I will not be cowed by a mob mentality," said Adele. "The shooting didn't even happen in the Bronx."

"Adele, they're not demonstrating about the Wickford shooting. They're demonstrating about what just happened. Right here. This evening. In the Bronx. That's why the news stations wanted to interview me just now. That's how I learned about the situation. From them."

"You mean some other cop just shot a civilian?"

"I mean your *boyfriend* just grabbed the granddaughter of the man he shot and dragged her out of a laundromat against her will. He's inside that charter school with her now and no one's quite sure what's going on."

"Jimmy? Yovanna? Why would either of them be in the Bronx?"

"I don't know. I thought perhaps maybe you did. But apparently, he's not even communicating with you." Tate raised an eyebrow. "So tell me, do you still want to go on that stage and defend him?"

Chapter 37

"You can't seem to visit the 'hood these days without getting in trouble, can you, *carnal?*"

Torres ushered Vega and Yovanna into the school lobby and locked the door behind them. He was still wearing a bulky hoodie and sweats from his basketball tournament earlier. "Now, what is this about?" he demanded. "And why in hell are you taking this kid anywhere against her will?"

Joy watched her father and Torres from a corner of the front entrance hall. Vega could tell by her sulky hooded expression that he'd failed her once again. "I'm sorry" wasn't going to keep cutting it anymore.

"It's not like it looks," Vega assured Torres and his daughter. "It's for her own good. She ran away from home. Her family's got no idea where she is."

Joy nodded to Yovanna who was looking sullenly at her wet sneakers. "Can't she answer for herself?"

"She doesn't speak English," Vega explained to his daughter. "She needs to come back to Lake Holly with us. That's where her family lives."

Yovanna exploded in a sudden burst of panicked Spanish that he and Torres could understand but Joy couldn't.

"He took something that belongs to me!" the teenager shouted, gesturing to Vega.

"What is she saying, Dad?"

Torres raised an eyebrow and answered Joy. "The girl says your father took something from her." Torres turned to Vega. "What's she talking about, Jimmy?"

"Nothing!" Vega didn't want to go into it here. He wanted to get the girl home and look at the evidence himself before turning it over to the police. "It's nothing. I'll return it."

"But what is it?" asked Joy. "Jewelry? Clothing?"

Torres asked Yovanna in Spanish. Yovanna told him. Even with Joy's limited Spanish skills, she could translate Yovanna's *"de-ve-de."* Vega wished the girl would just keep her mouth shut.

"You took a DVD from her?" asked Joy. "Why would you do that?"

"I'll give it back once I've had a chance to look at it, okay?"

Torres turned to Yovanna. "Perhaps I can hold it for you, *querida.* Until we can sort this out—"

"You can't do that," said Vega in English. "It's evidence in a police investigation."

"Work with me, *carnal,*" Torres muttered. "I'm trying to keep you from getting arrested for kidnapping, you dig?" Torres turned back to the girl, his voice soft and sweet in Spanish. "Would you like that, *querida?*"

"I want it back," she replied.

"And you will get it back, I promise," said Torres. "But you need to calm down."

Yovanna nodded. She took a deep breath and stopped arguing. Torres held out his hand to Vega. Reluctantly Vega reached into his jacket pocket and handed Torres the DVD.

"I need it back, Freddy."

"Of course. But right now, we're working on de-escalating the situation." Torres slipped the disc into a pocket of his zippered hoodie. "See? Wasn't that better than a show of force?" Torres shook his head. "Honestly, Jimmy. When will cops figure out that you can catch more flies with honey than with vinegar?"

"I'm usually dealing with manure," said Vega. "Vinegar and honey seldom come into it."

Torres turned back to Yovanna. "I will keep this safe for you, *querida,* until we can get hold of your family and figure out the best thing to do here, okay? In the meantime—" Torres switched to English and looked at Joy. "This girl really needs some mittens and an extra layer of clothes. You know that spare clothes room I showed you in the basement?"

"Sure," said Joy.

"Take her there and get her something warm to wear." Torres turned back to Yovanna and explained where Joy was taking her. To Vega's surprise, the girl willingly followed his daughter. Vega watched them walk off down the hall.

"Wow. I gotta hand it to you, Freddy. You know your stuff." Vega rapped a knuckle against his. "I'll take that DVD now."

"Don't you want to see what's on it?"

"When I'm out of here."

"Listen, Jimmy—if there's one thing I know as a principal, it's teenagers. That girl ain't going nowhere with you unless you give her back her DVD, know what I'm saying?" Torres had slipped into street vernacular. The neighborhood had that effect on people, no matter how they spoke elsewhere.

"No can do, Freddy."

"You're not using your gray matter, *carnal.* We can make a copy."

"I need the original."

"So? You keep the original and she gets the copy."

"I don't want to take a chance on compromising the contents."

"We're not going to *compromise* it. You think you're

going to get her home any other way? I bet you don't even have her mother's phone number. And she sure as hell ain't gonna give it to you the way you're acting."

Vega hesitated.

"Listen," said Torres. "Most of my computers are dinosaurs, but I have one up on the fourth floor that will do the job. Take a look. See what you think. If you're not down with that, fine, man. It's your call."

"All right," said Vega.

"And while we're up there," said Torres. "I want to show you the new roof gym I'm installing. Joy wanted you to see it before you left."

Vega didn't really care about the roof gym but he didn't want to say that to his old friend. "Will Joy and Yovanna be able to find us?"

"I told Joy I was going to show it to you." Torres grabbed his coat from his office. "C'mon, Jimmy. The front door's locked. You're safe. Besides, the longer you stay, the more likely people are to get cold, give up, and go home."

He had a point.

The Bronx Academy of Achievement had once been a tool and die factory and it still possessed an industrial sense of itself. The ceilings had exposed ducts running across them but everything was painted in cheerful blocks of color so it reminded Vega less of a factory and more of a modern art museum. Vega could still smell the fresh coat from yesterday as he and Torres climbed the stairs.

"What's on the DVD?" asked Torres.

"Can't tell you that."

"Ah. Police business." Torres chuckled. "Funny. Even after all these years, I still can't picture you as a cop, man. You don't have that killer instinct."

"The mob at your front door might disagree," said Vega. "And besides, having a killer instinct doesn't make you a cop. It makes you a killer. Most cops I know lead pretty tame lives off the clock."

He and Torres were on the fourth floor now. Vega squinted down the darkened hallway. "So, where's this computer I can make a copy on?"

Torres led him into a room and flicked on the light. He turned on a computer with two DVD slots. It looked old and painfully slow.

"It's going to take a couple of minutes to warm up," said Torres. "How about you come eyeball what I'm building on the roof. It'll just take a minute. By then the computer should be ready for action."

Vega hesitated.

"Listen, *carnal*." Torres was clearly getting frustrated with him. "You think I like being on lockdown like this? You got creds with me, man, but that only goes so far. You need to step up your game, you dig?"

"I hear ya." Vega would have to wait for that dinosaur to power up anyway.

The door to the roof was up six short steps. The passageway felt cold. Torres rummaged around in the pocket of his puffy down jacket for a key.

"A key?" asked Vega. "I thought all these exits were supposed to have emergency push bars?"

"Some of my students were playing hooky on the roof. It's better this way." Torres unlocked the door and pushed it open. A blast of cold air fanned their faces as Vega stepped outside.

"It's not finished yet," Torres apologized.

It looked barely started from what Vega could see. The nearest sides of the roof were enclosed by chain-link fencing but the far side was still open. There was no gym equipment, only bundles of metal joists and rods piled near a ventilation shaft and blanketed in snow.

"It's—nice," said Vega. It was freezing is what it was. He wanted to go back inside. The heavy steel door slammed shut behind them.

"See?" Torres slipped his key back in the door and turned

the lock. "I can lock and unlock the door from both sides to ensure no one gets up here without my permission."

"That's great, Freddy. So listen. Maybe we should—"

"Look at this view, man. You ever see a view like this?" Torres swept a hand to the unenclosed part of the roof. Sturdy tenements stood shoulder to shoulder, their grimy facades dressed up in the twinkle of traffic lights and neon signs. Even the high-rise housing projects took on a certain dark majesty set against the hazy accumulation of all that wattage. Vega wanted to appreciate it but all he could feel was the needles of ice pricking his face and the flakes of snow melting into his hair.

Something that sounded like a sheet of ice snapped behind him. Vega turned. At Torres's feet, he saw glittering shards on the compacted snow.

"What the—?" The DVD lay like a broken Christmas ornament between them.

Torres pulled a .380 Beretta out of his pocket and pointed it at Vega's chest. "It's loaded, Jimmy. Trust me, in this neighborhood, it's loaded. I know you're not packing. You wouldn't have run from that mob just now if you were."

Vega's insides burned with a mixture of rage and confusion. He couldn't believe the man who'd saved his life so many times could betray him so completely now.

"You're on the DVD." Vega had to say the words to believe them. "You killed my mother."

"Didn't want to, *carnal*. I swear. I tried to talk some sense into her on the phone that night. But all she kept saying was 'Turn yourself in. Get your head right with God.' I was outta options."

His mother's final phone call. It wasn't to speak to Martha. It was to speak to Freddy. A slow dawning crept over Vega. That's why his mother had an appointment with Detective Renfro in the Bronx homicide division. Luisa Rosario-Vega had evidence that Freddy Torres was involved in a murder, Martha's words at the nursing home came back to Vega:

You know what you did, yes? So does Luisa. And he knew.

"Donna." The name felt like a prayer on Vega's lips. Snow covered his shoulders and slipped inside his jacket. He felt the chill all the way down his spine. "She didn't fall from that window, did she? You pushed her."

Torres's face tightened for just a moment and then turned smooth and slack. Something went dead in his eyes. Vega felt as if a serrated spoon were digging out the lining of his stomach. Finding out about Donna was almost worse than finding out about his mother.

"Why, Freddy? For chrissakes, why? Donna never hurt anyone in her life."

Torres's voice turned steely when he spoke. "Who did you ever have to look after in your life, huh, Jimmy? You didn't have a drunken father you had to protect your mother from. You didn't have a sister with Down syndrome you had to watch all the time. It was all on *me.* Everything was always on *me!* And then my mother's Alzheimer's hit and I saw the future. I was going to be saddled with two dependents. *Two!* My mother *and* my sister. Their care was going to bleed me dry. Until the day I died, I would never be free. Jackie ran away. She got to live her life. When was it my turn?"

"So you *killed* your sister?"

"My sister's life insurance *paid* for my mother's home health care. It's still paying for her care now. You think Medicare picks up everything? Not for the kind of care she's getting, it doesn't," said Torres. "My solution was working. It made sense. If your mother hadn't gotten all up in my face. If Hector Ponce had repaid his loan instead of trying to get cute with me."

"So Hector knew that you killed my mother?"

"Then? No. I don't have a clue why he switched DVDs. Later? He probably ran the footage and figured it out. But he was a gambler who liked to borrow money so he wasn't about to rock the boat—until he had to."

"And then you killed him."

Torres steadied his gun with both hands. "Everyone who was a witness is gone now. It's over, Jimmy. No more."

"I'm a witness," said Vega.

Torres didn't answer. He took out his phone and punched in 911. A dispatcher came on the line. "This is Dr. Fred Torres," he said in his smoothest and most professional voice. The street vernacular was gone. "I'm on the roof of the Bronx Academy with a distraught police officer—the one who shot that dishwasher in Wickford? He's threatening to jump—"

"No!" Vega took a step forward. Torres leveled his gun and spoke into the phone again. "Please hurry. He's acting crazy. I don't—" Torres disconnected in midsentence. Which made it seem as if someone else had done it for him. Then he put his phone away.

"You see, Jimmy? I shoot you, it's in self-defense. Or maybe you just want to jump and save us all the trouble?"

Chapter 38

"The theme of this symposium is healing a divided nation," Adele reminded the hushed audience as she stepped on the stage at Keating Hall. "I suspect no one in this audience is more divided than I am at the moment."

There was a small murmur of polite but nervous laughter from the crowd. Adele saw no point in pretending that they wanted some canned speech or that they didn't know exactly who she was and how she was connected to the shooting. They thought they knew her—just as they thought they knew Vega. But they didn't. To go forward, she would need to summon the courage to look back. Publicly. It was something she never did.

"When I was a little girl," she began, "I was terrified of the police." Her voice sounded shaky to her ears but she needed to explain her position. If that meant walking off this stage and out of this line of work, so be it. She could not flinch.

She spoke about her childhood, living in fear that the police might one day break down her door and haul her parents away. Or that her parents might go to work cleaning offices one evening, get caught in a raid, and never come home. Blue uniforms terrified her. Sirens terrified her. She learned early not to talk too much about her family. If someone stole from her or cheated her, she quietly accepted it rather than chance anyone in authority asking questions that her parents couldn't answer.

"I was born right here in Port Carroll, New York. I'm an American citizen," said Adele. "And yet I've never felt that sense of birthright." She went on to confess how she learned early to shut down her emotions and not speak about things she couldn't change. She didn't go into all the silences she was asked to endure. Some were too deep to ever speak about and certainly not here.

She described her father's one visit to the police, when she was fourteen, after a neighbor stole her parents' business from them—and the ridicule the officers subjected him to.

"My father died two years after that incident," said Adele. "The doctors said it was a heart attack. But I think it was a broken heart." She had the audience spellbound now. She didn't really notice. She was lost in her own raw memories.

"My mistrust of the police only deepened after I became a defense attorney," she continued. "I saw cops lie. I saw them mistreat my clients. My fear and anger turned to cynicism. You could say I'd lost all faith."

She paused. "And then, one day, I met a police officer who changed all that. Not because he was perfect. I saw him make mistakes. Again and again, I saw it. But for the first time, I also saw behind the shield. I saw a man trying hard to do the right thing. Sometimes an impossible thing. In a world that is rarely fair or helpful, I saw a man get up every morning and try to be both."

Adele took a deep breath. "Does that exempt him from explaining his actions or having them scrutinized? No. But it does mean that we need to give him and all police officers the benefit of the doubt. We need to be as fair as we ask them to be. If the forensic evidence warrants a grand jury investigation, then I'll be the first to call for it."

She caught Tate's scowl from the audience. "Or maybe

the second, since my esteemed colleague, Ruben Tate-Rivera, will probably be the first."

That got a laugh. The audience was with her even if Tate wasn't.

"I do believe, however, that if we truly want to heal our divided nation, then we need to step away from the actions that divide us. We need to meet emotion with logic, hatred with justice. I would rather whisper my conscience to the wind than scream my fury with the mob. Thank you."

The applause was long and generous as Adele stepped down from the stage. Had she done it? Had she dodged a bullet and saved Vega from it as well? She wondered where he was right now. At a police station explaining why he'd grabbed Yovanna against her will? On his way back home? She felt too wired to stay for the dinner. Too light-headed and dizzy. She needed to hear his voice on the other end of a phone line. She walked out of the auditorium and found Gloria Mendez to apologize that she couldn't stay for the meal. Ruben Tate-Rivera caught up to her.

"Enough." She waved her hands in front of her face as he walked over. "I'm leaving." She backed away.

"Good thing you're a defense attorney," Tate hissed. "Your boyfriend's gonna need one. That is, if he survives at this point."

"Excuse me?"

"The NYPD just got a nine-one-one call from the principal of that charter school. Vega's holding him hostage."

"No!"

"It's coming over the police scanner," said Tate. "One of the reporters just told me. Your boy's finally gone over the edge, Adele. Nobody's going to defend him now. Or you, either. Don't let that polite applause fool you. You talk about whispering your conscience to the wind? That sounds a whole lot like spitting into it to me. And you know what happens when you do that."

Chapter 39

Two options. That's all Vega had: jump or get shot. Torres was a highly respected community leader and school principal. Vega was a disgraced cop with a pattern of emotionally unstable behavior. It was a no-brainer whose story the police were going to believe. Cop or not, Vega was the one the police would be gunning for. He didn't even have the DVD anymore to prove that Torres was lying. It lay shattered at their feet. Not that Torres was going to wait around to let Vega prove his case anyway. He planned to dispatch him long before that.

Vega had to get control of the situation. What he needed was a weapon. He spotted the pile of metal joists for the roof fencing. They were blanketed by snow. But still—if he could just get to one. He needed to keep Torres talking. He slipped back into the vernacular of the neighborhood, hoping to lull Torres into a false sense of security.

"Hey, *carnal*," said Vega, spreading his hands. "Chill, man. I'm totally down with what you're saying here. You were carrying the load. Most dudes, they'd have crumbled. Not you. You held it together. Kept it tight all these years."

Snow dusted the little bird's nest of dark hair in the middle of Torres's head. He shook it off. "I just want to be free."

"Put the piece down, hombre, and you are." Vega stepped forward. The snow was falling harder now. The roof was slippery.

"Stay where you are."

"C'mon, Freddy. The evidence is gone. You said so yourself. Ain't nothing to tie you to anything."

"There's you. You'll never let it go."

"Ain't nobody gonna believe a head case like me anyway, right?" Vega tried to inch his body toward the pile of metal joists. If he could just reach one, he might have a chance. "You'd be saving my ass once again. Like you always do."

One step. Then two . . .

"Dad? Are you and Dr. Torres okay?"

Ay, puñeta! Joy's voice tore through Vega, sharpening all his senses, derailing all his plans. She was on the other side of the locked door and Torres had the key. No way could he risk his daughter.

Do it now! Now is your only chance!

Torres shifted his gaze to the door. Vega lunged for the pile of metal, clasping his hand around an ice-cold rod about two feet in length. Adrenaline muted the sharp stab of frozen steel on bare skin. Vega willed his fingers to wrap themselves around it. Then he threw his full weight against Torres, hoping to knock him down before he could shoot.

Bam.

Bam.

Vega braced for the impact of metal tearing into flesh, the warm spurt of blood. A fitting ending. Live by the gun. Die by it.

"Dad!" screamed Joy on the other side of the door.

Torres's shots missed.

Vega's rod didn't.

He struck Torres hard on the shoulder of his thick down jacket. The sound was like a baseball landing cleanly in a catcher's mitt. No way could Vega do enough damage through that big puffy coat. But it was enough to jolt the gun from Torres's hand. The Beretta sank beneath the snow.

Joy rattled the door, her voice breathy with panic. "Dad! Are you okay? Say something!"

Vega couldn't. He was too out of breath. He raked the metal rod through the snow, hoping to find the gun. The cold sliced into his flesh like a filet knife. His limbs felt like they each weighed a hundred pounds.

He couldn't find the gun.

Torres landed a hard right to Vega's backside. The rod dropped from his hand. The two men rolled in a tumble of fists. The soft wet snow melted beneath them, soaking through Vega's pants and jacket. His hands were like slabs of stone he could swing but not feel. He and Torres hadn't fought since that day over thirty years ago when Torres took the can of black spray paint from Vega's backpack. Vega had been outclassed then—in weight, size, and skill. But he was in better shape than Torres now. And he had more to lose. His daughter was on the other side of that door.

Vega landed a hard right to the side of Torres's face. He was too numbed to feel the flash of pain as his knuckles connected with Torres's cheek. The blow stunned Torres, who fell back against the snow. It bought Vega enough time to sweep his arms through the drifts, willing his frozen fingers to find the gun. His small motor skills were fading fast. And then he felt the sharp outline of metal. He pulled up the gun and aimed it at his old friend as Torres was pushing himself to his knees.

"Stay down!" yelled Vega. "Hands behind your head!"

"Dad! Talk to me!"

Vega sucked in air and tried to catch his breath. He was soaking wet from the melted snow and shivering from a combination of sweat, fear, and ice water.

"Joy! Take Yovanna and go wait by the front doors.

The police are on their way. Tell them I'm on the roof. Tell them Torres pulled a gun on me. I'll explain later."

"I don't want to leave you," she cried.

"You've got to. Now do as I say."

Vega waited until he was sure Joy had retreated. "Get up," he ordered Torres. "Take the key out of your pants and unlock the door."

Torres got to his feet. His sweatpants and puffy jacket were dark and heavy with water. He shivered.

"Keep your hands where I can see them," Vega ordered.

Torres smiled. "Really, Jimmy? You think being the one holding the gun changes anything?"

"Get the key."

"You shoot me, you're going to spend the rest of your career with a cloud hanging over you, man. I'm a pillar in this community. And you? You're the pigeon crap that people scrape off their windshields around here." Torres shot a glance over his shoulder. "Don't count on a swift response from the boys in blue. People 'round here take care of their own—or have you forgotten?" Torres nodded his head to the street below. "Don't believe me? Take a look down there, *carnal.*"

Vega wasn't about to take his gaze off Torres.

"Unlock the door," Vega hissed at him. Already, his wet pants were freezing up stiff on him. His feet were soaked. His fingers had lost most of their feeling.

Torres reached into his pocket.

"Don't you hear it, Jimmy?"

And suddenly he did. A rumble of voices over the soft, compacted snow. Angry voices growing louder. Encircling the building forty feet below. Not police. There were no sirens. These people were chanting.

"Kill-er cop! Kill-er cop!"

"What do you think is going to happen," asked Torres, "if you shoot me up here? You think they're going to say it was all in the line of duty?"

"Open the door, Freddy!"

Torres pulled the copper-colored key out of his pocket. It was attached to a white plastic key fob. He dangled it in his hand for a second and then flung it over the side of the building.

"What did you do that for?" Vega demanded. "Now we're *both* locked up here."

"That's right, Jimmy. There's no escape. Either you shoot me and the Bronx mourns a fallen hero or I shoot you and they lament the tragedy of a cop who went off the deep end. Those are your only two choices."

Chapter 40

Adele left Fordham quickly, zigzagging through one-way streets, maneuvering around parked cars. Her GPS had told her the location of the Bronx Academy of Achievement. But she had no idea if she could get within a block of the building.

She wondered if she was already too late.

She parked her Prius on a cross street and raced back to the building. It was surrounded in front by several dozen people, all of them chanting, with fists raised in the air. The police had arrived, their flashing lights lending a circus atmosphere to the crowd. A woman watched the spectacle from the doorway of an adjacent laundromat.

"What's going on?" Adele asked her.

"This police officer went crazy. He dragged a young girl out of here and into the school. And now I think he's holding poor Dr. Torres at gunpoint."

Adele's head was spinning. None of it sounded like Vega. Then again, when he called her Friday night and told her he'd shot a man, that didn't sound like him either. Nor did that fistfight with a bunch of college students last night.

Nothing sounded like the man she knew and loved anymore.

She cupped a hand across her eyes to blot out the glare of the streetlights and stared up at the roof. The edge of the four-story building was too high to see over. She had no idea what was going on up there. Her feet had gone numb and soggy from the pavement slush. Snow fell down the back of her coat. She felt chilled so deep inside of her that she didn't think she could ever get warm. She fantasized for a moment that she could speak to these people and calm them down. But she was not Ruben Tate-Rivera. They might listen to him. They would not listen to her.

Conveniently Tate was nowhere to be found.

Four police officers began suiting up in flak vests and body armor. Adele felt the old fear returning, that sense of powerlessness in the face of authority. She tried to tell herself that this was different. Vega was a police officer—just like these men. But then she saw them checking their weaponry and she understood: These officers weren't here to rescue Vega. They were here to subdue him.

By any means necessary.

Vega heard the sirens split the night air. They had an odd compacted quality in the snow. He was near the edge of the roof now, with only a thin lip between him and a forty-foot drop to the basketball court below. He saw flashes of red and blue bouncing off the brick front of the tenements across the street from the school.

Torres stepped closer.

"Down on the ground," shouted Vega. "Hands above your head!"

Torres ignored him. "Shoot me, Jimmy. Go ahead. You know you want to. It's you or me. What's it going to be? You killed Ponce's brother. You know what it's like to take a life. You've tasted blood. Pull the trigger."

"Get down. Now!" Vega heard the hard, battle-ready voices of cops on the stairs. Not just uniformed officers, either. This sounded like a tactical squad. They were here to take down the shooter. And since he was the one with a gun in his hand, he qualified.

His feet had gone numb. His arm ached from holding up the gun. His fingers could barely feel the trigger. The snow had gotten a hard crystalline glaze on its surface, the pebbly slickness of moss-covered river stones. It had piled up along the edges of the roof so that the entire surface felt less defined. Plus, it was dark. The ever-present streetlights offered a hazy peach glow to the snowfall, but their pools of light petered off into shadows up here. One wrong move and forty feet of vertical drop guaranteed a quick and messy death.

"Get down!" Vega said to Torres again.

Torres remained standing. "What's the matter, man? Gun-shy now? Shoot me! I don't want to be locked up in some ten-foot cell. Shoot me!"

Every ligament in Vega's body stiffened. He felt paralyzed by his predicament. He could feel his blood rushing through his veins. He didn't want to pull the trigger. Not again.

Dear God, not again.

Civilians always think you can just shoot a person in an extremity and stop them. But it doesn't work that way. Moving extremities, even at close range, are hard to hit, and even when you do, the suspect is so charged up on adrenaline, they sometimes don't feel it and just keep moving anyway. He could miss and hit a cop coming through the doorway. The bullet could ricochet and hit some civilian having dinner in a building across the street. It could pierce an artery and Torres could bleed out anyway. Or Torres could use the seconds it would take Vega to re-aim the gun and push him right off the roof.

"Pull the trigger, *carnal.* You know you want to. Pull it."

There was no denying that a part of him did. There

would be a mild euphoria in shooting the man who bru-
tally beat his mother to death. Vigilante justice. So what if
the people below hated him for killing Torres? They hated
him anyway. As soon as he put on the badge, they hated
him. He was a homegrown son and they treated him like a
traitor. He couldn't win this one, no matter what he did.

Pull the trigger.

The police were at the door to the roof. "Open up!"
yelled a cop with razors in his voice.

"I'm a police officer!" Vega shouted back. "I have a gun
trained on the suspect. He threw the key over the building.
You'll have to break down the door."

Torres stepped closer. "It's a metal door, Jimmy. Your
buddies aren't going to be able to help you now."

Vega knew he couldn't hold out much longer. Torres
was about to pounce. Vega had to make the first move. He
had to take Torres down and try to restrain him. One
good headlock. Hard and fast. Like when he was a kid.
Vega sprang forward and grabbed Torres around the neck.
But Vega was cold and numb. His muscles weren't working right. Both men had slippery wet jackets on. Vega
managed the headlock but not completely enough to inca-
pacitate Torres. Torres fought back, elbowing Vega in the
ribs. Vega grabbed at Torres's hair. There were grunts and
kicks.

And then the door flew open.

Vega heard the clatter of duty holsters and handcuffs
behind him. Four cops in flak vests and headgear burst
through the door and aimed their weapons.

At Vega.

"Freeze, asshole!" yelled the man with razors in his
voice. "Drop the gun!"

Vega complied. "I'm a police officer!" he shouted. His
words had no effect. The four cops descended on him with
the force of a tsunami, tackling him to the ground, flipping

him onto his stomach, kneeing him in the back, and yanking his hands tightly behind to cuff them. Vega felt the slush soak through his clothes like he was swimming in ice water. He tried to speak but razor-man shoved his face hard into an icy embankment while he patted him down.

"Shut your fucking mouth, *hombre.*"

Vega burned with anger and humiliation. And a certain realization, too. There was only a tin shield separating him from the other side of this divide. At all times. In all situations.

Vega lifted his head just as the officer was about to snap a cuff on his wrists. He saw Freddy Torres back away from the officers. He saw every movement as if it were in slow motion. Torres swung a leg over the low upward curve of the roofline. Then he swung the other.

"No!" Vega forgot about the cops and their weapons. He saw only one thing. A man. Headed over a roof. About to plummet forty feet to his death. A man he hated, sure. But a life.

One.

Two.

Those same two seconds that had taken a life could now save one. Vega leapt for the edge of the roof and grabbed Torres by a sleeve of his puffy jacket. The cop who was about to pounce on Vega for moving saw at once what Vega was trying to do and latched on to the other sleeve.

"Don't do this, Freddy," Vega begged.

"Let me go, *carnal.* My way."

"No. You don't get to choose." Vega grabbed at his jacket. The cold wet nylon was slick in his hands.

"I want to be free."

"You *were* free. The door was open. You could have walked away at any time."

Torres tried to shrug out of their grip. They held tight. It was like playing a high stakes game of tug-of-war. Vega plunged his hands beneath Torres's armpits. He could feel the warmth thawing his flesh, giving him the circulation and strength to hang on.

Did he want to?

A life for a life. For many lives. His mother's. Donna's. Hector Ponce's. But a deeper part of him didn't want Torres dead. Death was a quick adrenaline fix. Life—life without freedom or options—that was justice.

And so Vega pulled. There was a thump, followed by four officers pouncing on Torres, cuffing him before he could try again. Torres lost a shoe in the scuffle. Vega heard it drop forty feet below onto the perfect white snow of the basketball court where it made a soft thud. But that was all that dropped.

Jimmy Vega had killed a man who didn't deserve to die. And now he'd just saved one who probably didn't deserve to live.

Chapter 41

A photograph graced the front page of the *New York Daily News* the day after Freddy Torres was arrested. It had been snapped the night before from a rooftop overlooking the Bronx Academy of Achievement. Jimmy Vega had no idea the shot had been taken.

It showed him and an NYPD officer (ironically, the same one who'd smashed his face in the snow). They were both sprawled on the ledge of the building's roof, halfway over themselves, risking their lives to save a man who would probably spend the rest of his in jail. It was a dramatic shot that made Vega and the other cop look like the good guys for once. Not heroes. Vega would never use that word. But it told the world at the very least that they'd tried to do the right thing when the right thing was damned hard to do.

The police charged Torres with Hector Ponce's murder. Not Donna's. Or Vega's mother's. Those two cases were older and would take longer to assemble. But even so, announcing to the world that Hector Ponce hadn't died by a cop's hand changed the spotlight. It turned Vega from the star of a drama he'd never auditioned for to a bit player. He welcomed the chance to step back and at least begin to reclaim his life.

Two days after Torres's arrest, Isadora Jenkins showed up at Vega's house in orthopedic shoes and glittery snowman earrings and gave Vega the news that the medical examiner's office had failed to find gun powder residue or metal particles in Antonio Fernandez's wounds—which pretty much put to rest the notion that Vega had executed the man. That, and the fact that Margaret Behring had abruptly recanted her testimony.

"You didn't *pressure* her into recanting, I hope," Vega said to Adele.

"Never," Adele assured him. "Let's just say, she uh, saw the light."

The media storm quickly faded from the Internet. By the third day after Torres's arrest, it was already back page news. An anonymous donor offered to bury both Hector and Antonio in St. Raymond's cemetery. The brothers would be together in death even if they never got much of a chance in life.

Vega thought he'd feel a great sense of relief knowing that his mother's murderer had been caught and that Yovanna was no longer in danger. The district attorney even floated the possibility that the case could be cleared in-house instead of being submitted to a grand jury. But something still gnawed at Vega.

Ricardo Luis.

He was at the center of everything that had happened. And he wasn't talking. Nor was Humberto Oliva. "I have made my peace with God," Oliva insisted. "And now, Luis must make his."

Vega refused to give up. He contacted a colleague in the FBI he'd once worked a joint investigation with to see if the Feds could press the case without Oliva's cooperation. But that too proved to be a dead end. Word came back that there was no proof Luis's victims had even died on the U.S. side of the border. The Mexican police had little interest in pinning such a heinous, twenty-year-old crime on a homegrown hero. Luis was free.

Not Vega. Antonio's death hung like a ghost around him. Even the news, five days after Torres's arrest, that the DA had declined to convene a grand jury, didn't offer Vega the relief he'd been hoping for. He was going back to work.

He wondered if he'd still be able to do the job.

"You know what you need?" asked Isadora Jenkins as Vega walked her to her car after their meeting with the DA.

"To shut my big, fat mouth?"

She laughed. "Always. But in this case, you need someone to keep you honest."

"I *am* honest."

"I mean honest about how you're doing."

Vega started to protest. Jenkins dismissed him with a wave of her hand. Today, she was wearing a big, flower-shaped ring encrusted with rhinestones. Vega's daughter had a ring like that back when she used to pretend to be a fairy princess. Isadora Jenkins apparently still thought she was.

"Don't you dare hand me those words *I'm fine,*" said Jenkins. "Ninety-five percent of cops who kill someone in the line of duty don't go to jail or face disciplinary charges. And yet something like a third of them quit their jobs within five years of the incident. Do you know why, Detective? Because they walk around with the same shell-shocked expression you've got on your face right now, saying, 'I'm fine.' And they're not."

Jenkins put a hand on his arm. Her eyes turned soft and maternal. "Keep going to therapy, Vega. And more than that, find somebody who gets what you're going through. Not your family. Lord knows, they never will. Just—somebody who's been there."

Vega nodded. "Okay. I'll keep that in mind."

She hugged him fiercely. He wasn't expecting that. "Thanks for everything," he said shyly. "See you around."

"Huh. Let's hope not."

And then she was gone with only her words still ringing in Vega's ears: *You need someone to keep you honest.* Fortunately or unfortunately, Vega knew just the man.

Every Friday at four P.M., Detective Louis Greco could be found at the Lake Holly 7-Eleven buying ten lottery tickets. Always ten. Always at the 7-Eleven on Fridays at four P.M. Louis Greco was nothing if not predictable.

Vega parked his truck next to Greco's white Buick and waited until the old detective barreled through the doors. He had a *New York Post* tucked under one arm. His face registered nothing—which meant he already knew everything.

"Get in." Greco sighed. "You want me to pretend I don't know? Or should we skip right to the 'get your ass back to work' speech?"

"The DA *just* cleared me," said Vega. "How could you know?"

Greco tossed the newspaper to Vega. The headline, RUBEN'S LAP OF SHAME, was splashed across the front page, complete with a picture of Tate recoiling from the very media that had made him a star.

Vega scanned the text. "So I take it his interns were getting private tutoring sessions from the professor. Whether they wanted them or not."

Greco chuckled. "Baiting cops, copping feels—it's all the same. Anyway, as soon as I heard, I figured there was no way the DA was going to make an example out of you now that Ruben Rapes-His-Secretaries was out of the picture. The political will was gone."

Vega folded the paper and handed it back to Greco. "So

how come I still feel like I'm carrying around a dead man on my shoulders?"

"Give it time, Vega. It's not going to get better overnight. I told you, you're different now. You always will be. Something good will come out of this eventually. You'll see."

"Not this time," said Vega. "Hector gave his life to bring his granddaughter over here. And now he and his brother are both dead and that poor kid's a mess. She's struggling at school. She's distressed at home. She needs help she's never going to get. And she's not the only one, either. Adele told me about this boy who just came over from Guatemala. He's sleeping in the restaurant where he works."

"You can't save the world, Vega."

"No. But I wish I could do *something*. These kids are *here*, Grec. They're not going away. And it's frustrating to know that they're not getting the help they need on any level."

"Yeah, well—help costs money. And you and I are working stiffs. What can you do?"

Vega bolted upright and put his hand on the door. He felt like a train was leaving the station and he had to run to catch it.

"Where are you going?" asked Greco.

"I think I may have just found my good."

It took a week to arrange the meeting. Luis was in Miami the first time Vega called. He was prepping to go on a concert tour. He had interviews to do for his new book. Gradually however, the realities of the situation became clear. If Ricardo Luis was ever going to be rid of Jimmy Vega, he was going to have to meet with him at his home in Wickford. Alone. Both men had much to lose by broadcasting their encounter. And so by mutual agreement, nobody else was informed. Not Luis's attorney. Not Vega's department. Not Adele.

Luis was on his cell phone when his housekeeper ushered Vega into his home office. Vega stood admiring one of Luis's guitars while he finished up the call. It was an acoustic Martin with an Indian rosewood fret board inlaid with mother of pearl.

"You are staring at that guitar like other men stare at a pretty girl," said Luis when he got off the phone.

"Sorry." For a moment Vega forgot himself, forgot why he was here. Music had a way of doing that to him.

"Would you like to play it?"

"May I?"

Luis nodded. Vega gently took the guitar from the stand and placed it in his lap. He strummed a few chords and felt transported. The strings were out of tune. Luis heard it, too. He made a face.

"Do you mind if I tune it up?" asked Vega.

"Please."

Vega turned the tuning pegs to pitch and tried out little riffs, running his fingers up and down the frets. The sound was deep and rich with a buttery resonance that Vega could feel all the way through his body like he was the amplifier.

"I can tell you're a real musician," said Luis.

"My first love." Vega kept his eyes on the strings, alternating between short riffs and chords. "But I'd be lying if I said that's why I'm here." Vega returned the guitar to its stand. "You shot Antonio Fernandez. I killed him. And we both know why he and Hector Ponce were really here."

"Under the advice of my attorney—"

"Your attorney can't do shit if this story hits the Internet," said Vega. "Take it from someone who's been there. It makes no difference what's true and what isn't."

Luis raised an eyebrow. "So now *you* want to blackmail me? Is that it, Detective?"

"No." Vega reached into his wallet and pulled out a picture of Marcela and Yovanna that he'd borrowed from Adele without telling her why. "This is Hector's granddaughter," Vega said slowly, pointing to the girl. "She's the reason Hector came to you for money."

"I know," said Luis.

"She's like a lot of children coming into the county these days to reunite with their families. These kids are traumatized," said Vega. "Their symptoms are a lot like mine were after the shooting. The difference is, I can get help. They can't. Their families don't have the resources." Vega's eyes locked on Luis's. "You do. You can help them."

"Help them, how?"

"Fund a program through La Casa to give these kids the support they need so their families can heal and they can stay in school."

"Do you know how many times a week people come to me for money?"

"You *owe* the Ponce family. I *owe* them."

Luis got up and paced the floor. All the glamour seemed to fall away. Those perfect teeth. Those dimples. That sparkle that ignited whenever a camera was pointed in his direction. There was no camera now. There was just the two of them—and a whole lot of past to reckon with. Luis massaged his forehead.

"I was a kid, you know. Nineteen. Stupid and scared. But not a monster. If I could do it over—"

"There are no do-overs," said Vega. "Believe me, I know."

"If I do this, I need your word that you will not talk about . . ." Luis's voice trailed off.

"There would be no purpose in that," said Vega. "I'm

sure your attorney has already told you that you can't be prosecuted. I'm not out to destroy your life. I'm out to save someone else's."

Luis perched on the edge of his desk and studied Vega for a long moment. Finally he extended a hand. His gaze was sober. "You've got yourself a deal, Detective. I'll ask my attorney to draw up the paperwork."

"Thank you." Vega shook his hand. "One final request."

"Oh?" Luis stiffened.

Vega saw the picture in his head of that fruit stand. Two hopeful men off to find their fortune in *El Norte*. And a teenage boy who never got the chance. "I'd like you to name the program 'Miguel's Place' after Hector's son."

"Miguel's Place. Okay. And may I ask what you get out of this, Detective?"

Vega felt something drain from his chest. A heavy weight he'd been carrying since the night of the shooting. It wasn't gone. It would never be gone entirely. But he could live with this ache. Maybe even learn from it. When he opened his mouth, he had only one word to offer Luis. The one thing he was hoping for.

"Peace."

The biggest gifts they all gave each other that season didn't come from a store. Adele gave Vega Diablo.

"My client took a live-in position and gave the dog up," said Adele. "I had a feeling she might. But don't worry. Sophia okayed Diablo moving in with you. So long as you bring him down for frequent visits."

It was the best gift anyone had ever given Vega. The dog made himself at home, taking over both the couch and three-quarters of Vega's bed. The house didn't seem lonely anymore with Diablo there to keep him company and go on runs around the lake with him.

Vega assembled a collection of his mother's photographs for Joy, along with a note that took him a whole day to compose about all the ways she made him proud, "tattoo and all—just don't get another." Now that classes were out for the December break, Joy drove up often, spending more time with her father than she had since she started college. The shooting had brought them closer together. Vega wasn't sure how or why but maybe Greco was right. Maybe something good really could come out of something bad.

Vega waited until a night when he and Adele could be alone in his lake house to give Adele her gift. They had already unwrapped a few silly trinkets and keepsakes for each other with Diablo sniffing and licking every one. They sat by the glow of charred logs in Vega's big stone fireplace with Diablo at their feet. Then Vega took out an envelope that he'd wrapped in shiny red and green foil and handed it to Adele.

"It's not a real gift," he said shyly.

"It's a gift certificate?"

"Uh, no. Open it."

Inside the envelope was the initial paperwork to start Miguel's Place, along with a check for $35,000 to La Casa to begin the funding.

Adele stared at it. "You got Luis to endow a program?"

"Yeah. In Hector's son's memory. For children like Yovanna and the boy you told me about who was living at Chez Martine."

"Omar." Adele touched his sleeve. "I can't believe you remembered his story. Jimmy, this is amazing. How did you get Luis to—?"

"Let's just say, this will put some demons to rest for both of us."

Adele put the envelope down and leaned into him. Vega felt her lips, pillow soft against his unshaven cheeks. A heat rose within him that he'd forgotten existed. It flooded all the empty spaces that had been floating around inside of him. All the loneliness and yearning. It filled them with an urgency and passion that made him hold tight to Adele, hold tight to this moment.

Outside, the trees danced in the December wind and the night settled in heavily for the long siesta. Vega welcomed the darkness beyond because here, between them, within them, he felt only light.

Acknowledgments

This novel would not be sitting in your hands right now if not for a very special group of people who made it possible.

My thanks first to Norma Roldan and her daughter, Lisseth Valverde, who shared with me the ten years they spent apart while Norma worked in the United States and Lisseth grew up without her in Ecuador. I'm indebted to them for their honesty and insights, especially about the difficulties they faced once they were reunited.

Thanks also to John Christy, a former Aurora, Colorado, police officer who wrote a wonderful memoir, *Sine Fratres: an officer involved shooting*. John's book and his gracious emails gave me a first-hand glimpse into what Jimmy Vega might experience after a shooting.

This book would have strayed badly if not for two very dedicated men who gave up so much of their time and energy to keep me honest. The first is Lt. James Palanzo of the Westchester County Police whose gut instincts are always right on target. The second is fire investigator and storyteller extraordinaire Gene West, who can take any ridiculous situation and turn it into something plausible and riveting. Gene—from my first book to this, my sixth, I could not have done any of it without you.

I would like to thank the incredible cast of people whom readers never see. My first reader, Rosemary Ahern, whose enthusiasm and story sense always guide me to my better self. My agent, Stephany Evans, and my editor,

Michaela Hamilton, both of whom always have rock-solid judgment. And the entire staff of Kensington Books who have gone all out for the series: Michaela, of course. But also Norma Perez-Hernandez, Morgan Elwell, the sales and publicity staffs, and Steven Zacharius who has thrown so much support my way.

My thanks most of all to the people who have to live and/or listen to me through the ordeal of writing a book: my husband, Thomas Dunne, my children, Kevin and Erica, and my dear friend, Janis Pomerantz. Thank you, as always, for putting up with me.